All the Way Through

By: Deb L. Lane

May all your
dreams come true-
♡ Deb Lane

For my children, who are my everything. Thank you to Nicole, Chris, Kara, and Connor for teaching me how to be a better person, and giving me the best of days, then and now.

Thank you to Walter, for being my rock and putting up with the endless tapping of my laptop keys.

My heartfelt appreciation to all of my family and friends who believed in me and took the time to read my story, even in its rough draft form. Thank you Elaine, Eileen, Chrissy, Sharyn, Sami, Adele, Lori, Barbara, Maria, Nancy, Rug, Louise, and especially to Beth, whose enthusiasm and anticipation of each chapter pushed me to finish.

Thank you, Ashley, for your fine tuning expertise, and Kara, for your artistic ability.

My appreciation to Number 13, whose example made me realize that if you believe in yourself and keep trying, anything is possible, no matter what your age.

I am also grateful to those in my life who disappointed me and let me down…without that heartbreak, I would not have experienced the growth and self-discovery that made this story possible.

Last, but certainly not least, thank you to God for blessing me with so much love in my life, and giving me the strength to follow my dreams *all the way through*.

Amen

CHAPTER ONE

Breathe in…breathe out…breathe in…breathe out…. This deliberate awareness of air entering and exiting my body becomes my coping mechanism as I drive my silver Maxima in the slow lane, one third of the way through the Squirrel Hill Tunnel eastbound out of Pittsburgh and about halfway *into* my panic attack. My hands are clutching the steering wheel, but it feels like they are going to fly off at any second and send me careening into the tunnel wall. I am fixated on the magical disk of daylight at the end of the tunnel, knowing that if I can find the strength to make it that far, I will swiftly be transformed back to my normal self…probably.

I've driven through this tunnel maybe a hundred times in my adult life without giving it a second thought. In fact, I've probably done it while refereeing my two children throwing punches in the back seat, changing the radio station, and chewing gum all at the same time. But in the last month or so, all it takes to make my heart race and my palms sweat is the army green sign gawking at me, the one that says, "Last Exit Before Tunnel." I know that once I pass that sign, I've come to the point of no return…I have to make it through to the other side.

I hate that this happens to me. I don't know how it started or how to stop it. All I can tell you is that the first time it happened I was driving my husband, Jack, home from the airport. He had been gone for several days on a business trip and was too tired to get behind the wheel. It was one of those warm summer nights that we appreciate in western Pennsylvania, and we were enjoying the ride with the windows down as I sped toward home on the parkway. One moment we were approaching the tunnel, discussing Steeler football training camp, and the next instant I was inside, transformed into a basket case.

I had begged Jack to grab the steering wheel from my hands as a feeling of anxiety consumed my whole body. I was

1

trembling and near tears. My heart was pounding and I felt like I couldn't breathe. His response was a look of total disdain, and his comment was, "What the hell is wrong with you, Ellen?" After we finally whooshed out of the tunnel, the sensation returned to my hands, and a feeling of foolishness replaced the panic.

Call me overly sensitive, but this incident has become my little secret. I have no desire to divulge that I can't drive through a tunnel without using my breathe in, breathe out mantra.

Today was another airport trip, one I've been dreading all summer, and not because of my tunnel issue. My youngest child, my daughter Casey, was leaving home today.

Casey is five-foot-nine inches of tall, blonde, and beautiful, a stark contrast to my five-foot-even of short, graying, and aging; however, we do share the same blue-green eyes that seem to change their tint depending on what color we're wearing. Aside from that, she is everything I am not. She's independent, self-confident, and a real go-getter. While I cringe at public speaking– I don't even like ordering out loud at a crowded deli– she thrives on it. In fact, that's sort of the reason she's leaving. Casey just graduated from the University of Pittsburgh Law School and has accepted an associate position with the law firm of Shaffer, Oates, and Spear, located in Orlando, where she can debate to her heart's content. I had my reservations about a firm whose initials spell SOS, but she has assured me that this is a wonderful opportunity, and with a starting salary of six figures, I guess I am assured.

She is leaving today, a week before her starting date in September, to get settled into her new apartment. I must have skipped the chapter in the mother's chemistry handbook that explains if you combine the elements of love, worry, and fear, you end up with a compound that really messes with your psyche. I want her to go, I want her to stay, I want her to be independent, I want her to need me…my inner turmoil is unceasing.

It wasn't this hard when my son, Adam, moved out. Maybe because, right or wrong, a mother doesn't have the same worries about a boy. Or maybe it was because he only moved thirty minutes away, instead of five states. Or maybe because, to some degree, I had Casey at home and could still function in my role as I know it: as a mom.

In any case, when I deposited Casey at the curb-side baggage check at Pittsburgh International today, I was not at my best. The airport security guards barely give you enough time to pluck the suitcases out of your trunk and give your passenger a hasty hug and kiss before they start giving you the evil eye and toying with their walkie-talkies. Don't even *think* about turning off the ignition.

"Mom, I'll be fine; now don't ruin my make-up," Casey said with a fake laugh, exclusively for my benefit. I breathed in the lovely scent that was totally Casey.
Hugging her tight, I could feel the dampness of my tears on her soft cheek as I pressed my face against hers. I pulled away, and we both forced a smile. Just to defy the security guards, I gave her an extra hug.

She heaved her heavy, red canvas suitcase over the curb, lugged it to the check-in counter, and then turned to look back at me.

"I love you! See you at Christmas!" we both said at precisely the same moment.

"Call me when you get there!" I added as I climbed back in to the driver's seat. I didn't care if the tears were flowing now…I didn't care if the security guy was coming my way. Things were changing, and I didn't like it.

Resisting the urge to look back, I put the car in drive and maneuvered my way out of the airport and back onto the parkway. Then I had to deal with this damn tunnel.

I stopped and did some window shopping at the mall in an attempt to lift my spirits, but my mind was too fuzzy to focus.

Halfway home, I decided that I really didn't feel like cooking. All I really wanted to do was put on my comfy pajamas and curl up in bed, but I knew that Jack would be expecting dinner.

As I waited at a traffic light, I tapped the Bluetooth button on the dash that connected to my cell phone and used the voice command. "Call DeLucci's," I said. Before the traffic light turned green, I had ordered two lasagna dinners, complete with salads, garlic toast, and their signature white chocolate raspberry cheesecake. With thoughts of dessert in my head, I actually started to feel better.

I live in Jeannette, a napping little city about thirty miles east of Pittsburgh. I don't call it a sleepy little town, because I think it's on the verge of waking up. In its heyday, Jeannette was known as "The Glass City" because it had so many glass factories. In fact, one of the founders of the first glass factory named the city after his wife, Jeannette. I always thought that was very romantic, although I've always been happy that her name wasn't Mildred.

I pushed my new Kenny Chesney CD into the player and tried to relax and picture myself on a beach somewhere. But after several miles and a few songs, I only found myself waiting at yet another traffic light in downtown Jeannette, with no tequila in sight.

I peered out my window at several vacant store fronts. In the same way that the decline of the steel industry had affected Pittsburgh's surrounding communities, the closing of the glass factories had left Jeannette pretty much a skeleton of what it used to be. Despite this, downtown still has a quaint, retro feel. We *do* have some primo restaurants, and one of them is DeLucci's.

The light turned green, and I drove up Clay Avenue past City Hall. A larger-than-life red and blue banner sporting a cartoon picture of a Jayhawk was strung across the front of the building, commemorating our high school football and basketball state championship victories. That's what I mean about napping. Good things are happening here.

I was lucky enough to find an empty parking space on the street in front of DeLucci's, so I parallel parked and went in to pick up dinner.

Ten minutes later, I pulled into our driveway with wonderful aromas escaping from white paper sacks. I grabbed my bounty, slammed the car door shut with my hip, and made my way to the back of our house. We live in a two-story red brick with licorice black shutters and snow white trim. It's very traditional, but very welcoming. I noticed the red impatiens lining the driveway were wilting and made a mental note to water them later. Usually I am a very attentive gardener and find it a great stress buster, but lately I just haven't had the energy or interest.

Jack was back by the garage waxing his black G35 Coupe, and he looked up as I approached. I saw his eyes look behind me up the driveway.

"Why don't you spend a buck and get your car washed?" he jibed. "Is that DeLucci's lasagna I smell?"

"Well, Jack, I had more important things to do today. And yes, it is lasagna."

"So, Casey got off okay?"

"Uh-huh, piece of cake. I told her to call when she gets there."

"Ellen, she'll be fine," he said. "It'll be Christmas before you know it."

Whatever. I carefully put the bags down on the picnic table. "Would you like to eat outside?" I asked.

"Okay with me. Grab me a beer while you're in there."

I opened the French doors from the deck and entered the kitchen, which has always been the gathering place in our home. It was earthy and airy and wonderful. We've had so many good

5

times in this room, and I was suddenly saddened again by the fact that things have changed.

I knew we would still have good times here, but it wouldn't be the same.

I tried to shake those negative thoughts from my head and quickly rummaged around in the cabinets for something special. I heaped a tray with white china plates, two place settings of my good silverware, cloth napkins, a blue linen tablecloth, and two frosted mugs filled with Iron City beer, then carried it out to the deck. I covered the picnic table with the blue linen, and began opening the steaming silver foil containers and filling our plates. I lit a couple of citronella candles, and *voila*!

Jack made his way up to the table just as I blew out the match.

"A little over-kill, huh?" he said with a note of sarcasm as he took in my efforts. I must have looked as dejected as I felt, because he smoothed it over with a hug and a peck on my cheek, then took his place opposite me at the table. "Looks good."

That's how it was with Jack. He could be the sweetest man *and* the most exasperating. You just never knew which one you were going to get. I'm used to it, but I don't always like it.

Jack and I have been married for nearly thirty years, and I have signed up for life. Our relationship started back when we were teens, precisely at the age when the raging hormones are shouting a lot louder than the sensible brain cells.

He was your typical tall, dark, and handsome, with sandy brown hair that had a mind of its own, and most of the time chose to fall into his chocolate brown eyes. He was slim, agile, and very sure of himself…quite appealing to someone with a more timid personality like me. He could get away with saying whatever was on his mind, and it didn't come off as being arrogant, usually. Looking back, he was probably overconfident even then, but I think it added a little bad boy allure to the mix.

Jack liked the best of everything: nice clothes, nice cars, and to his credit, he worked hard to get them. He was always able to find a way to come up with the money to take me on nice dates or out to dinner, even way back in our very early years.

But I wasn't attracted to those material things really. I just felt safe and happy when I was with him, and the electric physical attraction didn't hurt either. I thought there was nothing he couldn't do, and I suppose he thought so, too.

I remembered the first time I saw him. I was seventeen and working after school at the ice cream counter at Isaly's. He came in with a group of boys, sat down at a table, and looked my way. Our eyes met, held, and he winked. I said to myself, "That is the boy I'm going to marry." Cheesy, but true, I just knew.

Eventually he came up to my counter and ordered our specialty, a skyscraper ice cream cone. I remember how nervous I felt as I held the cone out for him, heaped high with chocolate fudge ice cream.

He handed me the money, winked again, and walked out of the store with his friends. I looked down at the bills he had placed in my hand and saw that he had also slipped me a napkin with a phone number and a scribbled message: Call me. Jack.

One phone call later, I was a goner. We went steady through the remainder of high school, and the year after graduation, I became Mrs. Jack Stern.

I looked at him as we started in on our dinner and tried to conjure up that heart thumping feeling of our first meeting. Wasn't happening. Somewhere along the way, the things that I had loved about Jack, I now sometimes found annoying. Oh, don't get me wrong, I still found him attractive. He was in great shape, even though his diet was horrendous, and although it was thinning a bit, he still had that great hair. Even the graying at his temples just made him look more distinguished. It is so unfair that men look great with gray hair, and women just look old. He was still a snappy dresser and usually wore a suit and tie to work every day.

I still feel safe with him, but not always happy. Especially lately. I love him heart and soul, but sometimes I just don't like him. *Geez, did I really just admit that to myself?*

We've been getting into the craziest arguments about trivial things, and no matter how right I feel I am at the beginning, I always end up floundering and feeling like an idiot by the time it's over. He just has this uncanny knack for turning the facts around, and somehow I always end up with the short end of the stick. So lately I try to choose my battles wisely, because what's the use if I can't ever win?

I used to admire his self-confidence, but it's beginning to border on rudeness, especially to me. I'm sometimes embarrassed in front of my friends by the way he speaks to me, so I haven't been inviting them over much. But...Jack's been very involved with work lately, so I try to overlook it.

I'm a little nervous about how it will be, now that it's just Jack and me. In fact, I'm just plain scared. I know we love each other, but I want us to *really* love each other. To enjoy being together and have it feel like it did before we had the kids. Maybe I've just read too many romance novels.

At any rate, I wasn't in the mood for any of his wise cracks tonight.

He was rambling on about some kind of investment seminar in Florida that he was planning on going to next weekend. Jack was a senior officer at an investment corporation. His job never used to require him to travel, but over this past year he's been gone at least one weekend every month.

I had just savored the last bite of cheesecake, when my phone started playing the theme song from *Legally Blonde*, the ring tone that signaled Casey was calling.

Usually I would never take a call while we were eating, it's one of Jack's pet peeves, but I snatched up the phone wearing my first real smile of the day.

"Casey! Did you get there okay?"

"Oh, yeah! It was a little bumpy over Atlanta because of storms, but the rest of the flight was fine. My apartment is *awesome*, Mom! I can't wait for you to see it! I met some really cool neighbors and they invited me to a poolside cookout tonight. Think I should wear my blue bikini or the green one?"

"Green. So, was the furniture delivered?" I recalled the many evenings that we had spent in front of the computer shopping for furniture online.

"Yep. At least I think it's all here. The bed needs put together, so I'll be crashing on just the mattress for tonight at least. A couple of the guys I met said they'd help me with the muscle stuff. At least I have a week to pull it together before I start work."

"That's super," I said, and I noticed that I was still smiling.

"Hey, Mom, I really need to get going now, but I'll call tomorrow. Oh, is Dad around?"

"Yes, he's right here, honey. I love you, and I'm glad you made it there okay."

"Love you too, Mom."

After handing the phone to Jack, I touched my fingertip to some cheesecake crumbs on my plate and licked them off while I listened to their brief conversation. He asked her about the security at her apartment and about the flight. Then he said, "I love you, too," and she was gone. I noticed that he was smiling too.

Suddenly, I felt very close to Jack. Despite our little differences, we *have* raised two great kids. We've been through a lot in our lives together, and now another chapter was about to begin. I got up and went to the other side of the table where he was sitting.

"I'm glad she made it safely," I said as I began to rub his shoulders.

"Of course she did. She's a big girl now, Ellen. I'll miss her too, you know," he added.

His cell phone rudely chirped that a text had arrived. He ignored it, as I kissed his neck. I sat down in his lap and wrapped my arms around him, and he held me close. As we kissed, his phone interrupted again.

"Damn phone," he mumbled, and I noticed that he didn't even check to see who the text was from.

Our kiss lingered a moment longer, and then Jack gently pushed me away, saying that he had some work to do inside.

I took my time cleaning up. I was still missing Casey, but she was starting her new life tonight, in a green bikini, and it was time for me to snap out of it. I always wash my good china by hand, but tonight I stashed it in the dishwasher without a second thought. Some things just didn't seem as important anymore.

After everything was put away, I went upstairs to Jack's office, where I found him sitting at his desk. He had been talking on the phone and hung up just as I came into the room.

"Hey," I said, smiling.

"Hey. Somebody's always got a problem," he grumbled, referring to his phone call. He pushed his chair back from the desk and went down the hall to our bedroom. I tagged along, and as he was getting a clean tee shirt out of his dresser drawer, I slid my arms around his middle. Stepping quickly out of my hug, he headed back down the hall to his office. I trailed behind, hoping to recapture that after-dinner moment of closeness.

"Now what are you gonna *do*, follow me around the house like a puppy?" he snapped.

I could feel the tears brimming, but what little pride I had left prevented me from letting him see them fall. Why answer? What answer did I have? I *was* following him around like a puppy, and I despised myself for practically begging like one for a scrap of affection. I silently turned and walked out of the room, down the stairs, and out onto the deck. I plunked down on the chaise lounge and let the tears flow. I don't know how long I cried, but I vaguely remembered hearing Jack move my car from the driveway, then the sound of his car stereo thumping and fading away as he drove down the street.

I felt exhausted and spent. I had nothing left. Between Casey's departure, my tunnel panic, and Jack's harsh words, I just couldn't take any more today.

I must have fallen asleep, though, because the next thing I knew Jack was gently stroking my hair, softly saying, "I'm sorry, Ellen." I opened my eyes and it was almost dark. My neck had a crick in it from sleeping on the chaise. I must have been out here for hours!

"Come on up to bed," he said, and led me silently back up the two flights of stairs with my hand in his. Once in our room, he sat me down on our bed and held me close, then without a word, our tender kisses turned into love-making. Afterward, as I snuggled next to him, I began to feel whole again.

Suddenly, Jack swung his legs over the side of the bed, stood up, and started picking up his clothes. When I realized that he was planning on putting them back on, I got up on one elbow and said pleadingly, "Jack, *please* come back. I need you!" Even to me it sounded pathetic, but it was the truth. I just wanted to stay safely in his arms for the rest of the night.

He sighed dramatically and sat down next to me, wrapping his arm stiffly around my shoulders. "Can't we do this later? I know you're missing Casey, but you'll get over it. I have a lot of paperwork to do for a meeting tomorrow."

"Fine," I huffed, and he wasted no time jumping out of bed, getting dressed, and leaving the room without even a glance behind.

Then, just when I thought I had no more tears left, I rolled onto my side and cried myself to sleep.

CHAPTER TWO

I was running in the woods and a giant bee was chasing me, hovering near my head, and making a horrible buzzing sound. The noise was getting louder and louder, and it just wouldn't stop. I swatted the bee with my hand and made a connection. BAM!

My eyes popped open. I didn't see any bees, but I could still hear the incessant, annoying buzzing sound, and my heart was pounding. I was all tangled up in my comforter and soaking wet with sweat. Freeing one arm, I swatted the alarm clock right off the nightstand, instantly squelching that obnoxious buzzing, and this time I killed the bugger. I made a mental note to buy a new alarm clock.

It was Monday morning. Jack always left the house early for work, and I had been sleeping so soundly that I hadn't even heard him getting ready. I had to be at work by nine and it only took ten minutes to drive there, so I was still in good shape.

I dragged myself into the bathroom and intended to start the shower. As I passed the mirror over the vanity, I stopped and looked at myself. I mean, *really* looked at myself. Was I pretty? I had always thought of myself as semi-attractive, although at the moment, I looked anything but. I had my share of crinkles and wrinkles around my eyes, but after crying so much last night, I also had puffy, dark circles under them too. Until recently, I have inwardly felt that I am still in my mid-thirties, when in reality, fifty was closing in fast. This morning I was shocked to see that my age was finally catching up with me.

The hair that framed my face and hung a bit past my shoulders was lacking in style, and I could see about a quarter-inch of gray roots showing. I hadn't had the energy to even do a quickie dye job lately; this morning it was dull and straggly and just made me look *old*. I wondered if Jack had looked at me before he left.

I plastered a pretend smile on my face, and it lifted about five years from my reflection. Sadly, it was too much of an effort to keep it there, so I gave up and headed to the shower.

Twenty minutes later, I was still standing under the hot spray, letting the water pelt its warmth on my skin. After finally convincing myself that looking like a prune wasn't going to help matters any, I turned the water off and wrapped myself in a huge, pink towel.

Actually, I *did* feel better, and after working some quick makeup magic and using lots of mousse on my hair, I looked tons better too. I pulled on a pair of jeans, a turquoise tee shirt, and a chocolate brown blazer, and as I fastened my earrings, my tummy started to rumble.

I used to have breakfast with Casey, and sometimes Jack, before we all started our day…usually I had whole grain cereal, wheat toast, and orange juice, but screw it. I grabbed a jelly donut from Jack's stash, tucked my purse under my arm, and headed out the door.

I turned off of Route 30 and carefully slid into a parking space at the Greengate Shopping Plaza with five minutes to spare. I noticed Abbey's champagne-colored Blazer already parked in her karma zone.

Abbey is my co-worker and my best friend. It's a standing joke that she always chooses the same self-designated parking space wherever she goes so she doesn't forget where she parked. A bad experience several years ago at the Stop & Shop was to blame. She had pushed a cart full of groceries around the parking lot for fifteen minutes trying to find her car and it had scarred her for life.

I chirped the remote to lock my car and walked happily through the door of Amazing Glaze, the ceramic studio where I work. I have always had a bit of artistic flare and enjoy creating with any medium, so when Abbey and her husband, Rick, opened this studio, I couldn't resist her job offer. That was five years ago, and I can't think of any position that could be more perfect for me.

The bells tied to the door jingled as I breezed in. Abbey was standing behind the counter at the register, readying the cash drawer for the day, and looked up with a smile. She was in her early forties going on twenty. Her auburn hair was usually pulled back in a ponytail, and her teenage daughter's cast off jeans and Limited tee shirts were pretty much her staple wardrobe. She hardly wore any makeup, but she didn't need to. Abbey was one of those lucky women who looked great with just a swipe of mascara and a touch of lip gloss.

She closed the register drawer with a thump and came around the counter to collect me in a bear hug. We rocked back and forth a moment, then she gripped my shoulders and held me at arm's length to look me in the eye.

"How are you, sweetie?" Not much gets past Abbey.

"I've been better. Just missing Casey," I said with a shrug. "I guess I just feel out of sorts...a little lost maybe. And if you say, 'It'll be Christmas before you know it,' I'm going to go move your car when you're not looking."

She giggled and dropped her hands. "How's Jack taking it?"

"He misses her too, in his own way. You know they've always been close. It's just that he's been so busy lately, and a little distracted."

"Yeah, well, let's get *you* busy and a little distracted with some window decorating," she said, and started toward the storage room at the rear of the studio. "We can probably get both windows done before the birthday party starts if we don't have too many walk-ins."

I stashed my purse under the counter and heaved a sigh.

15

Yes, that is exactly what I needed…work and distraction.

Abbey came out of the storeroom door pushing a large cardboard box with her foot and balancing another in her arms. I reached down and picked up the one from the floor and followed her to the front of the store.

We officially don't open until noon, and I wondered what kind of day it would be. School would be starting in a week, so most parents were already shifting gears. They were out shopping for new clothes and school supplies, so maybe we wouldn't be too busy.

"Halloween decorations already," Abbey said as she opened a box. "Can't say I'm not happy about it though. I'm tired of all the red, white, and blue holidays. I'm ready to move on."

"I agree," I told her. "Halloween begins the primo decorating season, and autumn is my favorite time of year."

We both dug into the boxes like kids on Christmas. Abbey's box contained garlands of artificial fall leaves, orange and purple twinkle lights, plastic red apples, and other assorted autumn goodies. Mine held large lengths of orange fabric, synthetic spider webs with black plastic spiders, and all the extension cords we would need for plugging in the ceramic decorations.

There were two display windows flanking the front door, and we each chose one and began working our magic in compatible silence. Abbey had put pumpkin pie scented wax chips in her warmer on the counter, and the scent was really inspiring me to think autumn thoughts…and making me hungry.

I adore everything about fall. I love the crispness of the air, the clear blue sky, the crimson, orange, and gold of the changing leaves and the way they crunch when you walk on them, fresh apple cider, roadside stands filled to the gills with plump, orange pumpkins, and the deep hues of fall mums. My spirits were beginning to lift just anticipating the change of season.

I covered the base of the window with yards of orange fabric, and strategically attached some loose leaves to the window glass as if they had fallen from a tree. After rummaging around in the storage room, I found a box containing our Halloween projects and carried it to the window. I chose a black cat with eyes that blinked red, a large, orange jack-o-lantern whose mouth was in the shape of an "O", a witch perched on top of a pumpkin, a scarecrow dressed in blue jean overalls, and a ghost that glowed a ghoulish green. After disguising the extension cords with more fabric, I planted twinkle lights in the folds of the material and then scattered some more loose leaves around as a finishing touch.

As I stood back to admire my work, Abbey climbed out of her window brushing fake cobwebs from her jeans.

"Are we good or what?" she said as she glanced at her watch. "Why don't you start unloading the kiln, and I'll go grab a couple sandwiches at Primanti's. My treat today!"

Primanti's was a few minute's drive from Amazing Glaze and was the best thing to happen to this neighborhood since sliced bread, or any kind of bread actually.

Abbey knew my standing order, so I just smiled and headed to the back of the store to unload the kiln. Yesterday, Abbey had worked a bridal shower on her own, and each guest had painted a mug, bowl, or plate as a gift to the bride.

In the summer, we usually run the kiln at night for the pottery painted that day because it makes the studio so hot. This way, by the time we get here in the morning, everything is done, and the air conditioning has had a chance to cool things down for us.

I put on a pair of gloves and opened the kiln. Because the temperature inside was still around two hundred degrees, the pieces were extremely hot. I carefully removed each one from its stilt and placed them all on a metal cart. I was pretty impressed with how they had turned out. Evidently the bride had some talented friends! I would let them cool a bit on the cart until after lunch, do a quick sanding on the bottom to get rid of the sharp stilt marks, then place them on the shelves ready for pick up.

I heard the bells on the front door jingling, and peeked out to see Abbey arriving with our lunch. I took off my gloves, hung them on the hook by the sink, and washed my hands with apple-spice soap that wasn't here yesterday. Abbey was really getting into the autumn thing!

She was already sitting at the table unwrapping her sandwich when I walked into what we affectionately call the lunchroom. It was really a card table and four metal chairs in the back corner of the storage area, but it was out of the customer's sight. One day last winter when business was slow, we got really creative and painted the walls a snappy lemon zest, then added some random polka dots. The result was a very relaxing and cheerful oasis in which to enjoy our meals.

I plunked down and greedily unwrapped my Pitts-Burgher cheese steak: grilled steak piled with fries, coleslaw, and tomatoes, all heaped between two slices of thick Italian bread. Heaven.

"Abbey, you sure know how to treat a girl," I said as I smashed the sandwich down so I could take a bite.

She wiped a bit of coleslaw from her mouth with the back of her hand. "I aim to please, sweetheart."

We both chewed silently for a few bites.

"So…how is it *really* going with Mr. Wonderful?" She fixed her eyes on me. "Did you have a romantic evening on your first night alone?"

I swallowed quickly and took a long sip of green tea lemonade. There was no love lost between Abbey and Jack. She thought he was arrogant and self-centered, and he thought she was a pushy neb-nose. I loved them both and walked a fine line trying to keep the peace between them.

"Well, actually we did. I brought DeLucci's lasagna home, and we had a nice picnic on the deck."

"And?"

"And…Jack had some work to do, so I went to bed early." There was no need to tell her the rest of the story. She would be furious.

"Hmm. Rick and I were on our way back from the grocery store and thought we saw the Batmobile pulling into the Backyard Grille. Thought maybe you guys were going out for a beer and some wings. I bet Jack will be *livid* to know there's another black G35 in the tri-state area."

I had to smile in spite of her attack on Jack. He *would* be livid, I thought as I munched on some stray fries that had fallen off my sandwich.

"So, when are you planning on going down to see Casey?" Abbey asked.

"Well, Jack and I haven't talked about it. He's been really swamped at work with all this financial crisis stuff going on and he's been working tons of overtime the last few weeks. I don't think it'll let up for a while."

"Why don't you just go yourself for a long weekend or something? It would make the time from now until she comes home more tolerable. I bet you'd love to see her place, and I bet she'd like to show it off to you."

I jerked my head up and looked her in the eye. "I hadn't thought of that. I've never gone on a trip by myself; I think I'd want to share that with Jack."

"Honey, Jack goes on business trips by himself *all* the time! I'm sure he won't feel too left out if you have some fun and go see Casey. He's a big boy and can take care of himself for a couple days. In fact, it would be good for him to miss you a little bit. I happen to know that your boss will let you have some time off," she said with a grin.

"Actually, Jack *is* going to Florida this weekend on a business trip," I said as I wondered if he had plans to see Casey. I hadn't been paying much attention to the details last night at dinner. "Maybe I *will* think about it."

"Good girl," she said as she crunched up her sandwich paper and threw it in the trash. "We'd better get that party set up before the birthday girl gets here."

We began preparing the front room for the party. It was reserved for twenty guests and would fit them, plus any stray parents, comfortably. We placed the brushes and paints on the tables, then filled small containers with water so they could rinse their bristles between colors.

Just as I placed a roll of paper towels on a table, the front door flew open, making the bells clang, and in breezed Mrs. Plumber with her entourage of seven-year-old girls marching behind her like a gaggle of geese. "It's Mary Frances' birthday! Say happy birthday to Mary Frances!" she exclaimed.

Abbey had her back to the door. She looked up at me and crossed her eyes.

"Happy birthday, Mary Frances!" we shouted in unison, enunciating just as a group of first graders would to their teacher.

Mary Frances had two long, blonde braids flung over her shoulders and was dressed in a cotton candy pink sundress with matching glittery jelly shoes. Mrs. Plumber had a perfectly coifed blond bob and was wearing white jeans, a Barbie pink tank top, and flashy rings on every finger.

The party was exhausting! Not so much because of the children, but due to Mrs. Plumber's demands, requested in her high-pitched, nasal voice. By the time it was over, both Abbey and I were hoping that next year Mary Frances would decide to have her party at Chuck-E-Cheese.

With a sigh, I grabbed my purse from under the counter and pulled out my cell phone to call Jack and see what he wanted for dinner. I was surprised to find a text message from him saying that he wouldn't be home until later. Well, that took care of that.

I hopped into the Maxima and found the air stifling. As I pulled out of the parking lot, I put all the windows down and let the cool breeze rush in, then negotiated into the traffic on Route 30.

I didn't feel like going home to an empty house. Impulsively, I clicked on my turn signal and exited off the highway and onto the PA turnpike. I was feeling maternal and needed a fix. Adam was like his father in that he wasn't much into phone calls, so I didn't bother to call first. I would take my chances that he was there. He was in between girlfriends at the moment and wasn't going out as much. About ten minutes later, I pulled into Adam's driveway, right next to his blue pickup truck. My lucky day!

Adam was two years younger than Casey. They both had the same way of looking at me like I was from another planet at times, but that's where the resemblance ends. He was taller than her, two or three inches over six feet. When he was a child he was dubbed the red-headed kid, but over the last several years it has toned down to a lovely shade of auburn, and lately he's been wearing it short and spiked.

I don't think he ever minded the red hair. In fact, it made him memorable. It was always an easy conversation starter because people were always asking him, "Where'd you get the red hair?" since it was pretty obvious that he didn't get it from Jack or me. I'm told that the red hair gene can actually skip a generation, which must be what happened in our family, because my grandfather was a redhead. But Adam got tired of explaining that and started to make up his own snappy comebacks.

"My mom ate a lot of strawberry ice cream before I was

born," was one of his favorites. "There was a back order on blondes," was another. Anything to get a laugh.

Once my own hair began turning gray, I starting dying it a color called brown sugar, which actually gave my dark brown hair a reddish punch. Now, Adam thinks it's hysterical when we're out together and someone says to him, "I see who you got your red hair from!" So far he hasn't embarrassed me with any one-liners to give my secret away, though.

I walked up the steps to his porch and rapped on the front door. His yellow lab, Cooper, began barking and prancing inside. A moment later, Adam opened the door, and Cooper scrambled out to greet me with a stuffed red Clifford dog in his mouth.

"Hi, boy!" I said as he put his front paws on my chest and wriggled his backside. I accepted his sloppy kisses and scratched him behind the ears. Then he dropped Clifford at my feet and went out to water a tree in the front yard.

I looked up at Adam who was leaning against the door jamb, holding a burger in his hand and still chewing. He was wearing jeans with holes in the knees, a Pitt tee shirt splattered with red paint, and a baseball cap turned backwards. He looked so grown up to me, but the sprinkling of freckles across his nose still gave him a youthful appearance, and would probably get him carded for years to come. His sky blue eyes looked at me in surprise.

"Hey, what's up?" he mumbled with a mouth full of burger.

"Just thought I'd stop by…Dad won't be home for dinner, Casey's gone, and I just missed you."

He stepped out on the porch and wrapped his arms around me. Nothing better than a hug, even one that smells like turpentine and charcoal. "I just finished painting the dining room. Come see!" He held the door open for me with one hand and lowered his other hand for an instant.

Cooper saw his opportunity and ran past us into the house, snatching the last bite of burger from Adam's hand and swallowing it on the run.

"*Cooper!* That's it buddy, you're in time out!" Adam said. Cooper immediately flopped down on the floor, and if a dog could look sheepish, he had it perfected.

I picked up the drool- covered Clifford and followed Adam into his home, shutting the front door behind me. The smell of paint and turpentine got stronger as we made our way into the dining room. Aside from a ladder in the corner, the room was empty.

"Wow!" I said. "This looks amazing!" All four walls were painted red with a vanilla cream crown molding.

"I wasn't really sure if I'd like so much red, but it's growing on me."

I nodded and asked, "What are you doing with the floors?"

"I'm leaning towards bamboo for the whole downstairs, but I'm not quite sure yet. What do you think?"

This is the third house that Adam has completely remodeled. Right after high school graduation, he used the money he received as gifts for a down payment on a real fixer-upper. He found that he really had a talent for home improvements and enjoyed doing them so much that he decided to forgo college and flip houses for a profession. Although I had my doubts at the beginning and wanted to see him get a college degree, it appears to be working out well for him. He is happy and loves his work. It's what I hope for both of my children.

He transformed that first home from a place I wouldn't enter without a respirator mask to a real showcase. Then he sold it and used the profit to purchase a neglected duplex located in a nice neighborhood in nearby Greensburg. Once again, he took the building down to the bare bones and worked a miracle with it.

He decided to keep the duplex and rent it, receiving two rent checks every month and netting a nice income for himself.

Then, a friend of a friend told him about an adorable Cape Cod that really needed a lot of work but was selling dirt-cheap. He went to see it and knew instantly what he could do with it. Fortunately, Adam was able to make the purchase, and he was ecstatic to move out of our house and make that one his home. I'm very proud of him for achieving so much at such a young age.

It's been fun for me because he randomly uses me as a sounding board for his ideas and color choices. He may have not gotten his hair color from me, but I like to tell myself that I had some influence on his artistic ability.

"I think bamboo is an excellent choice, sweetie. It's becoming very popular," I answered him.

"I just like the look of it, and I'm really trying to do everything as 'green' as I can. I have to research the bamboo a little more, though, before I make my final decision."

Adam may not have gone to college, but he's put in just as many hours of homework as any college grad. He intensely surfs the internet and trade publications for the latest building techniques and product information, and scopes out seminars and building workshops to improve his craft. He is very environmentally conscious and is adamant about incorporating sustainable products into his designs.

"The place is looking great," I told him. It was pretty sparsely furnished but coming along.

"Thanks, Mom," he said. "Do you want a burger? I have an extra on the grill."

"Sure, that sounds good."

We moved into the kitchen and he plated me up a hamburger on a toasted bun, poured two glasses of iced tea, and we both sat down at the table. Cooper gave me an accusing look, then sat next to me, putting his chin on my lap.

"Okay, I know this one was for you, but I'll save you some," I told him with my mouth full.

While I enjoyed my dinner, Adam told me about another house he was going to look at. It was a foreclosure, but apparently the woman who previously lived there owned over twenty cats and wasn't very clean about it, so the house was in pretty bad shape. He was actually excited about that fact, hoping that not too many buyers would be interested.

"Looks like I'll have to get the respirator mask out again," I thought to myself.

We chatted some about Casey, and about my work at Amazing Glaze, then he slipped in the fact that he had a date planned with a girl he met at a home and garden show. A year-long relationship he had been in had recently ended badly, so I was happy to hear that he was moving beyond his heartbreak and dating again.

I fed Cooper the last bite of my burger, which he gulped without even tasting it. What a waste.

"Well, I guess I'd better be going; it's been a long day. Thanks for dinner and the company," I said as I stifled a yawn. I was feeling relaxed and very happy that I had spent the evening with Adam.

He walked me out to my car and gave me a hug and a kiss on the forehead.

"Thanks, Adam."

"For what?"

"Just for being you."

He gave me an exaggerated shrug of his shoulders and a

25

silly grin in reply.

As I pulled out of the driveway, I looked back in the rearview mirror and saw Adam still standing there, thumbs hitched in his jean pockets, with Cooper at his side. I felt a tear trickle down my cheek. I don't know why I'm being so emotional. I just had a wonderful evening with my son, and I'm crying. *What is up with that?* Taking a deep breath, I wrote it off as just one of those Hallmark commercial moments and headed for home.

Just as I was preparing to merge onto the turnpike, a black G35 Coupe whizzed past me. All I saw was a blur, and it was gone, going much faster than the 65 mile per hour speed limit. Apparently, the owner of Jack's twin had a lead foot or was in a real hurry to get somewhere. Two trailer trucks zoomed by, and then I pulled onto the turnpike with my thoughts a million miles away. Or at least hundreds of miles, in Orlando, Florida.

CHAPTER THREE

I parked on the street in front of our house, because Jack was already home and had parked in the driveway. He usually made a fuss if I blocked him in, so I learned to avoid the hassle.

I was happy that he was home though, because going into a dark house alone isn't one of my favorite things to do. Also, I was looking forward to spending some much needed time together. As I passed his car on my way in, I could feel the heat still coming from the engine and heard the tick, tick of it cooling down.

"Well, look who finally decided to come home," Jack said as I walked in the front door. He was sitting on the sofa watching a pre-season football game.

"Hey!" I said, and shot him a smile. After I kicked off my shoes by the door, I plunked down next to him, kissing his cheek on the way. I had forgotten the Steelers were playing tonight.

As I put my head on his shoulder and settled in to watch the game, he said, "So, where have *you* been? I thought you only worked until six today."

"I stopped at Adam's for awhile. His place is really shaping up."

"That kid should be going to college to learn something useful. What happens when nobody can afford to buy a house from him, then what's he gonna do?"

This was an old argument, and I wasn't being pulled into it tonight, so I remained silent.

"So, what's for dinner? I'm hungry," he asked.

"Oh, I ate a burger with Adam."

"Give you an inch, and you take a mile. I tell you I'm coming home late, and you just go out and do whatever you please! I was working all evening; it would be nice to come home to something to eat once in a while."

"I'll go make you something. What do you want?" I said as I sat up.

"Don't worry about it," he said as he pushed himself up from the couch.

I watched, dumbfounded, as he went upstairs, and I could hear the jingle of keys as he got them from the tray on his dresser.

When he came back down, he grabbed his jacket from the hall closet and headed toward the front door.

"Where are you going?" I asked, still on the couch.

"Where do you think? To get myself something to eat! It's obvious that you had more important things to do than think about me tonight," he said as he went out the front door and slammed it behind him.

What the heck just happened here? Maybe if I would have just driven straight home from work like I usually do, the evening would have turned out differently, and we would be snuggling on the couch watching football right now. Jack probably figured that I'd come right home after work and make something for dinner that I could reheat right away for him. I know that being hungry always puts him in a foul mood. Why do I feel guilty though, when in my heart I don't really think that I did anything wrong?

I went into the kitchen, turned on the water faucet, and reached up in the cupboard to get a glass. All of a sudden, I felt that shaky, warm feeling that happens when I drive through the tunnels. I sat down at the table and took a sip of water. My hands were tingling, my body began to tremble all over, and I broke into a sweat. I started to feel like I might not be able to breathe, and that frightened me even more.

I grabbed my cell phone and pushed the speed dial for Jack. It took him entirely too long to answer.

"What?" he finally said.

"Jack, I need you to come home! I don't know what's wrong with me, but I feel like I'm having a panic attack, and I'm afraid I won't be able to breathe."

"Are you having chest pains or pressure?"

"No, I feel like I did that time when I was driving through the tunnel with you on the way home from the airport. I'm so scared...."

"Ellen, if it's just a panic attack, it'll go away. You sure you're not having heart attack symptoms or something serious?"

"Jack, this *is* serious!"

"Okay, I'll be home in about fifteen minutes," he said, right before he disconnected.

I tried the breathing and focusing techniques that I had learned a lifetime ago in Lamaze class. Staring at a daisy in a vase on the table, I concentrated on counting my breaths. Can your body forget to breathe? I sipped more water and could feel myself calming down a tiny bit just knowing that Jack was on his way home. I was afraid that I would pass out and no one would be here.

Slowly, the feeling returned to my fingers. My heart stopped racing and started beating a normal tempo. My breathing became automatic, and I took a chance on breaking my gaze from my focal point. The attack had subsided, but I felt exhausted. I crossed my arms on the table, rested my head on them, and closed my eyes.

About ten minutes later, I heard the front door open, and the deadbolt click shut. Jack was home.

"Ellen?" Jack shouted. I heard him walk through the living room searching for me, but I didn't have the energy to answer him.

"*Ellen!*" he said as he found me at the table. I lifted my head and looked at him.

"Are you okay?" He rushed over, sat in the chair next to me, and took my hand in his.

"I'm so scared, Jack. It stopped now, but I don't know why this is happening to me." Tears ran slowly down my cheeks.

He leaned over and gathered me in his arms. It felt so good to have him hold me. "Tell me what happened," he said as he pulled away.

Jack sat back in his chair and held my hand in his. I took a shaky breath and told him everything. All about my several tunnel episodes and how this one just seemed to come from nowhere. About how I keep crying at every little thing. He was stroking the top of my hand with his thumb.

"I think you should call Dr. Swanson tomorrow and make an appointment."

"I was thinking the same thing. I'll call first thing tomorrow morning…Jack?"

"Hmm?"

"I love you."

I thought I saw a pained look cross his face, but as fast as it appeared, it was gone. He smiled and said, "I love you too, Ellen. You know that."

We both jumped as his cell phone rang. He reached in his

pocket and turned it off without checking the call.

"Let's just go to bed," he said. "I'll lock up, you go on ahead."

I splashed some cold water on my face and patted it dry, then half-heartedly smeared on some moisturizer. I grabbed an old tee shirt out of my drawer and tugged it over my head, leaving my clothes in a pile at the foot of the bed. *Rats.* I remembered that I hadn't bought a new alarm clock. I picked up my jeans from the floor and grabbed my cell phone out of the pocket to set the alarm. I didn't have to go to work until afternoon, but I wanted to get up and call the doctor first thing.

There was a missed call from Casey. I must have hit the silent button by accident when I called Adam earlier. *Darn.* I sat on the bed and listened to her voicemail. I smiled as she briefly told me about her day and the friends she was making at her apartment complex. The name Chris was mentioned more than once, so he must have made an impression. I guess the green bikini was a good choice after all. She said she loved me before she hung up, and I whispered, "I love you, too."

I crawled under the sheets and just as my head hit the pillow, I heard Jack turn on the water in the shower. He poked his head into the bedroom, asked if I was okay, and said he'd be in shortly.

My next conscious thought was hearing my cell phone ring my wake up song. I grabbed it off the nightstand, and watched the little alarm clock on the screen doing the rumba, beckoning me to wake up.

I stretched and smiled, and then I remembered last night. As I slowly got out of bed and padded downstairs, I began to get anxious that I was going to have another panic attack today.

Jack was standing at the sink rinsing his coffee cup.

"Good morning," I mumbled.

He turned and looked at me. "Good morning. Boy, you were really out last night! How do you feel today?"

"Just nervous that it'll happen again."

"Ellen, you're going to *make* it happen again if you keep that up!"

Can a person do that? Great.

"Remember to call the doctor. Let me know what he says, okay?"

"They open at eight today. I'll call then."

He gave me a quick hug and a kiss, picked up his briefcase, and headed for the front door.

"I love you," I called after him.

"Love you, too," I heard right before the door slammed shut.

I filled a mug with water, put it in the microwave to heat, and picked up a jelly donut. I don't know how Jack eats stuff like this and stays in shape. The microwave beeped, and I made a cup of tea with honey as I munched on the donut. Then I ate another one as I sat at the table staring out the window.

Finally, it was time to call, and after two tries, I got through to the doctor's receptionist. They were able to squeeze me in at ten.

Now that I'd actually made the appointment, I was afraid to go. What if something was really *wrong* with me? Maybe they weren't panic attacks; maybe I had something really serious. My hands started trembling and the donuts churned in my stomach.

I tried to push those thoughts from my head as I showered

and got dressed. Still, when I arrived at Dr. Swanson's office, I wanted to turn around and run back out to the car.

Instead, I sat down on a hard, gray chair and picked up a magazine. I couldn't concentrate on reading it, just flipped through the pages over and over again.

"Mrs. Stern?" the nurse called.

I got up and followed her back to Examination Room No. 4. The white paper crackled as I took my seat on the table. After being satisfied that my vital statistics were performing enough to keep me alive for the interminable future, she told me the doctor would be in soon. I picked a tissue from the box and fiddled with it in my hand.

Fifteen minutes and three shredded tissues later, Dr. Swanson knocked on the door and came in holding his clipboard.

He eyed the pile of tissue in my lap and gave me a weak smile.

"So, Ellen, what brings you here today?"

I explained the feelings that I've been having, and he nodded and made some notes.

"How long has this been going on?"

"Well, for a little over a month, but last night was the first time it happened other than in the tunnels."

"Let's give you a complete physical, and I'll want you to get some blood work done just to rule out any physical problems. But I really think you have the classic symptoms of a panic disorder. Have you had any new stresses or major life changes lately?"

Oh yeah, big time. I told him about Casey moving.

"Hmm. How are things with you and your husband?"

33

"Pretty normal for a couple that's been married forever, I think."

"How about work? Do you have stress there?"

"Dr. Swanson, work is where I *de*-stress!"

He laughed. "I think I'm in the wrong profession then."

After my physical, he pulled up a chair to the desk and started writing on his clipboard again.

He cleared his throat, and began his monologue.

"Ellen, rest assured that from all indications today, you're physically healthy; however, you have all the classic symptoms of a slight panic disorder, most likely brought on by the major changes that are occurring in your life right now."

"Everyone has stress in their lives and feels anxiety from time to time, but when the anxiety escalates to the point of having repeated panic attacks, it may start ruling your life and interfering with your day-to-day functions. Then it's time to get help."

"I would like to give you two prescriptions today. One to take on a daily basis that will help you handle the overall stress. You may not feel the full benefits of it for possibly several weeks, but it's important to take it every day. Even when you start feeling better, you have to be very diligent about taking it every day."

"The other one is to take when you're going to encounter a very stressful event. It will immediately take effect to help you calm down, kind of like insurance."

"I would like to see you back here in six weeks. If you need to come in before that or have any questions about how the medication is making you feel, please call."

Just like that? I'm on medication? I wasn't liking this at all.

"Dr. Swanson," I began, "I'm one of those people who hates to take pills. I'd have a hard time even if you prescribed Flintstone vitamins!"

He peered at me over the top of his glasses. "I can't make you take the meds, of course, but I highly recommend it. Ellen, keep in mind that medication is only part of the treatment. These will only take the edge off to get you through this; it's a very low dose. The rest ultimately has to come from you. You should also speak to a psychiatrist and try to work out the feelings and stresses you're going through."

"I understand, but isn't there anything else I can try?"

"Let's do this. I will hand you the prescriptions today. My recommendation is that you begin treatment immediately, before this gets out of hand. It's up to you whether you take them or not. But I'm going to make an appointment with a psychiatrist for you, and I urge you to keep it."

Oh, Jack will love this one.

"Usually there's a several month wait to get an appointment, but let me see what I can do. I'll meet you out at the desk."

He quickly scribbled something down, then pushed his glasses up on his nose as he quietly left the examination room, closing the door behind him.

That's it. I'm crazy. What am I going to tell everyone? How could this happen to me? Jack will have a cow.

I trudged out to the reception area, and while I was fumbling around in my purse for my checkbook, Dr. Swanson poked his head around the window.

"Sarah is on the phone now trying to set up an

appointment for you with Dr. Burke. If you can wait a few minutes, she'll have that information for you. Also, here are a few samples of the meds. This is the one I mentioned that you only take before a stressful event…just in case."

He handed me a little white bag through the hole in the Plexiglas. I was expecting someone to say, "Would you like fries with that?"

I nodded. "Thank you for making the call for me," is what my mouth said. *"Get real,"* is what I was thinking.

I handed Sarah my co-pay check, and she handed me a pink appointment card on which she had written in purple ink, "Dr. Burke, October 1, 10:00 am"… *five weeks away.*

"It's the best I could do," Sarah said. "They're scheduled solid through December, but someone just cancelled this appointment today." And she grinned like she had just handed me a winning lottery ticket. "Do you want to schedule your next appointment with Dr. Swanson while you're here?"

Uh, no. I conjured up the most sincere smile I could, and thanked her for making the appointment for me. I promised to call about seeing Dr. Swanson again after I checked my calendar at home. Then my little white bag and I hightailed it out of there.

I sat in my car and expelled a whoosh of air as I tipped my head back on the headrest. What a relief not to have anything physically wrong with me! I opened the glove compartment and shoved in the bag of meds. Aside from my first gynecological exam, that had to be the most embarrassing doctor's appointment I've ever had. Pretty hard to admit that I can't cope with my own life.

Jack always makes fun of his friends who go to their weekly shrink appointments. I'm sure it would be open season on me if I told him I was going to see one.

I started the car and sat in the parking lot with the engine idling. I had some time before I had to be at work, and as I was sitting there deciding how to spend it, my cell phone rang. It was Casey!

I connected her to my Bluetooth and pulled out of the parking space and onto the highway.

"Hey you! Sorry I missed your call yesterday."

"It's ok, Mom, no biggie. I just figured if you didn't hear from me you'd imagine me in a gutter somewhere," she joked.

"Do they even *have* gutters in Florida?" I teased back.

"Mom, you know what I mean."

"I do, and I *am* glad you called. So, what's new?"

She filled me in on the happenings of her day, telling me all about setting up her apartment, and trying to get her bearings in the new neighborhood. We shared a laugh when she told me that she couldn't find her car in the parking lot at the grocery store.

"Mind if I share that one with Abbey?"

"At least *I* have an excuse! It's my rental and I've only had it a couple days. I was looking for my red Audi, not a blue midsize. I'm sure she'll love the story though."

Casey had left her new car parked in the second bay of our garage at home until she came home at Christmas, and then she was going to drive it down. Shaffer, Oats, and Spear was letting her use a company rental car for a few months.

. "Mom, it's *so* pretty here, and so *hot*! You'd love it!"

"Speaking of hot, what's up with this Chris that you keep mentioning?"

"Oh…well…he lives across the hall from me and has been really cool about helping me out and showing me the neighborhood. In fact, if he wouldn't have helped me find my car at the grocery store, I'd probably still be walking around there with melted ice cream dripping out of my bag. I'll send some pictures of my place to your email, and he might just be in one of them," she said smugly. "Make sure you check it."

"I can't wait! I'll check it as soon as I get home from work."

"Well, going to meet up with my friends for lunch, so I'll talk to you later, okay?"

"Okay, sweetie. Thanks for calling."

Somehow my car had ended up in Fat Boy's parking lot. Oh well, I deserve a treat today. I drove up to the speaker and ordered an FB special combo: burger, fries, and a chocolate shake. When they handed my order through the window, I remembered the meds in my glove box. I really don't want to have to take medication to get through this. Now that I know what's going on, I feel so much better about it. I smiled and took a big greasy bite.

Just as I was using my straw to slurp the last bit of shake, Jack called on my cell.

"Hey," I said.

"Are you finished at the doctor's?"

"Yes, I was just having some lunch and then I was going to call you."

"And?"

"Dr. Swanson said he thinks I'm just having some panic attacks due to the stress of Casey leaving and the changes in my life right now. He said that I'm physically fine."

"Well, I'm glad to hear that there's nothing wrong with you. See, I told you it was all in your head."

I sighed. "Yep, I'm fine and dandy. Good to go. All systems up and running."

"Could you pick up my suits at the dry cleaner on your way home from work today? I need them for the seminar this weekend in Florida."

"Oh." I had forgotten that he was going this weekend. "I work until nine. It's wine and cheese night."

"For Pete's sake, you mean no dinner again tonight?"

Silence. I have been working until nine every Tuesday for the past year.

"Well, I guess I'll just go out with the guys then. Maybe you can pick up my suits tomorrow."

"I thought you *always* went out to eat with the guys on Tuesday nights," I said.

"Why are you making this such a big deal? Drop it already. I'll see you when I get home," and he hung up.

The chocolate shake might not have been such a great idea. It felt like it was curdling in my stomach. I sighed and checked my watch. Didn't make sense to go all the way home and then leave again for work in an hour. I'd just appease Jack and pick up his dry cleaning now. Since I'd be passing the grocery store, I thought I'd check with Abbey to see if she needed any supplies for tonight's class.

"Hi, sweetheart," I said when she answered her phone.

She laughed. "Hi, honey. You'd better not be calling off! I can't face wine and cheese night alone!"

"I'm going past the grocery store and wondered if you wanted me to pick up the food for tonight."

"Oh, that would be great! I haven't had a free moment all day. We got a Christmas shipment in this morning and I can't wait until you see the new things! Anyway, Rick has been here helping me unpack some of the boxes and unload the kiln, but we haven't even been able to take a lunch break because we've had so many walk-ins."

She sounded exasperated, but I knew better. Abbey loved to be busy, and I knew she was excited about having her business doing so well.

"Well then, I will be the cheese wiz today. Anything special you want?"

"You choose. I expect a big crowd tonight though. Sort of the last week of summer blow out. Just pick what you want and bring the receipt. You know the drill."

"Okay, do you have a bottle of wine for us?"

"It's a surprise. Thank you so much, Ellen. I really appreciate it."

"See you soon."

Wine and cheese night was a favorite. It was a strictly over twenty one crowd, consisting mostly of moms looking forward to some grown-up time. Snacks were supplied by Amazing Glaze, and everyone brought their own bottle of wine.

We all gathered around the table, painting and sharing good conversation, and lots of laughs. It's kind of hard to find a place other than the bar scene where you can just hang out, have a glass of wine, and have some good constructive fun.

Have to say, though, that the pieces painted on wine and cheese night are the most interesting!

Within minutes, I was pushing my cart through the Super Dandy. I chose several varieties of cheese, a couple boxes of fancy crackers, and a long stick of pepperoni. Then I tossed in a huge bunch of red grapes. On my way to the checkout, a bag of foil-wrapped chocolates called my name. I figured, what the heck, and I put them in the cart, too.

After stashing my bags in the trunk, I walked two stores over to the dry cleaners. Even though I didn't have the receipt, the clerk found Jack's order easily. He pulled off a tiny envelope that had been stapled to the plastic bag and handed it to me.

"We found this key in one of the suit pockets," he said.

I handed him my debit card and opened the envelope while he was completing my transaction. Inside was a little key that I'd never seen before. Looked like it was for a desk or something, although it had 713 imprinted on it. Must be for something Jack used at work.

The clerk handed me my card and receipt, and I put them in my wallet along with the key. I grabbed Jack's suits and walked back to my car.

It was a beautiful, sunny day, and although the air had a touch of coolness to it, the car felt stiflingly hot inside. I started the engine and turned on the air conditioner. As I reached down for my sunglasses, I began to feel that all too familiar quiver in my stomach, and I knew it was going to happen again.

My hands started to shake, and beads of sweat were already forming on my forehead. I put my head down on the steering wheel and let the cool air from the vents blow on my face.

I tried to concentrate on my breathing and prayed that I would not die right here in my car. I kept repeating the mantra, *"I'm all right, I'm all right, I'm all right,"* over and over again, and in about five minutes, I was.

I lifted my head and ran my hands through my hair. I don't understand why this happens for no apparent reason. I know the hot car made me feel uncomfortable for a moment, but I've been in hot cars all my life and this has never happened.

I took a deep breath and exhaled slowly. So far this has only occurred when I'm alone, except for the two times with Jack. What if it had happened in the grocery store or dry cleaners? What if it happens when I'm at work? I would be so embarrassed.

These groceries needed to get to the refrigerator, so I started the engine and drove in the slow lane all the way to Amazing Glaze. After I unloaded the trunk, I carried the bags into the store, the jingling bells announcing my arrival.

Abbey was just handing a customer her change, and she looked up as I walked through the door. A concerned expression immediately replaced the smile that had been on her face.

As soon as the customer was out of ear shot, she asked, "Are you okay?"

"I'm fine. Just a little hot out there."

She came around the counter, grabbed the bags, and herded me into the back room. After we put the food in the refrigerator, she looked me in the eye.

"What's going on, Ellen? You looked as pale as a ghost when you came in."

"I don't know. I had a Fat Boy burger and a shake for lunch and I guess I'm just not used to eating that stuff anymore...then it was hot in the car, and I felt a little sick. I'm okay now though."

She gave me an appraising look and appeared to be having an internal struggle with herself not to say more.

"Okay," she said. "But if you don't feel well, let me know and I'll have Rick come back and help me tonight."

We both knew that Rick would rather have his fingernails pulled out with pliers than spend an evening among thirty cackling, slightly tipsy women with paintbrushes in their hands. The last time he helped us on wine and cheese night, he wore earplugs the whole time and consumed an entire bottle of chardonnay himself.

"I think I'll be fine," I said as I pulled out my wallet. "Here's the receipt for the groceries."

I handed her the paper cash register tape, and Jack's little key popped out of my wallet and landed on the floor with a clink.

Abbey bent down to pick it up for me. She turned it over in her hand and cocked her head to the side. "Since when do you have a post office box?"

"Is *that* what it's for? I thought it was to a desk or file cabinet."

"You don't know what your key is for?"

"It's not mine, it's Jack's," I told her, and relayed the dry cleaner story.

"So, Mr. Wonderful has a post office box. Let's go see what's in it today!"

"Abbey!"

"I'm sorry, honey. It's probably just girlie magazines."

My eyes opened wide.

"I'm *kidding*, Ellen."

"Well, we're not going to see what's in it. It has to be something for work because Jack has no reason to have a post office box. That might not even be what the key is for," I said, snatching it out of her open palm and tucking it safely back in my wallet.

Abbey persisted. "One more thing and then the subject is closed. Don't just leave it on his desk or something like I know you'll probably do...ask him what it's for, okay?"

Now that she's made such a big deal out of it, I *do* want to know what it's for. I tried to put on my disgusted face so she'd let it go, and told her I'd ask him.

"Okay, now want to see the new Christmas stuff that came today?" she asked.

The rest of the afternoon flew by, and I was so absorbed in the new merchandise that I forgot all about my lunchtime panic attack. The wine and cheese crew arrived, and consumed all of our energy and attention for the remainder of the evening.

Abbey surprised me with a bottle of champagne for the two of us to share. She said it was to celebrate the beginning of a new chapter in my life. Hmmm...I'd kind of like to skim over this chapter and get to the part where I feel like my old self again. Well, maybe "old" wasn't the right word choice.

Thanks to Abbey, I had a wonderful evening! It makes a girl feel pretty special to drink champagne out of a plastic cup! I was actually sorry when it was time to clean up and go home. I had really enjoyed the camaraderie of all the women tonight. We even sold some of the Christmas stock that had arrived this afternoon! Everyone was excitedly making lists of what they wanted to paint for gifts and making plans to return next week. Wine and cheese night was a huge success!

I'd only had one glass of champagne, so Abbey insisted that I take the rest of the bottle home. Being the instructors, we try to keep a higher level of sobriety than our customers. As a rule though, we require everyone to take a breathalyzer test before they leave. Not really, but we do make sure everyone is okay to drive home.

And so it was with a bottle of champagne in my arm and a smile on my face that I walked in my front door to find Jack sitting on the couch with his cell phone to his ear, scowling.

CHAPTER FOUR

I gave him a beauty pageant wave and tiptoed to the kitchen, not wanting to interrupt a phone call that was apparently causing him grief. Muffled bits of his conversation drifted in from the living room, and I listened as I got two glasses out of the cupboard.

"I couldn't check tonight...No, I told you the main office was already closed...I have no idea where it is...Have to go...Yeah, me too..."

A moment later, Jack padded into the kitchen. "Hey, Ellen," he said.

"Hey, Jack." I handed him a glass of champagne. "Looks like you could use this."

He accepted my offering and took a long swig. "Geez, Jack. You're supposed to sip it, not guzzle it."

"It's just been that kind of day."

"Sorry to hear that. I'm pooped too; we had a real lively crowd tonight."

"You call that work? Sitting around drinking wine and giggling? You wouldn't last a day in my world."

I winced. "My job *is* demanding," I told him. He wouldn't have lasted ten minutes at Mary Frances's birthday party. "Tonight was a lot of fun, though."

"Maybe you should get a *real* job to help out with the finances more around here, so *I* could do something fun once in awhile," he said as he drained his glass and poured himself a refill.

We've had this discussion before, and I wasn't going to get into it again. I have a job that I love, and even though I don't make a lot of money, I pretty much take care of my own needs and try to help with the household expenses. Jack handles all of our finances though, but we never seem to be lacking. In fact, I would say we're pretty well off.

I noticed that my glass was empty too and poured in the remainder of the bottle.

"Did you print me your itinerary for this weekend yet?" I asked. Jack always gave me a schedule of his flights and hotel information before his trips.

"No, I'll print it out in the morning and leave it on my desk. I may not have the hotel information though; it won't be finalized until the last minute this time. But you always just call on my cell anyway. I leave Thursday early and come back Tuesday late."

"Oh, I thought it was just for the weekend."

"Turns out it's longer than we originally thought. I'm going to drive my car and park it at the airport, then I won't have to wait for you to pick me up."

Hallelujah! I don't have to drive to the airport! Wait a minute.

"We?" I asked. "Is someone going with you this time?"

"No, just me. I meant *we* as in the people I'm meeting with down there."

"Oh. Where exactly are you going? Will you be able to see Casey?"

"Uh, no. I won't have any time for socializing. It'll be strictly business."

"I'll miss you, Jack," I said. And I realized that I really

46

meant it.

He gave me a calculated look. Setting his empty glass on the counter, he slipped his arms around me and held me tight.

"Let's go upstairs and you can show me just how much."

Feeling relaxed from the champagne, I took his hand and followed him up the stairs.

Thursday morning I kissed Jack goodbye and stood with the front door open, watching until he drove down the street and out of sight. The clouds were gray and hanging low, releasing an almost undetectable mist. It felt like summer had changed to fall overnight– Mother Nature must have gotten Abbey's memo. I clutched my robe closer around me and shut the front door.

Now what? Nothing to do until I have to go to work at four. I guess I could clean, but nothing really got messed up anymore with just Jack and me here. I could do some laundry…or not.

I wandered to the kitchen and stood looking out the window. The sugar maple already had a few leaves turning. In a few weeks, it would be breathtaking. And a few weeks after that…bare.

I made myself a cup of tea with honey and a bagel with cream cheese, grabbed a donut for good measure, and headed to the living room. I plunked down on the couch and turned on the TV. At some point, I was overcome by the down comforter that I had cuddled into. It has magical powers. It's a well known fact in our household that anyone who lies beneath that blanket will lose all battles with consciousness and fall asleep—it's that good. Really ticked me off this morning though. I had invested a good twenty minutes watching a newlywed couple trying to choose their first home. They had been living with the husband's parents so they could save up for a down payment, and we all know how that goes: "Thank you kindly, but get us the hell out of here."

We had been shown three properties, and I fell asleep before I found out which one they chose. That darn blanket.

It was a little after noon as I stood by the living room window and noticed that the only change in the weather was that the mist had turned to a good soaking rain. Lovely. Sometimes I do enjoy a nice rainy day or thunderstorm, but today wasn't one of them.

I moved on to the kitchen again and rummaged around for something to eat. I pulled out a box of graham crackers, broke a handful of them into bite size pieces, put them in a bowl, and squirted a very attractive design on them with a can of whipped cream. After all the years that have passed since my soda fountain days, I still had the knack. Then I went back to my nest on the couch and dug in.

I'd like to say that I outsmarted the blanket this time, but I fell asleep again and didn't wake up until it was almost time for work. My gosh, I'd slept the day away! No time for a shower; I struggled to shift gears and ran upstairs. I quickly applied my foundation and blush, and swished some mouthwash around while I did my eyes. Kind of hard to apply eyeshadow on lids that are puffy from so much sleep. I spit into the sink and ran a brush through my hair.

After pulling on a pair of jeans and a tee shirt, I slid on my Reeboks without retying them. I flew down the steps, grabbed my purse off the kitchen counter, my jacket out of the hall closet, turned on a light in the living room, and ran out the door.

At five minutes past four, I was stashing my purse under the counter at Amazing Glaze. Not bad.

Abbey just looked at me and laughed.

The evening went by quickly and before I knew it, we were locking up for the night. The days had gotten noticeably shorter, and it was already dusk. I was glad that I had remembered to leave a light on at home for myself.

Once again, I didn't feel like cooking, so I stopped at the drive-thru and picked up a chicken wrap and fries. Usually I get the salad, but I needed something resembling comfort food today. I added a hot apple pie to my order, just for the feel good factor.

Back at home, I tossed the possessed blanket on the floor and ate my dinner sitting on the sofa.

My cell phone rang and I jumped up to grab it out of my purse. It was Jack, calling to tell me that he had arrived safely and eaten dinner with his associates. He was joining them for drinks so he couldn't talk long and said not to bother calling again tonight unless it was an emergency, because he probably wouldn't hear the phone in the nightclub.

As soon as he disconnected, I punched in Casey's number.

"Hi, Mom!" she said, and I felt rejuvenated just hearing her voice.

"Hey, sweetie! Was thinking about you and thought I'd call to see how you're doing."

"Fantastic! But, Mom, I'm just walking into a restaurant with Chris. He was helping me hang some pictures today, so I'm treating him to a spaghetti dinner. Can I call you back?"

"No problem, honey. You enjoy and I'll just talk to you tomorrow. Oh, I was just wondering…your dad's in Florida on business, and I was curious to see if he'd made arrangements to visit you."

There was a slight pause, and she said, "No, I haven't talked to him since the first night I got here when you two were eating dinner on the deck. Remember? Where's he staying?"

"I don't know really. He said the hotel arrangements were made last minute."

"Well, did he leave you his itinerary?"

Duh, mental head slap. "He said he'd leave it on the desk. I'll go up and check."

"I'll give him a call on his cell tomorrow then," she said. "By the way, check your email while you're up there. Sorry, Mom, I have to go, we're about to be seated."

"Okay, talk to you tomorrow. I love you."

"Love you too, Mom. G'night."

I jogged up the stairs and flicked on the light in Jack's office. It used to be Adam's bedroom, but we converted it to an office for Jack a few weeks after Adam moved out. It was nothing fancy, just a desk and credenza, with a comfy chair positioned by a bookcase. We had given the walls a fresh coat of paint but hadn't gotten around to hanging any artwork yet.

True to his promise, Jack had left the computer printout of his flight itinerary under the paperweight right in the middle of his desk.

Tampa. I wonder how long it takes to drive from Tampa to Orlando. I wonder if he rented a car. Why didn't I ask these questions before he left? I've been too preoccupied with the stupid panic attacks to even think clearly. When I talk to him tomorrow, I'll get my answers.

I decided to check the distance from Tampa to Orlando on the computer, so I reached down and pushed the button to make it come to life. A moment later I knew that it would probably take an hour and a half to make the trip. If it were me, I would find a way to do it, but I don't know if Jack would. Seems crazy to be that close to your daughter and not see her.

I scanned my inbox folder for new emails. True to her promise, Casey had sent me one with the subject line, "Hottie for you!"

"Smart aleck kid," I mumbled to myself, and smiled.

Clicking on the attachment, I opened her pictures and started a slide show on my monitor. The first ones were of her living room. The furniture really did look awesome, and apparently Chris was very good at hanging pictures. The room already had a homey look to it. The next picture was the view from her balcony, overlooking a courtyard scattered with palm trees and a pool surrounded by umbrella tables and chaises.

I gasped when the next picture popped up. It was a close up of Casey in her green bikini standing by the pool. She looked tan and happy. I missed her so much I ached. All too soon, the picture faded and one of a handsome young man flipping burgers took its place. Ah, so that's Chris...no wonder she's been spending so much time with him!

The screen returned to Casey's email. I sent her a quick reply and turned off the computer. I sat there for a moment staring into space, then got up and headed down the hallway. Turning on the lights in Casey's room, I sat on her bed and the tears rolled down my cheeks. I felt empty all the way to the pit of my stomach.

My cell phone rang a few minutes later. I flipped it open and tried to say, "Hi, Adam."

"Hi, Mom!" he said, "What's the matter, do you have a cold?"

"Oh, uh, no, just little stuffy. How are you?"

"Couldn't be better. It looks like I'm going to get that property I told you about."

"The cat lady house?"

"Yep. It's *so* disgusting, but the place has great bones. I can't wait to start gutting it out. I'm going to have a *blast* on this one," he said.

I hope he didn't mean that literally. I couldn't believe he was so excited about cleaning up cat pee.

"That's wonderful, honey. When do I get to see it?"

"Lucky for you I took some digital pictures today, so you won't have to come until I get the smell gone. I'm going to load them on the computer tonight, so check your email tomorrow. Too bad they're not scratch and sniff pictures," he said.

I smiled. I really had some smart ass kids.

"Ha ha, very funny," I said. "All joking aside, I'm proud of you, Adam. I'd be happy to help you on this one if you need me."

"Thanks, Mom, I will definitely need you. Not sure if I'll be selling or renting it. We'll see how the market looks when I get it done. Is Dad on his trip?"

"Yeah, he'll be back Tuesday night," I said.

"I bet you're probably living it up while he's gone. Hey, if you need anything, call me."

"Yeah, I'm having a blast. Thanks, Adam."

"Well, I'll talk to you soon. Good night, Mom."

"Good night, sweetie," I said, and flipped my phone shut.

Well, that was a shot in the arm. I felt so much better now. Instead of focusing on what I don't have at the moment, I need to be thankful for what I do have. I still have Adam nearby and I have Jack. And I still have Casey; she's just a phone call or email away. I really need to think about redecorating this room as a guest room, as we had planned. That would be fun. Maybe tomorrow I'd look at some paint samples.

I turned out the light and headed downstairs. Sweeping through the kitchen, I picked up a handful of cookies on my way to the living room, then plunked down on the sofa again. Sitting there with an Oreo in one hand and the remote in the other, I surfed the channels. Funny how you can have a hundred channels and not find anything you want to watch. I did, however, feel a bit empowered to have total control of the remote for a few days.

On my second rotation, I paused on a home shopping channel. They were just about to end a segment called "Ring Bling." Boy, were those rings gaudy looking! Huge princess cut gems surrounded by tons of teeny, tiny diamond chips, on a thick sterling silver band. I would never find something like that appealing

After the commercial break, they only had one hundred of the blue sapphire and thirty of the emerald left. All of the ruby rings were gone. Seems they're selling fast! I leaned forward and took a closer look. A woman called in and gave a testimonial on the air about how she had bought one last year and was so thrilled with it, she was now going to buy two more…one for her daughter and another for herself.

I guess maybe they didn't look so bad nestled against the black velvet's caress. Lots of sparkle going on there. They were selling at a reduced price of $199.99, plus shipping and handling, payable in five easy payments. Quite the steal, according to the perfectly coiffed hostess. She held up her manicured, non-wrinkled hand, and turned it back and forth ever so slightly to make the ring shimmer and shine. She was wearing the emerald, and I have to admit that it was a great contrast to her crimson nail polish.

An announcement flashed across the bottom of the screen, *"Emerald Now Sold Out."* Oh my, now they only had blue sapphire left, and it was calling my name. I wanted that ring. I needed that ring. I suddenly couldn't bear the thought that it would be gone forever, or at least until the next time they had it on the show.

They broke for another commercial, and I sprinted to get my purse from the kitchen, pulling out my bank card before I even hit the living room threshold. Just as I got back to my seat, the show was coming back on. Down to the last ten minutes and then they'd be gone. I was urged not to miss out on a fantastic opportunity to own one of those delightful rings that would be the talk of any cocktail party. We're talking only twenty-five blue sapphire rings left.

I dialed the phone number and placed my order. Success! Now, if I ever attended a cocktail party, I would be all set. And if anyone ever tried to assault me, I could pop them one with it. Probably would be tons better than a brass knuckle! The bottom of the screen flashed, "*Sold Out.*" I felt accomplished and very smug.

The next segment, plugged as "Ear-Ring Bling," began. Oh, look! They had earrings with gems the size of half-dollars that matched the ring. Geez, the weight of that would pull my earlobe down to my shoulders. I could never wear that!

This time the blue sapphire ones were selling fast.

Maybe I could pull it off, if I only wore them for short periods....

Around dawn, I fished my bank card out of the empty Oreo bag, brushed off the crumbs, and put it back in my wallet to cool off. I trudged up the stairs and fell onto the bed without even pulling back the comforter.

The pattern was set for the remainder of Jack's trip. I would sleep until midafternoon, go to work, come home, and then not be able to sleep at night. I would watch the home shopping channel until daybreak, and then start the cycle all over again.

At noon on Tuesday, my cell phone rang and woke me up. It was Abbey.

"Good morning," I said in my raspy first words of the day voice.

Pause. "Ellen, were you still *sleeping?*" she asked.

"No, just have a little voice thing going on today."

"I see," she said, like she didn't really see at all.

"What's up?" I asked in a more normal tone.

"We're really busy today and I was wondering if you'd stop at the grocery store on your way in and pick up the stuff for wine and cheese night again."

Immediately I started to feel nervous. Last Tuesday I had my panic attack at Fat Boys, right after I stopped at the Super Dandy. What if it happened again in the same place? I haven't been back there since, and I didn't want to go.

"Abbey, I'd love to, but I really have some other errands to run before I come to work. I don't think I'll have time today. I'm sorry," I said.

"Oh, well, that's okay. Just thought I'd ask. I'll have Rick go, and hopefully he won't come back with cheese in an aerosol can and saltine crackers. See you later."

Flipping my phone shut, I rolled over, and pulled the comforter up to my chin. The nervous feeling was replaced by guilt.

I opened the door to Amazing Glaze very carefully, trying to walk in without the bells giving me away. Abbey wouldn't really care that I was fifteen minutes late, but I hadn't really thought up a good excuse yet.

Success! No one in sight. If I could just get behind the counter and slip my purse on the shelf, I could pretend that I've been here awhile straightening up.

As I silently rounded the corner and bent down to deposit

my purse, Abbey sprung up from the floor in front of me and we both screamed! A handful of brown paper bags flew from her hand like jumbo confetti.

"Holy cow, girl! Are you trying to give me a heart attack?" Abbey asked, putting a hand to her chest.

My own heart was pounding. "I didn't expect to see you down there restocking bags."

"And *I* didn't expect to see *you* sneaking in," she said as she began to pick up the mess. "What gives?"

I stooped, collected a handful of bags, and placed them on the shelf, trying to come up with something better than the fact that I just couldn't get myself out of bed. I came up empty.

"I wasn't sneaking," I said.

Abbey stopped in her tracks. "Listen, Ellen, something is going on with you and I'd like to know what it is. You just haven't been yourself lately."

I sighed. Abbey was my best friend. She deserved an answer.

The bells jingled, and several women bustled in, pausing in their conversation to greet us on their way back to the classroom.

"To be continued..." Abbey said, and gave my arm a gentle squeeze as she headed back to begin teaching her class.

Rick proudly dropped off the results of his shopping trip while Abbey was still in the classroom. I peeked in the bag and then looked up at him with wide eyes.

"What?" he said, his brow creasing.

"Oh, nothing," I tried to conceal my surprise. "I was just thinking that I'd better get busy taking the cellophane off all these cheese slices, that's all."

He expelled a deep breath. "For a moment I thought I bought the wrong thing."

"Rick, I don't know anyone who doesn't like American cheese…that would just be…uh, un-American!" I said. "Thanks for picking it up for us."

"Well, I'm outta here. Tell Abbey I'll see her at home."

Abbey was going to freak. I'd better think of a way to fix this, since it was really my fault. I should have just gone to the store like she asked me to.

I carried the grocery bag back to the lunch table, remembering something from one of Casey's elementary school parties that might save the day. I pulled out some small cookie cutters from one of the storage bins. After choosing a few shaped like leaves and pumpkins, I washed them up and used them to cut shapes on the cheese slices. Then I placed each shape on its own cracker. Once they were all arranged on trays, they didn't look half bad…for a kindergarten party.

I covered the trays with plastic wrap and put them in the fridge, just as Abbey was finishing her class.

Thankfully, the shop was full of customers the remainder of the afternoon, leaving Abbey no time to make good on her promise of continuing our conversation.

I knew when she opened the refrigerator though. Wine and cheese night had begun, and I was stooping down to get another pot of Harvest Gold paint from the bottom shelf when I heard, "What the hell?" reverberate from the lunch room. I paused with my hand in mid-air. Then I heard Abbey laughing hysterically.

"Well, ladies, looks like we have a real treat tonight!" Abbey said as she slid the cheese trays on the table. She looked over at me and shook her head, smiling.

Later, after everyone had cleared out and Abbey and I were cleaning up, she suddenly plunked down in one of the chairs and patted the seat of the one next to her.

"Sit down, Ellen."

Great. Inquisition time.

She pushed some stray hairs that had escaped her ponytail behind her ear and poured us each a glass of wine.

"So, what's going on, sweetie?" she asked.

I drained half my glass, and of course said, "Nothing."

She refilled my glass to the top and remained silent.

I took a few more sips.

"There's something I've wanted to ask you all night," she said.

I looked at her expectantly.

She grabbed my hand and inspected the bling on my ring finger. "What the *hell* is this?"

I looked down at the huge chunk of blue and silver. It had arrived this morning, and I had put it on right away. Suddenly it all seemed so very funny. I started to giggle and I couldn't stop.

I infected Abbey, and we both laughed until we had tears streaming down our faces. She reached over and gave me a hug, then refilled my glass again.

By this time, I was feeling more relaxed than I had in quite a while. Abbey sure knows how to run her inquisitions. I began by telling her that I was missing Casey, and then the rest just tumbled out.

I even told her about my panic attacks, but I made her pinky swear not to tell anyone…not even Rick. She urged me to keep the appointment with the psychiatrist and said that talking things out always helps. I have to admit that after talking to Abbey, I *did* feel better. She didn't make me feel inferior or embarrassed, like I felt when I told Jack.

Jack! Oh my gosh, he would be back from his trip by now and wondering why I'm so late getting home.

"Abbey, I have to get going. Jack's probably been home for an hour already."

I thought I saw her roll her eyes as I got up from the table to get my purse. I pulled out my cell phone and turned it back on. Four missed calls from Jack and one message. I listened to his voice saying, "I'm home. Nice to have you here to greet me."

How could I have let him down like that? I should have been home when he got there. I felt the tears welling up and stinging my eyes. The light-hearted feeling I'd just experienced was replaced by a dull ache in the pit of my stomach.

Abbey rushed over. "What's wrong?"

"Jack is upset because I wasn't there for him when he got home."

"Oh, honey, he just needs to grow up. You shouldn't feel bad about that. You were working, just like *he* was while he left you at home alone. Honestly, Ellen, I don't know how you put up with that arrogant SOB."

Lucky for me, I had left out all the parts about Jack when I was spilling my guts to Abbey. She just doesn't understand, and it would only have made her think less of him than she already does.

I searched my purse for my keys and couldn't find them. Abbey cleared her throat, and I looked up to see her swinging my key ring from her finger.

"I'm driving you home tonight, Ellen. I figured if my plan worked, you'd be in no condition to drive." Abbey looked a little sheepish.

I didn't know whether to be angry with her or grateful.

After a quick call to Rick to pick her up at my house, we walked arm in arm to my car.

"I love you like a sister, Ellen. Please let me help you through this," she said as we buckled ourselves in.

We drove in silence, and as she pulled up in front of my house, I noticed that there were no lights on. Even the outside light was turned off. She walked me to the front door and as I flicked on the hall light, we saw Rick's headlights reflecting off the garage as he pulled into the driveway.

"You okay?" she asked.

"I'm fine. Thank you so much, Abbey…for everything."

"You call if you need me, okay?"

"I will," I replied as I gave her a big hug.

I closed the door and kicked off my shoes in the hallway. Silently I padded up the stairs and peeked in the bedroom.

"Jack?" I said softly.

No answer. I turned on the nightlight and found Jack already sound asleep. He must have been exhausted from his trip. I turned off the light and retreated to the living room.

Even though I felt sorry he was already sleeping, a part of me was happy that I didn't have to deal with him being angry at me tonight. I'd make it up to him in the morning.

Still feeling a bit woozy, I plunked down on the couch

and grabbed the remote to see what my new friends had to sell me tonight.

Hours later, I was sitting cross-legged on the floor with a bowl of melting chocolate chip ice cream in my lap, totally engrossed in the demonstration of the super-duper vacuum scooper. What a handy gadget, and it came in six designer colors! I was so fixated on the TV that I didn't hear Jack come in to the living room, until he was standing beside me and shouting, *"Ellen!"*

I jumped, and the ice cream bowl flew in the air and landed upside down on Jack's slipper. I sat paralyzed with my eyes wide.

"What the hell!" he shouted.

I instantly sprang to life, reached over and used my hand to scoop the ice cream off his slipper and back into the bowl. The spoon was MIA.

"What the *hell* are you doing?" he asked.

CHAPTER FIVE

My late night TV watching was squelched. I'd go to bed with Jack whether I was tired or not. Some nights I'd lay with him in the dark for hours, and as he peacefully slept, my mind raced. No matter how early I did go to bed, I still wanted to sleep the day away until it was time for work.

As the weeks passed, I just couldn't get myself motivated to do much of anything. The few times that Jack wanted me to go somewhere with him, I made up an excuse not to because I was afraid I'd have a panic attack. He was working more, and it seemed the short amount of time we did spend together was spent arguing. And we were always interrupted by his damn cell phone ringing. It was as if someone had picked me up out of my life and placed me in someone else's. I felt that I just didn't belong anywhere.

Casey called several times a week, and even though I spoke to Adam occasionally on the phone, I hadn't seen him since the night I had stopped by his place. He was busy with the cat lady house.

Abbey was being very supportive, and sometimes picked me up for work since I didn't like to drive much anymore. I tried to hide how I was feeling from Jack, but I've been slacking on the housework and cooking, and he's been pointing it out to me daily. Especially this morning. I wasn't actually asleep, just lying in bed with my eyes closed, and Jack was ready for work, heading out of the bedroom.

"Ellen, you'd better snap out of this," he had said. "Go get yourself some happy pills or something."

My thoughts fluttered to the white bag still in my glove compartment.

I drifted back to sleep after he left and was jolted awake sometime later by the ringing of my cell phone. The screen showed me that it was an unknown number. I answered in my raspy morning voice.

"Hello?"

"Hello. This is Dr. Burke's office."

"Oh, hello," I murmured, but the voice just kept on talking.

"This call is to confirm your appointment at 10:00 a.m. tomorrow. If you are able to keep the appointment, please press number one now. If you need to reschedule, please press two now, and follow the instructions. Thank you and have a nice day."

For Pete's sake, I was trying to talk to an automated voice message. I hadn't planned on going to the appointment, but I was so tired of this whole damn thing and I wanted my life back. I made a bold move, and pushed number one.

"Your appointment has been confirmed for ten a.m. tomorrow. Thank you."

The call disconnected, and I lay there wondering, for the umpteenth time, why on earth this was happening to me.

The next morning, I dragged myself out of bed, showered, and tried to find something to wear. I now belong to the sisterhood of the shrinking pants, because lately I just can't seem to squish myself into them. I finally decided on a pair of gray sweats with a matching hooded jacket. I unzipped it just enough to show a bit of the pale pink tee I was wearing underneath. I didn't have the energy to decide what jewelry goes with shabby-chic gym attire, so I just didn't wear any.

I planned the route to Dr. Burke's office in my mind. No tunnels and it should only take about fifteen minutes to get there. I tried to reason with myself. If I'm going to have a panic attack, that would be the best place for it to happen.

Abbey was ecstatic that I was going today. She had even offered to go with me, and I was very tempted to call her right now and take her up on her offer. However, I mustered enough courage to get myself in the car and actually turn on the ignition and put it in gear. I drove past the place once, on purpose. I just wanted to keep on going until I was far, far away. But then that thought scared me even more, so I turned the car around and parked.

I sat in the car for another ten minutes. Finally, I just took a deep breath and made the plunge.

I signed the roster that the receptionist pushed through the glass window and checked the box by Dr. Burke's name. Then she traded me the roster for a clipboard with a questionnaire to fill out. I found a seat back in the corner, next to a potted ficus, where I hoped to be inconspicuous.

As I sat with pen poised, I checked out the room, which was pretty much filled to capacity. There were about twenty people of all ages, shapes, and sizes, and, I would suppose, degrees of craziness, as Jack would call it. I wondered why they were all here, and they were probably wondering the same thing about me. I guess it's too late in the game to pretend that I'm a pharmaceutical sales rep.

No one seemed to be paying any attention to me though, so I continued writing on the form.

"Ellen Stern," the receptionist called a little too loudly. I wanted to put my finger to my lips and tell her "Shhhhhhhh." Now all heads turned curiously as I walked through the door to meet Dr. Burke.

In my mind, I had imagined her as being a tall and gangly woman, having dark hair pulled severely back into a French twist, large framed glasses with thick lenses, and a face devoid of makeup with the exception of bright red lipstick. I couldn't have been farther from the truth.

A woman who appeared to be in her thirties, about my height, with pale blonde hair cut in a cute little updated pixie, a peachy complexion, and shiny lip gloss, greeted me with a smile and a firm handshake saying, "Nice to meet you, Ellen. I'm Dr. Burke."

She could have been someone I'd strike up a conversation with at the super market, and immediately I felt completely at ease.

We entered her office, which felt more like someone's den than a doctor's office. She motioned for me to take a seat in one of the two comfy looking chairs, and she sat in the other with one foot tucked under her bottom.

"I have my notes from Dr. Swanson, but I would like to hear from you just why you're here today. I hope you don't mind if I record our conversation; it distracts me when I have to take the time to write everything down while you're here. I would much rather participate in the conversation," she said.

I began talking, and had intended to give her a brief synopsis of the past few months, but in actuality I think I talked non-stop for a full twenty minutes. It was like once the spigot of confession opened, I couldn't turn it off.

When I finally came up for air, she gave me an encouraging smile and some advice.

"Ellen, when someone is feeling depressed or anxious, it's hard for them to focus on anything but themselves. They just don't have the energy to see outside their box."

I nodded my head, because I knew that I had been self-absorbed lately. I hadn't had the energy or inclination to deal with much of anything besides waiting for my next panic attack to hit.

"I want to give you a little assignment this week. Each day, I want you to do one nice thing for someone else. Now, I know that you do things for people all day, but really try to make an effort to go above and beyond something you would normally do. Maybe a random act of kindness for someone you don't know, or something unexpected for someone you do know."

I stared at her silently.

"It doesn't have to be grandiose. Perhaps send someone a card for no reason at all. Just buy a card, sign your name, address it, and put it in the mail. Not a lot of effort on your part, but it would make someone else happy. I think doing something for others will make you feel better about yourself. Will you try that?"

I nodded and felt the hot tears brimming again. I had always enjoyed doing things for others. She was absolutely right. I had been so focused on myself that I couldn't remember the last time I thought of someone else's needs.

"Great! That's a good start," she continued, "I also want you to start keeping a journal. Write down how you feel each evening, the things that upset you that day, the things that worry you, the things that make you happy. Always make sure you come up with at least one good thing that happened to you each day, even if it's only getting all green lights on your way to work."

"And lastly, I want you to get some exercise each day. Go for a walk, ride a bike, exercise to a video. Half an hour each day should help tremendously."

"Oh, and let's try to get you back to sleeping nights and not wanting to sleep the day away. In the evening, try some relaxation techniques. Avoid caffeine, listen to some calming music, light some candles…take a bubble bath. Write your thoughts down in your journal, then give yourself permission to put them away for the night."

"Let's make an appointment for next week, and we can see how things are going. You may call me if you need to talk before our next appointment."

I looked at my watch and then nodded. Our session was over.

I walked out onto the sidewalk, and a gust of wind whipped at the papers I held clutched in my hand. Dr. Burke had jotted down my instructions on violet– colored stationery. I liked Dr. Burke, I really did. I just don't know if sending someone a card was going to stop my panic attacks.

Remembering that my paycheck still needed to be deposited, I decided to swing by the bank on the way home. I pulled up to the drive-through window lane and took my place at the end of the line. A chocolate lab's head was hanging out of the window of the minivan in front of me, panting with his tongue hanging out. He was watching the teller's window expectantly. The cylinder whooshed down the tube, and he started quivering all over. I tend to get excited over money too, but his antics were cracking me up. The minivan's driver opened the tube. I saw her remove a white bank envelope, and then a bone-shaped doggy treat. The lab waited until she handed it to him, gulped it down, and then sat himself down in the passenger seat licking his chops.

I smiled as they drove away, and I pulled up to the teller's window. As the cylinder once again whooshed up the tube, I thought about what I had just seen. Maybe that's what Dr. Burke was talking about. Just a small gesture on the teller's part, but it made *me* smile, and I'm sure it really made the black lab's day. Go figure.

I had a sudden urge to see Adam. Maybe I could take Cooper a treat and cross off my nice thing for the day. I pushed the speed dial on my phone for Adam.

"Hey, Mom, what's up?"

"I was wondering if I could stop over for a quick visit."

"I'm not home, I'm working on my new house. Why don't you come over here and check it out…it doesn't smell anymore."

"How about I pick up some lunch for us?"

"Sure, that would be great. Let me give you directions."

I got on the turnpike and was already feeling better than I have in a long time. Going to see Dr. Burke was a positive step in the right direction. I was beginning to feel like I had some control of my life again.

As I slowed down for my exit, a black G35 Coupe whizzed past me. This time I noticed the license plate. It *was* Jack! I remembered the last time I came to visit Adam and saw a black G35. Could that have been him too? What the heck is he doing out this way when he told me he had meetings in Pittsburgh, totally in the other direction?

Despite my preoccupation with Jack, I followed Adam's directions and found his new house without a problem. I grabbed the sacks of sandwiches that I'd purchased at a fast food drive-thru on the way and made my way up the sidewalk.

From the outside, the house didn't look too bad. Really, it appeared that just some cosmetic improvements were all that was needed. When I was halfway to the front door, it opened, and Cooper bounded out to greet me.

"Hi boy! I brought something for you, too!" I told him as he sniffed at the bags.

Adam came to my rescue before he started jumping. "Hey, Mom, thanks for stopping by! There's a picnic table out back. Let's eat out there." He threw a tennis ball, and Cooper went charging after it.

I followed him to a nice-sized back yard and unpacked our food on the table. Cooper had returned with the ball and began sniffing the air. I told him to sit and give me his paw, then I rewarded him with a plain burger, minus the bun. He lapped it up in about five seconds, sat down, and raised his paw again.

"That's all, boy," Adam said. "Trust me, a little guilt trip is not going to get her to give up her sandwich."

Cooper stretched out next to my feet, just in case.

"I just saw your dad flying past me on the turnpike," I said.

Adam shrugged. "Anything unusual about that?"

"Only that he said he had meetings in Pittsburgh today. He must have had a change of plans and been really preoccupied not to notice that he was passing me."

"Probably. You know he always drives fast. He was probably on his cell or something."

"You're right. Funny thing is, I thought I saw his car the last time I was here, too."

"Well then, he probably has a client out this way."

I chewed thoughtfully. "I guess."

While we finished our food, Adam shared his renovation plans for the house with me, and I got caught up in the excitement. It felt good to be excited about something. He gave me a tour, and I could see how his ideas were coming to life. Before I left, I promised to help him pick out the new kitchen appliances.

I hadn't mentioned my doctor's appointment or anything about my panic attacks to Adam or Casey. Bad enough Jack and Abbey knew. No need to worry the kids or make myself more embarrassed.

I was feeling a burst of energy that felt almost foreign. It had been so long since I really felt like doing anything.

A little roadside market on the way home looked inviting, so I stopped and picked out two pots of bright yellow fall mums. They would look great on the front porch, along with the three plump, orange pumpkins and the corn stalks that I also bought. I crammed my goodies in the trunk of the Maxima and slammed it shut. Inhaling a deep breath of crisp fall air, I smiled. I was going to be okay.

After I decorated the porch, I still had an hour or so until I had to leave for work. I decided to check my email and send a quick note to Casey. Grabbing the mail from our mailbox, I took it upstairs to the office to sort.

I tossed the junk mail and began to open my bank statement. Jack and I had a joint account at International Bank, but I also had one in my own name at BNC, mostly for the convenience of depositing my paycheck and using for my own small expenditures.

Only this *wasn't* my bank statement. I turned over the envelope and looked again at the address. It was from BNC alright, but it was addressed only to Jack with a post office box *and* a sticker with our street address on it. What the heck?

I remembered the small key that was still in my change purse. I had forgotten all about it and had never mentioned it to Jack. I ran downstairs, grabbed my purse, and ran back up to the office. I fished among the coins and found the key: 713, the same number as the post office box on the bank statement.

Why would he have his own bank account without telling me? The staggering numbers on the page in front of me swam before my eyes. The beginning balance had been seven hundred fifty thousand dollars! Jack is always complaining that we have no money, and he has seven hundred fifty thousand dollars? There had been a couple large withdrawals, and the ending balance was fifty-five thousand.

Oh...my...gosh! My heart was beating wildly, and I was feeling a bit woozy. I just don't understand this. Where did all this money come from, and where did it all go? And why the post office box? There has to be a good explanation. Maybe he was planning a surprise for me, and I had just ruined it by finding the bank statement. If that was the case, Jack would be furious. He was going to be ticked at me for opening mail addressed to him anyway.

I stuffed the whole bank statement in the bottom of my purse. Jack was not going to know that I saw this, or that I have the key. I zipped it back into my change purse and put my head in my hands. I took deep, regular breaths, trying to calm myself down before a panic attack reared its ugly head.

After a few minutes, I felt calmer, but I still had no answers. Feeling exhausted, I dragged myself to the bedroom. I toppled onto the bed and a dozen possible scenarios raced through my mind, but none of them seemed viable. This was disturbing on so many levels. How could he keep something like this a secret from me?

My cell phone rang and interrupted my thoughts. I looked over at the clock. How did it get to be so late?

I flipped open the phone and heard Abbey's cheery voice.

"Hey, Ellen, want me to pick you up for work?"

Oh boy. "Abbey, I'm not feeling so well. I don't think I'll be able to come in today," I said.

She didn't answer for a couple of beats. "What's wrong, honey?"

The tears immediately welled up, and nothing would come out when I tried to answer her.

"Ellen?"

"I'm here," I managed to say.

"I'm coming over."

"No, don't–" I started to say, but she had already disconnected.

I dragged myself off the bed, went in the bathroom, and splashed some cool water on my face. I ran a brush through my hair, halfheartedly applied some lipstick, then picked up my purse and went to sit on the porch and wait for Abbey.

I didn't want to tell her about the bank statement. I needed time to digest that knowledge myself before she put her own negative spin on it.

So as Abbey pulled in the driveway, I put on what I hoped was a pretty convincing smile. I buckled myself into her passenger seat, but despite my efforts, a sigh escaped.

"Are you okay? You sounded like you were crying," she said as she put her hand on my arm, "And you look like sh–" She stopped herself from going any further.

"I'm okay now. I plead temporary insanity. I think I just tried to do too much today and got overwhelmed…thanks for coming to get me."

It seemed like she bought it, because she pulled out of my driveway and started talking about offering mosaic classes at Amazing Glaze. I stared out the window and tried to focus on the conversation, but other than offering a little requisite enthusiasm, I wasn't much of a participant.

The next morning, the blue sky and brilliant sunshine beckoned me to come out and play. I decided to take myself for a walk at nearby Indian Lake. After four laps around the half-mile walking track, I felt invigorated. I took a little detour through the woods on my way back to the car, picking some wildflowers and making a little bouquet to take home with me.

I swung into the driveway and saw Jack's car parked around back. What was he doing home at noon on a weekday? I opened the front door to the house and called his name. No answer, but I heard the closet door shut in the bedroom.

I ran up the stairs and into the bedroom to find Jack's suitcase open on the bed, and Jack standing there with a handful of socks, looking startled to see me.

"I thought you were going walking and then to work," he said.

"I'm just getting back from my walk, but I need to take a shower before work. What are you doing?"

He sighed and frowned. Then he puffed up his chest and said, "Ellen, I just can't do this anymore. I'm almost fifty years old now, and I want to live my life...not just exist."

"You're going on a vacation without me?" I asked.

"Ellen, you just don't *challenge* me anymore. You never want to *do* anything! You're so afraid of having a panic attack, it's making *me* crazy. Our lives are so predictable. I need a change. I need to be with new people in a new place. I'm sorry, Ellen, but I'm moving out."

There has to be a mistake. This could not be happening. As I stood there wringing my hands in disbelief, he grabbed a pile of tee shirts from a drawer and put them in the suitcase next to his socks.

"What are you talking about? How can you just come home one day and out of a clear blue sky say you're leaving?" I threw my hands up in the air.

He paused and looked at me as he was pulling boxers out

of the drawer. Then he slammed the drawer shut and threw them on top of the shirts.

"Surely you don't think I just decided this today. How out of touch with reality are you, Ellen?" He looked at me like I really *was* crazy.

I stood rooted to the spot, watching this nightmare unfold like it was a movie on Lifetime.

"I know it hasn't been great lately, but you're my husband, and we're supposed to get through hard times together. What can I do to make you stay?" I pleaded.

"Nothing you can do can make me do anything. I've thought about this for a while, and it's what I want. I just need a change."

My heart was pounding and my hands were quivering.

"Well, how about what *I* need? I need a husband who doesn't run away when the times get tough, and who loves me enough to try to work things out," I blurted.

He zipped his suitcase with a flourish and pushed past me out the bedroom door.

"Then maybe you should go find one," he spat at me.

I ran after him down the steps and grabbed his arm.

"Just when were you going to tell me about this? If I would've gone straight to work, I wouldn't have known until after you were gone! What were you going to do, leave me a note?"

He sighed dramatically. "No, *Ellen*, I was *not* going to leave you a note." His brown eyes met my tear-filled ones head on. "I was going to pack some things and then come back tonight and talk to you. I figured it would be easier on you not to see me packing."

"Well, *thanks* for the consideration," I mumbled.

He shook his head and huffed. "This is just the kind of drama I wanted to avoid."

"Where are you going to stay?" I started to cry and could hardly get the words out.

"With a friend for a while, then I'll see."

He paused with one hand on the doorknob and his suitcase in the other.

"Listen, Ellen, I need to do this. When was the last time we were really happy together? I want out. I want a new life. Someday, you'll probably thank me for doing this."

"Thank you for *leaving* me? Are you *kidding*? Why is it all about what *you* want? *I want you to stay!*" I sobbed. "What about the kids? You're breaking up our family!"

"Don't try to lay that guilt trip on me, Ellen. I stayed until they were out the door, and now that's where I'm going too." He opened the door and walked out, leaving it hanging open.

I ran after him and grabbed his arm again. "Just how long *have* you been thinking about leaving?"

"Don't make a fool of yourself, Ellen." He gave me a pitiful look. "I'm sorry. Really. I'll call you in a day or so, and we can talk things over when you're calmer."

When I'm *calmer*? He's leaving me, and he thinks I'm going to get *calmer* about it? My blood boiled, and then I did the unthinkable. I reached out and slapped his face. Hard.

If looks could kill, I'd be six feet under. I stood in disbelief as I watched him turn, put his suitcase in the G35, and slam the door. Then he noticed my car blocking him in the driveway. "Either move your damn car, or I'll run it over." He got in and revved the engine.

In a daze, I got in the Maxima and moved it onto the street. He squealed tire flying up the driveway, put down the passenger side window, and shouted out at me. "You'd better start looking for a full time job *and* an attorney." His tires squealed again as he sped up the street.

I sat in the car for a moment in disbelief. Then I ran into the bathroom and threw up.

CHAPTER SIX

I lay there for a long time with my cheek against the cool tile floor, just staring straight ahead. I didn't even have the energy to close my eyes. I kept replaying Jack's exit scene in my mind, and the hundredth time was as surreal as the first. I couldn't believe what had just transpired. How could this happen without me seeing it coming?

Yes, things had been difficult lately, and he was right that I haven't been happy. But I would never have left him. *Never.* I would have just plugged away and tried to make our marriage better. This is the time of our lives when we're supposed to be enjoying our time together now that the kids are grown. He's checking out just when the game is supposed to be getting good!

What am I supposed to do without him? He's the only man I've ever known. How can he throw away all those years that we've been together? A hundred "whys" and "what ifs" raced through my mind.

I started sobbing again and felt another wave of nausea creep up on me. I sat up and propped myself against the bathroom wall, putting my head in my hands. My heart was breaking into a million pieces, and it hurt like hell.

There was a pounding on the front door.

"Ellen? Are you in there?"

It sounded like Abbey. I felt so disoriented that at first I couldn't remember what day it was. I searched through the fog and remembered that Abbey was to pick me up for work today.

"*Ellen!*" Then more pounding.

I dragged myself to an upright position and staggered to the front door. I unlocked the deadbolt, then sat down on the hallway floor.

"Ellen, are you okay?" Abbey said as she opened the door. "You didn't answer your cell phone when I called to tell you I was on my way. Oh my! What's wrong?"

She hurriedly sat down beside me and gathered me into her arms. "What is it, honey? What's wrong?"

I started sobbing into her Abercrombie tee shirt. I couldn't get any words to come out.

"Are the kids okay?" she asked.

I nodded my head and continued to sob.

"Is Jack okay?"

I managed to utter one syllable. "Noooooo...."

"Is he hurt? Honey, you have to talk to me." And she pushed me away just enough to look into my eyes.

I couldn't say the words out loud. I just shook my head back and forth.

"Did he hurt *you?*" she asked a little more forcefully.

Oh yes, more than I can ever tell you, but I shook my head no again.

She pulled me close again and stroked my hair.

"Well, you just have a good cry then, and when you're ready, you can tell me what happened."

We sat like that, on my entry hall floor with the front door hanging open, for a very long time. The sun was shining brilliantly and slanting through the open door, warming my legs. I could see the bouquet of wildflowers that I had picked on my walk, in another lifetime this morning, on top of the hay bale on the front porch. How could I have been so happy a few hours ago, and then have my whole world fall apart?

My sobs were diminishing, my body sporadically shuddering in response.

Abbey got up and brought some tissues from the bathroom, and began mopping my face like I used to do to my kids when they were small. I took them from her and blew my nose.

I involuntarily shuddered again and took a deep breath. Looking Abbey in the eye, I told her in a small voice. "Jack left me."

Then I started to cry again.

"Oh, Ellen," she said, and sat down on the floor facing me. "Tell me what happened."

I took another deep breath, and replayed my conversation with Jack. I knew that I would never forget one word that he said, not ever. As I relayed the story to Abbey, I stopped crying, but my whole body started trembling uncontrollably.

"He is such a bastard," she muttered. "A self-centered, egotistical, good for nothing, arrogant bastard."

And for the first time ever, I didn't defend him.

She stood and shut the front door, then pulled me to my feet and led me to the kitchen table. I sat staring as she filled a glass with water and handed it to me.

"You've probably just about dehydrated yourself from crying, girl. You'd better drink this."

I was still trembling as I took a sip. Suddenly, I felt like I couldn't breathe. My heart was pounding, and I needed to get up and walk. I needed to get away. I stood abruptly, knocking over the glass of water, and started pacing across the kitchen floor.

"Ellen, what's happening?" Abbey asked me.

"Panic attack," I whispered, and tried to focus on my breathing. I just kept walking back and forth, and I felt like my vision was getting fuzzy.

"I'm calling Dr. Burke," Abbey said. She got up, grabbed Dr. Burke's magnetic card from the refrigerator door, and started punching numbers into her cell phone as she went into the living room.

A few minutes later when Abbey came back into the kitchen, I had calmed myself down to the point where I could sit back down at the table. I was still trembling, and I focused on the puddle of water, concentrating on just breathing.

"I talked to Dr. Burke and scheduled an emergency appointment for you tomorrow morning. I'd like to take you."

I continued to stare at the puddle and shook my head up and down.

"Meanwhile, she said that you probably should take one of the pills that Dr. Swanson gave you for stressful situations. Do you have them?" she asked.

I nodded again. I didn't care anymore, I just wanted this to stop. "They're in the glove box in my car," I whispered.

"Are you okay by yourself while I go get them?" she asked.

I managed one more nod.

By the time Abbey returned, the panic attack had subsided. I felt drained. She soaked up the spilled water with paper towels and refilled my glass. Then she sat down with me at the table and read the directions on the prescriptions.

"You've never taken any of these before?" she asked.

"No, I didn't want to."

"Do you want to now? I think you should, Ellen. Dr. Burke said it would just take the edge off."

"Okay," I said reluctantly.

She handed me the pill, and I swallowed, washing it down with the entire glass of water. I sighed deeply and looked at Abbey.

"Abbey, you're the best friend ever. I am *so* grateful to you for taking care of me like this. What would I do without you?"

"That's what friends are for, sweetie. You would have done the same for me. Now, I'm going to call Rick and see if he'll handle the store for a while until I get there. And then I'm going to call Adam to come and stay with you. You sit tight."

"No, Abbey, I don't want the kids to know yet. I have to come to terms with this myself before I tell them."

"Okay. Well, I'll go call Rick and then we'll talk about it."

She breezed back into the kitchen moments later. "It's all settled. Rick will take care of the shop today, and then Natalie can help her dad out after school. I'm spending the day with you. Why don't you go splash some water on your face and freshen up, and I'll meet you back on the deck."

My head was starting to feel weird, but I followed Abbey's instructions. A few minutes later, I found her on the deck reclining in a lounge chair with a glass of iced tea in her hand. I picked up the glass she had poured for me and sprawled in the chair next to her.

"Abbey, I just don't know what I'm going to do."

"Sweetie, you can't see it now, but you *will* be fine again.

Trust me, I know what you're made of. And pardon me, but you're better off without him."

I shot her a look.

"I'm sorry, Ellen, but he just broke my best friend's heart. He's slime," she said.

For some reason I found that statement hysterically funny, and I started to laugh…uncontrollably. It felt like I was in someone else's body. My head felt weird again, and I just felt like my whole body was loose and floating away.

"Abbey, I feel really odd."

"Maybe it's the pill kicking in," she offered.

I had completely forgotten that I'd taken it. That had to be it. I didn't feel the anguish anymore, but I didn't feel like *me*.

"So, tell me what's been going on with you and Jack lately," she said as she set her iced tea glass back on the table, leaned back, and closed her eyes.

I've never confided in anyone about the way Jack talks to me when we're alone, or the way I've been feeling about him, but suddenly this pseudo-person I've become started spilling her guts.

I told her everything. All the thoughts that I've been holding in for so long just tumbled out and became real. I must have talked for hours, and I thought maybe she had fallen asleep, because she let me ramble on, only interjecting an occasional, "Oh my" or "Bastard", during my whole monologue.

But when I got to the part about the bank statement and how much money had been in the account, she sat bolt upright. "You have got to be kidding me. I *told* you that was a post office box key! Where did he get all that money? And where is it now?" she shouted.

I just shrugged my shoulders.

"Well, what did he say when you asked him about it?"

"I didn't."

Abbey smacked herself in the forehead with the palm of her hand.

"Oh, Ellen, this is big stuff. If you're getting a divorce, you need to know these things."

I cringed at the word *divorce*, but I was still feeling the effects of the pill, and not much more. I didn't feel like we were talking about *my* life.

The sun was beginning to dip behind the trees, and without its warmth, I shivered as the damp autumn air settled over us.

"Let's go in and order some pizza," Abbey said.

I felt a little woozy when I stood up, so we walked up the stairs arm in arm.

I called DeLucci's and ordered a large veggie lover's while Abbey used the powder room. I gave them my charge card number over the phone like I've done a million times before, but they couldn't get it to go through.

"I don't understand what the problem is," I said into the phone, as Abbey joined me in the kitchen.

"Here, use mine tonight, my treat," she said as she handed me her card.

We made ourselves cozy on the couch and devoured the whole pizza, then the Sara Lee cheesecake that I had in the freezer. The blessed numbness that the pill had provided me with this afternoon was slowly starting to fade. I felt exhausted, and I stretched out on the couch, closing my eyes for only a moment.

"Ellen, wake up, honey."

I could feel someone gently shaking me. "You have to get ready to see Dr. Burke."

I pulled the magical blanket closer to my face and ignored the voice.

"Ellen, come on, wake up."

My head was throbbing, and I thought it must be from all the crying. But I couldn't remember why I had been crying. Then it hit me. Jack was gone.

I opened my eyes to see Abbey looking down at me. I was still on the couch, exactly where I had been last night.

"Did you stay here all night?" I asked Abbey.

"Yeah, we had a sleepover, but you missed it! I had Rick drop off a few things for me last night, and you didn't even budge."

I sat up and rubbed my eyes. I felt like my eyelids were lined with sandpaper.

"Why don't you go up and get a shower, and I'll make some breakfast, okay?

I noticed that she was already showered and dressed in a fresh pair of jeans and a clean Pac Sun tee shirt that didn't have my mascara stains all over it. Her hair was pulled back in the usual ponytail, and although she wasn't wearing a drop of makeup, she looked totally refreshed and ready for the day.

I stared in the bathroom mirror at the red blotches on my face and the dark circles under my eyes. The shower had felt wonderful, but nothing could wash away the pain I was feeling inside…and it showed on the outside. I just pulled on a pair of gray sweats and an old Pitt tee shirt and called it a day. I tried to follow Abbey's lead, and pulled my hair back and secured it with a rubber band, but my stubby little tail didn't look anything like Abbey's beautiful, long one, so I yanked the rubber band out and blew it dry. There was no way makeup was going to help these eyes today, and besides, I'd probably cry it all off anyway. I really needed to remember to invest in some waterproof mascara.

The smell of coffee wafted up to the bedroom, and it put a lump in my throat. Jack wouldn't be here anymore to share breakfast with me. I tried to reason with myself. *Take a deep breath, Ellen. Just breathe in and out and get on with your day.*

We had an uneventful ride to Dr. Burke's office. Maybe I'd cried so much that there were no tears left. I stared miserably out the window as Abbey drove, my mood matching the day. The gray clouds were hanging low, and the wind was whipping the leaves into chaos. If this kept up, the trees would be stripped bare by tomorrow.

I left Abbey in the waiting room, engrossed in the latest scandal magazine, while I followed Dr. Burke to her office. I told her word for word what happened yesterday, and all about my panic attack. I didn't cry until I got to the part where I slapped Jack's face.

"I've never hit another human being in anger before. I can't believe I did that."

Dr. Burke handed me a box of tissue. I dabbed at my eyes, blew my nose, and looked at her expectantly. I wanted her to give me the magic that would take my pain and humiliation away.

"Ellen, we haven't known each other very long, but I can tell a lot about a person's character in a very short time. You don't strike me as someone who would physically lash out without good cause. It's not a good practice to do that, but under the circumstances, I think it's excusable. Please don't give yourself a hard time about it. It happened, and it's over." She casually tucked a strand of hair behind her ear and continued.

"You're at a crossroads now; you have a choice to make." She put her hands out, palms up. "You can either wallow in self-pity, be depressed, feel sick, and keep on a downward spiral...or you can make a choice today to try and turn this unfortunate situation around."

"Don't get me wrong, you'll have plenty of sad moments, but if you make the choice now to overcome them, I think in time you'll be able to rebound from this. You are a strong person, I sensed that about you from the start. You can *do* this."

"But I feel so *empty* and sad. I want to make it through this, but I really don't know if I can. I just don't know what to do," I said as I shredded the tissue in my hand.

"When a marriage fails, it's like a death, Ellen. You have to grieve, and every person goes through those stages on their own timetable. Some people are back to their old selves in two months, some take a year, and some take longer still. You just have to understand what you will probably be feeling, know that it's normal, and know that it will pass. Time is a wonderful healer, Ellen."

"Dr. Burke, I don't know how I'm ever going to be myself again. I still can't believe Jack doesn't want to be with me anymore, and it hurts so much," I said, sniffing.

"Yes, I'm sure it does. Give yourself some time to digest what is happening, and don't be too hard on yourself. Although you have to begin to think about your future and make some plans, don't try to think of the big picture too much. Just concentrate on getting through one day at a time, or one event at a time. With every step you take, every obstacle you hurdle, you will feel more confident."

"I just want to go home and go to bed, actually. I don't want to think anymore."

"Well, then, that is what you should do...today. If that's all you want to do *every* day, then it wouldn't be healthy, and we'll talk. I'd suggest that you keep exercising every day, go to work as usual, and spend extra time with your friends. In other words, keep busy. An active body and mind don't have the time to sit and brood."

"Let's make weekly appointments, and call anytime in between if you need to, okay?"

"That's fine. Dr. Burke...should I call Jack and talk about it?" I asked.

"Well, you *will* have to speak to him at some point. Why don't you give yourself a day or so to collect your feelings and thoughts before you attempt to call him," she said. "If he would be willing to come to one of our sessions with you, it might be helpful."

I tried to visualize that, and all I could come up with were pigs flying.

I assured Abbey that I would be okay by myself, so she dropped me off at home and continued on her way to work. After waving goodbye to her as she pulled away, I walked up the sidewalk, key in hand. I inserted it into the lock, but I just couldn't make myself open the door.

Suddenly, I needed to put myself in motion...walk, run, drive...*something!* Anything but be trapped in this house with my thoughts and memories. I ran to my car, revved it to life, and drove toward Route 30.

I headed east, toward the mountains. The highway guided me away from the restaurant and shopping areas, and gently eased me through the rolling hills of Latrobe and on toward Ligonier. I loosened my death grip on the steering wheel and felt my shoulders relax.

The golden leaves that had weathered the rain and wind were still clinging to the trees and were gorgeous. They were the bright gems in this dismal, gloomy day. I drove at a steady pace, meandering through valleys alongside rippling creeks, and then up mountains and down the other sides. I didn't have a destination in mind, my mental GPS was malfunctioning. I just felt like I wanted to drive forever and not go back to face my life.

I had figured out one thing though. I *would* call Jack. I *needed* to call Jack. I craved answers, even if they were the ones I didn't want to hear.

The yellow glow of the fuel light on the dash caught my eye, so I pulled over at a small gas station and filled up. Inside, I poured myself a vanilla-caramel-latte and handed my credit card to the clerk.

"I'm sorry, ma'am, but this says it's declined," he said.

"There must be some mistake. Could you try again, please?"

He swiped the card, and we both stared at the screen while the sweet scent of vanilla drifted up from my Styrofoam cup.

"DECLINED," ominously stared back at us in red LCD.

I looked up at him, my face burning. "There must be something wrong with my card," I murmured. "I have cash though."

Thank goodness Abbey had paid me for the custom order of dinner plates that I painted for Mrs. Hinkle. I ripped open the envelope and handed him the hundred dollar bill.

"I'm sorry, ma'am, but we don't accept anything larger than a fifty."

I glared at him.

"But in this case, we'll make an exception." He handed me the change, and I turned on my heel and hopped back in the car.

What the hell…first last night when I tried to pay for the pizza, and now my gas card. What's going on? Then a red light flashed in my mind. He *wouldn't* have! Certainly Jack wouldn't have cancelled our credit cards!

Anger replaced the dismal feeling of despair that had been eating me alive for the past twenty four hours. I said, "Call Jack," to my Bluetooth. After the third ring, his voice mail picked up. This wasn't something I wanted relayed to Jack by a voice mail. I wanted to talk to him in person.

"Call me back," I snarled into the air, and disconnected.

I headed back toward home. I was on a mission now. I needed to get on the computer and check our bank account balance and find out what was going on with the credit cards.

This time when I put the key in the front door lock, I flung the door open with a vengeance, slamming it into the hallway wall. I ran upstairs to the office and tapped my fingertips on the keyboard while I waited for the computer to come to life.

Finally, I was online and typing in the password for our joint checking account. I blinked when I saw the balance…twenty dollars. *Shit.*

I clicked the mouse to view the account detail. Yesterday morning there had been nearly two thousand dollars in there, and in one transaction, all but a measly twenty had been withdrawn.

On an impulse, I opened the desk drawer. Just as I feared, the checkbook and box of checks were gone!

I returned to the main menu and, with dread in my heart, clicked on our savings account. We had been saving for a few years to do something special and had squirreled away about ten thousand dollars. Well, it looks like Jack had his own ideas of what the something special would be. There was an even five hundred left.

What was I going to do? I had the change from my hundred dollar bill that I got at the gas station, and about a hundred in my own checking account. That was it. What did he expect me to do now?

I speed dialed Abbey on my cell, and she listened patiently while I explained what had happened.

"Ellen, I'm so sorry this is happening to you. If Rick and I can help you financially in any way, just say the word."

"I'm just so angry that he did this to me."

"That's a good thing…the anger I mean. Use it! Hey, do yourself a big favor and make copies of all the files on that computer. You never know when all that information will come in handy. And you never know what's going to end up disappearing. I don't trust him as far as I can throw him."

"That's a good idea," I said as I slipped a flash drive into the USB port. "I may just sit here awhile and see if I can find out anything else that's been going on."

"Will you be okay by yourself tonight?"

"I'm fine now. Thanks, though. Abbey?"

"Yeah?"

"Thanks for being such a good friend. I don't know what I would have done without your help through all this."

I sat staring at the computer for a long time, trying to comprehend how a man that I had known for a lifetime could suddenly seem like a stranger to me. The Jack I've been married to, raised children with, and planned to spend the rest of my life with, was gone. In his place was this man who had left me all alone and apparently didn't think I needed any money to survive.

Just for kicks, I called Jack again. And again. And again. The bastard had to pick up some time. Finally my stomach was rumbling, and I remembered that I hadn't really eaten anything since breakfast.

I wandered down to the kitchen, turning lights on as I went. When did it get dark? I hated the way the days were getting shorter.

Deciding on waffles, I popped two in the toaster and rummaged around for the butter and syrup. After downing them and repeating the process twice more, I took a box of Girl Scout cookies from the freezer and ate a whole sleeve of Thin Mints. Then I went up to the bedroom, flopped on the bed, and hardly had time for a thought before I fell asleep.

CHAPTER SEVEN

The sun streaming in the window woke me up the next morning. How can it be such a beautiful day when I feel so crappy? Yesterday's blustery weather suited me better. I convinced myself to put on some blush and mascara and brush my hair.

Today I had to go to work. I couldn't let Abbey down again, and Dr. Burke had suggested it anyway. Before I went downstairs, I grabbed the flash drive that I had made last night and put it in my purse.

On my way to Amazing Glaze, I stopped at the bank and withdrew the entire five hundred dollars from our savings account. Damned if I'm going to let him have that too! Then I stopped for a dozen donuts and coffee.

As I sat licking jelly off my finger, Abbey was on a rampage about Jack. She held a donut in one hand and pounded the table with the other, bouncing stray sprinkles in the air.

"He's up to something, Ellen, and it can't be legal. We're talking lots of money here. You really need to talk to him about it. He not only took every cent the two of you had saved, he had that other bank account with tons of money in it."

"I can't imagine what he used that money for, or where it all came from in the first place," I said.

Abbey sipped her coffee thoughtfully. "You know, we could always go and check that post office box…."

"Do you really think we should?"

"Let's go right now," she said as she tossed her empty cup

in the trash. "Rick is still here emptying out the kiln. He won't mind watching the store for a few minutes."

We hopped into Abbey's Blazer and she had us to the post office in under five minutes.

"Is this illegal?" I asked Abbey as we walked in the front door.

"You're not breaking in, you have a key. It's *perfectly* legal."

Why didn't I believe her? My stomach was doing flip-flops as I tried to insert the key into the lock. "It won't go."

"Look how shiny the lock is. I bet they replaced it when he lost the key. Well, that sucks."

Now that actually brought a smile to my face. Abbey not only looked like a teenager, she sometimes talked like one too.

"It's a dead end," I said. "Let's get out of here."

Back at the studio, I tried to keep busy helping customers and unpacking some of the new Christmas bisque. For a while I would feel normal, then I would remember that Jack would never again be waiting for me at home, and tears would fill my eyes. Moments later, anger would engulf me as I thought about how he took all that money and cancelled the credit cards. I rode that emotional roller coaster all afternoon.

By the time we were closing the store, I was mentally exhausted. I promised Abbey that I would be fine though, and drove myself home.

I made a large stack of pancakes for dinner and stood next to the sink eating them, staring blindly out the window.

I needed to call Jack. I was missing him terribly, and the anger that Abbey had coached into me all day had dissipated and been replaced by a dull ache of loneliness. I wondered if he missed me too, and what *friend* he was staying with. Did he have a whole new set of friends that I didn't know?

I went upstairs to the bedroom to make the call to Jack, and I noticed that some things from the top of his dresser that had been there this morning were gone now. I opened his closet door, and there were only a few suits left hanging. He must have stopped by today while I was at work. That thought provoked a wave of nausea, and I sat down on the side of the bed until it passed.

I reached over and opened one of his dresser drawers, pulled out a tee shirt and held it to my nose. The scent of Jack flooded my senses, and I missed him so much.

I thought that I couldn't exist another moment without hearing his voice. I speed dialed his number, and he answered with a loud, "Hello!" on the second ring. My heart leapt in my chest at the sound of his voice.

"Hey, Jack," I said softly. I could hear loud music and voices in the background.

"Hey, Ellen. What do you want?"

"I just needed to hear your voice, Jack," I said.

"Hold on a minute," he replied, and the background noises faded away. "What did you say?"

"I miss you, Jack."

"First you slap me in the face, and then you miss me. That's a little hypocritical, don't you think?"

I cringed. "I'm sorry, I don't know what made me do that. I called you several times last night and you didn't return my calls."

"Ellen, get used to it. We're not together anymore. I'd advise you to find someone else to call."

I felt as if he had slapped *me* in the face this time.

"Who are you staying with?" I asked.

"Once again, you are on a 'need to know' basis. If I thought you needed to know, I would tell you. Don't be so concerned about what I'm doing; get yourself back on track."

"Have you talked to the kids about this yet, Jack?"

"I figured you'd be burning down the telephone lines as soon as I walked out the door, telling them what a rotten father I am."

"How can you say that about me? No, actually I haven't talked to either one of them since you left. I think you should be the one to tell them, or we should do it together."

"I haven't had time to call them. I've been too busy getting situated and trying to earn a living."

My loneliness was quickly morphing back into anger. "Well, you'd better *find* some time to talk to them about this. It was your decision. How can I explain it to them when I don't even understand it myself?"

"Is there anything else, or did you just call to whine?"

Good thing he was on the phone. I could feel my slapping hand twitching.

"Yes, as a matter of fact. I went to put gas in my car yesterday, and the charge card wouldn't go through. Then I checked the bank accounts, and you took all the money!"

"I took the money out of the account to pay the mortgage and utilities. What do you think I took it for? I'm still paying the bills, you know. Do you want me to put it back, and you can take care of everything?"

I did not.

As I sat there silently, he continued, "I couldn't chance that you would do what Karen did when Mark moved out. She cleaned out their bank accounts, charged their cards to the max for spite, and they ended up losing the house and going bankrupt because they couldn't pay their bills. How do I know that you wouldn't do that?"

"Jack, I wouldn't have done that," I said.

"How do I know that? You took the five hundred out of the savings account today, didn't you?"

So, he had checked the balance this afternoon. Why do I feel like he set me up for this conversation, just to accuse me and make his point? He left that money in there as bait and I fell right into the trap.

"Jack, you took thousands. I don't have money to survive on. I only took it so you wouldn't!"

"Ellen, I left that money in there for you to buy groceries or whatever you need this month. I needed the rest to pay our bills.

"And," he continued, "I needed money for a security deposit on an apartment and the first month's rent. Where did you expect me to live if I'm not living in my own home? I can't stay with friends forever; I don't want to inconvenience them."

"Oh, *please*! After what you did to me, you're worried about *inconveniencing friends*? Pardon me, but I don't see how that is relevant. Who are these *friends* anyway?"

"Sure, you're living in our beautiful home, and you're denying me a crummy, bare apartment," he said.

"You *chose* to move out of this beautiful home with all the furniture and may I remind you, more importantly, you chose to move away from *me*!"

"Ellen, it's not been good between us for a long time now. Tell me you haven't ever thought about leaving me!"

He had me there. There had been numerous times, after an argument, that I had allowed that forbidden thought to creep in. Although I never in a million years would have acted on it, I had entertained the thought.

My moment's hesitation was long enough for him to say, "I thought so. You are such a hypocrite, Ellen. You're blaming this whole thing on me, and you are just as much at fault. I just beat you to the punch, that's all."

"Jack, I married you for better and for worse. I actually *meant* those words when I said them!" My voice was getting louder and shriller by the moment.

"Ellen, this conversation is going nowhere. Call me sometime when you can talk calmly, without screaming in my ear."

There he goes again, and it made me madder than hell! I slapped my cell phone shut and disconnected the call. How can he turn this around to make it all my fault? He has an uncanny way of making all the things that he does wrong seem okay.

My phone rang, and I jumped. For a fleeting moment, I thought it was Jack calling back to apologize, but then I realized it was Casey's ring tone. She had called several times over the last couple days and I hadn't returned her calls. I'm sure she was getting worried.

I flipped open the phone and surrendered.

"Hi, sweetie," I said.

"Hi, Mom! Where have you been? If you wouldn't have

answered this time, I was going to call Abbey to go over and check on you guys. Neither you nor Dad have answered my calls, what's going on?"

I took a deep breath and tears filled my eyes. The words still got stuck in my throat, but somehow I was able to get a few out.

"Well…I have some news, but I don't know how to tell you."

"Mom, are you crying? What's wrong, is someone sick?"

Casey sounded so anxious! I felt so guilty for not calling her back. I know how worried I would be if she hadn't returned my phone calls.

"Yes, I've *been* crying for two days. No one is sick. Your dad…your dad…." And the rest just stayed lodged in my throat.

"Dad *what? Mom!* You have to tell me what's going on!"

I took a deep breath and let it all rush out. "I'm sorry, honey, but your dad has decided to leave me."

There was silence on her end.

"Casey? Are you there?"

"Leave you, as in *leave you*?"

"Yes, I came home and found him packing his stuff, and he said he doesn't want to be with me anymore. He wants a new life."

"You've got to be kidding, me. Please tell me that you're kidding, Mom."

"I wish I was, Casey. I'm so sorry, honey."

"What are *you* sorry about, Mom? He's the one who left! Are you okay? Does Adam know? Do you need me to come home?"

I was so proud of my daughter.

"No, you don't need to come home. But I may need some legal advice. You could help me with that. And no, Adam doesn't know yet."

"That's it. I'm calling Dad, and he'd damn well better pick up his phone! I'll call you back in a little while, Mom. I love you."

"I love you too, sweetie."

I flopped back on the bed with my arm over my eyes. It was a relief to talk about it to Casey, no matter how brief the conversation was. I've missed talking to her, and although I know the news hurt her, I was glad to have it out in the open.

Exhaustion claimed me, and I just lay there in the dark with my thoughts churning. I don't know if I fell asleep or not, but it seemed like only seconds had passed when I heard a knock, and then the front door opening.

"Mom!" I heard Adam call. "Where are you?"

I jumped up from the bed and made my way to the top of the stairs.

"I'm up here. I'll be right down."

I made a quick pit stop in the bathroom to make sure that I didn't look too scary, and it was a good thing I did. I looked like a zombie, with mascara smeared under my eyes.

I splashed some cool water on my face, cleaned up my eyes, brushed my hair, and practiced smiling. It seemed so long ago that a smile came without thinking about it.

I found Adam in the kitchen helping himself to a cupcake. As I entered the room, he put it down on the counter and gathered me in a hug. We rocked silently back and forth for a few moments.

"Casey just called me. What the hell is going on here? Why didn't you call me right away?" he asked.

"Oh, Adam…." I hugged him hard. "Let's sit down."

I put the tea kettle on, and as we sat at the kitchen table, I explained what had transpired over the last couple days. Adam sat quietly listening, until the tea kettle rudely interrupted me with its screeching.

"So, you had no clue this was going to happen?" he asked me.

"No, I really didn't. I was shocked!" I replied as I brought our tea and cupcakes over to the table.

"Well, I'm surprised, but not shocked," he said. "Sometimes the two of you would be arguing and I'd wonder why you were even together in the first place. I think you really want different things from your lives, Mom."

Now it was my turn to be surprised. I had no idea he had entertained those thoughts.

"We didn't argue *that* much."

Adam paused in unwrapping the paper from his cupcake and shot me an, "Are you kidding?" look.

"Adam, people don't always agree on things. It's normal for couples who love each other to argue from time to time," I said in our defense.

"Yeah, argue about things with some importance, not about whether you park the car in the driveway or walk on the grass in the front yard. It was the end of the world for him if you made vanilla pudding instead of chocolate for dessert. Seems to me like he always put his feelings before yours."

Adam was a very perceptive young man. He and Jack have had their share of disagreements in the past...over education, jobs, girlfriends. I knew that Adam was very happy when he moved out of our house into his own place.

"Don't get me wrong, Mom. He's my dad and I love him, but I don't always like him. And leaving you doesn't earn him any respect points on my scorecard."

"So what happens now?" he asked.

I stared blankly at the table, watching my finger lining up cupcake crumbs. After a moment, I looked up and met Adam's eyes.

"I don't know."

CHAPTER EIGHT

Adam answered his cell phone on the first ring. I could hear Casey's elevated voice from all the way across the table. He glanced up at me and rolled his eyes.

"I'm already here sitting with her. Let me put you on speaker and then we can all talk. Yes, she's doing fine."

Adam placed his phone in the center of the table and Casey's voice drifted out loud and clear.

"Mom, why didn't you tell me that you were having panic attacks?" she accused.

I didn't want to get into all this tonight, but since we were clearing the air, we may as well give it a good hose job.

"I didn't want to worry you guys...it's something I need to overcome myself."

"That's bullshit, Mom," Adam said. "You'd want to know if something like that was happening to *us*, wouldn't you?"

"Dad told me that you don't want to go anywhere because you're afraid you're going to have one. He said you can't even drive anymore. He said you're a basket case and have to go to a shrink," she said. "When you took me to the airport, I thought you were acting weird in the tunnel, but I thought you were just upset that I was leaving. Dad says you're just looking for attention and he can't take it anymore. He even said that you attacked him when he was leaving," Casey said.

I *attacked* him? That was almost humorous.

"I slapped his face, Casey. And he deserved it," I said. "I *was* upset that you were leaving that day, and yes, the panic episodes started when I drove through tunnels. Now they just seem to come for no reason. I can't explain it. It's just scary. And, yes, I've been going to a doctor to help me through this. Abbey knows and she's been helping me too."

Adam and Casey both started talking at the same time.

Casey was indignant. "Why would you tell Abbey and not us?"

"You've been going through this all by yourself and not telling us?" Adam echoed.

I ran my hands through my hair. I hadn't meant to betray my kids, I just thought I could handle it and it would go away. Hey, back up and rewind a minute. Jack said I was making it up and looking for attention? He's blaming this whole thing on *me*?

"Listen, Casey, your father is coloring the truth a bit here. I *can* drive! I just drove all the way to Ligonier by myself! It just makes me nervous that it's going to happen while I'm driving, that's all, but I'm trying to get over it."

"And it's very real," I continued. "It's hard to explain. Maybe it's something that can't be understood unless you actually have it happen to you, and I hope the two of you never do."

Adam reached over and put his hand on mine and gave it a little squeeze.

"That is *not* why your dad left! Is that what he tried to tell you, Casey?" I asked.

"Pretty much. He said that you were acting crazy, and he tried to make it work, but he couldn't take it anymore."

I started to fume. I jumped up and paced the kitchen floor.

"Where does he get off saying that to you? He wasn't even going to tell you guys he left! The dirty job of it was given

103

to me. I surprised him by coming home when he thought I was at work, and he was packing his suitcase. That's how I found out. He said he needed a change and hasn't been happy for a long time."

"He said you cleaned out the bank account," Casey said.

I stopped walking in my tracks. *I can't believe this!*

"You've *got* to be kidding, Casey! He said that? I took the last five hundred dollars out of the account after I found out that he took ten thousand and cancelled the credit cards!"

Adam shook his head. "Sounds like something he'd do."

As if on cue, my cell phone started ringing. It was Jack.

As soon as I answered, he started in on me. Just for fun, I put him on speaker.

"Well, Ellen, you didn't waste any time badmouthing me to Casey! She called me within minutes after our conversation. I guess you whined to Adam too."

"Actually, Casey called me right after I hung up with you, and she could tell I was upset. So I told her that you left and actually *she* called Adam and told him."

"Well, just for your information, I don't need to have my kids calling to pass judgment on me. I made a choice and everyone's going to have to live with it, so pass the word around." And the phone disconnected.

I looked at Adam. "What an ass," he said, and gave the finger to my phone.

"I heard him," Casey said. It seemed like the wind had gone out of her sails.

"Hey guys, this really has nothing to do with you. He's just angry with me, so don't feel bad. He's still your father and it will still be okay for you."

"Why are you defending him? I can't believe that after what he just did to you, and what he just said, you are still defending him!" Adam said.

I shrugged my shoulders. He scraped his chair back and stood to give me a hug.

"Hey, what's going on there?" Casey's voice filled the room.

Despite the situation, Adam and I both laughed. Casey hated to be left out.

"Group hug, Casey," Adam said to her.

"That's it, I'm coming home for Thanksgiving! It's only a few weeks away, will you be okay until then, Mom?"

"Casey, I would love to have you come home for Thanksgiving! That would be wonderful!"

"It's a deal then. Hey, Chris is beeping in. He knows I was upset and is probably calling to check on me. Call you later?"

"Sure, let's talk tomorrow. I'm so glad that I have you guys. I feel better already, just talking to you."

"Don't worry, Mom. We'll be here for you. Just don't keep any more secrets, okay?"

Adam stayed for a few minutes longer after Casey disconnected. I stood at the door waving goodbye, and actually had a bit of a smile on my face as I watched him drive away. It felt like a huge burden had been lifted from my shoulders now that my kids knew what was going on. Casey was right. No more secrets.

I shivered as I shut the door. Leaving all the lights on, I

went upstairs and plunked down on my bed. I crawled under the covers, once again with my clothes still on, and pulled the comforter up to my chin. I felt exhausted. Just thinking about dozing off seemed like an effort, but within seconds I didn't have to think about it anymore…I was blissfully asleep.

The next evening after work, I stopped at DeLucci's and got takeout lasagna and cheesecake for my dinner…again. I placed the bag down on the kitchen counter, and something white lying on the table caught my eye.

It was a note scrawled in Jack's bold handwriting. My hands started shaking as I picked it up and started to read.

It said that my cell phone bill was paid until the end of November, and then I would have to get my own service. Also, I would have to get my own car insurance after the first of the year. He said that he would continue to pay the mortgage and utilities until the house was sold, but the money from our savings account wasn't going to last forever.

I drew in a quick breath. *Sell the house?*

I continued reading. He wanted to know the name of my attorney, so he could have his attorney get in touch.

The room started spinning and I sat down at the table. This was all happening so quickly! I needed time to adjust to the fact that he was gone. Now I had to think about all these other things?

This is the home where we raised our children. I love my home! Where on God's green earth was I going to live?

I picked up my phone with trembling hands and called Abbey.

"Just take it one thing at a time, Ellen. First of all, you need to find an attorney. Why don't you call Casey and see if she can recommend someone? I'll go with you to the appointment if you want me to," she said. "Don't worry, Ellen. You're in a fog right now, but someday before too long, you'll come out of it and see clearly again."

"Abbey, you're such a great friend."

"Don't sweat it, kiddo. We'll get through this together."

I felt much better after talking to Abbey, so I ate my lasagna and polished off the piece of cheesecake. I knew that I needed to start eating better, but I was too tired to think about it. Maybe I would go for a walk tomorrow.

I wandered upstairs to use the computer to send Casey an email and was startled to see an empty desk in the office. *Jack must have taken the computer!*

My fingers immediately dialed Abbey again.

"I *told* you things were going to start disappearing! Did you make copies of all the files?" she asked me.

"Yes, I have copies. I can't believe he took the computer."

"You'd better check and see what else is missing. Ellen, he shouldn't be coming into the house when you're not there. He moved out, so I would think that would take away some of his privileges about coming into your home without your permission. It's not fair that you don't even know where *he's* living, and he can come and invade your privacy anytime he pleases. We need to get started on the lawyer thing."

I was fuming. What gives him the right to take anything?

"I'll call Casey right now. Thanks, Abbey."

Casey didn't pick up, so I left her a voice mail to return my call. Then I called Adam just to let him know that I was okay. I was intending to call Jack too, but didn't have the energy left for a fight with him. I'd save that until tomorrow.

I thought I'd better get a shower, since I couldn't remember how many days it had been since I'd actually gotten one. Afterward, I put on pajamas for a change, and went to my safe place under the comforter.

The next morning I had my weekly appointment with Dr. Burke, and I was actually looking forward to it. Now that I've told Adam and Casey everything, I didn't feel embarrassed about going. I needed to tell her what was happening with Jack and see if she could help me decide how to handle it.

Of course, she couldn't tell me what to do, but she did give me the courage to move forward.

"Ellen, you can do this. Just take one hurdle at a time," she said.

"But I feel so out of control…like it's not my life I'm living. I've finally admitted to myself that I've gained weight, and I don't even feel like putting on makeup anymore."

"Well, remember that you *are* in control of *yourself.* That's something no one can take from you. The most important thing is that you take care of *you* right now. It takes energy to accomplish all the tasks ahead of you, and you can't do your best if you don't feel well," she said.

"Have you been eating and resting properly? Are you still exercising every day?"

I shook my head. "Dr. Burke, I hardly have the energy to

get in and out of bed. I *have* been going to work though…mostly because I know that I need the money."

"Let's sit down and write up a plan for you then. I know that you don't feel like exercising, but once you get started, I promise that you *will* have more energy and it will help you stay focused too. You'll see. You need to get out with some friends and do normal things," she said. "Just try."

I tucked the list that we worked on in my purse and left her office with a new sense of confidence. Just having a plan made me feel better. I breezed into Amazing Glaze and tossed my purse under the counter.

"Wow!" Abbey said. "You seem happy today!"

"I just came from Dr. Burke's, and I actually feel better today than I have in a long time," I said.

I hung up my jacket in the back room and adjusted the waistband on my sweatpants. Even they had been feeling tight lately.

"I really have to start watching what I eat," I thought as I helped myself to a cup of tea and a donut from the box on the table.

"Abbey, do you want to come over tonight and watch a movie or something?" I asked, thinking of the list in my purse.

Abbey grinned, "Now, that's my girl! We haven't had a fun girl's night in a long time."

After work, I stopped at Primanti's, picked up two Pittsburgh Specials, and met Abbey at my house. I had experienced the best day that I've had in a long time! I felt ready to take control again. Jack or no Jack, I was going to be okay.

109

I draped a cranberry-colored cloth over the kitchen table and resurrected a couple pumpkin scented candles from the bottom cabinet drawer. Abbey retrieved two cold Iron City's from the refrigerator and poured them into frosted mugs for us, while I popped in an old Motown CD.

"This is nice, Ellen," she said before she took a huge bite.

I nodded in agreement, my mouth too full to speak.

A couple beers later, we were still sitting at the kitchen table chatting it up, the stories getting better with every sip.

Abbey started to imitate Mrs. Plumber. She held her nose and said in a whiny voice, "It's Mary Frances's birthday today! Everybody say happy birthday to Mary Frances!"

We both burst into a hysterical laughing fit. It felt so good to be wiping happy tears from my eyes for a change!

"Well, glad you miss me so much!" we heard a man's voice say.

We both jumped and turned around to see Jack standing in the hallway. I felt the blood drain from my face and the room start to spin.

"I stopped by to see how you were doing, and here you are having a party and laughing like a lunatic," he said, "You get the Academy Award for all those pathetic phone messages saying how much you miss me!"

I was so shocked to see him standing there that I couldn't say a word.

"You were laughing so loud you didn't even hear me knock," he continued.

Abbey found her tongue. "Get over it, Jack. What gives you the right to come walking in here without Ellen's permission?"

I could see her face getting red, and Jack's getting redder. I needed to step in fast.

"I'll come in any time I damn well please, and it's none of your damn business, Abbey!" he shouted.

"Jack!" I said as I got up from the table. "Let's talk in the living room. I'll be right back, Abbey."

He opened the hall closet door and took out his leather jacket.

"I was going to stay and talk, Ellen, but I see you're having too much fun, so I'll just leave."

"No, wait. I want to talk to you. I *need* to talk to you!" I reached out and touched his arm.

He jerked it away. "You blew it. I have someone waiting for me who actually wants to be with me. Have fun with your girlfriend."

He started walking toward the door. I ran after him and grabbed his arm.

"What are you saying? You're with another woman?"

He looked down at my hand on his arm and shook his head. "Ellen, this is getting old. Grow up already."

He shook off my hand and went out the door. I wanted to run after him, but I've already played that scenario. I wasn't chasing after him again.

I shut the door and heard the G35 speed up the street. Abbey was at my side and put her hand on my shoulder.

"He is such an ass," she said. "Don't pay any attention to what he says, Ellen."

But I felt guilty that he had come over to talk and see how I was, and now he thought that I didn't miss him at all. I stared down at the floor.

"Don't you see how he plays you? He knows just what buttons to push. No offense, Ellen, but he wasn't coming over to talk. He just wanted to pick up his leather jacket. He saw an ace in his hand when he saw you having a good time and decided to play it."

I jerked my head up and looked at her. "How can you say that? He thinks that I don't miss him."

"How can you miss someone talking to you like that? He makes me want to puke, and he was only here for five minutes. I can't imagine living with that every day," she said.

"Did you hear what he said? Do you think he's with another woman?" I asked.

"I heard every word. It's kind of hard *not* to hear Mr. Showboat! He didn't confirm or deny when you asked him about another woman. He just put it out there to get you upset, that's all. He can't stand the fact that you just might end up being happier without him."

She must have seen the look of terror on my face.

"He's only been gone a short time; I highly doubt he's with another woman. It's okay, Ellen."

The scent of coffee brewing mingled with the fragrance of pumpkin candle and drifted down the hallway. Abbey must have started the coffee maker, bless her.

We walked back to the kitchen arm in arm. I sat while Abbey grabbed two thick mugs from the cupboard and poured. Jack's appearance had sobered us more quickly than any cup of coffee could, but it felt good to wrap my hands around the hot mug and breathe in the familiar scent.

Abbey grabbed a sleeve of Lorna Dunes and we sat silently for moment, preoccupying ourselves dunking them in our coffee. Three cookies later, Abbey cleared her throat.

"Ellen…seriously, you can't have him just coming in any time he feels like it. You have to put a stop to it."

Part of me agreed with her, but part of me *wanted* him to come home. I didn't answer her; instead I just reached for another cookie.

"Did you ask Casey to refer an attorney?" she asked.

"I left her a voice mail yesterday, and I don't know if she sent me an email or not because Jack took the computer."

She huffed. "That's what I mean. He shouldn't be coming and taking things. What if he brings a whole moving truck while you're at work someday, and you come home to find the whole house empty?"

I sipped my coffee and thought about that.

"We're going to get you a new cell phone that has email capabilities. To hell with Jack!"

I put my cup down and yawned.

"Well, that's my cue," Abbey said. "Get a good night's sleep, kiddo, and call me in the morning."

After I waved goodbye from the front window, I unplugged the coffee maker, tossed our cups in the sink, and went up to bed.

I couldn't sleep, partly because of the caffeine, and partly because I had such unfinished business with Jack. I could hear the wind whipping the tree branches against the house. I felt so

lonely. I just wanted to be held. I wanted to cuddle up next to
Jack. I had to call him.

CHAPTER NINE

I picked up my cell with trembling hands.

The phone rang four times. "Hello?" a female voice said.

My heart was pounding and my ears were ringing. *Who* is answering Jack's phone? I looked down at the screen to make sure I had the right number.

"Hello?" This time it was Jack.

"Jack, who was that?" I asked numbly.

"Oh, it's you. Are you ready to put on another performance?" he asked.

"Jack, I'm so sorry about tonight. I *do* miss you! Can you come over?"

"Sorry, no can do. I'm with *friends*."

"*What* friends?"

"The friends who helped me move into my new place today. They're giving me a housewarming party."

My stomach flip-flopped, and my hand flew to my mouth.

"You have a new place? Where?"

"Hey listen, Ellen, you had your chance to talk before and you were too busy with *your* friend. Now it's my turn. We'll have to do this another time. Gotta go."

And he disconnected.

I was surprised that no tears were falling. This was something new! Instead, I was angry. *Very* angry! I'd heard enough about his new so-called friends. Let him have them!

I turned on the light and stomped down to the kitchen. I returned with a box of giant-sized black trash bags, opened every drawer in Jack's dresser, took whatever clothes were left in them, and stuffed them into the bags. Then I followed suit with the closet, shoes and all.

I made several trips out to our detached garage, wearing my pajamas, robe, and slippers, throwing all the bags on the garage floor. The wind swirled the leaves around my feet and the chilly air went right through my robe, but I kept going until there was not one stitch of Jack's personal things left in the house.

Then I went back up to bed and lay there in the dark, shivering. As an afterthought, I went back down and turned the deadbolt on the front door. Tomorrow I would tell Jack that he was no longer to come in without my permission!

I slept fitfully and woke up feeling like I really hadn't slept at all. I knew Jack would be at work, but I called him anyway. I was almost relieved when he didn't pick up.

"Jack, I took the liberty of packing up the rest of your clothes, and you'll find them in the garage. I don't want you to come into the house when I'm *not* here, and I *really* don't want you to come in the house when I *am* here. If *you* are able to talk calmly, then call me and we can discuss it further."

I slapped my cell phone shut. I could just imagine how angry he'd be when he retrieved that message!

So much anger was inside me, I needed to burn off some steam. I found comfort in putting on what had now become my standard, sweat pants and a hoodie, and slipped on my Reeboks. Then I let myself out the front door and took off at a fast clip, walking down the street.

Autumn was marching along, and the trees were now all bare. The air was crisp and cool, the sky azure blue. I admired the cornstalks and pumpkins and mums that decorated many of the yards in the neighborhood, and I kicked at the leaves congregated on the side of the road. My steps startled a huge flock of homely black birds that had gathered in someone's front yard, and they all took flight simultaneously, noisily scolding me. A little farther down the street, a chubby groundhog startled *me* as he scurried from the road into the brush.

I started to feel a little better and decided to call Casey again today for some help on finding an attorney. If Jack was going to file for divorce, I guess I should be prepared. Little by little, I had to move forward, which was easier to think about in the light of day. And having my mind move forward seemed to be easier when my feet were moving too. The walk had been a good idea.

Only a few more weeks until Thanksgiving, and then Casey would be home. I could make it. I *had* to!

A few days later, I found myself sitting across a sleek, black, conference table from Attorney Annee Slater. She was an acquaintance of Casey's from law school and had agreed to meet with me for a brief consultation at no cost, as a favor to Casey.

One thing I have learned… attorneys are expensive. I would need a one thousand dollar retainer just to get the ball rolling.

Considering that I have less than a thousand dollars to my name at the moment, the ball wouldn't be rolling for quite some time.

Annee was a bit older than Casey, maybe in her early thirties. She was wearing a navy pinstripe suit and her shoulder length, strawberry blonde hair was attractively pulled back with a tortoiseshell headband.

She was the picture of professionalism, while I, on the other hand, probably looked like a big dope. I had squeezed myself into a pair of dress khakis, but had to find a really long top to cover their skintight fit on my rear. I couldn't wait to get back to the car to unbutton them. I had, however, gone the extra mile today and actually put on makeup. I didn't want to embarrass Casey by having Annee think that her mom is a *total* frump. The reason I'm here is embarrassing enough.

Annee smiled and greeted me with a handshake, then got right down to business, proving that time is money.

I told my story briefly, listening to her silver Tiffany heart bracelet clinking on the table as she took notes. She asked a few questions, nodding her head or biting on her bottom lip, as she listened to my answers. As I focused on her French manicure, I involuntarily curled my own fingertips under. I couldn't remember the last time I did my nails.

I wondered if Casey's clients scrutinized her appearance the same way that I was doing to Annee.

I'm sure Casey also looked professional. She had bought several suits before she left, and I know that she spent a huge chunk of her first paycheck on clothing. Now I see why it was so important for her to dress the part.

"Well, Mrs. Stern, are you considering this a trial separation, or do you want to file for divorce?"

"I guess the ball is in Jack's court. He's the one who initiated the separation. I'm mostly concerned about him coming into the house without my permission. Is there anything I can do about that?"

"Yes, we can draw up legal separation documents with that stipulation, which I would highly recommend. You would be wise to list your assets and find out exactly what kind of settlement you could expect if you do file for divorce. Plus, you probably need money to live on, and that would have to be resolved. It's always better to have things like that in a legal document. When tempers flare, and from my experience, they will, things can get a bit messy."

"If we decide to get divorced, how long does it take?" I couldn't believe I was actually asking that question.

"Well, after you file, there is a three month cooling off period before it becomes final. That provides a little buffer in case someone changes their mind in the interim."

"I would be happy to represent you," she said. "I don't think your case would be very complicated. Take a day or so to think about it, and talk to Casey. It would be to your advantage to get a separation agreement started as soon as possible though."

After our meeting, I sat in the car for a while, trying to collect my thoughts. I hadn't talked to Jack since I left him the message. I happened to notice that his bags of clothes were gone from the garage. He must have come to collect them while I was at work.

I was riding this roller coaster of missing him so much that I couldn't breathe, and actually feeling more relaxed without him. I'm almost wondering if my anxiety was Jack-induced.

Dr. Burke actually feels that my panic attacks are not the result of chemical imbalance. They're probably from the stress I've had lately because of Casey leaving, and then Jack. I had refused medication from the beginning, but I did take that one pill the day Jack left. I understand how it can be necessary and helpful in some cases, but I really want to try to work through this myself first. However, it's nice to know there is a Plan B available if I need it.

Since Jack has left, I know that I'll have to do everything for myself, and I think that knowledge has given me something resembling strength. It's sink or swim, and I wasn't planning on being the guppy going down. I *have* been feeling some of my old energy returning in sporadic little bursts. I'm still not feeling very creative, and I could probably stay in bed all day without too much persuasion, but there *have* been a few moments during the last few days when I actually felt focused. I'd like to think maybe the fog was lifting just the tiniest bit.

There are so many details to be taken care of, and so much about the way I do things is changing. Most days I'm still overwhelmingly hurt and confused, but just like driving through tunnels, I'm trying to focus on the light at the end.

I decided that I wasn't in any hurry to retain an attorney. I would wait and see what Jack's next move was. Maybe he would get tired of his "new friends" and want to come home. Maybe he would realize that he made a grave mistake and miss me so much he would beg me to take him back. Maybe it's just wishful thinking…but it's what I do best.

I watched the windshield wipers flicking back and forth intermittently all the way home. There was a heavy mist in the air, and the sky looked like it would open and drench me at any moment. It was another one of those gray, damp days with just enough hint of coolness in the air to remind you that before long, winter would be knocking on the door, and it would be white stuff falling from the sky.

As I pulled up in front of my house, the clouds made good on their threat, and huge drops of rain pelted down mercilessly. I decided to sit and wait it out in the car, instead of getting soaked and chilled to the bone. Usually cloudbursts don't last very long.

I noticed a white minivan bearing a Nester's Realty logo, parked across the street. There appeared to be someone sitting in it, also waiting out the downpour.

The insides of my car windows had steamed up, and I rubbed my sleeve across the door window to see the van more clearly. A woman was sitting in the driver's seat, and she waved over at me.

I waved back, and let the window fog over again. I leaned back against the headrest, closed my eyes, and tried to clear my head. The rain thundered on the car roof, drowning out my troubled thoughts. I sat in my safe little cocoon, willing myself to think happy things…so I thought about Casey coming home for Thanksgiving.

We could cook a big turkey dinner together, just like we always have. Adam could come over and bring Cooper, who would run around the house sniffing every square inch, adorably begging for treats.

Then I thought about Jack. Would he come? *Should* he come? Did I even *want* him to come?

A knock on my window interrupted my downward spiral, and I opened my eyes to see the woman from the Nester's van standing beside my car, ducking under a black umbrella. The rain had slowed down to a drizzle again.

I put down my window a crack. "May I help you?" I asked.

"You must be Ellen Stern," she said, and without waiting for confirmation, continued, "I'm Nancy Hodge, from Nester's Real Estate. Jack had scheduled a two o'clock meeting to appraise your home, but I'm running a little ahead of schedule and thought maybe you could take me through. I tried to call Jack and tell him I was early, but he didn't pick up."

I looked at the clock on my dash and saw that it was one-thirty. Wait a minute! Jack scheduled an appraisal without even confirming it with me? We seriously needed to talk.

I opened the car door and stepped out. The water was still streaming down the street, and I could feel it seeping through my shoes. I shivered as the damp, cool air penetrated my jacket.

"I'm sorry, Nancy, but there must be some mistake. I didn't know anything about an appraisal today," I said.

She looked confused. "Jack said you would probably be working, and he was going to meet me here at two."

How *dare* he!

"Well, *Nancy*, you can tell Jack that he needs to confirm any future appointments with me. I'm sorry to have wasted your time, but there will be no appraisal here today."

She put a smile on her face that didn't quite reach her eyes.

"Oh, I see. Well, I'll give Jack another call. There must have been some miscommunication."

Miscommunication, my foot.

"I'm really sorry, Nancy, but I'm just not prepared to have this happen today."

"I understand," she said as she held out her hand to shake mine. "It was nice meeting you, and I hope we can work this out." Then she and her black umbrella turned and walked back across the street.

Nancy got back into her white van, and I retrieved my purse from the car and let myself into the house. *My* house. If I wouldn't have taken the afternoon off to go to the attorney, I *would* have been at work. Jack and Miss Nancy Hodge would have been traipsing through my house and I would have been none the wiser. How could Jack do something like this to me? Has he changed so much that he has no regard for my feelings at all?

I needed to get out of my damp clothes, get a hot shower, make a cup of tea, and make two phone calls. One to Annee Slater to get that separation agreement underway, and one to Jack to give him an attitude adjustment.

I peeled off my clothes and threw them in a damp pile on the bathroom floor. The heat of the shower felt so good, and the scent of my lavender shower gel made me feel more relaxed. I was glad that I had taken Dr. Burke's suggestion and tried it. Oh, I was still good and mad as I pulled a thick towel from the shelf and dried myself off, but I felt ready to make my phone calls in a civilized manner.

I wrapped the towel around me and opened the door to the

bedroom. For a split second, it seemed normal to see Jack sitting on my bed. In the next instant, I realized that it wasn't. I stopped dead in my tracks, hugging the towel closer to my body.

"What are you doing here? You scared the life out of me!" I said.

He didn't answer right away, just looked me up and down. My heart was pounding in my chest and I still hadn't moved.

"I stopped by to talk to you, Ellen. You didn't answer the door when I knocked, so I tried your cell. When you didn't answer that either, I got worried and came in to check on you."

Well, I guess that made sense.

He looked so handsome sitting there in his navy suit, wearing the red and blue striped tie that I had bought him last year for his birthday. The scent of his cologne mingled with the lavender still hanging on the mist from my shower, and it all felt so familiar and so right.

He tipped his head to the side and gave me a smile.

A sudden wave of nostalgia and yearning ebbed inside of me.

Still standing in my wet towel, I could feel goose bumps springing up on my body, and I shivered involuntarily.

"Come here," he said, and held out his hand to me.

I put my cool hand in his warm one, and he gently pulled me down to sit next to him on the bed. He wrapped his arms around me and held me close.

Oh, how I've missed his touch! I could feel the tears springing to my eyes, and willed them not to tumble out.

"You feel good, Ellen." He had his head buried in my

hair, and was gently caressing my back.

"Jack..." was all I could manage.

I felt the towel slowly drop and his warm hands on my skin. I was melting. My still hands began to move over his muscular back, and despite the warmth I was feeling inside, I shivered again.

"Let's get you warmed up," he said. Pulling the comforter back, he carefully pushed me down on the pillows, lying down next to me. He held me close and replaced the comforter over us.

I felt warmer immediately and snuggled close to him. Our cheeks touched, and then he slowly moved his face, ever so lightly brushing his lips on mine. I felt a fire burning inside me and pressed my lips against his in a heated kiss.

His warm, practiced, hands touched me all over, and I was breathless with desire. Jack knew me well, and within moments, I was panting in ecstasy.

Afterward, Jack held me close, stroking my hair. I wanted to stay in his arms like this forever. With Jack, my husband. I allowed myself the first real, heartfelt smile I've had for a long time.

I reached down under the covers and pulled at his shirt. His hand reached down and covered mine, stopping my progress. I pushed slightly away and looked at his face.

"Sorry, Ellen, no can do," he said.

"Why?" I asked. I could tell that he was just as aroused as I was.

"It's complicated. Believe me; I've never wanted you so much as I do right now, but I just can't."

I felt the cold air rush under the comforter as he stood up

beside the bed.

"Go ahead and get dressed. I'll put on some tea," he said, and walked out of the bedroom.

I lay there, not knowing what to think. I stretched out under the covers, pointing my toes and reaching my arms above my head, more relaxed and happy than I'd been in months. I would love to just curl back up in this safe place and sleep the rest of the day away, but Jack and a hot cup of tea were waiting for me downstairs.

I hurriedly dried my hair, put on minimal makeup, and slathered on some lavender body lotion as an extra touch. Then I slipped on a powder blue sweat suit and bounced down the stairs with a newly acquired spring in my step. Maybe everything was going to be fine now.

As I entered the kitchen, I smiled at Jack, who was already seated at the table with a pad and pen in front of him. He was scratching some numbers on it, and looked up when he heard me come in.

My cup of tea was steaming in my favorite mug, and I was sure it was made exactly the way Jack knew I liked it. I smiled. It felt good to be taken care of again.

It was so great to see Jack at the table…just like old times. I sat in the chair across from him and took a sip of tea, holding the warm mug with both hands and inhaling its fragrant vapors.

"We need to talk," Jack began.

I looked up expectantly. Maybe he was embarrassed to ask me about coming home. I smiled again to encourage him to continue.

"Nancy Hodge said you cancelled our appointment for an appraisal today," he said.

I felt myself tensing up, remembering my confrontation with Nancy Hodge.

"That's right, I did. Why did you make the appointment without consulting me?"
I asked, gripping the mug a little tighter.

"I figured you'd be at work, and then you wouldn't be stressed out about it. I thought it would be upsetting for you to be here…like maybe it would throw you into a panic attack or something," he said.

"Of *course* it would be upsetting, Jack! We're talking about our *home* here!" I was struggling not to turn into the raving maniac.

In an attempt to distract myself, I got up and plucked a bag of chocolate chip cookies from the cupboard. Jack watched me with interest as I consumed one on my way back to the table.

"Cookie?" I offered as I sat back down.

"No thanks, and maybe you should cut back on the sweets a little yourself. When we were upstairs, I noticed there was a little bit more of you," he said.

My previous euphoria was pretty much squelched now. I ate another cookie in defiance.

"I'm rescheduling the appraisal. Do you want to be here for it or not?" he asked.

"What I *want* is for things to go back to the way they were, for you to come home and be my husband, and for us to live together in this house and be happy," I said. "So what exactly are we doing here, Jack? What's happening?"

"I didn't want to get into this today. I just wanted to take care of the house situation, not have another battle with you," he said.

"Listen, Ellen," he continued as he reached across the table for my hand, "It's just not going to ever be the same for us. I'm happy in my new life. Sure, there are days when I miss you, and I'm dealing with that in my own way. But I'm moving on, and you need to do that, too."

Well, gee, he missed me. Thank Heaven for small favors.

"So, what was that upstairs?" I asked.

He looked at me with troubled eyes. "You really seemed like you needed some affection, and I was happy to help you out with that. I want us to be friends."

I snatched my hand away from him and stood up.

"So, what does that mean? I'm an orgasmic charity case?" Forget keeping my anger in check. The raving manic was ready for a comeback.

"Call it how you see it, Ellen. You weren't exactly pushing me away up there. You seemed pretty satisfied to me."

I stood there with my hands on my hips and stared into his eyes. How could I have given in to him so easily? Why would I think he had changed his mind? How could one smile from him draw me in the way it did?

Because I love him, that's why. But something Adam had said the other day came back to me. Maybe my love for him wasn't enough. I really haven't *liked* him for a long time. I felt like I just took one more step out of the fog.

"Ellen!" he said, sharply pulling me out of my thoughts.

I took my seat back at the table.

"Jack, you can rest assured that I won't be troubling you to help me fill my affection quota in the future." And I wondered where he was getting his affection quota filled.

"Well, you don't have to get all huffy about it," he said.

"So, Jack, are you seeing someone else?" I was feeling a new bravado.

"Ellen, I don't want to get into this with you today. Let's try to get the financial things going before we both go bankrupt."

"Where are you living?" I shot back.

He slapped his hands palm down on the table and leaned forward toward me.

"I'm living in the Townhouses at Penn, if you must know. I'll write the address down so you can come over and spy on me. We *are* separated now, so we are both free to see other people if we want to, and that's all I'm saying about it right now. Case closed."

"So, you *are* seeing someone." I felt like the cookies were stuck in my throat.

He pushed his chair away from the table and gathered up his pad of figures and pen.

"I guess you still can't get through a conversation without going crazy. Go take a pill and call me when you're ready to talk."

I called after him down the hallway, "My attorney will be drawing up a legal separation agreement, so I *will* need that address of yours."

He walked back to the kitchen.

"Sure...you have an attorney."

I stood up and faced him.

"Yes, I do, as a matter of fact. That's where I was this morning. Her name is Annee Slater, and she will need your address and also that of your attorney. She also asked for a list of our assets, and your income information." And after I thought about it a moment I added for good measure, "and your bank account information too."

Now it was his turn to stand and stare at me.

"Don't even think you're going to rake me over the coals, Ellen."

"Jack, you were the one telling me to get an attorney, and the one making plans to appraise the house. Did you think I was just going to sit here and have you rake *me* over the coals? I can't even email Casey anymore because you took the computer!"

He shook his head.

"How juvenile, Ellen. I have to pay the bills online for all the utilities *you* are using in this house, and make the mortgage payment for the house *you* are currently living in, and pay all the credit card bills that *you* had no trouble racking up. I think that is a little more important than emailing. Call her on the phone to do your bitching."

There he goes again, making something that he did wrong seem like it's okay.

"The point is, you have no right to just come and take what you want without consulting me first, Jack."

His cell phone rang, delaying his response. He looked at the screen and exhaled deeply.

"I'm done talking today. I'll get you the information you need. You don't have to get all hot and bothered about everything, Ellen."

His cell phone interrupted again. This time he answered it, "I'll be right there. Give me a minute here," and he flipped it shut.

"Jack, I think we need to have a meeting with both of our attorneys present to straighten this whole thing out."

"You're probably right, because *one* of us can't just talk without going nuts," he said as he walked out. "I'll be in touch."

"Fine," I said to the closed door.

CHAPTER TEN

Casey would be home in three days! I plopped down my magazines and DeLucci's takeout bag on the table and put the tea kettle on. After rubbing my hands together to warm them, I reached up to turn on the light above the stove.

I think that's what I dislike about winter the most, the short days. Here it was only six o'clock, and it was pitch black outside. Dr. Burke suggested putting on tons of lights in the evenings to keep my spirits up. Even though they weren't the broad spectrum kind, it was more beneficial to my psyche than sitting in the dark, although sometimes that's what I felt like doing.

The last couple weeks have been a struggle, but I've gotten through them mainly by focusing on Casey's homecoming. I haven't seen Jack since the day we argued about the home appraisal, but he did call me to swap information about our attorneys.

Since I haven't been able to save up enough yet for the retainer, I haven't officially hired Annee as my legal counsel. I didn't tell Jack that, though. I was planning on getting Casey's help when she came home, and I just needed to take a break from all the drama for awhile.

Jack had agreed not to come into the house without my permission, and also to postpone the house sale until after the holidays. I don't know why the attitude change, but I'll take it. I've learned the hard way that Jack's moods change like the wind, so if a calm breeze was blowing, I would just accept it until the next hurricane blew in.

I still missed him, sometimes so much I ached. Just as Dr. Burke had said it would though, the pain began to get a little easier to manage with the passing of time. Some days were better than others, although one day I cried all afternoon because I heard the song we danced to at our wedding play on the radio.

Another evening, when I was watching TV and a commercial came on for cemetery plots, I cried for two hours because I didn't know if I would spend eternity buried next to Jack. I even had to call Abbey to console me on that one. She wasn't much help though. She told me she would tap dance on his tombstone! I knew she was kidding though…probably.

Abbey has been my guardian angel. I honestly don't know what I would have done without her since Jack left.

It's funny; I measure time in two segments now, before Jack left and after Jack left.

Adam has been busy working on his house, but he's stopped by every few days to visit, and we've had dinner together once a week. As far as I know, he hasn't talked to his dad at all about this mess. I think Adam is waiting for Jack to call and talk to him, and I'm more than sure Jack feels Adam should be the one to call him.

The tea kettle screeched, and I made my cup of tea and carried it back to the table. DeLucci's lasagna has become my addiction, and I opened the steaming container to enjoy. I stopped on the way home from work and bought some new cooking magazines, so I leafed through them while I ate, looking for some new recipes for our Thanksgiving dinner.

Abbey, Rick, and Natalie were going to join Casey, Adam, and me for Thanksgiving. I had been feeling generous and invited Jack, but he said he had other plans. It probably was a good thing. Jack, Abbey, and a carving knife in the same room probably wasn't one of my better ideas.

Abbey and I had made plans to grocery shop together tomorrow. I already bought the turkey though, and it has been defrosting in my refrigerator for two days now and still feels as hard as the frozen tundra. Every Thanksgiving it's the same story. I'm always chiseling away ice to release the bag of frozen gizzards from inside good old Tom. I guess it's tradition, just like the au gratin potatoes boiling over in the oven and setting off the smoke alarm every Christmas. It wouldn't be a proper holiday without it!

Casey called just as I was finishing off my other addiction, a slice of cheesecake. I've given up on just buying single servings. Now I just get a whole one and it lasts me the entire week…usually.

"Hey, Mom, only three more days!" Casey chirped.

I smiled. "I know, I can't wait!"

"Can you make that strawberry pretzel Jell-O salad?" she asked.

"We'll be having pumpkin pie, but if you want that too, we can make it."

"Yes, I would like it, and green bean casserole, those mashed sweet potatoes with the crumbly brown sugar topping, and homemade applesauce!"

It had always been Casey's job since she was a little girl to make the homemade applesauce. I started to feel very nostalgic remembering her as a child cutting up the apples and eating as many as she put in the pot.

"Oh, and Chris said we have to have corn bread *dressing*, so he's giving me a recipe to try. Apparently, southerners don't eat *stuffing*."

"That sounds great. What's he doing for Thanksgiving?" I asked.

"Oh, his grandpa lives nearby and his family is going there."

I miss having my family together for the holidays. Ever since my parents passed away, my brothers and I don't seem to get together for the holidays like we used to.

Both of my brothers live in Montana now running a ski lodge, so they don't make the trip east very often, especially in the winter. I hadn't told them about my situation with Jack, but I know they will call for Thanksgiving, and I'll have to tell them...how embarrassing.

Jack is an only child, and his parents retired and moved to Arizona, so I couldn't imagine what his plans were for the holiday. I don't think I really want to know.

"Mom, will you be okay picking me up at the airport?" Casey asked.

I'd already thought about this and I knew my answer.

"Yes, I will be wonderful," I replied. "I think I can do it if I put my mind to it."

I've been trying to face my fears. I've been able to go to the grocery store by myself again, and I even had lunch with Adam at Fat Boys, the scene of a panic attack. Once I knew that I could eat there and nothing bad would happen, the fear went away. It would be good for me to tackle the tunnel, especially when I knew that Casey was on the other side.

Just as Casey and I were saying goodbye, the doorbell rang. As I flipped my phone shut, I went to the front door. I surely wasn't expecting anyone, and since it was already dark out, I was feeling a little apprehensive.

I peeked out the window and could see a man standing on the front porch with a flower arrangement, and a florist truck parked in my driveway.

Huh? I opened the door and accepted the delivery. Who could be sending me flowers? It was a beautiful Thanksgiving table arrangement, full of yellow and orange mums, with a few spikes of fall leaves and gourds tucked in here and there. There was a fat, cranberry-colored candle in the middle of it all that would just look gorgeous when lit.

I placed it in the center of the dining room table and fumbled with the tiny card. I recognized the handwriting before I started to read the message, and my eyes brimmed with tears. I sat down on the floor and read.

"I am thankful for all the years with you. I hope you have the best of holidays, because you deserve to. I'm sorry all this had to happen, Ellen. Happy Thanksgiving. Love, Jack."

I drew a shaky breath, and then read the card over and over again. He's thankful for me and he loves me. What does all that mean?

I grabbed my cell phone from the kitchen table and called Abbey.

"It means that he's being a weasel, that's what it means," Abbey said when I told her about the flowers.

"Could it be that he's having regrets and wants to come back?" I asked.

"Ellen, I hate that he does this to you. Just when you get yourself on the right track, he throws you a curveball and makes you rethink things. I think you should just take it at face value. He's sorry and he loves you in his own way. I don't think he's coming back, Ellen. Enjoy the flowers or throw them in the trash, but don't hinge any false hopes on them, okay?"

"For once could you give him the benefit of doubt, Abbey? Maybe he's changed."

"Honey, the only thing he changed was his address."

I sighed. Of course Abbey was probably right, but I just had that tiny hope in my heart that things were still going to work out.

After I hung up with Abbey, I wanted to call Jack and at least thank him for the flowers. What I really wanted to do was give him a hug and look into his eyes. I think I would be able to tell if his words were sincere if I saw him face to face.

I sort of had a feeling that it was the wrong thing to do, but I grabbed my jacket and headed out the door anyway. I had previously done a "drive-by" of Jack's rented townhouse, just so I could see where it was. Tonight I was going to go one step further.

I pulled into the parking lot, turned off the ignition, and just sat there with my heart pounding, looking at the front of his building. The G35 was in the lot mocking me, and the lights were all on inside the townhouse, so I was pretty sure that he was home. Did I dare to knock on his door?

Just as I had mustered up enough courage, and had my hand on the car door handle, a dark-colored SUV pulled into the lot and parked across from me, right in front of Jack's place. I took my hand off the handle and sat in the car holding my breath. I leaned against the steering wheel and squinted for a clearer view.

A woman about my age exited the vehicle, carrying a sack of groceries. I heard the SUV beep once and saw the lights flash as she locked it with her remote. She started up the steps, and Jack's front door opened before she reached the top. I heard her laugh as she handed the groceries through the door to someone. Was it Jack?

From my vantage point, I was angled so I could only see a man's arms reaching out to accept the groceries before the door was closed. What the hell?

I felt a new emotion, extreme jealousy mixed with a dose of anger. I had entertained the thought of him being with someone else, but I really didn't think in my heart that he was. I still didn't have absolute proof, but the evidence was pretty strong.

Part of me wanted to march right up there and knock on the door and see how he liked that! But the sensible part of my conscious knew the only person appearing to be a fool in that scenario would be me. I settled for my second choice.

I flipped open my phone and speed dialed Jack. No answer. I pressed redial.

A shadow crossed in front of his window, and then his voice broke through the silence in my car.

"Hello?" he said.

"Hey, Jack,"

"What's up?"

"I got the flowers you sent this evening, and I wanted to thank you."

"Oh," he replied, and after a long pause, added, "You're welcome."

"That was very sweet of you. They'll look lovely on the dining room table for Thanksgiving dinner. Are you sure you won't join us?"

"No, I told you I already have plans."

"Oh, will your parents be in town?" I asked.

"No."

"Oh, I see. Well, I'm sure you'll want to see Casey while she's home."

"Sure. Hey, listen, I have to go. I'm in the middle of a business meeting."

"Gee, working late tonight then?'

"Yeah, have to work extra to keep paying those bills."

I ignored the jab and answered sweetly, "Well, don't work too hard. Thanks again." And I disconnected.

The lying bastard. Abbey was right, he was a snake. I was so angry, I lost my mind. I got out of the car and slammed the door hard behind me. I marched up the steps and rang Jack's doorbell. My heart was pounding and my adrenaline was pumping.

A few seconds later, Jack opened the door, holding a glass of red wine in his hand and wearing a big smile on his face, a smile that was immediately replaced by a look of shock, then disbelief, then anger.

Who *was* this person standing in front of me? This man, whom I thought I knew inside and out, and was married to for nearly thirty years, now looked like a stranger to me.

Later, in retrospect, when I replayed that moment in slow motion, I realized how much I had observed in the several seconds that I had stood there. The aroma of garlic-infused spaghetti sauce wafting out of the open doorway…the strange new scent of Jack's cologne…the shirt he was wearing that I'd never seen before…beyond him, a new sofa with a woman's coat flung over the back….

However, the feeling I had when he opened that door was the same one I get when I ride the Phantom's Revenge coaster at Kennywood Park. There's always the moment when I near the top of the highest peak, after climbing the hill slowly, slowly, then creeping just over the ridge, that I want to change my mind and not really ride the coaster at all. Then I realize that it's too late to change my mind, and the coaster plunges at breakneck speed, plummeting down into a deep valley with my stomach still at the top of the hill, and my hands clenching the rails.

As he stood there and looked at me, I wanted to jump out of the coaster before I lost my stomach, but realized that I had to stay in my seat until the ride ended.

He appeared to be speechless, and I didn't say a word to

him. I just cocked my head to the side and stared straight into his eyes for a moment. Then I turned on my heel and walked purposefully back to my Maxima. He was still standing in the open doorway as I pulled out of the lot, and as an afterthought, I shot him the finger. It was so dark that he probably didn't see it, but it made me feel better to do it.

When I got home, the reality of what I'd just done hit me, and I started trembling. I was still on an adrenaline rush though. I grabbed that flower arrangement and tossed it in the garbage can. Then I felt sad about it, and pulled it back out.

I straightened out a few of the bent mums and set it back on the table. My love for flowers won out over my loathing for Jack. I would enjoy them just to spite him.

This whole evening exhausted me. I trudged upstairs and flung myself across the bed.

I must have been chilled during the night, because when I woke up the next morning, I was snuggled deep in my comforter. My alarm was ringing me awake for my grocery shopping trip with Abbey.

I showered, had a little piece of cheesecake for breakfast, and was ready and waiting for Abbey when she came to pick me up.

Telling Abbey about the things that happen with Jack may not always be the wisest thing to do, because it just fuels her fire of dislike for him, but I *had* to tell her about last night.

She was filling a plastic sack with yams when I dropped the bomb.

"You *what?*" she shrieked.

"I went to his place," I repeated.

139

I told her the whole sordid story, and she stood rooted to the spot, holding the bag of yams, during the whole tale.

"Holy nuts! Who stole my shy little friend and replaced her with this bold new woman?" she joked. "Ellen, you sure had guts to do that! I'm proud of you! Even though you didn't say anything, he knows that you caught him in a lie."

I actually felt pretty proud of myself, almost an alien feeling to me anymore.

Abbey and I had a great time shopping together, and by the time we reached the check out, our cart was bulging over the top. We had agreed to split the cost down the middle, and even that was stretching my budget.

I've been getting some holiday custom orders, like personalizing Christmas ornaments and painting Thanksgiving platters, and that money has been keeping me afloat. I really have to start thinking about this budgeting thing, but I refuse to ruin the holiday over it. I figured I'd talk to Casey when she got here about all the legal stuff.

Abbey helped me put the groceries away that were staying at my house and took the rest home to create the dishes that she was bringing over.

I was so busy chatting with Casey, I didn't even realize that I was driving through the tunnel until I was halfway through.

"Mom, are you okay?" Casey asked when I stopped talking.

My hands clenched the wheel, and I focused on the light at the end, but I wasn't getting the palpitations and the cold sweats. I shook my head up and down.

"I thought you said you were okay with this now?" she asked me.

I couldn't answer, just focused on driving.

A moment later we emerged into the bright sunlight, the amazing view of the Pittsburgh skyline welcoming Casey home. I gave her a brief glance and smiled.

"I *am* okay with this now. I *did* it!" I exclaimed as I drove over the bridge and maneuvered into the correct lane heading toward the parkway.

"If that's being okay with it, I'd hate to see how you *used* to be with it!" she offered.

I shot her a look, but I was smiling on the inside.

We decided to stop at the mall, have some lunch, and do a little shopping afterward. Casey ordered a salad, and out of guilt, I ordered the same. However, just to make me happy, Casey agreed to share a piece of caramel apple pie a la mode.

She pulled out her new Coach purse and took out a crisp fifty. "Lunch is on me, Mom," she said.

Normally, I would never let her take the check, but today I would accept the gesture. I had seen my checkbook balance.

I really needed to buy a new outfit to wear tomorrow though. My uniform of sweats just wasn't going to cut it for Thanksgiving dinner.

We went to Dante's Drawers, my favorite store at the mall.

"What size, Mom?" Casey asked as she sifted through a rack of gray wool slacks.

"I honestly don't know, Casey. I just know that my pants

at home won't fit anymore."

She handed me a stack of pants. "Here's a bunch; just try them all on and see what you like."

I went into the dressing room with trepidation. I've been denying my weight gain, and now I had to face the music…in front of a triple full length mirror to boot.

I sucked in my belly, but still couldn't get the button fastened on the first pair. Geez, these were two sizes larger than what I normally wear, and they *still* didn't fit! Maybe it was the cut.

Casey knocked on the dressing room door. "Mom, try this sweater on with them. I love it!"

I opened the door a crack and stuck my hand out.

"I've seen you changing before, you know," she said as she put the sweater in my hand.

I snatched it from her and shut the door.

Finally getting a pair of pants to zip and button, I slipped the teal, cable knit sweater over my head. I loved it too. Unfortunately it wasn't long enough to cover the butt that I *wasn't* in love with at the moment.

I stood staring at my reflection, listening to Burl Ives singing Frosty the Snowman through the store's speakers, feeling like I was auditioning to be one of the helium balloons in tomorrow's parade. I felt like crying. How did I let this get so out of hand?

Casey knocked on the door again. "Here, try this."

I opened the door again and Casey jokingly put her hand over her eyes, and handed me a dress, of all things. I tugged off the pants and folded the sweater back up. Then I slid on the dress. It was soft, black cashmere, and felt so comfy. It fit perfectly. The v-neck clung to my slightly larger boobs and then fell softly over my much larger bottom. Best of all, it had no zipper or buttons to battle with.

I still wasn't happy with my profile, but the dress took at least ten pounds off my appearance. God bless Casey! It *was* perfect! Just dressy enough, without overdoing it.

I opened the dressing room door wide.

"Ta-da!" I said, and twirled around once.

Casey smiled at me. "It looks great! Do you have shoes to wear with it?"

"Actually, I do…providing my feet haven't increased two sizes!"

I emerged from the dressing room with the bundle of pants that I wanted to forget about in my arms.

"I'll hold the dress for you," Casey said.

I placed my discards on the rack and met Casey at the checkout just as she was signing the receipt.

"Casey, what are you doing?" I asked.

"It's my gift to you, Mom. It's a Happy Thanksgiving present," she answered.

"Oh, honey, that's too much!"

"Mom, I don't want any arguing. Just say thank you."

"Thank you, sweetie," I said as I gave her a huge hug.

She smiled and handed me the bag. This was all new to me. I'm used to being the one to provide for my children, not the other way around. I wasn't sure how I felt about this, although I loved the dress and was so appreciative. I looked at my daughter in a new light. She would always be my little girl, but she had grown into a wonderful young woman.

Later that evening, we decided to park ourselves on the couch and have movie night, just like we used to. Casey was at one end of the sofa, and I at the other, with our feet touching in the middle and the big magical blanket shared between us. I didn't want to fall asleep this time though. My times with Casey were too precious to miss even a small moment of them.

About halfway through the movie, Casey hit the pause button. I thought maybe it was time for a bathroom intermission, but she didn't move.

"Mom, can we talk?" she asked.

"Sure," I replied. Somehow I knew what was coming. We hadn't talked about the situation between Jack and me at all today. I think it was a silent, mutual agreement not to flaw our time together this afternoon by discussing it, but I knew that she would be curious and demand the answers that she so deserved.

"It feels sad without Daddy here," she began.

With that one sentence, this professional young woman turned into my little girl in pigtails. My heart went out to her. I hate to admit the fact that I've been so wrapped up in my own feelings, I haven't genuinely thought much about how it really was affecting the kids.

I got up and went to sit beside her, embracing her in a hug. I could feel the wetness on her cheeks from the tears she had finally let fall.

"I'm so sorry, honey," I said as I pulled back. I took her face in my hands and said, "It's going to be okay. You and your dad can still have a relationship. It'll just be different, that's all."

"You won't mind if I see him while I'm home?" she

asked hopefully. "I feel like I'm betraying you."

"Honey, this isn't a competition between your dad and me for your loyalty. It's just something we need to work out. We're still your parents, just living under different roofs, that's all."

Did I really say that? I impressed the hell out of myself by actually verbalizing something so coherent on this subject. I must be making progress! I was suddenly glad that Casey had been away for the beginning of this mess. It spared her the heartache of witnessing the actual breakup, and gave me a chance to come to terms with the situation myself before dealing with her emotions. I couldn't have handled anyone's grief but my own during those first few weeks.

"Thanks, Mom. He invited Adam and me to come over to his place on Friday for dinner, and I didn't want to go if you were going to be upset about it."

Well, now, there went the coherent thoughts right out the window! My stomach did a flip-flop and I could feel that sneaky fellow named Jealousy worming his way into my good intentions. So, he's been talking to the kids. I wonder what he's saying to them.

"Casey, I think that would be nice to visit your dad. I'm sure he's missing you too."

I lied. A part of me really wanted the kids to say, "The hell with you," to Jack, but I knew deep down that wasn't the healthy thing for anyone. I could deal with this…one more step out of the fog.

That night, while I was lying in bed, I had a tremendous feeling of well-being, just knowing that Casey was sleeping in her bed right down the hall. Sure, I was upset more than a tiny bit that the kids were having dinner with Jack on Friday, but I decided to just absorb the wonderful day that Casey and I had today and concentrate on looking forward to our Thanksgiving together tomorrow. It sure was nice to have someone in the house with me again. Very nice….

CHAPTER ELEVEN

I actually woke up before my cell phone alarm had a chance to startle me awake. It must have been the smell of coffee brewing and...could that wonderful aroma be cinnamon rolls?

Wrapping my robe around me, I padded down to the kitchen to find Casey stooping to take a cookie sheet out of the oven. She turned and smiled at me.

"Happy Thanksgiving, Mom!" she said. "One of my best memories of Thanksgiving morning was always waking up to the great smells of all the things you were already cooking in the kitchen. So, I wanted to do that for you this year."

What did I ever do to deserve this daughter?

"Casey, you're amazing! Thank you *so* much. I will never forget this Thanksgiving morning." And I meant it.

We sat together at the kitchen table in our pajamas, eating breakfast and planning our day. Adam would probably arrive early, but Abbey and her family wouldn't be here until around three. We had plenty of time to get the dinner preparations underway.

Before long, the tantalizing scent of onions and celery being sautéed in butter filled the kitchen. Casey started frying sausage to add to the dressing, and I tackled the turkey preparation.

"Hurray!" I shouted, holding up the bag of giblets triumphantly. For the first time ever, they came out without using an ice pick.

Casey, wrist deep in her bread crumbs, grimaced.

"That is so gross, Mother."

"Ah, you won't be saying that at dinner time," I answered.

We turned on the TV in the kitchen and watched the Macy's Thanksgiving parade while we cooked. Just as I slid the pumpkin pies in the oven, Casey grabbed my hand and thrust a spatula in it.

"Follow me!" she hollered.

She had grabbed her own spatula and began marching around the kitchen in time to a marching band's version of "Santa Claus is Coming to Town." I fell in behind her, twirling my spatula and lifting my knees high. We paraded through the dining room, then the living room, completing the circle back to the kitchen and collapsing onto the floor in a fit of giggles.

Before we had totally composed ourselves, I heard the front door open. Within seconds, Cooper was joining in the fun, jumping all over us and washing our faces with his wet kisses.

"Cooper, give them a break," I heard Adam call. "Sit, boy!"

Immediately, Cooper went to Adam's side and plunked down next to him. He sat there panting, with his tongue hanging out and his nose twitching, apparently intoxicated by all the good smells in the kitchen.

Adam offered me his hand and pulled me to my feet, planting his own wet kiss on my cheek.

"Happy Thanksgiving, Mom! What the heck are you guys doing sitting on the floor?" he asked.

Casey stood up and gave her brother a hug, and Cooper a pat on the head.

"Oh, just having some fun," Casey told him. "We were having the annual Stern Thanksgiving parade."

Adam rolled his eyes.

"Sorry I missed that…got anything to eat?" he asked as he glanced at the plate of cinnamon rolls.

"Help yourself," I said.

Adam, Cooper, and the plate of cinnamon rolls took up residence on the couch, tuning in to watch football, while Casey and I set the table.

I lit the candle on the centerpiece and stood back to admire our work.

"It looks like something out of a magazine," Casey said. "Where did you get the centerpiece?"

"Actually, your dad sent it."

"Really?" Casey asked. "That's a good sign, isn't it?"

I didn't want to give her any false hopes, but at the same time, I didn't want to ruin her day.

"Doing nice things is always a good thing," I replied.

The pumpkin pies were cooling on the counter. The turkey, sweet potato casserole, and the green beans were in the oven. The coleslaw and strawberry salad were made and chilling in the refrigerator. The potatoes were boiling on the stove. The only last minute thing to do would be to heat up the dinner rolls and pour the wine.

Adam was telling Casey all about the cat lady house, and as I was walking up the stairs, I heard Casey's voice.

"Eewwwwwwww!"

I smiled as I turned the corner into my bedroom and sighed. The only thing missing was Jack.

I hadn't allowed myself time to think about what he was doing today, but as I stood in the shower with the hot water pelting my body, I granted myself permission to cry. The sadness had come upon me suddenly. I had been feeling so happy all morning. Having Casey home has been so good for me.

Dr. Burke had warned me that the holidays may make me feel a little sadder and that I should just go with the flow…and then let it go. So I stood in the shower and cried my sadness out, then I was ready to move on with my day.

I fixed my hair and put on a full face of makeup for a change. Then I slid on my new dress and felt like a new me!

Adam whistled when I walked down the stairs.

"Way to go, Mom! You look great!" he called out from the living room.

I actually *felt* great, and I was so thankful to be spending this holiday with my children and my best friend.

As I was taking the turkey out of the oven, I heard the commotion at the front door and knew that Abbey and her family had arrived.

Abbey burst into the kitchen, her arms loaded with her special creations for dinner, and put them on the table. Rick followed her, carrying two bottles of wine, and Natalie brought up the rear bearing a luscious double layer chocolate cake.

"Happy Thanksgiving!" we all shouted at the same time.

"Don't you look wonderful today!" Abbey told me.

"Thanks! The dress is a gift from Casey," I said as I did a slow spin.

A short time later, as I sat gazing around my dining room table, I felt the true joy of being with the people I love and care about the most. I lifted my glass for a toast.

"To the best family and friends a person could ever have...I am truly thankful."

A round of "Cheers" echoed around the table as we clinked our glasses.

And a "Woof!" came from somewhere near Adam's chair.

After the leftovers were stashed in the refrigerator and the kitchen was restored to its normal state, we all sat in the living room playing Monopoly. Of course Adam, with his real estate expertise, was the winner by a landslide. Casey used to hate losing to him when they were younger, but she took it pretty well today.

At the end of the evening, Abbey gave me a big hug at the door.

"It's so nice to see you happy again, Ellen," she said. "Thanks so much for inviting us today."

I truly loved this friend of mine.

So I simply said, "Abbey, I love you!" and hugged her back.

Adam decided that he and Cooper would spend the night. Evidently he and Casey had an early morning shopping mission. I'm not into fighting the Black Friday crowds, so I told Abbey that I would help her in the shop.

Casey delegated her room to Adam and Cooper, and she bunked with me. After the lights were out and the house was quiet, except for Casey's even breathing, I once again had a feeling of contentment. It felt like old times having both of my kids under my roof, safe and sound. I was exhausted, but in a good way...and I fell asleep with a smile on my face.

I felt Casey kiss my cheek and give me a little shake. I opened one eye, but it was still dark.

"Mom...we're leaving to go shopping now. Adam let Cooper out already, but he wants you to let him out again before you go to work, okay?"

"Mmmmmm-hmmmmmm," I mumbled, then closed my eye and fell right back to sleep.

When my alarm went off at nine, I opened both eyes to see Cooper stretched out next to me hogging the extra pillow. He lifted his head and watched as I pushed the snooze, then plopped his head back down on the pillow and promptly fell back to sleep...my kind of bed companion.

I wasn't so lucky this time though, and I lay there replaying Thanksgiving Day in my head. It had been a wonderful day, and I hadn't really let any bad thoughts creep in to ruin it.

However, today was another day, and already I was feeling nauseous just thinking about the kids going over to Jack's. Would he be alone, or would another woman be there? I hadn't mentioned that to the kids; it was just too hurtful to talk about yet.

I turned off the alarm before it had a chance to chime again and jumped in the shower. Today would be another sweatpants day. I was starting to get disgusted with myself. It had felt so good yesterday to dress up and look nice, although it did take a lot of effort and energy that I just haven't had.

After letting Cooper out, I grabbed a piece of Abbey's chocolate cake for breakfast and maneuvered through the Route 30 traffic to Amazing Glaze.

It turned out to be a very busy day. We didn't have any formal classes scheduled, but the bells on the door jingled all day

152

with walk-in customers. It would be a mad dash from now until Christmas, with everyone trying to complete their projects in time for gift giving or decorating.

Abbey had set out plates of cookies and cakes for everyone and had a punch bowl in the middle of the painting table. We strung multi-colored twinkle lights randomly throughout the store and hung our hand-painted ceramic ornaments on an artificial tree by the checkout counter. Abbey had painted a red and white striped bowl and filled it with peppermints next to the register. The festivity factor here was pretty high today, and I was sad when the work day was over and I had to go home.

"Would you like to come over to our house for dinner tonight?" Abbey asked.

"No, I think I'll just go home. I'm not sure what time the kids are getting home and Cooper may need to go out again."

I pulled my coat up to my chin as I walked to the car. It was already dark, and the wind was whipping and swirling the leftover leaves around the parking lot.

Blah.

When I pulled up in front of my house, there were no lights on. I let myself in and flicked the switch in the hallway.

"Cooper?" I hollered, but it was quiet. No furry greeting…no sloppy kisses.

I went to the kitchen, turning on every light I passed. There was a note in Casey's handwriting left on the table.

"Went to dinner at Dad's. Shouldn't be too late. Took Cooper back to Adam's house this afternoon. Love you!"

Huh.

I opened the refrigerator and looked at all the leftovers, but the only thing I pulled out was the pumpkin pie. I sliced a generous piece, covered it with whipped cream, and then parked myself under the blanket on the couch.

Suddenly not having the energy to even pick up the remote, I sat there eating my pie in silence. Then I snuggled down in the warmth and drifted off to a troubled sleep, with visions of Jack dancing in my head. I wanted to be with them tonight. I wanted us to be a family again.

I sat up when I heard Casey coming in the front door.

"How was your dinner?" I asked as I rubbed at my eyes.

Casey came right over and slid in beside me, pulling the blanket up to her chin.

"I can't believe how cold it feels out there. That's one thing I haven't missed."

"I can appreciate that," I replied.

"Well, dinner was actually good. We had pasta, and Dad said he made the sauce by himself from scratch! I don't remember ever seeing him in the kitchen cooking before."

"That's because he never did," I replied. My skin was beginning to feel prickly.

"Oh. Well, he served a salad, garlic toast, and wine. Then apple pie and cinnamon ice cream from King's Restaurant for dessert."

"That sounds nice," I was starting to clench my jaw. I knew that Adam's favorite dessert was apple pie and cinnamon ice cream from King's.

"His place is pretty cool. He bought new furniture so it didn't feel like home, but it felt cozy."

I had to ask the burning question, "So, it was just you guys and Dad?"

Casey stared at me. "Who else *would* there be?"

"Just wondering," I answered feeling pretty foolish.

"It just feels weird, Mom, going somewhere else to visit him."

"How did Adam do?" I asked.

"He seemed fine. Dad actually asked him if he had any new projects, and he laughed with him about the cat lady house."

"I'm sure that made Adam feel good. So, no arguments tonight?"

"No, Dad seemed different. Like he actually paid attention to what we were saying."

"It's about time," I couldn't resist; it just popped out of my mouth.

"Mom…maybe he just needs some time away, and then things will work out."

I was staring at the floor, watching my tapping foot making the blanket quiver up and down. I know that I should be happy things went well for them tonight, but I had secretly hoped it would have blown up in Jack's face.

What was it about *me* that brought out the worst in Jack? Why didn't he ever cook *me* dinner if he had such a burning desire to make spaghetti sauce? They should have checked the trash can, it was probably from a jar. This whole "new Jack" thing wasn't sitting well with me.

While I was preoccupied with wallowing in my self-pity, Casey put her hand on my foot to stop my tapping.

"Are you okay, Mom? What did you do tonight?" she asked.

"Oh, you pretty much saw it. I just plopped here after work and slept the evening away…my usual."

I wasn't intentionally trying to make her feel bad, but maybe the little devil sitting on my shoulder was. He wanted to inflict pain on someone so I wasn't the only one hurting.

Then I immediately felt bad, so I added, "I guess I was just tired from all the hoopla at work today. We were really busy. If I see one more ceramic tree with the little plastic lights on it, it will be one too many!" And I forced out a little laugh.

Casey smiled at me and took the bait. "Are they still making them? Wow, I remember painting those way back when I was a kid! Do we still have mine somewhere?"

"Casey, they were popular way back when *I* was kid! And of course we still have yours! I just haven't put it out for a few years."

Casey kissed my cheek and went up to bed, with me trailing not far behind her. I slipped beneath the covers and lay there in the darkness trying to process the events of the day.

I could hear Casey's muffled voice coming from her room. She was probably talking to Chris. Suddenly, I needed to hear Jack's voice. I knew that I shouldn't, but I picked up my cell phone and dialed. It connected on the third ring.

"Abbey, is it too late to talk?"

"No, sweetheart, we were just watching a movie. What's up?" Abbey said.

I gave her a rundown of the kid's dinner with Jack and how I was feeling about it.

"Don't beat yourself up about how you feel, Ellen. Who

156

wouldn't feel left out? You're all alone, and he's got his new place, and his new life, and he's learning new things. He's moving on, and you're still spinning tire."

"Well, thanks for making me feel so damn good about myself!" I replied with a huff.

"Oh, sweetie, you know what I mean," and she laughed.

"I wanted to call him tonight."

"Why give him the satisfaction? Ellen, he can't keep up the nice guy pretense for long. You know that better than anyone. The kids will see through him eventually. Adam and Casey love you. Just concentrate on that and getting yourself back on track. Jack will trip himself up soon enough."

"Thanks for letting me vent, Abbey."

"No problem, kiddo."

Abbey was right. I needed to start focusing on getting myself back on track, or finding a new track.

I put on my robe and went down to the basement. Rummaging around in the plastic bins, I found what I was looking for and climbed the two flights back upstairs. I opened Casey's bedroom door and peeked in. She was sound asleep.

I placed the ceramic Christmas tree on the middle of her dresser and plugged it in. A warm red glow filled the room, and I smiled.

CHAPTER TWELVE

"Are you coming, Mom?" Casey yelled from the foot of the stairs.

I finished tying my shoe and slipped a sweatshirt over my head, then grabbed a tossle cap out of my dresser drawer and pulled it down past my ears.

"Coming!" I called as I bounced down the steps.

Casey loved to walk, and we used to go together nearly every day when she lived at home. She picked up a fast pace as we headed down our sidewalk and out onto the street. We walked for a bit in compatible silence, our breath making foggy little puffs from the cold.

"Thanks for finding my Christmas tree! That was so sweet," she said after we had circled the block once and started up the hill toward the elementary school.

"You're welcome," I replied. I was starting to feel a little winded, and I was happy when we reached the level walking track. Last summer I was able to walk at this pace and carry on a conversation, but right now I couldn't muster more than those two words.

After we completed two miles on the track, we headed back down the hill toward home. Even though I felt tired, I also felt invigorated and clear-headed. I sheepishly remembered all the times that Dr. Burke had reminded me to exercise, and I had filed her advice in my mental trash can.

Once we were home and showered, we sat down to have breakfast. Casey was making two bowls of oatmeal for us, and as I reached for the orange juice, I almost grabbed the pumpkin pie out of the refrigerator again, but thought better of it.

I sprinkled a handful of raisins on my oatmeal and handed

the box to Casey.

"Adam and I have a surprise for you today! It's an early Christmas present, but I can't tell you what it is until he gets here."

I looked up with my spoon poised halfway to my mouth.

"Oh, *really?*"

"Yes, and you're going to like it," she replied with a grin.

"Is it my old size six body, by chance?" I asked, only half kidding.

Casey raised her eyebrows.

"Mom, if you don't like the way you look, then do something about it."

Wow. That hit home. *Do* something about it. *Do something about it!* Now that's a great idea. Why didn't I think of it?

I swished my spoon around in the oatmeal, swirling the raisins and brown sugar. Why *couldn't* I do something about it? No one was stopping me. It would be my choice.

"Will *you* help me do something about it?" I asked her softly.

Casey got right down to business. I could see her morphing into counselor mode right before my eyes.

"I've read in my fitness magazine that you should write down everything you eat for a week, and then you can see how you're taking in the extra calories," she gushed as she bolted out of the room. I half expected her to return wearing a two-piece suit and pumps, but she returned with a pencil and notepad instead. She plunked down on the chair across from me, pencil poised and ready for action. I noticed it was a pretty pencil, turquoise with yellow polka dots…very un-lawyer like, and I wondered where she got it.

"Okay," she began, "What did you eat for breakfast yesterday?"

I searched back in my fuzzy mind for the answer, and, proud that I had remembered, blurted out, "Abbey's chocolate cake!"

The yellow polka dotted pencil began tapping against the table top, and I sensed disapproval. Maybe that wasn't the million dollar answer.

"Well, then…" she continued, "What did you eat for lunch?"

I readily knew the answer for round two, but my response was a little more subdued. I was visualizing the spread of goodies that Abbey had provided at Amazing Glaze yesterday.

"Cake," I squeaked, deciding not to include the peanut butter kiss cookies in my answer. "But it had real strawberry filling," I added, hoping to score some nutritional value points.

Casey wasn't buying it.

"Mother!" she cried, totally exasperated, "Please tell me you didn't eat cake for supper too?"

I was silent for a couple of pencil taps, and then I tilted my chin up and replied, "No. I had pumpkin pie."

"*Mom!*" she shrieked, and the pencil flew into the air, pinged off the wall behind her, and rolled under the refrigerator.

Casey cringed and looked at me like I was single-handedly responsible for toppling the entire food pyramid.

"And you wonder why you're gaining weight?" she asked.

"I guess it sounds pretty bad, but I don't eat like that *every* day. Usually I do get take out though. I haven't had the energy for cooking, and it's no fun to cook for one."

"Well, *I'm* only one, and I can do it. You used to be the only healthy eater in our family! Remember the grief you used to give Dad over his donut fetish every morning?"

I should have saved my breath. Let him eat all the donuts he wants! And I never could understand why he didn't swell up to blimp proportions from all the crap he ate.

The mention of Jack sealed the deal. I *would* lose weight, and I *would* start being healthy again. Like a lightning bolt to my brain, I realized that I had let his actions control me, even when he wasn't here. I would do this for *me*.

"Okay, Casey, I want to do this! I want to make this happen," I said.

"Good for you, Mom. I'll help you make a menu before I go home tomorrow, and you'll see how easy it'll be!"

Later that afternoon, Casey, Adam, and I were sitting around the kitchen table, with steaming cups of hot chocolate all but forgotten, as our fingers were flying over the sleek keys of our new cell phones.

I think a little bird named Abbey had mentioned to Casey that I would be needing new phone service soon, and the kids decided to combine their efforts and get me the newest one, complete with internet and all the goodies. Of course once the temptation was there, they each had to have one, too.

"Listen to this ring tone, it's crazy!" Adam said. Immediately the sound of dogs barking filled the room.

"That's crazy all right," Casey replied. "It'll drive *Cooper* crazy."

Casey added me to her phone plan, so I would have a minimal payment and we could all call each other without using any minutes.

I'm usually not a gadget kind of gal, but I have to admit that I was loving this little gizmo! It was so nice to have the internet and email back again!

I dialed Casey's number. She looked amused and answered.

"Hi, Mom! Haven't talked to you lately!"

"Hi, Casey! I just wanted to thank you for my early Christmas gift and for helping me with the phone service." I spoke into my phone and met her eyes with a smile.

"My pleasure, Mom."

I disconnected and looked at Adam, who was still engrossed in selecting his ring tone.

"Adam, thank you, too, for a wonderful Christmas gift," I said.

"You're welcome," he said without looking up.

We made turkey sandwiches and finished up the last of the Thanksgiving leftovers for dinner, including the last of the pumpkin pie.

"Enjoy your dessert, Mom! It'll be the last for a while!" Casey jibed.

"Actually, I'm looking forward to eating healthy again," I said—and I meant it. I felt like I had a plan now. I felt like I was gaining a little bit of control over my life again.

I dropped Casey back at the airport without a hitch. It wasn't nearly so hard saying goodbye when I knew that she'd be coming home in a month for Christmas. I felt rejuvenated and sensed some of my old spunk returning.

A little apprehension threatened as I approached the tunnel on the way home, but I made it through by only regulating my breathing and singing to the radio. When I emerged on the other side, I wanted to shout out loud! Casey had knowingly kept me engrossed in conversation on the way *to* the airport, so I did just fine then too. Maybe I have this panic attack thing beat! I think it helped me just to know that the people important to me are aware of what's happening to me.

I decided to swing by the Stop and Shop on the way home and buy some fruits and vegetables to replace my stash of cookies and cakes. Swinging by the deli department, I picked up a rotisserie chicken and a small container of parsley potatoes, then cruised through the rows of vegetables. While I was inspecting a bunch of broccoli, I heard a familiar voice. My heart started beating wildly and a wave of heat ran the length of my body.

I turned around slowly to see who he was talking to. There was Jack, on the other side of the green peppers, holding up jar of garlic cloves in one hand and fresh garlic in the other, acting like he was doing a commercial on Food Network. The woman he was with laughed hysterically, then took the fresh garlic and put it in the shopping cart. They moved toward me to select a long stick of French bread from the bakery department, and I threw my broccoli in the cart and hid behind a table stacked high with bananas.

She wasn't anything over the top in the looks department, from what I could tell at my vantage point. (although she could have been super model material and I still would have found fault). I wanted to flounce right over there and rip her dyed blond hair right out of her head. She had a killer body though, if you like that kind of thing, with great big cha cha's that she wasn't shy about letting peek out of her red v-neck sweater. She was wearing skin tight jeans tucked into cowboy boots, and she had her hair pulled back in a high pony tail. It was hard to tell her age from this distance. I squinted. Was she the same woman I had seen at Jack's apartment?

She began to push their cart, with Jack beside her and his hand at her waist. A fruit fly went up my nose and I sneezed, quickly crouching down in case they looked my way.

"Bless you!" I heard a woman say in a country drawl.

Oh geez. I looked under the banana table and waited until their legs were out of eyesight. Then I stood up slowly to make sure the coast was clear. I should have just gone directly to the checkout, but of course I couldn't help myself. Even though it was shocking and something I really didn't want to witness, I couldn't pull myself away. Of *course* I had to follow them. It was like I had become someone else…a supermarket stalker, no less. There was no one who could stop me from doing this.

"Ellen!" I turned around wide-eyed to see Abbey pushing her cart my way. "Wait up!"

"Shhhhh!" I motioned to her as I crouched back down behind my cart.

Abbey looked alarmed. "Ellen, are you having a panic attack?" she asked.

"No! Get down!" I grabbed her hand and pulled her down with me.

I turned around and stood up just enough to see Jack and the mystery woman over in the floral area. I pulled Abbey up to my level and pointed.

"Look," I said.

She looked at me like I was bonkers, then focused over the donuts to where I was pointing.

"Holy mistress!" she whispered.

We watched as Jack chose a bunch of autumn flowers wrapped in cellophane and held them up for the woman's inspection. She shook her head, and he replaced them with a bunch of red roses amidst green pine and white baby's breath. The bimbo nodded, lifted them toward her nose to sniff, and then stood up on her tiptoes and *kissed* him. Right on the *lips*. Right in Stop and Shop. *Right in front of me!*

I sat down right there on the floor, oblivious to the other shoppers milling around me. I started feeling the shakes, my telltale sign that I was on the verge of a panic attack. But instead of the usual uncontrollable wave of panic that comes next, I experienced a wave of determination. I was *not* going to let Jack set me back after I had come so far!

Abbey sat down next to me.

"Are you okay?" she asked gently.

"I *will* be," I replied, still trembling and trying to regulate my breathing.

"Hey, we're drawing a crowd here," Abbey said.

I guess two women sitting on the floor wasn't the norm at the grocery store. We were creating our own train wreck, and people were approaching us to see if we needed help. Nice to know there are still caring people in this world, but I didn't want to draw Jack's attention, that's for sure.

I stood up, pulling Abbey with me.

"Thank you…no, we're fine. I just lost something, but I've found it now, so we're good to go," I addressed the whole semi-circle of people that had gathered.

I looked back toward the floral department as the crowd disbursed, half expecting to see Jack glaring at me over the clearance pumpkin pies, but they must have rounded the corner already and were nowhere in sight.

Abbey started four-wheeling up the aisle. "Come on! We're going to lose them!" she said in an exaggerated whisper.

I grabbed the back of her shirt. "Wait a minute. I don't want them to see me."

I yanked my cell phone out of my pocket and called Abbey. "You be the scout and I'll follow an aisle or so behind you. Tell me on the phone when you find them."

She accepted the assignment and took off up the aisle, giving me a thumbs up as she rounded the corner.

I proceeded slowly up the aisle, cell phone poised next to my ear.

"Ceramic Mama to Scorned Woman. Are you there?" I heard her whisper in my ear.

Despite my inner turmoil, I smiled. I was very glad to have Abbey here to help me through this.

"Affirmative," I answered, getting into character.

"Suspects sighted in the pasta aisle. I'll hold position until you get here."

Evidently the man only has one recipe in his box.

I made it to Abbey's side, and we watched as they selected their noodles and proceeded to the checkout. Once they were in line, we made a bee-line over to the entertainment section where we could peek undetected over the shelves of videos.

All of a sudden, Abbey pushed a button on her cell phone, put it in her pocket, and took off.

"Leave your phone on," she called over her shoulder.

I couldn't pull her back without drawing attention to myself, so I stood frozen to the spot.

She slowed down when she got to the checkout lines and of course chose the one Jack was in. They had their backs to her, and I could sense her frustration at not being seen. She *wanted* Jack to see her.

She reached past them to choose a pack of gum, then bumped into Blondie. I held my breath.

"Excuse me," I heard Abbey say through my phone.

Wow. She was a great detective. She had her phone on speaker!

"That's okay," I heard the southern drawl again.

"Oh my gosh... Jack!" I heard Abbey mimic surprise.

I could see Jack's face getting red, even from this distance, as he turned around to face Abbey. Good for him. What did he expect parading around with her in the neighborhood grocery store, that he wouldn't bump into anyone he knew? I wonder what he would have done if it had been me there instead of Abbey.

"Abbey," Jack said nodding, then turned around, snubbing her.

Abbey wasn't to be defeated. She addressed the southern belle, who was still looking at her.

"Looks like you're eating Italian tonight," Abbey offered.

"Yes, it's our favorite. My Jack makes the *best* sauce!" she said as she touched him on the back.

"Is that right, Jack?" Abbey tried to draw him back into the conversation. "After all these years, I never knew that."

He reluctantly took the bait, probably not wanting to appear rude in front of Miss Clueless.

"There are a lot of things you don't know about me, Abbey," he said dripping sarcasm.

"Apparently," Abbey replied in the same tone.

They were both smiling at each other, but I could practically feel the electricity between them crackling through the cell phone.

"Aren't y'all going to introduce me?" I heard Chesty say as she grabbed Jack's hand.

I saw Jack's shoulders slump. *Ha!*

"Jessica, this is Abbey, a friend of the family," Jack tried.

"Yes, Jack and I go *way* back," Abbey offered. "I take it you're not from around here?"

"No, did my accent give me away again?" she replied, laughing.

Oh, brother.

"Abbey, it's been fun, but now it's done. Gotta go here," Jack dismissed her and started putting their groceries on the conveyer belt.

Leave it to Abbey to get the last word in.

"I'll give Ellen your regards," she said, turning her cart around and heading away from me back toward the vegetables, where this whole debacle had begun.

I stood there and watched until the happy couple exited

the store hand in hand, then I doubled back to meet Abbey.

"Did you hear that?" It was Abbey's voice in my cell phone.

"Every word. Stay put and I'll be right there," I replied and sprinted.

"It's a wonder they didn't check her for shoplifting melons!" Abbey said when I got there. "Do you think they're real?"

Leave it to Abbey to make me laugh.

"Ellen, you need to get your butt back to the attorney and get things moving. I don't think this problem is going away, honey."

"I was just thinking the same thing. I'm so hurt, yet I'm so angry. I'm so mixed up right now."

"*I'm* angry and it's not even *my* husband!" Abbey said. "You're too nice. If that was Rick, I would have marched right up there and smacked him on the head with his loaf of bread."

I needed to go home and sort out my feelings about this. I left Abbey to finish her shopping, threw a bag of shiny, red apples in my cart, and called it a day.

CHAPTER THIRTEEN

Placing my pen down on the table, I took a bite of my warm baked apple. It would have been much tastier with a scoop of vanilla ice cream melting on top, but I'm determined to change my ways.

I'd been sitting eating my dinner and trying to process the events of the day. To say that I was confused would be a gross understatement. I was trying an exercise that Dr. Burke had suggested a while back, one that I hadn't had the courage to do until today.

Looking at the paper beside me, I stared at the two columns. One labeled, *Good Things About My Relationship With Jack,* and the other, *Not So Good Things.*

The *"Not So Good Things"* list went all the way to the bottom of the paper. The *"Good Things"* list, well…it was rather sparse, and the reasons were flimsy to say the least.

Seeing Jack with another woman had lifted the last shred of fog. I finally felt like I was seeing things clearly and rationally for the first time. I still felt nauseous when I visualized him kissing her. That was disturbing on so many levels. But at the same time, it made me realize that I didn't want to be with him after he'd been with someone else.

I really *didn't* want to go back to my old life. If I had Jack back, I'd want him to be different. But I knew that his ways wouldn't change; amazingly, the change was coming from within *me*. A new Ellen was emerging…a person that I've always been inside but was never able to develop because of Jack's overbearing presence. Always trying to be careful of what I said, always trying to please him, never standing up for myself. That wasn't a healthy way to be, and it was my own fault for not realizing it sooner. I just don't like to make waves, but now I was ready to rock the boat.

I picked up my cell and called Casey.

"Hey, Mom, what's up?" she answered cheerfully.

"Well, I have a very difficult question to ask you. I've decided that I'm ready to hire your friend, Annee. I'm embarrassed to say, though, that I don't have the money right now for her retainer. Do you think I could possibly borrow it from you until I get the financial things here settled?"

There was a moment's pause, and I held my breath.

"Mom, are you sure that you want to do this?" she asked. "Why the sudden rush?"

"Yes, I'm sure," I answered. I enlightened her on the fact that Jack was seeing someone else, sparing her the 007 supermarket incident.

"I'm really disappointed in him," she replied.

I felt sad for her, and I was angry with Jack all over again for putting everyone through this.

"I don't have a lot of money put away yet, but I'm sure I have enough to lend you for that, Mom. How about I just call Annee and get it squared away for you tomorrow?"

"That would be great, honey. I can't tell you how much I appreciate your help with this."

Now that my decision was made, I felt more focused and in control of the situation. I fell asleep in my safe place under the comforter, daring to think of what my new life might be like.

The next morning I felt inclined to exercise, but one peek out the window convinced me that it wasn't a great day for a walk. It was really cold and the sky was a dismal gray. I wandered into Casey's room and rummaged around in her closet.

An old exercise video caught my eye, and I pulled it out and blew off the dust. Oh geez, how long had it been since anyone has used this? Next to it was a yellow stretchy rubber band type thing with black plastic handles. I read on the video cover that this was called a "firming cord" and it would give my muscles "star quality" when I used it to tone up to Broadway tunes. Well, if there was ever anything I wanted, it was star quality muscles.

It must have been the healthy dinner from last night talking, but I thought, *"What the hell."* I went back to my room and pulled on a pair of sassy pink sweat shorts and a white tank top that had "Cupcake" written on it in sequins, a wise-guy gift Casey had left for me. I felt ridiculous, but Casey insisted that I needed to try some new "youthful" things, so I endured just to appease her…and besides, no one was here but me.

I carried the video back to the living room and popped it into the ancient VCR. Of course it needed rewound. Apparently Casey had obtained her star quality muscles and hurried away to show them off. I patiently waited while the VCR hummed and squealed as I tried to get the hang of the firming cord. I pulled it back as if shooting a bow and arrow. I pulled it up high and down low. Yeah, I could feel that. Just then, the VCR clicked, the music began, and I was transported to Broadway.

I began singing and dancing along with the tunes…I have always been a sucker for Broadway hits. I was really getting into it, stretching and strutting myself around the living room to the pulse of the video. It felt good to actually "feel" something again. Was I actually *smiling*? Evidently, positive endorphins like Broadway hits too.

Just as I had finished "Cabaret" and was gearing up for the big finale, the yellow rubber stretchy thing decided that it had enough. I pulled it back into one of my bow and arrow poses and – SNAP! It flew across the room and ricocheted off the flower arrangement that Jack had sent!

I just stood there with my jaw dropped, while the girls on the video began prancing around to "Don't Cry for Me Argentina." Water was splattered everywhere, and the flowers were strewn all over the table. The candle was spinning on the floor like a top. I could just hear Jack's voice in my head saying, "You idiot!"

And that's when I started to laugh. Instead of feeling stupid and being afraid of what Jack would think, I found the humor in the situation instead. What a revelation!

The next two weeks flew by. I exercised in some capacity every day and resumed my healthy way of eating. I was feeling so much better. I was sleeping well again and getting some of my old energy back. Amazing Glaze was thriving, and we had full classes every day. Abbey had been giving me extra hours, not only to help me out financially, but because she really needed my help. I was lucky enough to have lots of holiday custom orders too, so I was able to earn some extra cash for Christmas gifts.

I hadn't received any more money from Jack, but since he was still paying for the mortgage and utilities, I was earning enough on my own to handle my personal expenses.

Last night I had carted two dozen ornaments home to paint. I would take them with me to work this afternoon to be fired in the kiln, but for now they were spread all over the kitchen table.

I had just dipped my brush in the red glaze and was preparing to stripe a candy cane, when I was surprised to hear the house phone ring. It actually made me jump! Since we've all been using our cells, I had almost forgotten that we had a landline.
Leaning back, I reached up and plucked the receiver from the wall phone.

"Hello?" I said, paintbrush still in my hand and phone cradled between my ear and shoulder.

"Hello. May I speak to Jack Stern?" a young female voice purred into my ear.

I set the brush down and gripped the receiver.

"He's not here at the moment, may I take a message?" I snipped back.

"It's important that I reach him today. Should I try his cell number?" she asked.

"May I ask who's calling?" I replied.

"Oh, I'm sorry. This is Maggie from Nestor's Realty."

"If this is about rescheduling the appraisal on our house, I have to tell you that Jack and I haven't discussed a time frame for that yet.

"No…it's not about an appraisal. Nancy left me a note to call Jack for her and tell him that she was able to set up the closing for tomorrow if that would be convenient for him. Evidently it wasn't supposed to happen until after the first of the year, but Nancy was able to smooth out the complications, and she thought he'd be happy to hear that he can move before the holidays after all."

What is she talking about? Did Jack have a buyer for this house without even telling me?

"So, you have a buyer for our house?" I asked.

It was quiet for a few beats, and then *she* sounded more confused than *I* was! I think she was realizing that she had just made a mistake of gigantic proportions.

"Maybe I should just try the cell phone number listed here for Jack," she said.

Maggie was a big fish, and I didn't want to let her get away. Something was up and I wanted to know what the hell it was. I tried to regain her trust.

"I'm sure Jack will be *very* happy to hear about the closing tomorrow. He probably would appreciate a call from you on his cell phone, but if I see him today, I'll make sure he gets the message to call you."

"Thanks! That would be great. I'll try his cell now." She sounded relieved.

"I keep forgetting...what's the address of the new house again?" I asked innocently.

"Let me see. It says here that it's 2105 Saxon Lane."

"Thank you so much," I muttered, and we disconnected.

Where is Saxon Lane, and what house is he closing on? I forgot all about my painting project and dug out my cell phone. I punched the address into Map Quest and found Saxon Lane in a new housing plan about an hour away, in Cranberry Township.

Jack built a new house? How could he have built a new house? That takes time...and money! He's only been gone two months. Then the words he said the day he was leaving gave me a mental head slap. *"Do you think I just decided this today?"*

He must have been planning on leaving for a long time...that explains the post office box and all the money. He was building a house and didn't want me to find out! If the twerp from Nestor's hadn't called the home phone by mistake, I probably wouldn't have found out for a long time, if ever! I just can't believe that he did all this right under my nose!

Now *I* don't even have enough cash to pay for my attorney, and he has a brand new house? I stood up and paced back and forth across the kitchen.

I had been in touch with Annee, and she'd been having trouble with Jack's attorney. He didn't return phone calls or respond to her letters. She had requested financial information, and so far had received none.

No wonder Jack had said we wouldn't put the house up for sale until after the holidays. He didn't expect his house to close until then, and he didn't want anyone digging through his finances until his new house was a done deal. That also explains why *he* hasn't filed for divorce yet. He figured I'd be happy and complacent enough just living in the house and getting by on my own earnings, and once again, no one would be in a hurry to have him disclose his finances.

How naïve I have been.

On an adrenaline rush, I grabbed my purse and headed out the door. Forty-five minutes later, I turned off the turnpike at the Cranberry exit. I followed my GPS to Saxon Lane, slowing down to a crawl when I reached the home with 2105 in gold numbers above the triple garage door. I stopped the car and cut the engine.

It was a beautiful home. Tudor style, always Jack's favorite. No one was around except for the construction workers up the street, so I decided to have a peek in the front window. I carefully made my way through the rocky front yard—they probably couldn't landscape until spring—and stood on tiptoe, cupping my hands between my face and the window to get a good look.

Of course the room was void of furnishings, but I could see gleaming hardwood floors and a mammoth stone fireplace that practically took up an entire wall. Just past that I could make out what appeared to be a dining room with glass doors opening onto a deck.

I sighed. The urgent need to see Jack's new home was now replaced by snooper's remorse. I was almost sorry that I had come…Jack had planned and schemed to build this home with every intention of living in it without me. Would his girlfriend live here with him? Had she helped him choose the kitchen cabinets and paint colors? Had they come here together and watched excitedly as the foundation was dug, and then later walked through the rooms when they were only framed out, envisioning how each room would look? Did they stand arm in arm on the street and smile as they gazed at the completed home? After the closing tomorrow, would they drink champagne and christen the bedroom? Would Jack rip off her shirt and let the enormous girls out to play?

I wanted to puke right there in front of the window.

I walked slowly back to my car, eyeing the brick pillar with the enclosed mailbox next to the street. One of the construction workers was walking down the road carrying a green metal lunchbox.

"That one's sold I hear, but there's a model open up the road a little farther if you're interested," he shouted over at me, and smiled pleasantly.

"Thanks," I hollered back.

I watched him as he continued walking down the road to a gray pickup truck. He flung the lunch box onto the front seat, then got in and drove away.

I shivered as the wind began to pick up. I knew that I would never come back here. Not ever. I didn't want to see Jack in his new life. It was hard enough just to see his actual home. I knew that I didn't want to witness him living in it. It was bad enough that I would always see it in my mind's eye.

On an impulse, I decided to let him know that I knew. I just wanted him to know that I was here. I opened the mailbox, took off my wedding band, and placed it way in the back. Shutting the mailbox with a decided thump, I got in my car just as the snowflakes began to fall.

There is something magical about the first snow of winter. After all these years, I still feel the same excitement that I felt as a child– when we'd be in school and flock to the classroom window to catch a glimpse of the first white flakes. Of course today would just be flurries, and the ground was probably too warm for it to lay. But even in my utter dismay, the lacey crystals worked their magic, and a tiny seed of joy began to grow inside me.

I stood in my front yard, face upturned and eyes closed, letting the soft, white flakes land and melt on my cheeks. I had cried most of the way home, and the coolness felt comforting and refreshing on the heat of my tear-streaked face.

Opening my eyes, I looked up into the gray sky, mesmerized by the swirling frenzy above. A hushed calmness enveloped me, and I was sure that I could hear the wet plop of the snowflakes at they landed. My hands were shoved in my pockets– I hadn't remembered to bring my gloves. I moved my thumb across my empty ring finger, still feeling the indentation of my wedding band.

I prayed silently that I would have the strength to embark on this new life of mine. I knew in my heart that I didn't want to go back to the way things were, but I was afraid of what was to come and felt very much alone.

CHAPTER FOURTEEN

Later that afternoon, after loading my ornaments in the kiln, I sat down at the lunch table with Abbey. She had made us both cups of tea, and in honor of my new healthy eating plan, had cut up two red apples instead of the usual plate of donuts. I picked up a slice and dipped it in the fat free caramel sauce. If I ever needed a piece of cake, though, it was today.

"So what happens now?" Abbey asked, referring to the divorce.

"I've signed all the documents that I need to, but Jack's attorney won't return Annee's phone calls. I'm going to call her tomorrow and let her know about his house," I replied.

"Something's just not right, Ellen. How was he able to get a mortgage on that house before your house was sold?"

"I don't know. Casey has told me all along to just be patient and trust Annee to do her job. She'll get to the bottom of this."

"What did the kids say about the house?"

"I didn't tell them yet. I just found out about it myself this morning. Besides, *technically*, I'm not supposed to know about it."

I didn't have to call Annee the next day though, because she called me bright and early.

"Well, the big guns are coming out now, Mrs. Stern. I finally got a response from Jack's attorney. Jack is demanding that if you are requesting spousal support, then, effective immediately, you pay for half of the mortgage, half of the home owner's insurance, all of the utilities, and half of any outstanding debts such as credit cards, retroactive from the day he moved out.

"I don't have money to pay for all those things! I just make enough to pay for the expenses that I have *now*, I can't add any more to them!"

"The letter says that if you agree to put the house up for sale on January 1st and don't require him to pay spousal support, then he will continue making the payments as he has been until the house is sold," Annee said.

Oh sure, now that the ink is dry on his new house mortgage, he's in a hurry.

"He knows that I don't have any money. Why is he doing this?" I asked.

"It's his strategy to get out of spousal support for years down the road. If you sign off on it that will save him a lot of money in the long run. It appears that he wants to split the assets and call it a day. I assume that you have equity in your house, and once it's sold we can negotiate on the percentage that each of you get. So if you decline the support money, we can negotiate perhaps a seventy-thirty split, in your favor, on the house proceeds."

"How much support am I entitled to?"

"I don't know. The one thing they didn't include was Jack's income figures."

"Well, I know where a lot of his income has been *going*." I told her all about the house in Cranberry.

"I'll put some pressure on Jack's camp to give us some income and asset figures. However, be aware that anything he's purchased since you've separated is not considered in the divorce settlement."

"But he used money he had during our marriage to buy

it!" I stammered.

"Don't worry, Ellen. We'll work all this out for you," Annee said calmly.

I didn't have to be at work until mid-afternoon. I needed a happy distraction from this mess, so I made an impulsive decision to take a trip to Spangles Christmas tree lot to buy a live Christmas tree. One of my fondest memories from my childhood is the smell of pine from our live trees. Jack always claimed that he was allergic, so I haven't had one in over thirty years. Since he had no other allergies, I highly suspect that he just didn't want the mess of all the needles in the house, but I had never confirmed my suspicions, just went along with the flow.

Feeling almost giddy with excitement, I phoned Adam.

"Hey, kiddo, want to come with me to buy a Christmas tree? I need your truck to bring it home," I asked as soon as he answered.

"What's wrong with the tree you have?" he asked.

"It's a fake," and I wanted to add, "just like your dad," but I didn't.

There was silence on the line.

"Adam?" I asked.

"I don't understand, Mom."

"I want to go to Spangles and buy a live tree."

"Oh…we never *had* a live tree. Why do you want one now?" he asked.

"I'll explain on the way. Are you in or not?" I was getting impatient to get going. "I'll buy you lunch," I threw in as an added enticement.

"Well, you just sealed the deal. When do you want to go?" he asked.

"Now?"

I heard laughter on the line. "I'm laying tile in the bathroom today, so lucky for you that I'm not knee deep in grout! I'll be there in about twenty minutes."

I felt like my whole body was smiling. I ran upstairs and grabbed a clean pair of navy sweatpants out of the drawer. After a moment's pause, I replaced them and pulled out a pair of jeans. I wonder....

"Eureka!" I yelled out loud, drowning out the click of the snap. My three weeks of hard work had paid off! Granted, these weren't my "skinny" jeans, just the pair I used to reserve for those bloated days of the month. But, hey, my whole butt was in them, and that was one more cheek than I could have fit in them last month!

I ran back downstairs and grabbed my cell phone.

"Casey! I fit into my jeans!" I exclaimed when she answered.

"That's great, Mom! Congratulations! I'm just about to meet with a client, so I'll call you back later, okay?"

Temporary insanity had made me call Casey when I knew darn well she was at work, but no harm done.

Running back upstairs, I took two steps at a time. I chose an emerald green turtleneck sweater and pulled on my black, shiny, waterproof boots. Then I even applied a bit of eyeshadow and mascara. No time to do my hair though, so I quickly brushed it and tucked the ends up under a black cable knit tossle cap.

Zipping up my parka and flinging my purse over my shoulder, I gently closed the front door behind me and stepped out into the hushed, white wonderland. Although I thought the ground would still be too warm for the snow to lay much, Mother Nature had proven me wrong. I stood on the front doorstep and looked around.

The streets were only wet, but at least two inches of pure white snow blanketed everything in the yard. Still undisturbed, its only flaw was a trail of footprints left by an energetic little rabbit, and some indentations where the melting snow had plopped off the telephone wires above.

Walking slowly to the end of the driveway, my boots made a squish, squish sound as each step turned the snow to slush beneath my treads. In stark contrast to the clean, white of the ground, the sky was just a huge sea of gray.

Within minutes, Adam arrived, and before I knew it, I was choosing my first real Christmas tree! Adam seemed just as excited as I was as he held trees upright and tapped their trunks on the ground to shake off the snow. After much debate, we finally decided on a six-foot Douglas fir. We watched while the tree was pushed through a netting machine and emerged from the other side tightly bundled for the journey home.

While Adam was loading it into his truck, I ran inside the store and purchased a green and red plastic tree holder. I had almost forgotten that real trees need to be watered!

Adam held me to my promise of lunch, and we bought some chili cheese dogs on the way back to my place. We laughed and struggled getting the tree through the front door. I have to say it looked a lot larger in my living room than it did on the Christmas tree lot! We pushed an end table into the dining room to make room for it in front of one of the large living room windows. Finally, after we had maneuvered it to stand up straight, Adam tightened the large screws in the base to hold it in place, and I added water to the basin.

Handing Adam the scissors, I gave him the honor of cutting off the netting. He bowed and said, "I hereby christen thee, the first live Christmas tree to grace the Stern household.

May you glow with the true spirit of Christmas and hold your needles until New Year's!" Then he cut the net and the branches gently swayed down into place.

I clasped my hands in front of my chest and grinned. I had done it! I had made a decision and made something happen…albeit only a Christmas tree, but it was much more than that to me. It was a symbol that I would think of over and over again in the months and years to come. The first building block of confidence in this new structure of a life that I had to construct for myself. I felt empowered.

A glance at the clock told me that I needed to leave for work. Adam offered to stay and clean up the little branches that we had to cut off to make the tree fit in the stand.

I stood on tiptoe and kissed his cheek.

"Thank you so much, Adam, for helping my dream come true today!"

I wrapped my arms around him and hugged with all my strength. I squeezed my eyes shut and held my breath for a few seconds before releasing him.

"Anything for a chili dog," he joked. "Seriously, Mom, I think it's great. I can't wait to see it all lit up. By the way, is it okay if I bring Mya over on Christmas day? Her parents will be in India visiting family over the holidays."

I knew that he had been seeing a lot of Mya lately, but I had never met her. Adam had showed me a picture of her though, and I recalled her long, dark, hair and beautiful almond-shaped eyes. Quite a beauty.

"Adam, anyone you want to bring will always be welcome here, you know that. I can't wait to meet her."

I left Adam to his clean-up mission and hopped in the car. The sun had never penetrated the clouds today, but the warmer afternoon temperature had melted the snow from the windshield, so I didn't have to get out the scraper.

My six hour shift at Amazing Glaze sped by. The customers were, for the most part, in good spirits, with the exception of Mrs. Heasley, who mistakenly painted her Rudolph's nose hot pink instead of red and didn't notice until after it was fired. She wasn't a happy little elf.

Abbey had greeted me with a slap to my behind saying, "Look who's back into her jeans! You go, girl!"

Before I knew it, I was going through my second drive-thru of the day– only this time I ordered the more sensible grilled chicken salad with fat free dressing. I was anxious to get home, a feeling that had been foreign to me. For the longest time, the thought of going home to an empty house had filled me with dread, and before that, the thought of going home to Jack's ridicule had been equally unappealing. This evening, though, I couldn't wait to get home to decorate my tree.

I turned the key in the lock and pushed open the front door. I've heard that scents are the most powerful memory inducer. In that moment, as I inhaled the fresh scent of pine, I became six years old again– sitting in front of the Christmas tree, cozy in my red flannel pajamas, rosy-cheeked from a day of playing in the snow, while my brothers and I wrote our lists for Santa with red and green crayons.

I smiled and breathed in deeply, taking it all in. Then I turned on the hall light and made my way to the living room. The tree was beautiful, and next to it were bins of Christmas lights and decorations from the basement. That Adam! Bless his heart.

I tossed my coat on the couch and quickly stashed my salad in the refrigerator. Snapping off the lid to the bin and unraveling the lights, I immediately began to string them on the tree, starting at the top and weaving them in and out of the branches. Then I turned off all the other lights in the room and plugged them in. Breathtaking! After retrieving my salad, I sat on the floor in front of the tree to eat my dinner, just like when I was

185

a kid, only with a glass of lambrusco and a salad instead of milk and cookies.

Christmas was right around the corner, and Casey would be home tomorrow. Adam was picking her up at the airport since I was scheduled to work for a full day. I was so excited to see Casey again! We had become even closer since her Thanksgiving visit. She had called every day to check on me, and encouraged my healthy eating by sending her favorite recipes. I was anxious for her to see my weight loss.

I had just finished eating my chicken cacciatore when I remembered that I hadn't checked the mailbox on my way in. It had been a particularly grueling day at work with everyone trying to get their projects finished before Christmas, so when I got home I had just wanted to sit and have dinner in front of the tree.

I've lost the anticipation of seeing what the mailbox held anyway. Usually I can't wait to get Christmas cards. This year it was depressing to see all those envelopes addressed to "Mr. and Mrs. Jack Stern." When the first cards arrived, it brought tears to my eyes, but after a couple weeks I was becoming immune to it. I just ripped open the envelopes without even looking at the address on the front.

I opened the front door and a whoosh of frigid air swept past me and rustled the ornaments on the tree. Adam came over one evening and helped me put on the decorations, and he also strung some lights on the bushes outside. Usually I have every room in the house decorated, but this year I just didn't have the energy for it. My tree was all I needed.

As I stretched my arm around the door frame to open the mailbox, a movement in the darkness caught my eye.

"You scared me!" I said, as my hand flew to my chest. My heart was pounding so hard I could hear it beat in my head.

"I'm not that scary, am I?" Jack said.

I stood shivering, watching as he walked up the sidewalk to the open front door where I stood. He was wearing his worn, black leather bomber jacket that I've seen a million times, looking so familiar it made me ache.

The times I'd seen Jack lately, he had seemed foreign to me– new clothes, new surroundings– he had become almost a stranger. However, as I watched him walk up our sidewalk in the soft glow of the Christmas lights, wearing his worn jacket, I was instantly transported back to another lifetime when everything was fine. The wind tousled his hair, and I felt the urge to reach out and touch it. The scent of his cologne rode the breeze to touch my soul with its familiarity, and my heart skipped a beat as he stopped in front of me and smiled a smile that lit up his whole face.

"Long time, no see," he said softly.

I didn't reply, just stood there holding the door partially open with one hand and clutching the mail against my chest with the other. I was feeling confused by his presence. Part of me wanted to slam the door in his face, and another part of me wanted to wrap my arms around him and welcome him home.

"May I come in?" he asked. He was holding a bag which only partially concealed a bottle of champagne.

I hesitated for a beat, then opened the door wider, stepping back into the warmth of the house.

He came in, stomping his feet on the mat and handing me the champagne.

"I thought it might be nice to share a Christmas drink together," he said.

What the hell? I wasn't sure how I felt about this. I can't turn my feelings off and on like a light switch. Just when I get to the point where I can distance myself from him and start moving forward, he pulls a quick one like this, and I go back two steps.

I responded by not responding at all, just waiting for him to shake off his jacket. Underneath was a navy blue knit sweater that I'd never seen before; the moment of familiarity was beginning to evaporate, and I felt a little wary. He swiftly moved to the kitchen and removed two glasses from the cabinet.

He expertly popped the cork on the champagne, then filled our glasses and handed one to me. I had just been standing next to the table silently observing this crazy turn of events. How could someone be so much a part of me, yet not a part of me at all?

Jack pulled out one of the chairs for me, and then abruptly chose a chair for himself across the table. He held his glass in the air, inviting me to toast, and as our glasses clinked, he said, "To our new lives."

I almost choked as I swallowed. To our new lives? I wasn't following this at all.

"You're looking good, Ellen. Better than the last time I saw you."

"Thanks," was my response to his back-handed compliment.

My cell phone began to ring, announcing a phone call from Casey. I felt the old nervous feeling creeping up my spine, knowing that Jack would disapprove of me taking a call when we were at the table.

I answered anyway. I explained to Casey that her dad was visiting and asked if I could call her back shortly. Then she asked to speak to Jack.

"Mom, let me talk to him. I haven't heard from him since I was at his house for dinner."

"Casey wants to talk to you," I said, holding my phone toward Jack.

He accepted the phone from me, and I could tell by the disgruntled look on his face that he wasn't pleased by this.

"Hmpph," he huffed, inspecting my new phone. "Must be nice...."

I wasn't about to explain that it was a gift from Casey and Adam. Let him think what he would.

"Hi! I thought maybe the phone lines were all broken in Florida!" he said to Casey.

Of course he would blame the lack of communication on Casey.

"Yeah, I've been busy too," he continued.

"Sure, we'll get together when you're home for sure. When are you coming?"

"Call me later and we'll set up a date. Love you, too," and he disconnected, handing the phone back to me.

"Jack, why are you here, really?" I couldn't help myself. I had to ask.

"Geez, I just wanted to tell you Merry Christmas, Ellen. I try to be the good guy, and this is the thanks I get?" he said as he drained the champagne from his glass.

"Jack, we haven't had a civil word in months, then you show up with a bottle of bubbly, and I'm not supposed to be confused?"

He stared at me a moment, then sighed.

"Ellen, it hasn't been easy for me either. Some days I really miss being with you. I want us to still be friends."

He had a sad little boy look on his face, and I highly

189

suspected from his mellowness that he had tossed back a couple beers before coming over.

I thought about his new house. I thought about his girlfriend. I thought about all the money taken from the account. I wasn't ready to be friends.

"Jack, we need to get our divorce finalized, then maybe we can work on being friends. Why did it take so long for your attorney to get back to mine?"

"He's a busy guy, Ellen. He has more important things to do than chit chat about our divorce."

"Chit chat? This is important, Jack!"

"Oh, don't get on your high and mighty horse already, Ellen. Can't we just have a conversation without fighting?"

He got up from the table and plucked his jacket from the closet. Reaching into the pocket, he pulled out a red envelope with my name written on it. He handed it to me and shrugged into his jacket.

"I'll see myself out. Merry Christmas, Ellen," he said, and he stooped down to plant a kiss on top of my head.

I sat frozen in the kitchen chair, listening to him walking down the hallway and not moving until I heard the front door closing. Then, in a rush of regret, I jumped up and flew to the front door. Just as I put my hand on the knob, the memories of all the times I'd chased him down that sidewalk came back to me, and my hand dropped to my side.

I stood at the window watching his headlights disappear as he pulled out of the driveway and headed down the street. I put my head in my hands and sobbed. Why did I chase him away? Why *couldn't* I just be friends? The sobbing had stuffed up my nose, and it was hard to breathe. I started to feel panicked. What if I couldn't breathe and I was here all by myself?

For the first time in over a month, a panic attack reared its ugly head. I sat on the floor in the hallway until I talked myself out of it, feeling drained and disappointed in myself at its conclusion. Then I looked over at my Christmas tree, and gentle tears rolled down my cheeks…not tears of sadness, but of hope.

I gathered strength from the vision, and I knew that I could move forward. It's just that I sometimes feel so alone and sad.

I took my cell phone out of my pocket and called Casey.

Just hearing her voice saying, "Hi, Mom!" healed the wound in my heart that Jack had just opened up.

"Hi, sweetie. Sorry I didn't talk to you before, but your dad stopped by unexpectedly."

"What's up with him coming over?" she asked. "I thought you two weren't speaking."

"That's what I thought too! He brought champagne and wanted to wish me a Merry Christmas."

"Well, that's pretty strange. Are you okay?" she asked.

"Actually, I had a panic attack after he left, but I'm okay now."

"Well, hang in there, Mom. I'll be home tomorrow."

"Can't wait!" I said, and I meant it.

"By the way, Dad called me back a moment ago," Casey said. "He invited me and Adam over for dinner the day after Christmas. He said he had something to show me and someone for me to meet. I told him if it was his girlfriend, then I did *not* want to meet her under any circumstances."

I was shocked into silence. Jack wanted to introduce the kids to his girlfriend?

"Mom?" I heard the concern in Casey's voice.

"I'm here. I'm just surprised, that's all," I managed.

"Well, I don't want to meet her and I'm sure Adam doesn't either."

"Where are you having dinner?" I asked.

"He said he'd pick us up at Adam's house and drive us to somewhere special."

Jack was taking them to his new home. I hadn't told the kids about his house. I just hadn't had the strength to discuss it.

"Casey, I found out last week that your dad's built a new house. I'm guessing that's what he wants to show you."

"How can he afford two houses?" she asked.

"That's a question you'll have to ask him. I told Annee about it and she's working on it."

"Hey, Mom, I have to go now. Chris is beeping in and I want to take the call. His grandfather had an accident and was in surgery, so he's calling to tell me how it went. I'll see you tomorrow, and we'll talk this all out."

"I love you, sweetie," I said before we disconnected.

I walked slowly back to the kitchen to make a cup of green tea. After filling the tea kettle and setting it on to boil, I turned around and spied the red envelope still sitting on the table. I had completely forgotten about it.

I picked it up and held it to my nose. I could smell Jack's cologne gently clinging to the paper. Slowly I slid my finger under the flap and removed the card…it was one of those elongated cards with a muted picture of an evergreen on the front and a fancy script message written over it.

"Merry Christmas to Someone Special," it said at the top. My hands shook as I continued to read the rest of the rhyming message on the front…"so many good years…thankful for the special times…joys of Christmas past…hopes for the future." A tear plopped when I read, "Even though we are apart, I'll hold these memories in my heart."

What does he *want* from me? He doesn't want to be with me, but he wants me to accept him in his new life and welcome him with open arms when the mood suits him?

I opened the card, and through my blurred vision, I saw five one hundred dollar bills tucked inside. Jack's signature was scrawled beneath the words Merry Christmas, and he had written "Santa's Elf" under his name.

The tea kettle screamed, and I jumped, but stood fixed to the spot, holding the card and the money.

This was an incredibly kind thing for him to do! But what was I supposed to think? I know that Abbey would say he probably had a visit from the "Ghost of Christmas Past" and feared for his soul, but I would like to think that he sincerely just felt guilty and wanted to try to make it better. He didn't want to fix it, just make it feel better for a little while.

I finally turned around and shut off the tea kettle. I was working on a headache from all the crying, and the screeching wasn't helping. I dunked my teabag in the cup, wondering what to do. Should I return the money? It wasn't like I didn't need it; I did. I added a dollop of honey to my tea and stirred. It wasn't like I didn't appreciate his gesture; I did. Leaving the money and the card on the table, I carried my tea to the living room and parked myself in front of the tree.

I held the warm mug in both hands and leaned back, closing my eyes, breathing in the warm vapors. Then I remembered that Jack would have closed on his new house by now. Maybe that was the tipping point for his guilt. But why wasn't he celebrating and drinking champagne with Jessica?

I wondered if he found my wedding ring in his mailbox, and if not, whether he would have told me about the house if things had gone differently tonight. Over the years, Jack had always seemed to need to show me the new things he bought, so he could hear me say, "That's really nice," or "What a good price," or "Good job, Jack." Although he made his decisions independently without a concern to my opinion, he always needed my reinforcement and a pat on the back after the fact. I wondered if he really just stopped by to tell me about his nice, new house and hear me congratulate him on it.

I finished my tea and pulled the comforter up to my chin.

CHAPTER FIFTEEN

Today was my last day of work for the year. I'd scheduled tomorrow off since Casey would be home, and Abbey always closed Amazing Glaze between Christmas and New Year's.

It had been a heck of a day. There had been two birthday parties and a never-ending flow of customers picking up orders. Abbey was counting out the cash drawer, and I was rinsing the paint brushes when the bells on the door jingled. I looked up and saw Casey, tan and smiling, prancing through the door, followed by Adam, who was tickling her from behind.

"Now, now children– behave! No running in the store!" Abbey teased.

Adam stopped to chat with Abbey, and Casey continued her reindeer prance back to greet me with a big hug and kiss.

"Hello, Mama!" she laughed. Then she picked up the jars of paint on the table and began replacing them on the rack. Casey had worked here part-time a few summers ago and knew the drill.

"Thanks, sweetie. The last birthday party was crazy," I told her. I was overjoyed to see her again and just couldn't get the smile off my face.

We all looked toward the door when the bells jingled again, hoping it wasn't another last minute customer.

"Looks like the gang's all here! Hello, everyone!" Rick said as he and Natalie breezed in.

We all shouted our greetings and went back to finishing our tasks. Natalie hopped up on the counter next to the cash register and sat there with her long legs swinging back and forth, as Rick went to the back of the store to check on the kiln.

Casey and I finished up just as Rick emerged from the back room, and we all walked up to the front of the store together.

"Natalie and I think we should all go ice skating tonight," Adam said as he put his arm around Natalie. Evidently they had been conspiring while we were all working. Natalie blushed.

"Can we, Mom?" she asked Abbey. "Some kids from school are going, and it would be fun if we could all go, too."

"Count me in," Casey sounded enthused.

Abbey looked at me and rolled her eyes. "Are you up for a little ice skating, Ellen?"

I hadn't been skating in twenty years. Jack and I had taken the kids, but we'd never skated because he was sure we would fall and break a leg.

That thought alone was enough to push me over the edge.

"Sure, I can hug the side, can't I?"

"You can hug anything you like, sweetie!" Abbey said good-naturedly.

Rick, who had been silently watching our banter, finally spoke up.

"I'm only going on one condition, and it's that we walk over to Market Square afterwards and get a sandwich and a beer."

We agreed to meet Abbey, Rick, and Natalie at the skating rink at PPG Place in Pittsburgh. Although Adam was dressed warmly, Casey and I needed a change of clothes, so we had to stop home to raid the closets.

After a quick pit stop, we were driving down the parkway, and Casey told me about Chris's grandfather.

"I feel so bad for Chris, Mom. He's really worried about his grandpa, and he's so upset that he'll be in the hospital for Christmas. His family always spends the holidays at his grandpa's house near Orlando. In fact, his parents were due to arrive yesterday, and Chris was going to introduce me to them."

"So what happened to his grandfather? Is he going to be okay?" I asked.

"All Chris told me is that he fell and broke his hip. He had the surgery already and is recovering. He won't be able to go home for a long time though. He'll be in a nursing home for rehab for a couple months."

"How old is he?" I couldn't help asking. Jack's past warnings of breaking a leg while ice skating were taunting me.

"Older than you," she answered with a smile.

After leaving Adam's car on the sixth floor of the parking garage, we walked the two blocks to PPG Place. The city was amazing! White twinkle lights graced the branches of the leafless trees lining the sidewalks, and some of the store windows were filled with homemade gingerbread houses and electric trains. As we rounded the corner, I caught my breath. I had stepped right into a fairy tale! The center of the courtyard housed a fountain in the warmer months; during the winter though, it was frozen over and turned into a circular ice skating rink. In the center was a huge artificial Christmas tree, several stories high, all decked out in brilliant lights and gigantic ornaments. A live brass band was playing carols as skaters glided around and around the tree. I felt like I was walking into a Christmas card! The scene transfused Christmas spirit into my veins, and I was very glad that we had come.

The tall PPG buildings, with their reflective exteriors and pointed peaks, always made me feel like I was in the Land of Oz. Tonight it just felt surreal to be in such a beautiful place.

We met up with Abbey at the skate rental counter, and although I had my reservations about going out on the ice, I decided to go ahead and give it a try. I fastened the last latch on my royal blue rental skates with a snap and walked like Herman Munster toward the ice, holding hands with Abbey.

The kids and Rick had already done a few laps by the time we ventured onto the ice. Abbey was a good skater, but she stayed by my side as I gripped the railing the whole way around.

"You're doing great, Ellen!" she said with a smile. "Isn't this fun?"

I returned her smile, but was too busy concentrating on not falling to answer her.

Rick glided up beside Abbey and grabbed her hand.

"Mind if I take her for a spin, Ellen?" he asked.

"Go right ahead. You know where to find me!" I replied.

I watched as they skated off, Abbey's red mitten held snugly in Rick's black leather glove.

I skated slowly, still gripping the railing, to the far side of the tree and just stood against the side taking it all in. Natalie raced by with her group of friends, waving at me as she sped past.

Adam and Casey were engrossed in conversation as they passed side by side, not even noticing me. Abbey and Rick were doing another lap, and she looked like she was going to join me again, but I waved her on. No need for her to babysit me.

I felt that now familiar pang of loneliness. It's odd, but I most commonly feel it when I'm not alone. I can be in a room full of people, or, for instance, tonight with family and friends, and this lonely feeling just creeps up on me. I suppose maybe it's not being part of a couple, or having someone special to wink at me or grab my hand and tell me everything will be okay.

The band started to play "Sleigh Ride," one of my favorite songs. How can anyone be sad listening to that snappy beat? I decided to go for it and let go of the side. I started off tentatively, but by the time I had completed one circle around the tree, I was gliding along at a pretty good clip, with my red crocheted scarf tails flying behind me. The wind in my face was invigorating, and the speed was intoxicating. I just wanted to keep going and going! I felt free, and very much alive!

Casey and Adam caught up to me and slowed their pace a bit to skate alongside me. We didn't have to speak. The smiles on our faces said it all! I was living in the moment, and what a wonderful moment this was. I would pull it out of my memory box to savor many times in the future.

I felt so thankful that I was able to enjoy things like this again. I know that many people who suffer from panic attacks and depression aren't able to get out and do things. I also know that a couple of months ago, I would not have had the strength or courage to do this.

I was so grateful for Dr. Burke's help and the support of my children. Of course Abbey has been my rock of Gibraltar. I don't know what I would have done had she not been there to literally pick me up off the floor.

Although I had such a loving circle around me, Dr. Burke insisted that my progress has been the result of the strength I have found within myself. It's been my choice to swim and not sink...to fight and not fly. I suppose there is some truth to that. With every baby step forward and with every small accomplishment, I feel stronger and more confident to rise to the next level.

After an hour of skating, it was time for the zamboni to come out and clean the ice. It was also time to see that we kept our promise to Rick. We all returned our skates and walked across the street and down the block to the restaurants at Market Square.

Later that night, after lights out, Casey called out from her bedroom.

"Mom?"

"Yes, sweetie?"

"Thank you for tonight. It was great! I love you!"

"Thank *you* for tonight, Casey. I love you too," I replied. Lying in the dark, I fell asleep feeling truly blessed.

Christmas Eve and Christmas Day went by in a flurry of activity. Adam, Casey, and I attended the candlelight church service on Christmas Eve, something we've always done as a family. I felt a pang of emptiness without Jack, and I wondered if he was attending church tonight. I had never called him after his visit the other night. I thought it only right that I thank him for the gift, but I just couldn't force myself to make the call. Maybe I would just send him a thank you card. After all, I *do* have his new address.

Adam and Cooper slept over Christmas Eve, and we all opened our gifts in the morning. Although they had already given me the phone, Casey surprised me with a salon gift certificate to receive a new hair style and color. She had already scheduled me an appointment for the next day.

"You'll just love Emilio. He works magic! Just let him have his way with your hair," she gushed.

While Casey and I were preparing our dinner, Adam left Cooper with us and went to pick up Mya. By the time the house was filled with the aroma of baking ham and au gratin potatoes, they had arrived.

Mya was as nice as she was pretty, and she got along famously with Casey. After dinner, we gathered in front of the tree and played Scrabble.

Adam was victorious, and after some friendly gloating, he packed some leftovers in a bag and left with Mya. Casey and I curled up under the comforter on opposite ends of the couch, with our feet touching in the middle– our customary position. The glass of wine I'd had while we were playing the game coupled with the warmth of the blanket to put me in a complete state of contentment.

"Thanks for a great Christmas," Casey said sleepily.

"It's so nice having you home, Casey. And thank you so much for the gift certificate. I can't wait until tomorrow!"

"You deserve it. Think of it as your reward for taking care of yourself again."

I smiled in return. I have to admit that I've been feeling so much better the last several weeks, although I was already dreading how lonely I was going to be when Casey left. At least when she went back to Florida after Thanksgiving, I knew that she was coming back in a month, and I had the distraction of preparing for the holidays to keep me occupied.

But now it probably would be several months until she would come home again. I was also dreading the end of the holidays for another reason. Jack would be pressuring me to get moving on the home sale and the divorce. It had been nice to file all that away in the "to do later" part of my brain.

Even though these life-changing events were looming in my immediate future, I didn't want to think about them today. I pushed them aside and focused on the moment I was in.

I took a deep breath of pine-scented air and snuggled down deeper under the comforter.

"So, tell me more about Chris."

Casey smiled. "Well, I really like him. He's so much fun to be with, and he's very smart…and he can cook!"

"Well, he sounds perfect then!"

"Seriously, Mom, he really is a great guy. I wish you could meet him. Maybe he can come home with me sometime."

"I'd like that," I replied.

Casey drove us to Pittsburgh and pulled up in front of Emilio's salon.

"I'm going to park in that garage over there," she said, pointing down the street a few blocks, "but I'll drop you off here. We don't want to keep Emilio waiting!"

I stepped out of her red Audi and onto the curb. She immediately pulled back into traffic, and I was on my own. I took a deep breath and pushed open the heavy glass door.

I was feeling a bit embarrassed about the state of my hair. There was so much gray in it now, and I hadn't had a good cut in a long time.

By the time Casey poked her head around the corner, I had already been ushered into the back room, draped in a lavender smock, and given a steaming mug of coffee laced with chocolate liquor. I peered at her over the top of the mug as I took a sip.

"Wow! Looks like they're treating you right!" she said as she plopped down in the empty chair across from me and began leafing through a book of hairstyles.

Just as I drained the last yummy drop from my cup, Emilo

breezed in. He was wearing faded jeans, a white, baggy turtleneck sweater, and brown leather boots. His shoulder-length, jet black hair was pulled sleekly back in a ponytail. Casey has been coming here for years, and she stood up and kissed him on both cheeks. She enthusiastically introduced me, and he stooped down to give me a hug, smelling good enough to eat. The next thing I knew, he was fluffing up my hair with his fingers and smiling.

"Ah, great hair…great hair. I can do as I please?" he asked.

I gave Casey a quick glance, and she was shaking her head up and down.

"Well, yes, but nothing crazy," I replied. I was starting to get a little nervous about this.

"I'm thinking about this length, yes?" he said as he grabbed my hair right above my collar bone.

"Okay," I said meekly. I haven't had it that short in a long time– maybe never.

"Lots of layers, lots of sexy layers…a warm auburn with subtle red highlights….I'm seeing this…you will like," he insisted, still running his hands through my hair and looking at me with a very persuasive smile.

Did he say sexy? That might be nice.

"Emilio, I'm trusting you," I replied.

He started commanding color numbers and portions to his assistant, to concoct my sexy new color. I sat patiently while the base color was applied, then felt a little silly-looking while the highlights were brushed on and wrapped in foil.

Emilio kept checking under the foil to see if I was "done," and finally, he exclaimed, "Perfecto! Rinse!"

I reclined in the cushioned chair and had my hair rinsed by a girl with extremely short, spiked, pink hair, and a nose ring. She struck up a conversation with Casey, but I wasn't paying much attention to what they were saying. Having one's head massaged is one of life's heavenly experiences, and I was enjoying it to the max.

All too soon, she rinsed the fragrant conditioner from my hair and wrapped it in a huge white towel. Then I was marched out to another room for the cut and Emilio began his magic. Hair was falling to the floor with great speed, and I resisted the urge to put my hand up to my head and see how much was still left. I hadn't been offered a mirror to see my new color yet, and I kept being reprimanded by Emilio for trying to look on the floor to see what color the clippings were.

"Trust me, yes? You will be one hot mama!" he said as he put his index finger under my chin and tipped my head upwards.

Finally, he spun me around to face the mirror.

I almost gasped out loud! I *loved* the color! He was still snipping away, perfecting the sexy layers.

"I see you with a bit of a fringy bang. Not too much, just to frame your face a bit, no?"

"Emilio, whatever you want to do. I am in your hands," I said with authority. I no longer felt nervous; in fact, I was feeling a tiny bit daring.

He pulled out the blow dryer and the magic show continued. Casey had just come back in the room, and she was grinning.

"Way to go, Mom! Look at you!"

Emilio whooshed the smock off of me with a flourish. "Voila!"

I couldn't believe it was me! I mean I knew it was me, but when I looked in the mirror I saw a reflection of someone else. Someone who actually looked pretty, stylish, and yes, sexy!

"I just love it, Emilio! I'm overwhelmed!"

Casey gave me a big hug. "Merry Christmas, Mom!"

We all exchanged cheek kisses, and after thanking Emilio profusely, I followed Casey back through the heavy glass door.

"Mom, you look amazing! Do you like it?" she asked.

"Like it? Are you kidding me? I can't believe it!" I was feeling skip-down-the-street-and-turn-a-few-cartwheels happy!

I had my doubts about reproducing this look by myself. I can't wield a blow dryer and styling brush like Emilio, but he assured me that it was a low maintenance cut. That's me: low maintenance.

Casey dropped me off at home, then left to meet Adam for their dinner with Jack. So here I was, all "sexied up" and nowhere to go. I went upstairs and tried on a few more pairs of my jeans. They were a little tight yet, but I didn't feel discouraged. I was determined. And I felt like a million dollars right now.

I settled for some sweats, bounced down the steps, and put in the new walking DVD that Abbey had given me for Christmas. I selected the two-mile walk, and before I knew it, a half-hour had passed and we were doing the cool down. My stomach was growling, so I figured I'd better make something healthy to eat before I was tempted to just have Christmas cookies for dinner.

I downed an eight-ounce glass of water while I prepared a salad, tossing in some cubed ham from yesterday's dinner. While my small portions of leftover au gratin potatoes and green bean casserole were heating in the microwave, I grabbed the mail from the box and placed it on the table to sort through while I ate.

Munching away on my salad, I flipped through a magazine, stopping to read an article on organization. That would be one of my New Year's resolutions– to organize my life.

I turned the page, and a photo of a house that was the clone of Jack's new Tudor mocked me. I hadn't been thinking about Jack's dinner with the kids– an accomplishment in itself, since I remembered how gloomy I was when they went to his place the day after Thanksgiving.

I rinsed my plate and loaded it into the dishwasher. Grabbing two thumbprint cookies, complete with green icing and sprinkles, I sat back down at the table to go through the rest of the mail. Feeling very deserving of a treat, I nibbled happily on cookie number one.

At least there shouldn't be any more Christmas cards arriving. I noticed an envelope with Jack's name on it from Hercules Gym. It had been addressed to his post office box, but now sported a little yellow sticker over that address, forwarding it here. It was probably an advertisement, so I figured I may as well just open it.

I was surprised to see a statement for his January monthly dues. Apparently, judging by the information on the paper, Jack has been going to the gym this whole year! Why didn't he tell me about this? No wonder he could eat those donuts for breakfast every day and still be in shape!

I tossed it in the trash can, then pulled it back out. Maybe I should tell Annee about this. The information might come in handy for some reason. I just can't understand how I could have overlooked or missed completely all the things that Jack was doing right under my nose. Was I so absorbed in myself that I hadn't seen the warning signs that my marriage was failing, or was Jack just that good at hiding?

I felt so betrayed about so many things. I had never actually asked Jack face to face about the money in that bank account, although I know now that more than likely he used it to buy his house. But I still don't know where he got that kind of money in the first place. I didn't ask him at the time because I knew in my heart that I probably couldn't handle the answer and didn't have the courage or strength for the verbal battle.

Looking back, I seemed weak, even to myself. No wonder Abbey was so upset with me for not pursuing the bank account issue…and the post office box key…and so many other things. Now that I'm feeling better, I'm beginning to see the whole picture, instead of the little freeze frames that I've been dealing with for so long. I know that I'm on the right track to being healthy in mind and body, but I'm not totally there yet. I'll just keep feeding all the facts that I can to Annee and let her do the best she can for me.

I put a few Christmas CDs in the player and took my cup of tea to the living room, plunked down on the floor in front of the tree, and that's where Casey found me when she returned from her dinner with Jack.

"Hey, Mom," she said as she stooped down to give me a hug. She smelled of fresh air and fireplace smoke.

"Hey, honey. Have a good time?" I asked.

"Yes and no," she replied as she hung her coat in the closet and sat down next to me, pulling the comforter from the couch and putting it over her lap.

"It was nice to see Daddy, but it's different now, Mom. He's different."

"How so?" I asked.

"I can't explain it, really. He's still the same person, but it's just weird to think of him as an individual and not as the other half of you."

She put into words what I've been trying to figure out for months. It's very difficult to think of us not being a couple. Our names just "went" together. Jack and

Ellen…JackandEllen…almost as if it were one word. I totally understood where she was coming from. It wouldn't be mom-and-dad, anymore.

"It was so strange to be in his new house and know that you weren't going to enjoy it. I kept thinking about how much you would love it. You deserve to live in that house, Mom."

I sat silently watching the ornaments on the tree swaying slightly from the warm air blowing from the heating register.

"Anyway, it was fine until after dinner, when he mentioned that he was seeing someone, and he wanted Adam and me to meet her. He was actually going to have her there tonight, but she had an emergency and had to go out of town. I told him that what he does in that respect is his business, but I don't want to be involved in it. I don't want to meet her."

"I'm sure he wasn't happy not to have your blessing," I said.

"No, especially when Adam agreed with me. I mean, how can he already be involved with someone else? And I still don't understand how he bought that house, Mom. It must have cost a mint!"

"Annee's looking into that for me."

"I'm going to give Annee a call and maybe meet her for lunch before I go back, to talk off the record about this. He's my dad, but I don't like what he's doing to you, Mom."

"Did he tell you that he's insisting we put this house up for sale…this week?"

Casey looked at me with tears in her eyes. I took her hand and gave it a squeeze.

"I'm guessing he can't afford two mortgage payments," I offered.

"Mom, that's awful. What are you going to do?"

"Well, I don't really have a choice, Casey. I have no money, and if I don't agree to sell the house– well, I just can't afford to live here."

"I'm calling Annee tomorrow," Casey said firmly. "I'm sorry, Mom. I had no idea it was so bad for you."

I put my arm around her, and she rested her head on my shoulder.

"Sometimes I'd just like to get in the car and keep on driving until I'm far away from here and all this heartache," I confessed to her as the lights on the tree glistened through my tears.

CHAPTER SIXTEEN

The next morning after our walk, Casey and I sat at the kitchen table eating our breakfast. Her cell phone rang, and her face lit up as she answered.

"Hi, Chris!" she said excitedly.

I rinsed my bowl in the sink and went upstairs to shower, giving her privacy to take her call. After dressing in my big jeans and navy turtleneck, I used a blow dryer on my hair and gave it a quick flick of the curling iron. I just loved my new style!

After hearing the water running in the spare bathroom, I went downstairs to wait for Casey to finish showering. I opened the morning paper to look at the apartment rental advertisements.

Fishing a pen and notebook from a top drawer, I made a preliminary budget to see how much I could afford to pay in rent. I heaved a heavy sigh and put the pen down just as Casey was walking into the kitchen.

"What are you doing?" she asked, looking over my shoulder.

"Just trying to figure out a budget," I responded.

"Well, wait until later for that. I just called Annee, and she scheduled us an appointment for noon today. She said she has things to discuss with you anyway, and it would be a bonus to have me along."

I felt so much more at ease having Casey with me as I entered Annee Slater's office this time. She and Casey embraced, and after a moment of catching up on their personal lives, we all sat down at the familiar glossy table.

Annee opened a manila folder and extracted a few papers, setting them on the table in front of her. Then she picked up her pen and sat with it poised over her legal pad.

"Mrs. Stern, I've received some financial information from Jack's attorney; however, it's not very favorable. Since you and Jack had taken a second mortgage out on your home, there won't be much equity to distribute once the home is sold. According to Jack's personal tax records, he's also showing a near loss for last year."

"I don't understand, Annee. What do you mean he's showing a loss?" I was dumbfounded. "How can you have a loss when you bring home a paycheck every week?"

"Well, he's saying that he's not an employee of Antiquity Investments; rather, he's on the payroll as a consultant—sort of like owning his own business."

"That's news to me!" I was getting exasperated with this! *What is going on?*

I snuck a look at Casey, and she was looking as angry as I felt.

"In other words, he's saying there won't be very much money, Ellen."

"So, would I be better off going for the spousal support?" I asked.

"Well, let's wait and see what it looks like when all the figures are in. Let me ask you a few questions to clear a few things up in my mind," Annee said.

She asked me some things about my income and finances, then placed her reference papers back in the folder and folded her hands on top of it.

"Ellen, I'm going to do the best that I can for you. I would suggest that you go ahead with the sale of your home.

Even if it's minimal, the income from the profit is something you need right now and will only diminish if you drag your feet on this. Are you agreeable to Nester Realty handling the sale?"

I looked to Casey for advice.

"Annee, if you can be sure everything will be on the up and up, then I think that would be fine. We want to be advised of every offer and anything at all that happens. I don't want him sneaking anything else by my mom," Casey said, looking Annee in the eye.

"I'll have everything come through me, then I'll give the information to you, Ellen. That way we'll be sure this will be handled in a professional manner, and you won't have to deal directly with Jack. Would that be agreeable to you?" Anne asked me.

"Yes, I would appreciate that. Will you make the arrangements for the sale then?"

"I'll call Jack's attorney today and let you know the details."

She rose from her chair and we followed suit.

Annee extended her hand to me, and I shook it firmly.

"Thank you so much for being my advocate," I told her.

She nodded in reply, and then Casey gave her a hug. "I'll keep in touch."

We were the only two in the elevator, and Casey let loose as we passed the fourth floor.

"Mom, I just don't believe him! How can he do this to you? Obviously he has money if he just built that house. What's he trying to pull?"

"Casey, I haven't a clue. That's the problem. I've been clueless this whole year," I replied.

"Don't beat yourself up about this. I wish I was still living at home and could help you more. *I'd* like to see his financial records, that's for sure."

A little light clicked on in my brain. "Well, I did make copies of all the computer files before he took it. I have them on a flash drive at home."

Casey smiled. "Wow, Mom, you pulled a Sherlock Holmes! Have you looked to see what's on them?"

"I don't have a computer, remember? Besides, I wouldn't even know what to look for, honey."

"Mind if I take them home with me then?" she asked.

"Not at all," I replied. "I'd welcome the help."

That evening Adam came over for dinner, and as the three of us sat at the kitchen table eating our grilled chicken salads, Casey filled him in on the events of our meeting with Annee.

"Anything I can do to help, I will," he said. "You can stay with me. I have two spare bedrooms."

"That's so sweet of you, Adam." I was deeply touched. "If I would take you up on that, it would only be very temporary."

After the table was cleared, I pulled out the want ads again.

"I guess I'd better start looking for a full time job that pays enough to keep food on my table and a roof over my head."

"Did you talk to Abbey?" Adam asked as he munched on one of the last thumbprint cookies. "Maybe she could give you a

213

raise and more hours."

"Abbey knows the situation. She's already been giving me more hours than she should be, and the next few months will be our slow season anyway. I can't impose on her generosity any more than I already have."

"Mom!" Casey startled Adam and I with her shout. "I may have the answer! Let me make a phone call and I'll be right back!"

Adam and I just looked at each other as Casey flew past us and raced up the stairs to her room. I put on a kettle of water and pulled some mugs from the cupboard, placing a teabag in each. Just as the kettle whistle began to shriek, Casey bounded back into the kitchen and embraced me in a huge hug.

"Mom, just say yes to this. I know your first impulse will be to say no, but hear me out and then say yes."

Has my daughter lost her mind? "What on earth are you talking about, Casey?" I asked.

"Come sit down, and I'll explain," she replied.

I poured hot water into the three mugs and set one in front of each of us at the table.

"Okay, Sis, what's up your sleeve?" Adam asked.

Casey put her palms down on the table and leaned forward.

"Remember when I told you that Chris's grandpa had an accident and broke his hip? Well, he owns a very nice home on Lake Juliet, about an hour away from where I live in Orlando. He and his wife ran it as a bed and breakfast before she passed away. Anyway, Grandpa's going to be in a nursing home for physical therapy for maybe a few months, and he's very worried about his house being empty that long. Chris was telling me that they were considering a house sitter. Mom, it would be the *perfect* job for *you!*"

"Oh, Casey, I don't–" I began, but Casey interrupted me.

"Don't say no, Mom. Think about it. You said yourself that you'd like to just get in the car and drive someplace far away. You'd be in sunny Florida all winter, only an hour away from me. I could see you every weekend. Wouldn't that be fun? And I just checked with Chris, and he said they'd pay you very well. Plus, you'd hardly have any expenses while you're there. You'd be living in the house rent free, and Grandpa would want you to use his car so it wouldn't be sitting idle for months. The only thing you'd have to buy is food…and sunscreen!"

"You could drive down with me! How much fun would a road trip be, Mom?" And with that she sat back in her chair and took a sip of tea, looking quite smug.

"But, Casey, I have all this unfinished business here. I can't just pick up and leave in the middle of a home sale. I couldn't keep track of what was going on when it was right under my nose; how am I going to be aware of the situation when I'm hundreds of miles away?" I asked her. I had to admit though, she had given me a tiny spark of her excitement.

"I could look out for things here," Adam offered.

"Annee said she'd handle the home sale anyway. She can call you on your cell phone just as easily in Florida as she can here," Casey interjected.

"Won't I have to be at the closing or sign papers?"

"That's what FedEx is for," she replied. "I have clients do that all the time. We just use a notary to authenticate the signatures."

"Oh."

"Maybe it *would* be easier on you if you weren't here while buyers were coming through the house," Adam said.

215

"But how could I get all this stuff packed up?" I asked.

"Is it all yours or do you have to split it with Dad?" Adam asked.

"I'm not sure, actually. I guess I'll have to call Annee on that one."

"Well, we have a few days until we leave. We can pack up all of your personal things and put them in storage at Adam's until you get back. We'll call Annee tomorrow and see what she says about the furniture." Casey's voice was elevated with excitement.

I was beginning to think this actually might work. The spark of excitement was being fanned into a flame by Casey's enthusiasm. It wasn't like I was leaving forever, just taking a working vacation while the dust settled. I wanted to sleep on it though, and I had to check with Abbey to see if she could manage without me for a while. I couldn't imagine the possibility of leaving my house for the last time at the end of several short days, but on the other hand, it wouldn't be any easier leaving it in a month when it was sold. The kids were right; it would be hell to be here with buyers coming through.

"Can I give you my answer in the morning?" I asked Casey.

"As long as the answer is yes," she replied, and stuffed the last thumbprint cookie into her mouth.

The next morning I awoke to the sun streaming through my bedroom window and a feeling of anticipation streaming through my body. I was going to do this crazy thing! I was going to Florida! It wasn't a conscious, weighed decision, and if I would have had more time to make my choice, it might have been a different one. But circumstances being what they were, I wasn't granted the privilege of procrastination. I just knew in my heart that I needed to do this. It felt *that* right. I jumped out of bed with intent and purpose. I had a million things to take care of, and I felt more alive than I have in years.

Ironically, my regularly scheduled appointment with Dr. Burke was this morning. She was going to be flabbergasted! I was glad to have the opportunity to see her again before I left, and to maybe benefit from her insight.

I showered quickly, chose a jade green sweater, and made short work of styling my hair and applying a bit of makeup. I followed the smell of coffee brewing and found Casey sitting at the kitchen table, already dressed and reading the morning paper. She had her coffee mug poised near her lips when I breezed into the kitchen.

Taking a quick sip, she put down the mug and the paper and eyed me suspiciously.

"Mom?" she said, tilting her head to the side.

I was grinning from ear to ear and could barely stand still. I threw my hands up, punched the air, and yelled, "*Yes!*"

Casey rocketed out of her chair and grabbed me in a bear hug. "Mom, I can't believe it!"

She released her grip on me and grabbed both of my hands, jumping up and down. "This is wonderful! You won't be sorry. It'll be great! I'm so proud of you!"

I joined in the jumping until we both became breathless and plopped down on the kitchen chairs. What was it about this daughter of mine that could elicit such wonderful, childish behavior in me? The last time I jumped up and down like that was…well, I don't remember!

I reached behind me and pulled a tablet and pen from the drawer and began to make a list. "I still don't know how I'm going to get everything done in such a short time," I stammered as I began to write.

"Adam and I will help. I bet it won't be as bad as you think," Casey said.

"I have my appointment with Dr. Burke this morning, then I'm going to see if Abbey can meet me for lunch, then I think I need to talk to Annee about the legalities, and then stop and get some packing boxes, and–"

"Wow, Mom," Casey interrupted, "You really are getting into this!"

I stopped writing and jerked my head up to look at her. I shrugged. "Casey, I feel like I've just had a shot of adrenaline! I feel like I have a purpose and a goal now, instead of my life spiraling out of control, and it feels damn good!"

Casey smiled her approval, folded up the newspaper, and deposited her cereal bowl and mug in the dishwasher. "I guess I'd better get started packing up the things in my room and give Chris a call and have him tell Grandpa that he's hired himself a house sitter!" She planted a kiss on my cheek as she passed by me on her way upstairs.

As I ate a bowl of oatmeal, I quickly filled three sheets of paper with notes that I would end up carrying with me constantly for the remainder of the week.

Emerging from Dr. Burke's office, I felt even more confident of my choice. She had been ecstatic to hear of my plans, and when I stepped onto the sidewalk outside of her office I was armed with her list of things for me to remember and the peace of mind that I could call her anytime I felt the need. She had shaken my hand firmly at the conclusion of our session and had given me her heartfelt blessing.

Mark one thing off my list!

I had called Abbey on my way to see Dr. Burke, and we made a plan to meet for lunch at a small café in Greensburg. I told her that I had a bit of a surprise, but didn't give her any clues because I wanted to witness her expression firsthand when I told her.

Abbey was already seated and sipping on green tea when I arrived. She caught my eye and motioned with her hand in the air.

"Ellen! Over here!" she called to me.

The café was an area favorite, and all of the white, wrought iron bistro tables were filled with men in suits and women in heels enjoying lunch away from the office. I pulled out my chair, scraping it against the terra cotta tile floor, and sat down across from Abbey.

"What a great idea to have lunch, Ellen. Although I'm more than intrigued about your surprise…did you win the lottery or something?" Abbey asked.

I picked up the menu from the glass table top and quickly scanned it. "Let's order first, and then I'll tell you."

As if on cue, the waitress appeared. She took our orders without writing them down. It never ceases to amaze me that people can do this; I can barely remember what I've ordered myself. Once she left the table, Abbey's curiosity got the best of her.

"Okay, sweetheart! Fess up!"

I took a deep breath and blew it out. "Abbey, you're not going to believe this, but I'm going back to Florida with Casey!"

Her jaw dropped, and then she broke into a smile. "Yay! I think that's great! You need a little time away."

"Well…it will be more than a little. I need to know if you can spare me at Amazing Glaze for a couple months."

"Holy vacation! That's some serious time off!" she replied.

The waitress appeared and placed two steaming bowls of French onion soup in front of us. I picked up my spoon and toyed with the melted cheese on top.

"Well, you know that we have to put the house up for sale, so I would have to start looking for a place to live very soon. Casey came up with this great idea that I should take a temporary job house sitting for her friend's grandfather in Florida, who is recovering from a broken hip. My first impulse was to say no, but when I woke up this morning, I just knew that I wanted to go. Do you think I'm running away, Abbey?"

Even though Dr. Burke had dispelled the thought when I asked her, a tiny part of my brain was still unconvinced and needed the person who knew me best to affirm my motives.

"No, I don't think you're running away at all. Actually, I think the opposite. You're starting a new life, not running from your old one. You were pushed into this crappy situation without a crash helmet; it's nice to see you finally taking charge and doing something that you feel good about. I *will* pull the selfish card and tell you how much I'm going to miss you though," she replied.

"I'm glad to hear you say that! I don't *feel* like I'm running away, but I guess I needed to hear it from someone else. I'm sorry to leave you in a lurch for help at the store though."

Abbey made a noise that sounded like someone extinguishing a candle. "Pfft! Don't think twice about that. The next couple months are slow anyway. I'm sure I can find someone to fill in for you. Maybe I can convince Natalie to help me with the birthday parties on weekends. Now, tell me more about this house you'll be babysitting."

I stopped with my spoon in midair and took a mental inventory. I knew nothing about the house that would be my home for the next couple months.

"Abbey, I was so excited about the whole prospect of going that I didn't even think to ask Casey an important question like that!"

Abbey laughed at me. "I'm sure Casey wouldn't throw you to the dogs. It's probably magnificent!"

I searched my brain. What had Casey said exactly? I tried to give Abbey a coherent reply.

"All I remember is that Casey told me that it was a really nice house on a lake called Juliet, and it's about an hour from where she lives."

"Doesn't that sound romantic...Lake Juliet! Maybe you'll find your Romeo there!" Abbey suggested.

"That's the last thing on my mind right now!" I shot back at her.

During this whole ordeal, I had never thought of myself being with someone else, and I found that thought a little disturbing. I didn't need that complication. I didn't even know how one goes about dating these days, and I found *that* thought a little frightening. At any rate, it was much too soon to entertain those kind of thoughts.

"Whoa, girl! I was only kidding! But seriously, Ellen, you have to open yourself up to new relationships in the future. Promise me if Romeo shows up on your doorstep, you'll give him a fair chance."

I rolled my eyes and pushed my empty soup bowl aside. "Abbey, I promise if Romeo shows up I will not push him into the lake, fair enough?"

By the time we had finished our turkey club sandwiches and were lingering over our tea, I once again felt secure in my decision. Abbey had given me the encouragement I needed. I knew that I would stick to my choice, but her approval meant a lot to me.

I pulled my list out of my purse and checked off "Lunch with Abbey." Next up was to call Annee and then to pick up boxes. Abbey snatched the list from the table.

"Glad to see I made the top ten!" she teased. "Hey, I can help you with boxes and packing material. I saved most of the nice boxes from the Christmas shipments and you're welcome to them. We can stop by now and fill up both of our vehicles if you'd like."

An hour later, Abbey trudged through the front door of my house with the last stack of boxes and dumped them in the hallway.

"I have to get back to the studio now, but call me if you need anything else. By the way, why don't you, Casey, and Adam come over for New Year's Eve? We could make it your send-off party!" she tossed back over her shoulder as she was heading out the door.

"That sounds great to me! I'll have to check with the kids though," I yelled back from the living room.

"Fair enough. I'll call you tomorrow!" And with that I heard the front door slam.

I pushed my way past the maze of empty boxes and went upstairs. I looked into Casey's room and found it a picture of chaotic organization, if there could be such a thing. There were piles everywhere, but they appeared to be arranged in some sort of order that I'm sure would make sense only to Casey.

I found the house deafeningly quiet as I retraced my steps back to the living room. Turning on the CD player, the soothing sounds of Kenny G's "Silent Night" filled the room. Christmas seemed so long ago, although it had only been a matter of days.

So much had changed in such a short amount of time. Needing to hear something a little more upbeat, I popped out the CD and tuned the radio to 13Q, the station Casey and Adam used to listen to as teenagers– I needed something with a beat to keep me going.

Annee's receptionist cheerfully answered on the third ring and asked me to hold for a moment. While I waited, I wandered to the dining room and gazed out the picture window at our backyard. Eyeing the snow-covered flower bed surrounding the deck, I realized that this year, someone else would be watching the crocuses rushing to be the first to poke their heads out of the cool spring earth, trying to beat the daffodils and tulips that would be hot on their heels. I wondered if the new owners would even appreciate their beauty, or just walk by them on their way into the house. I wondered if they would know not to cut them down after they were done blooming, but to instead let their green stems and leaves remain until withered to let the nutrients go back into the bulbs to be stored for next year.

A senseless little thing, but it filled my heart with sadness.

"Hello, Ellen," I heard Annee say.

I turned away from the window and pulled myself back into the moment. "Annee, thanks for taking my call. Do you have a moment for a few questions?"

"Actually, I have a client coming in a few minutes, but I'll try to help you. What's going on?"

"To make a long story short, at Casey's recommendation, I'm taking a temporary job in Florida and I'm planning on leaving with her in less than a week. I was wondering if that would be a problem with the house sale and all the divorce proceedings."

"If Casey recommended the job, then I feel confident it will be a good strategy for you. If I recall, all of the offers on the sale of your home were to come through me, so I would be able to call you on your cell wherever you are. If we are lucky enough to have a closing while you're gone, then I'll just overnight the paperwork to you and have you sign and overnight it back to me. I can draw up some documents that you can sign before you leave, giving me permission to handle certain aspects of the sale on your behalf if you'd like."

"Oh, that sounds wonderful! Would it be all right if I have Casey give you a call too? She understands all this so much more than I do, and that way the two of you can work this out for me."

"No problem, she may call anytime."

"One more thing, Annee. Obviously, since I won't be here for several months, I need to pack things up before I go. Is Jack entitled to half of everything, or how does that work?"

"Well, the best answer I can give my clients when they are divorcing is that the more they can decide by themselves, the better. In other words, if you and Jack can agree on who gets what, then it's better in the long run. However, if you don't feel comfortable with that, then we'd have to draw up an agreement between the attorneys, and that can tie things up awhile."

"So, what you're telling me is that if I say I want the sofa, for instance, and Jack agrees to it, then the sofa is mine, no questions asked."

"Pretty much. Only you need to write everything down and give it to me. Then I will prepare a legal document stating such and give it to Jack's attorney to have him sign as well."

"Time is of the essence; do you think we can accomplish that in just a few days?" I asked doubtfully. I'd seen how slowly the other paperwork was going.

"That's up to you and Jack."

Great.

"Well, then, I guess I have my work cut out for me.

Thanks so much, Annee."

I disconnected, and before I lost my nerve, pushed the speed dial for Jack.

CHAPTER SEVENTEEN

"Hey, Ellen."

Those two words, said in such a familiar greeting, made my insides quiver. How could he still have such an effect on me?

"Hey, Jack," I replied. "Do you have a moment to discuss something?"

"Go on," he said without hesitation.

I drew a quick breath and tried to blurt it out before I lost my nerve.

"I was wondering if you could come over. I mean, since we're selling the house, we need to decide on who gets what. It makes more sense to decide between ourselves, instead of involving the lawyers, don't you think?"

There. I said it. I don't know why I'm so nervous about this! Surely I could get through a couple hours of being with him.

"Is tonight good for you?" he answered immediately.

I knew his voice so well that I could tell he was smiling when he said it. And I'm sure he knew *my* voice so well that he was enjoying how uncomfortable this conversation was making me.

"Sure. Casey and Adam will be here, just so you know."

"Well, then, I'll bring a pizza. See you around six."

What? He's bringing dinner? Is he joking? Why does he do this?

"Ellen? Is pizza okay?" I could tell that he was enjoying

this entirely too much, and it was really ticking me off.

"Fine…see you at six then," I replied gruffly.

It was hard to tell how the kids really felt about Jack coming over. Casey agreed with Annee on the fact that Jack and I should try to settle as much as we could on our own. She knows firsthand how expensive legal advice can be, and she also knows my budget. Adam had just said, "Fine," and then went about his business of shoveling the snow from the sidewalk.

The rest of the day quickly evaporated into evening, as Casey and I methodically packed up our bedrooms and labeled the boxes. Adam loaded them into his pickup and then unloaded them again in his garage.

Since I had removed all of Jack's personal belongings and clothes from our bedroom in my previous rampage, it only took me a few hours to pack up my own things. The hard part was deciding what summer clothes to take on my Florida trip, what winter clothes I'd need handy for the remainder of this week, and then tagging the box with the clothes I'd need first upon my return home.

Casey had put a large box in the hallway labeled "Goodwill" that we had been tossing things into all afternoon. I dumped an armful of tee shirts on top of the pile and turned to heave a box of books into the hallway for Adam's next trip to his garage. I love to read and have accumulated quite a library over the years. I just couldn't part with my books. However, in the past several months I hadn't had the urge or energy to pick up a new novel. Maybe that's something I'll be able to do while I'm house sitting.

With my hands on my hips, I spun around to survey the room. Only the bed and furniture remained, except for a couple items I had left out to stage the room. Hey, I've watched enough HGTV to know that you need to stage a house if you want to sell it. But did I *want* to sell it? I think part of me was hoping that it wouldn't sell, and then I might be able to buy Jack out and keep it. But on the other hand, did I really want to stay here with all the memories lurking in every corner? I could already feel myself distancing from this house. As Adam had said, "It's only an address– a place becomes a home from the people who live there." Realistically, why did I need a big house like this if it was only going to be me living in it? *Well, isn't that a cheery thought.*

Satisfied that I had vacuumed all the dust bunnies out from under the bed and scoured any soap scum lurking in the master bathroom, I turned on my heel and turned out the light.

Poking my head in Casey's doorway, I scanned the neatly labeled boxes lined up against the wall that were waiting for their trip to storage and spied Casey's rump sticking out behind the closet door. She was down on all fours vacuuming the floor and couldn't hear me over the din. She had already taken her most important possessions when she left for Orlando in September, so her afternoon efforts had left her room showcase ready.

Leaving Casey and the hum of the vacuum behind, I shuffled down the hallway and into the office. Not much here really to pack up either. Jack had pretty much cleaned it out when he left. It struck me again how we have all left this house, first Adam, then Casey, and of course Jack. I suppose now it was my turn too.

I heard the front door open and thought that it was Adam coming back for more boxes, but then I caught the aroma of pepperoni and green peppers and knew darn well that Jack had let himself in. I don't know why that perturbed me, but it did. He should have knocked.

My stomach was churning, and I wasn't sure if I could even force down a piece of pizza. I just wanted to get this meeting of the minds over with. I grabbed a notebook and pen from the desk drawer and retreated back to Casey's room.

Even though she had turned off the vacuum, my ears were

still ringing...or was that from my nerves?

"Casey, your dad's here– I can smell him," I said from the doorway.

Untying the purple bandana that was holding her blond hair captive, she shook her head, releasing the strands to once again frame her face.

"You are implying that he has food?" she answered with a smile.

"Precisely," I said, although the phrase, "I smell a rat" also came to mind.

"Let me wash up and I'll be right down. I'm starving!" she said.

So, I was on my own.

Jack had put two pizzas in the center of the table and was cracking open a can of Iron City when I walked into the room. In one quick glance, I took in his snug-fitting boot cut jeans, complete with new black leather cowboy boots. Evidently the influence of Boobzilla.

He was wearing his hair a little longer these days, the tips curling over his ears and to the middle of his neck. Was he tan? *Ha!* Well, I would be tan in another week, too.

It appeared that he was taking in my appearance as well. By the time my eyes got to his face he was wearing a bit of a smirk.

"Hey, Ellen."

"Hey, Jack," I answered as I accepted the chilled can he held out to me, making sure my fingers did not touch his.

"Hi, Dad!" Casey said, and she enveloped Jack in a hug.

I busied myself getting out the paper plates and napkins. Jack released Casey and searched in the refrigerator for the Parmesan cheese. I found this equally as disturbing as letting himself in. Why did he assume that he could walk in here and act like nothing had happened?

The front door slammed and Adam stomped down the hall.

"Mmm… I smell pizza! Hi, Dad," Adam said as he entered the kitchen. He extended his right hand to Jack, and after a brief shake helped himself to the six pack that Jack had brought.

Adam put three slices of pizza on his plate and perched himself on the kitchen counter, while Casey, Jack and I sat at the table. *Well, isn't this just cozy.* Just what I thought I wanted– all of us together how it used to be– a family, a pizza, and an evening together…but it wasn't right at all. As I sniffed Jack's new cologne, I admitted to myself that I really didn't want this anymore. It would never be the same. I was too angry…and perhaps jealous?

I chewed methodically while Jack talked to the kids. The green peppers could have been anchovies for all I could tell. The pizza felt like sawdust in my dry mouth, and I swigged down the last drop of liquid from my can.

Appearing to be the only one in the room distressed by this situation, I helped myself to another beer, and no one missed a beat in their conversation– until I snapped the can open– then I felt three pair of eyes on me.

"What?" I said innocently.

Everyone knew that one beer usually lasted me all night, and as I eyed the two empty cans next to my plate, I amazed even myself. How did that happen?

Jack laughed, then the kids joined in. "Looks like our

little Ellen is learning to live a little!" he said, and I noticed the smirk on his face was a lot more apparent.

Okay, so I did have a tiny buzz going. I'm not sure if I even cracked a smile at his comment, but I did feel that I could handle the rest of the evening with Jack. And then I burped.

Pushing my reading glasses up on my nose, I focused on the lined tablet in front of me. Jack and I had walked through each room side by side, very mechanically and methodically, and I had taken inventory of the contents, placing items in one of two columns....mine being significantly longer than his. He was being very cordial– to the point of even cracking a few jokes, which I of course let crash and burn– and he didn't seem to want much in the way of furnishings. At first I thought he was being very generous, but then the thought occurred to me that he probably had all new pieces for his new house, so why would he want this stuff hanging around?

I was *so* ready for him to leave! The kids conveniently took off right after dinner to take a load over to Adam's place, leaving Jack and me alone. The house felt very crowded with just the two of us. His presence seemed to dominate every atom of space, making me feel very tiny and obscure. Placing the tablet in front of him I handed him the pen.

"Please sign this and I'll drop it off to my attorney tomorrow."

"My, aren't we being efficient! Don't you trust me?" he said as he picked up the list. After scribbling his signature at the bottom, he slid the tablet back across the table to me.

I resisted the urge to dignify that question with an answer. How could he be so clueless?

"The 'For Sale' sign will be going up next week. I assume that you'll have everything gone by then?" he asked.

"I'm going to leave a few pieces here to stage the rooms, then I'll get them when the house is sold, unless I need them beforehand," I replied.

"Won't you need them in your new apartment?" he hedged.

Suddenly, I didn't want him to know where I was going. There was no need for him to know. It gave me a victorious feeling of satisfaction that I didn't have to tell him of my plans!

"Not sure what I'll need yet," I replied vaguely.

"Don't you have a place yet?" he persisted.

"I'm working on it."

I stood up from the table, dismissing him.

Jack glanced at his cell phone, checking the time as he illuminated it with a touch of his thumb. "Well, I have to get going. I'm picking up Jessica at the airport."

I bit my tongue. I didn't want to give him the satisfaction of asking. Oh, what the hell.

"Traveling on business?" I asked, trying not to sound too interested.

He had been dangling the bait in front of me, and judging from the smile on his face, was feeling very smug about the fact that I jumped on it.

"She travels quite a bit. She's from Tennessee and has a business there, but she's also working on some investments for me."

Well, la-de-da.

"You working on getting a new job, Ellen?" he tossed in for effect.

How dare he compare me to her! He was goading me, and I was playing the game.

"Actually, I do have a new job lined up."

I almost wanted to plug my thumbs in my ears, wiggle my fingers, and stick my tongue out at him. Must be the beer buzz.

I hooked my thumbs into my front jeans pockets instead and puffed out my chest...enough of this juvenile banter.

"I guess you'd better be going then, you wouldn't want to be late," I said.

Jack rose, pushed his chair back to the table with a rumble across the floor, and straightened the tablecloth. He shrugged into his jacket and followed me down the hall towards the front door. No one had bothered to turn on the lights in the living room; the Christmas tree was the only illumination. It still looked beautiful, and as I glanced at its soft, intimate glow, I was immediately filled with calmness. I had successfully finished my business with Jack tonight and hadn't felt one drop of anxiety...only annoyance.

That thought brought a smile to my face. I was making progress.

"Happy to see me go?" Jack asked.

My head jerked up to look him in the eye. He was standing uncomfortably close. Close enough for me to smell the leather of his jacket.

He reached up, and I felt the warm palm of his hand rest softly on my cheek. I jumped at his touch.

"You look great, Ellen. I'm glad to see that you're taking care of yourself." His voice was soft.

While his eyes were locked with mine, he slid his hand

down my throat, fingers gently massaging little circles on my skin, until he reached the boundary of fabric.

I sucked in a quick, shaky breath as I felt the burning pad of his finger slide beneath and trace an imaginary line just below the neckline of my sweater.

I was turning to mush inside…my brain was screaming, "Stop him!" but my body betrayed me and screamed louder, "Yes!" I heard a gentle moan. Was it me?

Abruptly, Jack pulled back his hand.

"Get everything ready for next week then, and we'll get this puppy sold."

All gentleness was gone from his voice and was replaced by…uncertainty? Stepping away from me, he opened the front door, offering me his parting words, "Make sure you vacuum up all the pine needles from that tree."

The rest of the week was a blur of activity, and it seemed only a blink in time before I was standing in Abbey's living room clinking my glass of champagne to hers in a toast. We had all just counted down the New Year, and everyone was hugging and cheering, drowning out "Rock'n New Year's Eve" on the TV. The younger kids had taken Abbey's old pots and pans outside and were banging them with wooden spoons, competing with the neighbors who were setting off firecrackers they had squirreled away from the fourth of July.

Abbey grabbed my hand and pulled me out onto the porch. A blast of cold air hit my face as we joined the others who had gathered outside to be a part of the celebratory energy. As I lifted my face to watch a Roman candle light up the sky, Rick came to stand behind us and wrapped his arms around Abbey. She leaned back into him, resting her head on his chest and covering his hands with hers.

I involuntarily shivered and folded my arms around my middle to stop the quivering. Heaving a sigh, I wondered if I would ever get used to being a single. I felt my eyes getting misty. Nothing like a holiday to start the tear factory. Where's a positive endorphin when you need one?

They say the first year is the hardest in any kind of grieving. Getting through the first holidays and special days alone for the first time is very difficult. Well, I'd made it through Christmas and now New Year's Eve. I bet Valentine's Day was going to be a real bitch.

I was saved from a full blown self-pity party by the ring on my cell phone. Holding it to my ear, I made my way back inside.

"Happy New Year, Mom!" Casey's voice rang loud and clear. She and Adam had been at Abbey's party earlier but had gone their separate ways after dinner to spend the evening with their friends.

"Happy New Year to you too, sweetie!" Her happiness was contagious and I felt better immediately. In the next instant, Adam was on the phone shouting his New Year's greeting over the commotion in the background.

I was reminded that I *wasn't* a single. I've been yearning to be part of a *couple*, and I may not have that. But I *was* a part of something bigger: I was part of a family, and no one could ever take that from me.

As I helped myself to a cup of coffee, Abbey and the rest of the guests made their way back inside. The kids were running around with those crazy noisemakers that sound like an elephant in heat, and the men had gathered around the pool table, loudly challenging each other to a game. Someone pulled the string on a party popper behind me, and I jumped as tissue paper streamers cascaded through the air. Chaos, but I loved it!

This was my life, and these were my friends. At first I felt awkward being around them for the first time without Jack, but after the first round of drinks, no one really missed him. It was almost refreshing to be around my friends and not have to worry about any snide comments or putdowns. I could be imagining it, but they seemed more at ease too.

I say "my" friends because Jack had abandoned them as well. After all, he had his "new" friends now. So we were all in the discard pile together.

A piece of nut roll was calling my name, and I obliged, slowly savoring each tasty bite. Abbey was a superb baker. I would gladly add an extra mile to my walk tomorrow to enjoy my treats tonight.

I spied Abbey making her way across the room, balancing a paper plate full of goodies as she weaved her way through the crowd and successfully dodged Rick's pool stick as he bent over to make a corner shot.

She plopped down next to me on the sofa, offering a share of her bounty. I selected an apricot filled pastry and as Abbey took a bite of a pecan tassie, she slumped down and put her head on my shoulder.

"Great party," I said as I popped the final morsel of cookie into my mouth and rested my head against hers.

"Thanks! I think it turned out pretty well. I'm exhausted, and that's a good sign."

We sat silently for a few beats, then Abbey straightened up and looked me in the eye.

"I'm going to miss you, my friend," she said, and I could see a tear in her eye.

"I'll be back before you know it," I replied, plastering on the fake smile that I now had perfected.

"I've been thinking that Rick and I need a vacation," Abbey continued, scratching her cheek absentmindedly. "Maybe we'll take a trip down to Florida to visit you when Natalie has her spring break."

My eyes opened wide and a genuine smile replaced the pseudo one. "Really?" I gave her a big hug, almost smashing the remaining cookies on her plate. "I would *love* that!"

"I'll have to talk to Rick about it, but I feel pretty confident that I can persuade him," she said as she caught his eye and blew him an imaginary kiss through the air.

She pulled a small silver package out of her sweater pocket and handed it to me. "This is something I want you to have, so you know that you are not alone in this journey, Ellen."

I gently touched the shiny box, fingering the loops on the satin bow. "Oh, Abbey, this is so sweet…." The gift began to swim before my eyes as tears welled up.

"You need to open it," Abbey reminded me with a gentle shove of her shoulder.

I pursed my lips and looked at her from the corner of my eye, then carefully unwrapped the small box.

I gasped. "Oh, Abbey! It's beautiful! It's just perfect!"

Nestled against the black velvet of the jewelry case was a silver cross hanging from a dainty silver chain. One tiny diamond glistened from the center of the cross.

One of my tears plopped on the crinkled wrapping paper as Abbey took the box from me and removed the necklace.

"Turn around and lift up your hair," she ordered as she fastened the necklace with a click. "Now, let's see how it looks."

I brushed the remaining tears from my cheeks and turned to face her.

"Abbey, you're the best friend ever! But this is too

much," I said as I turned for her inspection.

"Ellen, listen to me. Nothing is too much for my best friend. I want you to remember that you are never alone. Even though you'll be far from me and far from home, you are not alone."

I wrapped my arms around her and clung tightly. "Abbey, I've prayed so hard that things would work out."

"They will, sweetie, they will… just you wait and see. Have faith."

One of the kids pulled the string on a party popper right behind the couch. Abbey and I both jumped, jolted from our own little revelry back to the crowded party.

"Well, I guess I'd better go check on the food supply in the kitchen. The kielbasa and sauerkraut probably needs replenished. Wanna come?" Abbey asked.

"Actually, as much as I'd love to, I think I'll be going. I have tons to do tomorrow, or I guess I should say *today*." I stole a quick glance at my watch.

"I understand. I'll meet you in the hallway after you've said your goodbyes and I've refilled the buffet table."

I made my rounds, accepting good wishes from everyone. Rick paused in his game to give me a big hug, the first masculine hug, other than from Adam, that I've had in a long time. It felt so good to have his sturdy arms around me, and I felt so happy to have such wonderful friends.

Abbey was waiting in the hallway for me as promised, with my coat flung over one arm and a bag filled with plastic containers of food in her hand.

"Here are some goodies for your trip. You never know when you may need a cookie or two."

I shrugged into my coat and wrapped my scarf loosely around my neck. After I'd tugged on my black leather gloves, I accepted the bag.

"Abbey..." but I couldn't get any more words to come out.

"It's okay...it's okay...I know..." she crooned as we once again hugged each other tight.

Then she held me at arm's length.

"Listen, kiddo, call me when you're on your way. I want a full report when you get there, you hear me?" she said with a serious look on her face.

"Abbey, you're number one on my speed dial," I managed to get out.

"And remember what I said about Romeo," she added with a wink, and I rolled my eyes.

As I sat bundled in my wool coat waiting for the car windows to defrost, it really hit me that the time had come. Shortly I would be leaving this life behind and embarking on a new adventure. I turned up the heat another notch and pulled out into the darkness, and into the new year.

CHAPTER EIGHTEEN

It felt strange coming into my house alone so late at night. Casey wasn't coming home from the party. She was spending the night at her friend's place. Adam went home to feed and take care of Cooper. So this is what it would be like if we weren't selling the house…coming home to this big empty place all by myself…all the time. I suppose it was a good thing that we were selling it. At least that was the thought I was trying to wrap around my brain.

I turned on lights as I went through each room, my steps almost echoing in the hollowness. I'd left a few pieces, but for the most part the furnishings were pretty sparse.

After I'd wandered aimlessly through each room, I retraced my steps, turning the lights back out as I went. I made a cup of tea and sat on one of the boxes in the dining room.

I couldn't fathom that this could be the last night ever in my house. I'd been in such a frenzied state of preparedness trying to pack everything that I wanted to keep and making lists for Adam of all the things I wanted to sell or donate, that exhaustion had claimed me every night. I'd been tossed into a deep slumber the moment my head hit the pillow…a blessing. Without the distraction of the Florida trip, I'm afraid I would have driven myself mad with grief.

But now, in this moment of being alone, in this single moment of quiet, I was consumed by sadness.

I glanced at the kitchen. When Casey was little she would open the two bottom corner cupboard doors until they touched, and the tiny triangle of space would become her hideout. Later, in her teenage years, when she wasn't tap dancing across the tile, she would recline in the doorway between the kitchen and dining room with her back on the floor and her legs and stocking feet vertical to the door jamb and chat with me while I prepared dinner.

A tear rolled down my cheek, and I gripped the mug tightly, letting the warmth radiate to my chilled fingers.

The kitchen table had doubled as a tent for Adam too many times to count. He would drape it with a blanket and take up residence underneath, lugging his backpack filled with important things like comic books and action figures, immerging only when "nature called" or we evacuated him so we could eat dinner.

So many good things have happened in this house. When did it all start to change?

Gentle sobs had their way with me, even though I tried to hold them back. My shoulders trembled and I cried unabashedly like a child. This wasn't only about the house. I knew that. I felt like everything and everyone around me had changed– moved forward– and I was the only one without a place or a purpose for myself.

My children were grown and independent. Just what a parent strives to achieve, and I'm very proud of that. But I've come to realize that I hadn't personally grown *with* them. How is it that at my age I still don't know what I want to be when I grow up? I still want to make dinner for them, play board games, stay up late and watch movies with them. Hell, I wouldn't even mind a night of helping with algebra homework!

A realization hit me that maybe that is partly why Jack left me. I had stagnated and remained the same; maybe I *wasn't* interesting and challenging anymore. I had in essence become what everyone needed me to be and lost myself somewhere along the way.

I blew my nose into a tissue that I had stuffed in my pocket earlier. The waterworks subsided, and I sighed heavily. I guess when parents deal with the empty nest, they lean on each other and take the time to enrich their relationships. Heck, some of my friends couldn't wait to have their kids move out. But now I had no one to lean on and help bear my burden. Jack had flown the coop, and all he wanted to do was kick me out of the nest too…and then sell it. The bastard.

I had no husband, no kids to take care of on a daily basis, and now no house. Not to mention the fact that my bank account was so nearly empty that if I wrote a check to buy a pack of gum, it would probably bounce. I was wallowing in self-pity up to my chin, and I was afraid I was going to drown in it. I fingered the silver cross hanging on the delicate chain around my neck. And I was going to miss my best friend.

I turned to look out the window in the dining room, fixating on a gigantic icicle hanging from the rain gutter on the back of the house. I had noticed it this afternoon when I was sweeping the dining room floor and had marveled that it was so large, hanging halfway down the outside of the window. Now it had grown to nearly reach the bottom of the window ledge.

It was illuminated by the porch light, and I watched as yet another drop of water made its journey down the icicle and immediately froze at the tip to create a new layer and extend its length. All day long, the cycle had been repeating, layer upon layer, the icicle growing with every frozen drop. It was a thing of beauty, glistening and shimmering, sturdy and rock hard, yet so fragile that it would shatter into many pieces if someone knocked it to the ground.

I could relate; each stage of my life has been a new layer: my childhood, marriage, motherhood…feeling strong in my relationships and knowing exactly where my life was taking me…then being suddenly shaken from my foundation and lying shattered in pieces, unable to be assembled exactly the same way ever again.

I flicked off the light switch and forced myself to move. Once upstairs, I flopped across the bed, pulling the comforter up to my chin, and for the first time in a long while, I just slept in my clothes.

The next morning dawned gray and gloomy, with a biting wind that was wreaking havoc with the bare tree branches outside my bedroom window. It was taking every ounce of willpower I had to make myself get up and shower and start my day. I really just wanted to hide under the covers and turn the clock back five months, before this nightmare started.

I hadn't expected Jack to call and wish me a Happy New Year. I don't really think I even *wanted* him to, but I felt ticked off all the same that he hadn't. I wasn't expecting a call today either. He didn't know I was leaving for Florida. He didn't know that I wouldn't be around. I felt strangely proud of that knowledge, but also a little sorry that I couldn't share my adventure with him. Hard letting go.

Casey had come home early, and I heard the water running in her shower. We had decided to just use one bathroom this week so we would only have to clean one today before we left. Everything was ready, my bags were packed...the furniture and my personal belongings were stored...Annee was all set with the legalities of the home sale and divorce...I had said my goodbyes to my friends...all that was left to do was...go. "Going" was one thing; "letting go" would be another.

I heard the water stop and the shower door slide open and slam against the wall. Taking a deep breath, I pushed the covers off my body and shivered as I reached for my robe. I stripped the sheets from the bed and pulled the comforter back up, tossing on a few decorative pillows.

Casey already had her sheets in the washer, so I just added mine and a capful of detergent and that was that. I showered, dressed, and cleaned the bathroom in record time. Just as I was making a final inspection of the bedrooms, I heard the front door open, and the smell of coffee found its way up the stairs.

"Hey, Mom!" Adam called. "Breakfast is served!"

Okay, I can do this. Stealing one last look behind me, I trudged down the stairs. Adam and Casey were already devouring the bag of bagels and cream cheese that Adam had brought. I accepted the Styrofoam coffee cup with eager hands, desperately needing some caffeine reinforcement, and used a plastic knife to slather fat-free cream cheese on my cinnamon raisin bagel. Adam had even thought to have them toasted. What a guy!

Which led me to another dilemma. Even though it was only going to be a few months, I was going to miss Adam. He's been such a help in this whole ordeal, and now he's going to handle things at the house while I'm gone.

I chewed silently while Casey and Adam chatted about the party the night before. My eyes wandered to the dining room window, and I noticed that the icicle had fallen to the ground. Quickly I looked up at the gutter and found that it was already growing back, but not nearly as long as it was yesterday. I took a moment to watch a drop of water run from its base to the tip and, once again, freeze. The cycle had begun again.

And that's how it was going to be with me. I would persist. Start all over, just like that icicle, adding new layers…*great* layers…and I would once again be whole. Maybe not exactly the same, but none the less a whole person; who knows, maybe even better.

I was tired of crying, I was tired of being sad and afraid, and I was tired of being lonely. Shit. I was just plain tired!

Suddenly, I was just ready to get on with it. I wiped my mouth with the brown paper napkin and tossed all the trash in a paper bag to put outside in the can. Everything was done. It was time.

Casey went outside to warm up the car and help Adam clean off the fresh snow.

I tugged on my boots and grabbed my purse, looking back over my shoulder one last time before gently closing the door behind me.

Adam tossed the ice scraper in the trunk. "You guys

won't be needing this anymore," he said with a grin.

That's right! I was going to Florida! I've been so obsessed with what I'm leaving behind that I almost forgot there was a ray of sunshine to look forward to…literally!

Adam wrapped his arms around me, and his cold nose nuzzled my neck. "Have fun, Mom, and don't worry about anything at all here. I'll keep an eye on things and keep Dad in line."

"I know, sweetie. I'll mmmiss you," I squeaked.

"I'll miss you too, but when you come back you can bunk at my place and we'll have lots of time to catch up, okay?"

I smiled my reply and settled myself in the front seat. Adam winked and closed the door for me. Casey gave him a hug, then climbed in the driver's seat and backed out of the driveway.

"Drive carefully and call me when you stop tonight!" Adam called after us.

I didn't have the heart to look back…I just couldn't. And I couldn't help the sobs that escaped my throat.

Casey put one hand on my leg. "Are you okay, Mom?" she asked gently.

I nodded, then rested my head against the soft, leather seat and stared out the window, leaving Casey to navigate the snow-covered roads.

CHAPTER NINETEEN

We rode in silence for awhile, Casey focusing on driving while I stared at the passing scenery and perfected my pout. After a few miles, the snowy white landscape and the continuous blast of heat from the vent must have lulled me to sleep.

I felt the car slowing down, opened my eyes, and stretched, wiping the drool from my cheek.

"Good afternoon, Sleeping Beauty!" Casey teased.

I really had to pee. "Good afternoon? How long was I out?"

"Well, we're already to Beckley, West Virginia, so at least four hours."

"You're kidding!" I was incredulous.

Casey maneuvered into a parking space in front of a family-style restaurant, and I reached down to the floor and picked up my purse.

It seemed that she cut the engine and opened the driver's side door in one fluid motion. "Race you to the ladies room!" she giggled, sprinting down the sidewalk.

I smiled, locking the car behind me and taking off at a fast clip right behind her.

After a bathroom trip and a nourishing lunch, I felt much better. The first glimmer of excitement was stirring in my belly...kind of like the butterflies I remember feeling on the first day of school.

Casey had peppered our lunch conversation with descriptions of her apartment, her friends, and funny anecdotes about her job. In between bites of chicken and noodles, I found myself looking forward to the experience of seeing the places she had described.

While I stripped off my coat and tossed it in the backseat, Casey popped five CDs into the changer.

"These should keep you entertained while I snooze," she said with a yawn. "We haven't been able to get a good radio signal for the past couple hours."

Casey shrugged out of her coat, then used it to cover herself like a blanket. Balling up a sweatshirt, she propped it against the window and leaned her head on it. I fastened my seatbelt and pulled back onto the highway.

I drove my four hour stretch, taking I-77 through Virginia and into North Carolina, occasionally nibbling on a few of Abbey's chocolate chip cookies from the plastic container, listening to Casey's gentle breathing, and trying to concentrate on the music and driving.

After a quick pit stop, Casey drove the last leg of the journey for the day, and by the time we pulled into the Gongaware Inn near Columbia, South Carolina, we were both ready for a hot shower and a bed. I never knew that sitting in a car all day could be so exhausting!

We grabbed a speedy dinner at the hotel restaurant, and while I waited for Casey to finish in the shower, I decided to give Adam a quick call and let him know that we had gotten this far safely. As I flipped open my cell, the screen notified me that I had five missed calls and a voicemail from Jack. My stomach lurched as I listened to his message.

"Hey, Ellen. I don't know if you're ignoring my phone calls or if you're too damn busy to pick up the phone, but I wanted to let you know that Nester's will be putting the lockbox on the front door and the sign in the yard bright and early tomorrow morning. Figured I'd warn you so you don't flip out or something."

And that was it. Nothing like a little dose of reality to warm the cockles of my heart. He must've called when we were in the mountains of West Virginia and phone service was a little sketchy. Not even a "Happy New Year, Ellen." Well, what did I expect?

My thumb grazed over the "Return Call" button without putting any pressure on it. I didn't want to call him back, and you know what? I wouldn't.

I called Adam to check in and let him know where we were, promising to call from Casey's apartment tomorrow. Then, while Casey lay across her bed flipping through a magazine, I jumped in the shower and let the hot water pelt against my body.

Minutes later, I was crawling between the cool sheets, and as I closed my eyes I still felt like I was in a moving car, seeing the road in front of me. I set the alarm on my cell phone to ring early. We still had another eight hours on the road tomorrow.

Chris had called Casey while I was in the shower, and I fell asleep smiling, listening to her soft conversation.

We left behind the mountains and our winter coats, replacing them with sweatshirts and the red clay of Georgia. Although there was an early morning chill, I could feel the sun beaming through the window and warming my leg.

My mood had improved immensely; I had slept soundly. Casey said that I snored, but aside from that, we both woke up with renewed energy and an eagerness to be on the road again.

We decided to switch off driving every two hours today. There would be no sleeping; we were energized with excitement! I was behind the wheel as we sped over the border from Georgia into Florida.

"Yippee!!!!" I yelled. "Look, Casey, there's my first palm tree! Let's stop and get a picture." I pulled into a spot at the welcome station and rummaged through my purse for the camera.

Casey beamed at me, highly amused. "You are *so* funny, Mom! I predict there will be tons of palm trees in your immediate future."

"But not this one. This is my *first!*" I don't know why it was so important to me, but at that moment it was.

I grabbed the camera and opened the door, and Casey grabbed our empty Styrofoam coffee cups and tossed them in the trash. Never one to back away from a photo session, she got into the spirit of things and had me do a couple funny poses, snapping my picture with enthusiasm. After the one of me hugging the palm tree, which I would probably delete when I got back in the car, she asked a passerby to snap one of us together.

At the next exit we picked up chicken wraps at a drive-thru, neither one of us wanting to take the time to stop and eat inside. We were on a mission now, and my stomach was fluttering with anticipation.

Casey was right. The farther south we traveled, the more palm trees I saw, tall ones and stubby ones, fat ones and slender ones. The land was surprisingly flat, and I could see that the soil had a sandy appearance. We passed an area where the trees were blackened from a brush fire a couple of years ago.

I adjusted my sunglasses and sipped the iced green tea lemonade that we had purchased at our last stop. Casey opened the sunroof, and fresh warm air circulated through the car, gently blowing strands of hair around my face and rustling the magazine pages in the back seat. Was it really January?

Finally we were on I-4, and this time it was Casey who said, "Yippee!" Apparently she was happy to be almost home. It struck me as funny that she had adjusted so quickly. After all, she had just moved here four months ago.

Eventually she maneuvered from the highway into a residential area.

"Welcome to my home, Mom," Casey said proudly as she pulled up to a gate and punched a series of numbers into a black keypad resting on a shiny, silver pillar. The gate opened and we continued slowly down a driveway lined with lush vegetation and beautiful flowering shrubs.

"Casey, there are flowers blooming!" I exclaimed happily. "I wonder what they are!"

We rounded the corner and I recognized the front of Casey's building from her pictures. She pulled into her designated parking space in the lot and turned off the engine, looking at me with a smile. "It's a different world here, isn't it? Aren't you glad you came?"

"Casey, I am *very* glad I came! Thanks again for bringing me."

I couldn't wait to get out of the car and investigate.

Opening the door, a blast of hot air smacked me in the face. "Wow, this sure is different from what we left behind yesterday!" I said, remembering the frigid air penetrating my coat as I hugged Adam goodbye.

Since I was only going to be here two nights, I left my large bags in the trunk and just grabbed my overnight case, following Casey up the sidewalk. We entered the courtyard, and I felt like I had stepped into a postcard. The swimming pool sparkled and beckoned me from behind a row of comfy looking lounge chairs covered in green and white striped fabric. Waist-high terra cotta urns were strategically placed, spilling over with some kind of green vine and, once again, those beautiful flowers I had seen in the driveway.

I recognized everything from Casey's pictures, even the barbeque area. It felt surreal to actually be here in person, and I shivered with excitement.

Casey's apartment was on the second floor, so we

climbed the stairs, lugging our bags with a thump on each step. When we reached the top, I heard a door open and saw a handsome, dark-haired young man, wearing khaki shorts and a sky blue polo shirt, peek his head around the corner.

Casey dropped her bag on the spot and ran down the hall. Chris picked her up in a bear hug and spun her around several times before setting her down and kissing her hard on the lips.

Casey grabbed his hand and led him toward me.

"Mom, I'd like you to meet Chris. Chris, this is my mom," she said, grinning so broadly that I thought her cheeks were going to split. She had it bad.

"Mrs. Stern, it's a pleasure to meet you."

Chris shook my hand firmly, and then I couldn't help myself from reaching up and giving him a brief hug as a thank you to someone who makes my daughter so happy.

Chris grabbed our bags with a smile as bright as Casey's, and we followed her down the hallway to her apartment. It was just like the pictures, obviously, but so much nicer in person. I couldn't believe that my daughter actually lived in this beautiful place.

I was so proud of her! She had worked so hard in college and then law school, and now she was reaping the rewards of her labors.

Casey motioned for me to follow her into the bedroom.

"You can stay in here, and I'll camp out on the couch," she said as she propped her suitcase against the wall.

"No, *I* can sleep on the couch," I replied.

"I *insist!* You are my guest." Casey tucked her hair behind her ears and grinned at me, clearly proud of her home, and she had reason to be.

Her bedroom furniture was wicker, and her comforter and curtains were a sea mist green and cream print. A Monet print hung above her bed and a large conch shell resided on the glass-topped nightstand. Coffee-colored pillows rested against the headboard and a papasan chair sat in the corner just asking to be curled up in. It was lovely! So fresh, inviting, and utterly relaxing. French doors opened up to a view of the courtyard. Yes, I would take her up on the offer to sleep here!

I wandered into the bathroom that was done in the same colors as the bedroom, with matching wicker accessories. My thoughts trailed back to the summer nights we spent huddled over Casey's laptop choosing furniture and other decorations. It was very gratifying to see it all in place and looking so appealing.

Casey handed me a chilled bottle of spring water as I seated myself at the granite-topped island in the center of the kitchen, and I swigged it gratefully.

"Chris is going to make us his famous burgers for dinner, and look, Mom, he even stocked the fridge. Isn't he a sweetheart?" Casey gushed as she put her arms around his belly and gave him a hug.

Chris blushed a bit, but took the compliment in stride. "I knew that you didn't have anything fresh here since you've been gone so long. Just figured you'd rather spend time with your mom and not grocery shopping."

"That was extremely thoughtful of you, Chris," I told him. He was scoring lots of points with me.

After a delicious dinner, Chris and Casey shared a lounge chair while I sat poolside, dipping my feet in the water. It felt incredible to be here, and I was smiling as I gently manipulated the water into tiny waves.

Chris's cell phone announced the arrival of a text.

"It's Andy. He's having a few people over to play poker and we're invited."

"You can go. I don't want to leave my mom," Casey replied.

I knew how much Casey enjoyed the game, and I was actually tired and would turn in early anyway.

"Go ahead and go, Casey. I'll just sit here and relax for a little while longer, and then I think I'll be ready for bed. I'm exhausted!"

After she asked me if I was "sure" about ten times, I finally convinced her to go have fun. Casey ran up to get her purse, and a moment later reappeared with fresh lip gloss and her Coach wallet.

"Good luck!" I hollered as I waved goodbye, and they disappeared behind the foliage. I settled back on the chaise they had abandoned, letting the softness of the cushion envelope my body. Hard to believe that two days ago I was shoveling snow, and now I was sitting poolside in shorts and a tee shirt.

It was pretty quiet for a Friday evening. Casey assured me that tomorrow night would be a different story. The complex held a weekly Saturday night event with live music and a dinner buffet. Although the music and dancing were complementary, the cost of the meal ticket was minimal and included drinks from the Tiki bar. Casey had already purchased them for us, saying that it would be a good welcoming party for me.

As for now, I closed my eyes, enjoying the quiet and listening to the hum of the pool filter and the gentle splashing of the fountain at the far end of the patio. In the distance I heard a girl laugh, then a door shut. The faint scent of chlorine mingled with the remains of my coconut infused sunscreen…and then something else…sort of smelled like Old Spice.

I opened my eyes and was startled to see that the chair

next to me was occupied…by a man! He was wearing plaid Bermuda shorts and a white muscle shirt, and he definitely had muscles to show off. Even though his hair was gray, it was cropped in a stylish buzz, and he had a very youthful and fit appearance. His eyes were a deep brown and the tan of his skin set off the brightness of his perfectly aligned, super white teeth, most of which were in plain view as he flashed me a brilliant smile.

"Hi! I hope I didn't scare you," he stated simply, with a hint of an accent, but I couldn't place it.

I wondered how long he'd been sitting there. It took me a couple of beats to take a mental inventory of my appearance, and once I decided that I didn't look that bad, I replied with a confident, "Hello! A bit surprised maybe. I didn't hear you walk up."

He held up a tanned leg to reveal bare feet. "I was traveling in stealth mode."

I laughed easily, surprising myself.

His gold chain bracelet flashed as he extended his hand to me.

"I'm Brooklyn."

I put my right hand in his, opening my eyes wide.

"Like the bridge," he said.

Ah, a New York accent.

"Oh," I said and laughed again, although maybe a little nervously this time. "I'm Ellen. Nice to meet you."

His handshake was brief, but he continued to look my way.

"I'm not intending this to be a pick-up line, but I haven't

seen you around here before."

"That's because I haven't *been* around here before," I replied in a playful voice.

He just continued looking at me with an amused smile on his face, perhaps calculating his next move, or just trying to figure me out.

"I'm visiting my daughter," I said, deciding to give him a break.

"I find it hard to believe that a woman as young as you has a daughter old enough to be on her own!"

What a flattering thing to say. I'd better be very careful around this one!

I just smiled in return.

He swung his shoeless feet over the side of the chaise and sat up, facing me.

"So, how long are you visiting?"

What a complicated question. I really didn't want to get into my life story with this stranger, so I gave him the least amount of information without appearing rude, or at least I hoped I wasn't being rude.

"Just the weekend this time."

It was just an innocent conversation with a person, with a man, but this was new territory to me. I felt like we were sizing each other up. I wasn't even divorced yet; could I date? *Did I want to?* This was all very confusing. I decided to treat it for what it was…just a conversation.

"Well, Ellen, that's a shame! You definitely improve the poolside scenery."

"Okay, now that *was* a pick-up line!"

Did I really say that out loud? Was I flirting? It must be like riding a bicycle. It comes back to you even if you haven't ridden for thirty years!

Now it was his turn to laugh, and it was a pleasant sound. It made me feel good that I could bring that out in someone.

"Ellen, you are a treat! Are you coming to the party tomorrow night?"

Oh boy, now what do I say?

"Actually, I'll be here with my daughter and her friend."

He rose from his chair and picked up my hand, grazing it with his lips before releasing it.

"I will look forward to chatting with you again tomorrow then. Rest well, and enjoy your stay."

And with that he silently padded around the pool and disappeared down one of the paths toward the front of the complex.

I expelled a deep breath. Maybe it was time to turn in. I had a smile on my face that I just couldn't wipe off, and it was still there even after I had showered and was snuggled in Casey's bed. It felt good to have the attention of a man, but I didn't know what to do with it.

This was an entirely different ball game than teenage dating, and I didn't feel like I was ready to get involved with anyone yet. I know that Dr. Burke would say that I still needed some healing time, and she would be right. But it felt good anyway...nothing wrong with a conversation.

I lay there under the covers wondering though; when I dated in high school, we held hands...we necked...a boy might slip a hand under your shirt– and that was a big deal! Now that

I'm an adult, I'm sure things progressed a little more quickly than first, second, or third base. Maybe men wanted a home run on the first date! I tried to imagine having a man see me naked. I shuddered. No, I was *not* ready for that!

I must have fallen asleep while mulling it over, because the next thing I knew, the aroma of bacon was wafting through the apartment. I used Casey's bathroom and met her in the kitchen, noticing her pillow and blanket still rumpled on the couch as I walked by.

Casey removed the bacon from the microwave and began picking it off the paper towel that she had placed under it.

"Why does this always stick?" she asked, clearly frustrated.

"Here, I'll do that while you flip the pancakes," I said as I took the plate from her.

"I wanted to make you a nice breakfast," she pouted.

"Casey, it was great to wake up to those wonderful smells. Thank you so much! Look, the bacon is fine."

Casey's smile brightened as she put two pancakes on each of our plates and poured orange juice into crystal juice glasses.

I lifted my glass and tipped it towards her. "Cheers! Here's to a great day!"

She clunked her glass against mine, and we gobbled our breakfast in record time.

The plan was to have Chris drive us over to New Hope Personal Care Home so Hal and I could meet, and he could give me instructions on taking care of his home. As I finished my makeup, my stomach began to feel a little upset. What if he didn't like me and sent me packing?

Also, what if I promised this man that I would do the job,

then I hated living in the house? What if it was dirty and neglected? I guess it was too late for those kinds of thoughts now. Abbey would tell me to, "Suck it up and get on with it." I smiled thinking of her and I touched the cross at my neck lovingly. I owed my girl a phone call.

We arrived at New Hope around eleven o'clock. I was pleasantly surprised that it looked more like a resort than a hospital. The siding, trim, and hurricane shutters were done in muted earth tones, and the building sprawled on grounds that were impeccably manicured.

As we entered the lobby, I once again had the feeling that I was in a hotel; while Chris signed us in with the attendant, I surveyed the royal blue and gray color scheme, including sofas and chairs that were arranged in several groups throughout the room. It felt very inviting and calming.

Chris had been here many times to visit Hal and was able to lead us to the screened-in Florida room where we were told Hal was currently playing Scrabble. As we walked down the hallway, we passed what appeared to be a workout room with various pieces of exercise equipment. It was the only indication so far that this was a place for rehabilitation.

Chris held the French doors open for Casey and me, then slid them closed against the air conditioning once we were in the screened room. A group of several men, who had been huddled around a Scrabble board, looked up.

"Chris!" a handsome, white-haired man exclaimed. "And look what you brought me today! Two beautiful women! Much better than the slippers you brought me on your last visit!"

The other men snickered good-naturedly, and as Hal pushed his wheelchair away from the table he said, "Boys, we'll have to continue our game later, I have business to attend to."

This brought another round of laughter, a few adding their own comments.

"Don't do anything I wouldn't do, Hal!" a man on crutches advised.

"Hey, Hal, how about sharing your good fortune!" came from another wheelchair occupant.

"Well, if you don't want the slippers, Hal, I'll take 'em!" said a man with a cast from his ankle to his hip.

Hal waved his hand backwards in the air, dismissing them. Chris bent down and gave him a hug and kissed the top of his head.

"Don't pay any attention to those ones," Hal said, jerking his head in the direction of his Scrabble buddies. "I know they're going to look at my letters while I'm gone anyway."

We all laughed, and Chris introduced us.

"Ellen, what a pleasure it is to finally meet you. I'm truly blessed that you are willing to do this great favor for me. Thank you so much!" and he took my hand in his and gave it a squeeze.

"And, Casey, I've heard many wonderful things about you, my dear. You are making my Chris here a happy boy."

"I'm a *man,* gramps," Chris teased him.

"Well, then, show me your masculinity and wheel me out to the patio, would you?"

Casey and I followed Chris as he pushed Hal's wheelchair out to a patio surrounded by tropical greens. There were those flowers again! I stopped to examine a flamingo pink one, the blossom as big as the palm of my hand.

"So, Ellen, you are an admirer of hibiscus?" Hal asked me.

I turned my head to look at him as I released the flower.

259

"Is that what these are? I've been seeing them everywhere, and I love them!"

"Yes, they *are* beautiful! You'll see many of them at my house." A bit of sadness crept into his voice. "Could it be that you enjoy gardening, Ellen?"

"Enjoy gardening?" I replied with a grin. This job was getting better by the moment. "My hands have just been itching to be in a pair of gardening gloves! Unfortunately, where I live it's time to wear fur-lined ones!"

"My mom *loves* flowers," Casey interjected as she and Chris got comfortable on a wooden glider. I chose the huge matching rocker and plunked myself down, crossed my legs at the ankles, and began to rock slowly.

Hal was so easy to talk to, and it was clear that he was enjoying our visit. He included each one of us in the conversation, asking questions and telling amusing stories, some to Chris's chagrin.

Although he looked a little tired, he was a very attractive man. I could see dark circles under his eyes, and maybe a little paleness. His skin tone was more like my "up north winter white" than the golden glow that Casey and Chris had. Even dressed in his comfortable sweat pants and Marlins tee shirt, he exuded an aura of class. I could picture a youthful Hal in my mind's eye as he told us how he had met his wife, Louise, and a little about how they came to live at Lake Juliet. I could sense his feeling of loss as he spoke of her, even three years after her passing. Once he winced as he straightened up in the chair, and even though he was disguising it well, I could tell that he was also in physical pain.

We all looked up as a young woman who appeared to be about Casey's age joined us on the patio. She was wearing jeans, sneakers, and a hot pink polo shirt with the New Hope logo on the pocket and a gold rectangle pin with the name "Lindsey" written on it in white block letters.

"Sorry to interrupt, but looks like it's time for Hal's afternoon therapy session."

She had very curly, golden blond hair pulled back in a tight ponytail, and a sweet smile that lit up her whole face. "Are you ready, big guy?"

I couldn't imagine anyone refusing her. She just appeared to be such a sweetheart.

"Just a moment, my dear."

Hal grinned at her, then whispered to us loud enough for her to hear, "She puts on that angel disguise for company, but when she gets me in there she really cracks the whip!"

"I heard that, Hal! You're looking at five extra minutes on the treadmill for that comment!" she said with a smile. "He'll be about an hour. Y'all are welcome to wait for him if you'd like."

"Actually, we need to be going anyway," Chris spoke up.

He bent down to give Hal a hug. Casey and I followed suit, each giving him a quick squeeze. When I stood up, he grabbed my hand and turned it palm up, placing a key in it and closing my fingers around it.

"Now you take good care of Miss Juliet, Ellen," he said with a wink.

"I will, Hal. Don't you worry about a thing, and I'll come back to visit you soon too," and I meant it.

CHAPTER TWENTY

Casey suggested an afternoon swim since we missed our workout walk this morning. I squeezed into my new tank style swimsuit, a cute little solid black number that I picked up on clearance at Macy's last summer. At that time I had the idea that Jack and I might plan a romantic getaway to somewhere exotic; well, that fantasy sure had bitten the dust. I pulled the latex up over my bosom and let the straps go with a snap, surveyed my silhouette, and was surprisingly pleased. The strategically placed padding made the girls look pretty good! I just had to tone up my thighs and buttocks, where all those late night deposits of cakes and desserts had compounded interest daily.

A tan would probably help to hide those nasty little spider veins that were beginning to road map the back of my calves, and I intended to work on that right away.

I slathered on sunscreen and breathed in the happy scent. In the past, I've been known to crack open a bottle in mid-winter just to get that "on the beach" high. Just one sniff would transport me to sunshine and summer. But now it *is* the middle of winter and here I *am,* in sunshine! How about that!

Casey, wearing her familiar green bikini, was waiting for me in the living room with two fuzzy beach towels and two refillable water bottles, the ice cubes clinking around as she handed one to me.

We swam compatibly, silently, completing lap after lap. It felt good to stretch my muscles and push them in new ways. The sun glistened off the surface of the water, shimmering as each of my arm strokes broke the surface, pulling down and back, pushing the water away and propelling me forward.

Later, as we stretched out on the lounge chairs, I felt invigorated and renewed. The sun was therapeutic as its warmth seeped into my body, and I was overwhelmed by a sense of wellbeing that I hadn't experienced in a long time. What a day it had been! It was such a pleasure to meet Hal. I finally feel like this job is important and has merit, and I'm not just running away from my troubles, although my troubles did seem a million miles away. I'm actually helping someone, and it feels mighty good.

I had seen the frustration in Hal's eyes as he sat in the wheelchair, wanting more than anything to be home and not bound to the nursing home for the required regiment of physical therapy. But the spunk in his attitude was evident, and I knew immediately that he was a fighter and would embark on his journey to recovery with vigor.

I also saw the mutual admiration between Chris and his grandfather, and it warmed my heart to witness that kind of family affection. Even after only knowing Chris for such a short time, my instincts and mother's radar had honed in on his kind, gentle ways, especially where Casey was concerned. Although he radiated self-confidence, it was different than the self-confidence that Jack had emitted. Jack's registered high on the arrogance barometer and held people at bay, but Chris just seemed self-assured in a way that made you feel like you could trust him with anything, and it drew you in. I sensed that right off about Hal, too.

My eyes were closed, my mouth was smiling, and my ears were hearing someone approaching.

"Hello, Casey. Good afternoon, Ellen!" a male voice with a New York accent greeted us. "What a pleasant surprise!"

I opened my eyes and peeped over the top of my sunglasses.

"Hi," I heard Casey say warily.

I took a breath and expelled it in one swoosh. "Hello, Brooklyn."

He had a green plastic grocery bag in one hand and a six pack of beer in the other.

Casey was looking at me with a perplexed look on her face.

"Save me a dance tonight, will you, Ellen?" he asked, not expecting an answer as he grinned and walked past us, once again disappearing behind the shrubs.

I could feel Casey's eyes burning on me, and it only took her a second to pounce.

"How the heck do you know Brooklyn the bridge, Mom?"

I laughed out loud.

"Brooklyn the bridge?"

"Every time he introduces himself to someone he says, "Brooklyn, like the bridge" as if no one could figure it out on their own.

"Well, he stopped by and introduced himself when I was at the pool yesterday. He seems nice enough."

"I leave you alone for one evening, and you already have guys hitting on you!" she teased.

I smiled over at her, adjusting my sunglasses. I could feel beads of sweat dripping down between the happy girls.

"Well, he seems harmless. How do *you* know him?" I asked, giving her the squinty eyed look this time.

Casey shrugged.

"He owns the place. *Everyone* knows Brooklyn, and he makes it *his* business to know everyone."

I raised my eyebrows. Huh. He owns the place...interesting.

After the sweat and chlorine were rinsed off in the shower and replaced by a spritz of Jessica McClintock, I tugged on a pair of white capri pants and slid a silky, black sleeveless blouse over my head. I fastened a silver ankle bracelet around my left ankle, tucked my feet into black leather sandals, and surveyed myself in the mirror in Casey's bathroom.

My skin already had a bit of color from my afternoon in the pool, and I could see a red blotch on my chest where I had evidently missed a spot with the sunscreen. Amazing how much stronger the sun was here.

I leaned in toward the mirror and attached silver hoops to my ears, applied a bit of bronze lipstick, and I was ready for the party. My stomach was growling, and the scent of charcoal and barbeque had been riding the breeze up through Casey's windows, teasing me for the past half hour.

Just as I emerged from Casey's room, Chris came through the front door.

"Guess what? Brooklyn Bridge hit on my mom!" Casey blurted out before the door even shut behind him.

"If I wasn't already taken, I'd hit on her too!" Chris joked.

Casey punched him in the arm, and he playfully grabbed her by the wrist and pulled her close, dropping a gentle kiss on her forehead before releasing her.

"Casey, he's not hitting on me! We've probably only exchanged twenty words total!" I said shaking my head, but all the flattery was feeding my starving ego.

"I'm just teasing you. You're a free woman now! You can date if you want. It seems kind of weird though."

"I'm nowhere near ready to date, so you don't have to worry about that. I *am* ready for dinner though. Let's go!"

I followed Casey and Chris down the steps toward the wonderful aroma. Quite a crowd had gathered around the Tiki bar, and even though it was hardly dusk, the poolside torches were lit, and tiny white lights that had been draped through the tree branches were twinkling a greeting.

Chris took our drink orders, and while I stood next to Casey waiting for him to return, I found myself nonchalantly scouring the crowd for Brooklyn. Who was I kidding; I was looking forward to seeing him tonight. I felt a flutter in my chest as I spied him coming around the corner, carrying a bucket of ice. I reached up and tucked a strand of hair behind my ear as I accepted my drink from Chris. Brooklyn continued on his mission, dumping the ice in a huge bin behind the bar without even a glance in my direction.

Dinner was delicious! It was a beautiful buffet of barbecued chicken, salad greens, parsley potatoes, a hollowed-out watermelon full of fresh fruit, and feathery light rolls with cinnamon-honey butter. Just as white almond cake with raspberry filling was being served, a steel drum band began to play softly in the background.

Darkness had fallen, and the ambiance was over the top romantic. I had noticed Brooklyn tending bar, once again replenishing ice and overseeing the barbeque area. I felt a pang of disappointment that he hadn't sought me out. I knew he was taking care of business, but, well, I guess I expected he'd be looking for me too. I hadn't even caught his eye.

The buffet was cleared and the tables moved to allow room for dancing. Chris and Casey were swaying to the music, his hands low on her back and hers wrapped around his neck. They made a handsome couple.

I was standing poolside, sipping my third "sex on the beach." I loved the taste of them but was always too embarrassed to order them out loud for myself. Casey wasn't inhibited in that way. "Mom, it's only the name of a drink," she told me, "They name them like that so it's more fun to order!" The shock factor wasn't wasted on me, so she was taking it upon herself to keep me well-hydrated tonight, or she was trying to get me sloshed. Both scenarios were holding merit.

The hair on the nape of my neck prickled as I sensed a presence behind me, and before I could turn around, two hands came out of nowhere and tried to wrap around my middle. I reacted with lightning knee-jerk speed, pushing my elbows straight back as hard as I could. Reflecting on this later, I was shocked that I actually had reflexes that weren't covered in cobwebs. Abbey and I had taken a self-defense course at the YMCA a few years back, and I guess my fight or flight instinct was still set on automatic pilot and resurrected the practiced move.

Three things happened in that blur of a moment. My bony elbows connected with flesh, my tumbler of sex on the beach flew in the air and became sex in the pool, and I heard a loud splash. My heart was racing as I quickly turned around to face my attacker.

My hand flew to my mouth as I stared at Brooklyn bobbing in the water, his orange and lime green flowered shirt billowing around him.

"Oh my gosh, Brooklyn, I'm so sorry," I said as I stooped down beside the pool.

We were drawing a crowd, and I heard Casey's voice.

"Way to go, Mom."

Was that sarcasm?

"Are you alright?" I asked him as he swam to the ladder.

"Perfectly fine," he said as he climbed out of the pool. He stood for a moment wringing out the tail of his shirt, and then shook his head like a wet dog, spraying a few of the onlookers with water.

I was afraid he was going to be angry and make a scene, calling me stupid or other more descriptive adjectives, but to my astonishment he started to laugh! Then everyone started laughing with him.

A few of the guys teased him about being thrown in the pool by a woman, but he took the comments good-naturedly. I was still rooted to the spot, and I felt a hot flush all over my body. Oh, no, not a panic attack here in front of all these people.

Brooklyn stood by my side. "I guess I have to stop traveling in stealth mode," he said sheepishly.

"You scared the living daylights out of me!" I said in my own defense.

The crowd had disbanded, and everyone went back to their dancing. Only Casey and Chris remained nearby.

"You okay, Mom?" she asked, the ridicule gone from her voice.

I smiled a weak smile, feeling better. No panic attack; it must have just been my nerves settling down after such a shock.

"I'm fine," I answered. And I was…embarrassed, but fine.

The rest of the evening went by quickly. Brooklyn changed into dry clothes, and we spent the remainder of the night in conversation. He was a very interesting man. Even though his name seemed to lack a little masculinity to me, he exuded testosterone. He informed me during the course of the evening that his parents were inspired to name him after the place where he was conceived, and I didn't ask for details. After having made a career of the military, he had retired at an early age and invested in real estate. He still had the hard, muscular body of a Marine, and the short, neat haircut as well.

He asked me to dance. He said I owed it to him after knocking him in the pool, and what could I say to that? I was still feeling lucky that his Marine self-defense training hadn't kicked in when I gave him the double reverse elbow technique.

It felt really strange to be in another man's arms. He felt so different from Jack. I can't say that I didn't like it, but I can't say that I was crazy about it either. He was nice enough, and very attractive, but I would have been happy just to sit and talk instead of having this physical contact.

At the end of the evening, he walked me to Casey's door and gave me a hug. I was afraid he was going to go for the kiss too, so I nipped it in the bud and gave him a tiny peck on the cheek. He gave me a quizzical look, but didn't comment.

"May I see you again sometime? I really enjoyed my evening with you, Ellen…even the unexpected swim. There's something attractive about a woman who can take care of herself," he said.

I paused a moment, my insides shaking again.

"It was fun, Brooklyn, and I am *so* sorry that I knocked you in the pool. I just don't think that I'm ready to date yet. I still have some healing to do."

He nodded his head. "I understand, but no reason why we can't get together as friends. I'll look you up next time I'm out your way. I have some properties near Lake Juliet and get out that way from time to time."

During the course of our after-dinner conversation, I had become more relaxed with him and told him a little about my job. I hadn't told him that I would be in the house alone though; I didn't know him *that* well.

"How about I give you my cell number and maybe we can have lunch or something after I get settled in. Or maybe I'll run into you next time I visit Casey."

He pulled his cell out of his pocket and punched in the numbers as I recited them.

"I'm a patient man, Ellen. Patient, but persistent."

Somehow I knew that would be true.

I smiled. "Goodnight, then."

He took my hand and squeezed it. "Goodnight, Ellen."

I let myself into the apartment, closed the door, and then leaned against it with a silly smile on my face. Casey and Chris were still at the party, so I slipped into my pajamas, curled up on the bed, and pulled out my cell phone.

"How the heck are you, kiddo?" Abbey's voice was so clear, she could have been sitting next to me.

"I have so much to tell you already! You're not going to believe this, but I kind of had a date tonight."

"Holy moly! Well, isn't *that* a flip of the switch!" I could sense Abbey smiling through the phone. "Will the real Ellen please stand up?"

I laughed out loud.

"Seriously, you've only been gone a few days and you've met someone already?" she asked in surprise.

"Sort of but not really…I don't know if it qualifies as a real date…I threw him in the pool…we danced, and he hugged me…I kissed him on the cheek…."

"Whoa, Ellen, let's take a step back and start at the beginning, please."

I took a deep breath and relayed everything that had happened since we arrived. I still couldn't believe that I'd only been here for two days. Jeannette, Pennsylvania felt so very far away. When I finished my story, Abbey was quiet for a moment.

"Are you still there?" I asked into the seemingly empty phone line.

"Yes, honey, I'm here. Just thinking, that's all. I want to say the right thing here, and not offend you."

Okay, now I *was* offended, and the silence was on my end of the line.

"Ellen?"

"I thought you'd be *excited*...."

"I *am*! I'm just worried about you. I don't want you to get hurt, that's all."

"Well, talk about a *flip of the switch*!" I became indignant. "*You're* the one who told me to keep my options open and not to be afraid to meet someone new! *You're* the one who said to watch out for Romeo!"

"Yes, but never in my wildest imagination did I expect you to do it in forty-eight hours! Just because I told you not to throw Romeo into Lake Juliet, I didn't mean to throw him in the pool instead!"

Abbey's laugh jingled across the miles, and as usual, it was infectious. I wanted to be upset with her, but instead began to smile, which led to a giggle...then Abbey snorted and I cracked up.

I laughed so hard that tears were running down my cheeks, and I could tell she was doing the same.

"Ellen, you amaze me."

Abbey was finally able to get words out. "I'm so proud of you for putting yourself out there. Just be careful and don't get too serious right away, okay?"

"Yes, Mom!" I teased. I knew where she was coming from; I would have given her the same advice, and actually Dr. Burke had given me the same caution before I left. It was all so new, after being married for so long, to suddenly be free to think about men from a different point of view. "I promise to take it slow. It's all just so weird, Abbey. I don't really think I'm attracted to him, but he is very nice, and I have to admit that it feels good to have the attention."

"Well, it sounds like you're doing fine, then. Just keep the brakes on for a bit and see where it goes."

After we disconnected, I curled up and fell asleep, but only after I'd replayed the scenes from the evening through my head time and time again.

I had already met some very interesting people. Hal was wonderful, and Brooklyn was interesting…good thing, though, that I was going to Lake Juliet tomorrow. I needed some time to collect my thoughts, and I was really ready to get to work!

CHAPTER TWENTY ONE

In the morning, the three of us piled into Chris's Jeep, Casey riding shotgun and me tucked snugly in the backseat next to my luggage. I welcomed the blast of air conditioning that was quickly chasing away the stuffy, stagnant air of the interior. Pushing my sunglasses up on my head, I leaned forward to peer into the front seat.

"So how long does it take to get there again?" I asked Chris.

Casey burst out laughing. "Geez, Mom, why don't you sit back and sing ninety-nine bottles of beer on the wall, and by the time you're done, we should be almost there."

Now I knew why the kids always groaned when we told them that on road trips. I guess I was getting a little impatient, considering we hadn't even pulled out of the parking lot yet. I lowered my sunglasses, settled into the backseat, and fastened my seatbelt.

"It's less than an hour, Mrs. Stern," Chris answered much more politely than my smart aleck daughter.

I decided to pay close attention as he drove, knowing that I would have to learn how to navigate to and from Casey's apartment during my stay here. Gazing out the window, my mind was suddenly racing as quickly as the scenery was flying by the window. Although I was still very excited about my new job, especially after meeting Hal yesterday, a tiny bit of nervousness was trying to sneak into the cracks in my self-confidence. Was it really wise for me to be alone in a strange, huge house all by myself? Would I get bored or lonely? What if I started having panic attacks again? What the heck was I going to do all day?

Apprehensive thoughts that hadn't had time to gel because I had been so focused on packing up the house finally caught up with me. I was playing the "What If?" game, and Dr. Burke had warned me not to go there. She told me that I may second guess myself at some point, and if that happened, to just remember how excited I was when I made my decision and to focus on my goal and be happy in the moment.

Then my mind changed tracks and I started thinking about Brooklyn. Would he really call me again? What would I say to that?

"Mom, are you sleeping?" Casey had turned around in her seat and was tapping my leg.

Listening to my inner dialogue, I hadn't heard a word she was saying, nor had I been paying attention to the directions.

"No, I'm not sleeping…just thinking," I answered.

"We're almost there now."

This time it was Chris's voice booming from the front seat.

I sat up straighter as we exited from I-4 and the Jeep slowed down, adjusting to the reduced speed limit. Chris made a left at the end of the ramp onto a two-lane road with orange groves on either side. A gas station, large enough to accommodate the big rigs from the highway, was to our immediate right. Out front, big white billboards splashed with bold neon print, advertised freshly squeezed orange juice, homemade ice cream, and souvenirs.

I made a mental note of the homemade ice cream.

We drove for about five minutes with nothing but rows of orange trees lining the sides of the road. I was beginning to wonder if we'd ever see a house, but I dared not ask Chris if we were almost there. My hands were clenched tightly in my lap.

Just as I thought my resolve was going to crack, Chris tapped the brake pedal, slowing us down to almost a stop, then made a slow right turn, navigating onto a paved driveway. I was glad Chris was at the wheel; the driveway was so obscure that I surely would have missed it completely.

He maneuvered slowly around a bend, then Casey and I both exclaimed at the same time, "Wow!"

A sprawling red brick home with white trim was nestled beneath mature oak trees, dripping with Spanish moss. The house was neither pretentious nor showy, but was elegant and welcoming at the same time. It appeared to be multi-level, most of it being two stories with tons of single pane windows, and the rest a one-story sunroom with floor to ceiling tinted glass.

A lush, green lawn met the driveway and meandered about fifty yards past the house, carpeting the way to Lake Juliet. Who would have known all this was hiding behind all those orange trees?

From what I could see from the car, the lake was much larger than I had expected. I had envisioned something like Indian Lake at home, maybe a half-mile's walk around. I think it would take me two days to walk around Lake Juliet!

Chris pulled up next to a detached garage and turned off the ignition.

"Well, what do you think?" he asked me.

"Chris, it's wonderful! I can't wait to see the inside!" I exclaimed, my hand already on the door handle.

I clambered out, standing beside the car with my arms folded around my chest, taking it all in. A slight breeze swayed the Spanish moss, and I could almost swear I heard it whisper, "Welcome home, Ellen."

All of the misgivings I had in the car were gone and were replaced by a sense of contentment.

"Let's leave your things in the Jeep, and I'll give you a

tour first," Chris said as he took Casey by the hand and started walking toward the back of the house.

I followed close behind, stopping occasionally to admire the beautiful landscaping surrounding the home. My feet sunk into the crisp, thick zoysia grass, so different from the soft grass back home.

"Does Hal take care of the gardens himself?" I asked Chris.

"He used to. Now he hires someone to mow the lawn. But I think he still putters with the flowers."

A screened enclosure ran the length of the rear of the house, and I could see very comfy looking white wicker furniture with turquoise and chocolate brown cushions arranged inside. Was that a swimming pool?

"Oh my gosh, Mom! A pool!" Casey had noticed it at the same time I did, and she ran up to put her face against the screen. A tiny green lizard skittered right in front of her nose and disappeared into the garden.

"Ew!" she screamed and jumped back.

"They're harmless," Chris laughed at her. "We used to try and catch them when we were kids. They're pretty quick!"

Casey gave a quick shudder and flashed me a pathetic smile.

Chris led us across the lawn to where the green of the grass met a small patch of white sand, slightly littered with dried moss and twigs, before it disappeared into the lapping ripples of the lake. Tall grasses lined the shore, and I spied a slender white bird with a long beak standing at attention, as if we were intruding on his secret hiding place.

Hand in hand, Chris and Casey walked about twenty feet to the edge of the wooden planked dock. I stood a moment listening to the whooshing sound of the tiny waves slapping against the shore, then I joined them. Shading my eyes with my hand, I squinted to see the opposite side of the lake. Most of the homes had docks, some quite large. Even though they appeared tiny from this distance, it was apparent that the owners of those houses were very well-to-do.

There were also what appeared to be some mobile home parks, along with some smaller houses sporadically sharing the lake view. A few rowboats, complete with fishermen, were scattered out on the water, and the hum of a motorboat could be heard, but I didn't see it.

Although it was apparent that we had neighbors, the property was very secluded, and I felt as if the lake was my own.

"Mom, you are so lucky to be staying here," Casey said, turning to me. "This is awesome!"

I sighed. "Yes, I think I can get used to this. Chris, your grandfather has a beautiful home."

"You haven't even seen the inside yet!" Chris said with a smile. "Now you can see why he didn't want to leave it unattended."

"Absolutely," I replied. "And I can see why he'll be so anxious to return."

A white duck came squawking out from the brush and swam over to the dock expectantly.

"Hey, Dora," Chris crooned as he stooped down. "Nothing for you now, but I'll bring you something later."

"Dora?" Casey asked with a giggle.

"Yeah, there are lots of ducks around, but Grandpa and this one took a liking to each other. You should see how she follows him around the yard. She's really attached to him, and he has a soft spot for her too."

Dora swam under the dock and came out the other side, quacking her displeasure at Hal's absence. I have no experience with ducks, but I hoped that Dora would like me too.

We trooped back to the front of the house. I wanted to stop and admire each wonderful thing that caught my eye along the way. Pausing to touch a canary yellow hibiscus blossom, I heard Casey scold me.

"Mom, come on! You'll be here for months so you'll have plenty of time to check everything out."

Chris led us up several wide, flagstone steps and unlocked the front screen door. Once again, I followed behind them, taking in the beautiful screened-in front porch. It was much smaller than the huge one out back, but charmingly decorated with more wicker furniture, this time painted black with lime green and salmon colored cushions.

After Chris punched a code into the keypad, he opened a brass trimmed glass door, and we followed him into the main living area. It was a very spacious room, and even though I could tell the furnishings were high-end, they looked comfortable and welcoming. A large sofa, two loveseats, and a few wingback chairs were arranged near a glass topped coffee table, all gathered around a flagstone fireplace. I immediately felt right at home.

Every room was delightful! Chris was probably getting weary of hearing Casey and me oooing and ahhing, but it really was fabulous. I couldn't wait to tell Abbey about it!

After climbing the stairs to the second floor, we found a hallway with four bedrooms. One, apparently, was Hal's, housing a huge four poster maple bed draped with a royal blue comforter, and delightful antique dressers.

"Mom, you get to pick what room you want to stay in!" Casey exclaimed. "Or you can sleep in a different one every night!"

Peeking in the doorways, I found each one of them charming, but I knew which would be my choice the moment I saw it.

Located on the back side of the house facing the lake, a queen size brass bed was positioned between two tall bow windows, with ample built-in seats at their bases. I walked over and sat down on the plump, celery colored cushion and gazed out at the lawn and Lake Juliet. I smiled.

"I'll go out to the Jeep and get your things. It looks like you've made your choice," I heard Chris say from the doorway.

Casey came and sat down beside me. I took her hand in mine and looked her in the eye.

"Thank you so much, Casey, for giving me this opportunity. It's exactly what the doctor ordered."

Casey leaned in to give me a quick hug.

"I'm just glad that Chris mentioned the job to me when he did. It's all working out perfectly for you *and* his grandpa, isn't it?" she asked. "I think I'll go and pick out where I'm staying tonight," she said as she flounced out of the room.

She must have chosen the room next to mine with the antique canopy bed, because I heard Chris come up the hallway and pause at the door. Then I heard a clunk as he dropped off Casey's overnight bag and continued down the hall to *my* room. Even though I'd only chosen it a few moments ago, it already felt like *mine*. Leaving my large suitcase on the floor, he retreated for another load.

I tore myself away from the view and lifted my suitcase to the luggage rack. By the time Chris returned with my two smaller bags, I had already placed most of my clothes in the bureau drawers and was hanging the few dresses I brought in the closet. I stashed the empty suitcase on the closet floor and quickly unpacked my other two bags.

Grabbing my duffel of toiletries, I made my way down the hall to the bathroom and left the bag on the floor. I could put them away later. The upstairs was quiet, so I went in search of Casey and Chris.

I found them in the kitchen. Chris dumping a container of sour milk down the drain, and Casey hovering over a tablet, with pen in hand.

"All settled in?" she asked as I entered the room.

"Yep. I think I could just live in that room forever!" I replied. "What are you doing?"

"Chris is cleaning out the fridge, and I'm making a grocery list. He thought it would be a good idea to take you into town so you would know how to get there, and we could stock up on some food for you."

Fifteen minutes later, Chris made a right at the end of the driveway onto the familiar two lane road. Eventually the trees gave way to a more residential area, and we passed several new housing developments.

"All of this used to be orange groves, but they've been sold in the past few years," Chris explained.

We were only about ten minutes into our journey when I spied another lake. It was more the size I had expected Lake Juliet to be. There was a paved walking track around it, picnic tables set under magnificent cypress trees, and a children's playground, which at the moment was being enjoyed by lots of kids in shorts and sneakers. My thoughts drifted back to Pennsylvania, picturing the neighborhood kids all bundled up in snowsuits and boots.

The road paralleled the lake, and once we had driven all around its perimeter, we found ourselves in the town shopping district. Before we pulled into the grocery store parking lot, Chris circled around the block, pointing out the places he thought might interest me– the library, the movie theater, several small boutiques, and a bakery. It was an adorable place, and I envisioned myself leisurely strolling down the sidewalk window shopping, with an ice cream cone in hand. No, make that a cupcake...the bakery looked awesome!

The pungent mixture of ripening produce, deli meats, and Mr. Clean hit my nostrils the moment I stepped through the front door...not an unpleasant scent...just that of a small grocery store where things are fresh, in contrast to the pre-packaged big box store I was used to.

Ever since I arrived in Florida, I've had a craving for oranges. I chose about two dozen, placing them in two separate plastic bags in my cart next to the green grapes and bananas that Casey had already tossed in.

"Look, Mom! Fresh strawberries!" Casey exclaimed as she inspected several green plastic baskets before making her choice. "I'm getting a basket to take home with me, too."

"It's just about the beginning of strawberry season," Chris said. "You should be able to have fresh berries the whole time you're here, Mrs. Stern. We'll have to take you over to Plant City to the Strawberry Festival in March. I think you'd get a kick out of that."

In March...two months away. Would I still be here? I pushed that thought aside and tossed a bag of lettuce into the cart. A salad sounded delicious.

Chris accepted the brown paper package from the butcher, containing three fresh T-bones for our dinner. I peered through the glass front of the refrigerated case and also ordered several chicken breasts and two pounds of lean ground beef. May as well be prepared.

I paid cash for the groceries, which reminded me to have Chris show me the nearest Citrus Trust Bank on the way home. Casey had taken me to the branch where she does banking near her condo to open a new account, so that part was already done.

Now all I needed was money to put in it.

"Is it typically this warm in January?" I asked Chris. Casey and I were admiring his grilling expertise from our vantage point in the pool. We had done a few laps and were both flung over a lime green raft, lying on our bellies and slowly paddling with our feet.

Chris used his tongs to turn the steaks and sprinkled them with his secret seasoning mix. "Today was a bit warmer than usual, and I heard on the radio that it's supposed to be really warm all week, so you came at a good time. We get cooler weather too, but nothing like what you're used to."

"Well, this is my first winter here, too! I really didn't know what to expect," said Casey. "Even though I do miss seeing the snow at home, have to say it's not really breaking my heart to be swimming in January! Aren't we the lucky ones?"

"These beauties will be ready in a few minutes," Chris told us as he set the tongs on a plate beside the grill.

Reluctantly, Casey and I climbed the steps out of the pool and wrapped ourselves in oversized pink and white striped beach towels. I watched as she went over to Chris, stood on tiptoe, and gave him a quick kiss.

I sighed, then went inside to get the salad. Goosebumps prickled my arms as the air conditioning assaulted my damp skin. Grabbing the bowl from the refrigerator, I scurried back out into the warm, humid air.

Dinner was wonderful. I enjoyed everything, from the steak that almost melted in my mouth to the luscious strawberries that were probably just picked this morning. We all worked together to clean up and put the kitchen back in order, then Chris went out to light some candles on the porch. Casey turned back to look at me as she was going back outside.

"Coming out, Mom?"

I decided to give them a little privacy, and actually I was really anxious to try out the soaker tub in the upstairs bathroom.

"You go on ahead. I think I'm going to get out of this damp suit and try out that monstrosity of a tub upstairs," I said as I refilled my wine glass.

She smiled over her shoulder as she shut the sliding glass door. I stood a moment and watched as she cuddled next to Chris on the chaise, then I took my wine and climbed the stairs.

I turned the brushed nickel handle to start the water flowing and rooted through my toiletry bag that I had left on the floor. After adding a capful of pomegranate bubble bath to the churning water, I padded back to my bedroom and pulled a white tank top and gray lounge pants out of the drawer and carried them back to the bathroom.

As I slipped down through the iridescent bubbles, I succumbed to the gentle caress of the warm, scented water. Tipping the crystal goblet upwards, I savored the last sip of wine, then rested my head against the coolness of the porcelain tile, closing my eyes.

In the complete silence, I could hear the tiny bubbles popping like muted Rice Krispies in milk. My mind's eye replayed the events of the day…my new life in the forefront, nice and shiny. I didn't want to think of the past, didn't want my mind to wander down the all too familiar road back to Jack. Shaking my head, I tried to banish his face from the slideshow playing in my head. I opened my eyes to make it go away.

Picking up a handful of bubbles, I blew them into the air. Dr. Burke had told me way back at the beginning of my therapy to allot myself a certain amount of time– say fifteen minutes– to be sad, or cry, or think my scary thoughts…and when that time was up, to put them away and not burden myself with them until the next time. This process had definitely worked, and I haven't needed to do this exercise in a long time.

Deciding on a five minute curfew, I let myself think about my house back home and all the prospective buyers wandering through the rooms where so much of my life had happened. It saddened me to think that it was more than likely that I'd never set foot in it again. Picturing Jack in his new home, once again I found it hard to imagine how he left our home with such ease and no apparent signs of regret, and moved into his new place without so much as a glance behind.

But even more confusing was that after only being gone several days, I was already moving on as well.

I checked the clock on the vanity, took a deep breath, and brought myself back to the present. Closing my eyes again, I conjured up a beautiful lake, lined with tall grasses and a sprinkling of palm trees. Warm air cloaking my body and sun glistening on gentle blue waves. Casey's muffled voice saying, "Mom, are you okay in there?"

My eyes snapped open, and I sat up straight in a flurry of bubbles and sloshing water.

"I'm fine, Casey! I'll be out soon."

"Stay as long as you want. I just wanted to make sure you hadn't fallen asleep in there! We're putting on a movie in the den if you want to join us."

"I think I might just go to sleep, sweetie, I'm exhausted! Would you mind?"

Casey laughed. "No, I don't mind. Sleep tight, and I'll see you for breakfast."

"Good night," I called to the closed door as I heard her footsteps retreating down the hallway.

I lost myself in the pillow top mattress, and with the combination of wine, bath, and excitement of my day, fell asleep almost as soon as my head hit the pillow.

At dawn, I woke up a little disoriented. I groggily turned on my side and was treated to a glimpse of Lake Juliet from the window, immediately jogging my mind into consciousness. The lake was on the west side of the house, promising engaging sunsets, but its early morning beauty was also dazzling, prompting me to swing my legs over the side of the bed and rummage around in the drawer for something to wear.

I hastily pulled a sweatshirt over my tank top and slipped my feet into flip-flops, made a speedy bathroom pit stop, and scurried down the hall. Casey's bedroom door was open and she was still sound asleep, as was Chris, who was bunking in Hal's room. I tossed a mug of water into the microwave, feeling too impatient to wait for the tea kettle to boil. After what seemed like an interminably long two minutes, the buzzer obnoxiously broke the morning silence. I dunked a tea bag, added a squirt of honey, and scampered out the door.

The morning dew was cool against my feet as they sunk into the thick grass. I clunked down the wooden planks and stopped at the end of the pier, gazing out over the lake. There was a delicate mist rising from the water and the reflection of the sunrise behind me colored it a rosy hue. Setting my mug down on the bench, I stretched my arms above my head, breathing deeply. This was magnificent! I tipped my head and gazed upward into the first light of the day. "Thank you," I whispered softly.

The mist concealed the houses across the lake, but as I took a seat on the bench I had a clear view of our neighbors' homes. Technically speaking, anyway. The nearest pier was at least the equivalent of two city blocks away. There were no human noises, only the chatter of birds, an occasional splash of a jumping fish, and the hushed lap of the water against the shore.

I sat transfixed for quite a while, watching a spider diligently repairing a web on the crossbars beneath the other bench, the fibers glistening as he worked his magic.

The sun had now moved well above the horizon and burned off most of the mist, taking with it the enchantment and tranquility of the first light and promising another exceptionally warm day.

The engine of a motorboat revved to life somewhere in the distance, and a moment later I spied it zooming across the lake. The screen door slammed and I glanced back at the house to see Chris coming toward me toting a fishing pole and a bucket.

"Good morning!" Chris called out.

I held my hand up and waved a greeting. "Hi!"

"Thought I'd try my luck this morning," he said as he reached into his bucket and made short work of baiting his hook. Tipping the rod behind his shoulder, he brought it forward with a quick swoosh and I heard a little plop as the bobber hit the water. He grinned. "Nothing like fishing in the morning to calm the soul."

He pulled plastic baggie out of his shorts pocket and shook it up and down, its contents making a muffled rattling sound. A few seconds later, I heard, "Quack!"

Dora, or who I suspected was Dora, came swimming out of the grasses and waddled up onto the shore.

"Come on, sweetheart," Chris told her, confirming my suspicions.

He continued shaking the bag, and when she got to within a few feet from us on the pier, he opened it and asked me to hold out my hand.

"I want to introduce you to Dora, and there's no better way to get on her good side and gain her trust than to give her a treat," Chris said as he filled my palm with cracked corn. "For today, just let her see you setting it down for her, and before you know it she'll be eating out of your hand."

I reached down and scattered the corn, and watched, amused, as Dora gobbled it up. When she was through, she waddled over to Chris, quacked loudly, and made herself comfortable by his feet, completely snubbing me.

I laughed out loud. "Looks like I'll have to sneak her a few cheese puffs or something to win her over."

"Ah, I have a feeling she'll love you. Wait and see! The only person I've ever seen her not like is my mom…and the feeling is mutual. Maybe she senses that. Remind me to show you where grandpa keeps the cracked corn when we go in. Oh, by the way, Casey said she was going for a pre-breakfast lap fest in the pool if you want to join her."

I said goodbye to Chris and gave Dora her space, making my way back up to the house. Casey was ready to jump in the pool, so I quickly ran upstairs, got into my suit, and was able to join her for lap three.

We had a delightful day exploring the grounds, and all too soon it was time for Casey and Chris to go home, leaving me alone in the house for the first time.

I hugged Chris, then Casey a little longer.

"Are you sure you're going to be okay?" she asked me.

"Sure," I answered, although I really wasn't. Everything had been wonderful all weekend, until Casey started packing her overnight bag. Then I started to get a little shaky about this whole thing again.

"You can call me any time, and drive over to visit any time too. We'll get together next weekend for sure."

"Please feel free to drive the car; it's better for it not to sit idle," Chris joined in.

"Maybe tomorrow I'll go into town then," I replied.

I knew that Chris had taken Hal's car for a spin this afternoon, filling the gas tank and making sure that it was running properly. He had left me directions to Casey's apartment written in a notebook on the kitchen counter, along with the security code to the house, and other things he thought I should know.

Casey closed the door to the Jeep and sat with the basket of strawberries on her lap, then Chris started the engine. I waved goodbye as they backed down the driveway. Casey called out the window, "I'll call you tonight!"

I watched until they were out of sight, then I sighed heavily and strolled down toward the pier. Once again I sat on the bench, listening and watching. I heard a "Quack!" and saw Dora slowly sashaying towards me. She circled around, eyeing me up, then came to sit right next to my feet, with another "Quack!"

I'll be darned.

CHAPTER TWENTY TWO

My first full day on the job went well. After spending another dawn on the pier and doing some morning laps, I poked around in the garage and found some gardening gloves, then spent the afternoon tidying up the front flower beds and making friends with the little lizards scampering around. After a dinner of grilled chicken breast and salad, I settled myself in a cozy chair on the back porch and ate my bowl of strawberries while I watched the sunset. Then I parked myself inside once it got dark. Surprisingly, I wasn't afraid in the house, probably because of the security system, but I felt a little apprehensive yet about sitting outside alone after the sun went down.

On the second day, after enjoying what had become my morning rituals, I once again did some gardening and found a real gem on the side of the house. A lemon tree full of fruit! I picked a basketful and made fresh lemonade for lunch. After that I called Abbey to gloat.

"Oh, that's just super, Ellen. Thanks for sharing. I just harvested a whole batch of snowballs," Abbey had snapped back.

By day three, even though I had talked to Casey every evening and spoken to Adam and Abbey yesterday, I needed face to face human contact. I decided to take a trip into town.

I left early in the morning and neatly parallel parked Hal's Subaru in a spot under a huge cypress tree on the circle surrounding the lake in town. After locking the car and placing the keys in my shorts pocket along with my cell phone, I began my first lap on the paved track. Even though the early morning air was still cool, I knew from my experience of the last couple days that before long the heat would be radiating off the pavement, making walking at a fast clip very uncomfortable.

I suppose that's why so many people were out so early on a weekday. There were tons of people, all shapes and sizes and age groups. I lapped baby buggy mama as she struggled to push her infant in a carriage with a toddler hanging on the back, and felt pretty good until yellow shorts co-ed chick with her iPod lapped *me* twice.

After my walk, I crossed the street and took a stroll down the sidewalk, window shopping and getting acquainted with the town. Passing an art supply store, I stopped and looked in the window. I had a sudden urge to sketch. In my younger days I always carried a sketchbook with me, but I hadn't thought of that for many years.

I purchased a turkey and swiss bagel sandwich and a large iced green tea, after I had made my selections at the art store, and took them back to a picnic table by the lake, diving into the paper bag holding the pad and pencils first. I had almost completed a sketch of the lake and trees before I even unwrapped my sandwich.

Buggy mama with her baby and toddler in tow walked past and smiled.

"You're really good!" she said as she glanced over my shoulder.

"Really? Thanks!" I replied, smiling. I wondered if she was just being nice, or if I still had some talent lurking in there somewhere. At any rate, it was relaxing and probably good therapy. I think it would be Dr. Burke approved.

I finished my sandwich, took my art supplies to the car, and began the drive back home. I decided to stop by the gas station we had passed on the first day. Homemade ice cream sounded delightful!

While I waited my turn, I pulled a handful of postcards from the black metal revolving rack. I could have some fun sending these. I indulged in an orange creamsicle flavor on a sugar cone, well worth doing a few extra laps in the pool or on the track.

Feeling a little lazy, I decided to forego the gardening today, gathering my art supplies and postcards and making myself comfortable in the turquoise print cushion of a white wicker settee on the back porch. I had taken a photo of the lake on my cell phone, and I was using that to add the finishing details to my sketch.

I could hear the gentle waves lapping against the shore, an occasional bird squawking, and…someone's flip flops coming up the sidewalk?

I peered over the top of my reading glasses and saw a woman in jungle print capris, a lemon yellow tank top, and a matching plastic yellow sun visor walking down the sidewalk. Her white hair was cropped in a short, spiked style and tinted on the ends with shades of hot pink and baby blue. She flopped up to the screen door and walked right in, like it was something she did every day.

I stared at her, my charcoal pencil poised above my drawing.

"Hi y'all, is Hal here?" she said with an engaging smile.

"No, not at the moment," I replied, setting down my project and quickly standing up.

"Is he back from his vacation? I saw the lights on over here the last few nights and figured he was back."

"Are you a friend of Hal's?" I asked.

"You might say that…are *you*?" she shot back.

"I'm more like an employee."

She took off her pearl white framed sunglasses and looked speculatively at me with beautiful light blue eyes. She had a kind face, and even though I knew she had to be old enough to qualify for the senior citizen discount coffee at the Burger Express, I couldn't pinpoint just how old she was. The blue and pink tints were throwing me off. She had a tan that definitely didn't come from a tanning bed or a bronzing potion, and a slim, well-maintained figure. Her style was eccentric meets elegant, but she really made it work.

"Is that so?" she asked putting her hand on her hip, exuding an "I take crap from no one" attitude.

I decided to trust her– mostly because I figured she'd slap me silly if I didn't spill the beans.

"I'm house sitting for Hal. He fell and broke his hip while he was on his trip."

Her demeanor changed instantly.

"Oh my stars! I'm so sorry to hear that! Is he goin' to be okay?" Her hand went from her hip to splay over her chest.

I briefly filled her in on the pertinent details.

"By the way, I'm Sylvia," she said, extending her hand, which had a ring on every finger. "I live next door."

"I'm Ellen," I accepted her handshake. "Next door?"

"In the trailer park on the other side of the orange grove. Only we call them modular homes. Mine's the pink one. You can kind of see it from here."

My gaze followed her perfectly French manicured finger. I could make out about twenty modular homes in various colors about a half-mile beyond the orange grove to my right, mostly hidden from view by palm trees and tall grasses growing at the lake's edge. And yes, when I squinted, I could see one in pastel pink.

"You're from up north, aren't you?" Sylvia asked, assessing me.

Once again, I wasn't sure how much I really wanted to

tell a stranger about my situation, so I tried to give her the abbreviated version of my story.

"Yes, I am, near Pittsburgh. My daughter lives in Orlando and is friends with Hal's grandson, Chris. That's how I came to be here."

Sylvia cracked her gum and looked pensive. Her scrutiny was a little unnerving.

"So, how long are you goin' to be here?" she finally asked.

"A few months maybe. I'm not really sure," I answered shrugging my shoulders.

A smile suddenly lit up her face, signaling that she had dismissed whatever negative thoughts about me that she had been struggling with.

"Well, maybe *you'd* like to come then!"

I was confused. "Come *where*?"

"Oh, I thought I told you." She swished her hand through the air like she was backhanding a fly. "I'm turning into my forgetful sister!"

"I came over to ask Hal to go to the prom with me Saturday night, but since he's not here, maybe you'd like to go?"

If I was confused before, now I was over the edge.

"To the prom?"

"You're looking at me like I'm daffy! Don't they have proms up north?"

"Well, yes," I answered, "When you graduate from high school."

"Same thing. Over at the clubhouse we're havin' a buffet dinner, a band playin' fifties music, and some raffles. You can dress up in a gown if you like, but you don't have to. I wouldn't imagine you brought one with you anyways."

"No...I left all my gowns at home."

She squinted at me, then smiled again. "I like a sense of humor, Ellen. You and I are goin' to get along famously!"

I was curious about something. "So, are you and Hal dating?"

Her face registered shock. "Mercy, no!" she exclaimed, putting her hand to her chest again. "Although he *is* a mighty handsome man, and as gentlemanly as they come. He's had a hard time of it, though, since his Louise passed. We're just friends is all. I met him last summer up at Biggley's. We were both buyin' fresh squeezed orange juice, and I noticed him looking a bit lonely and struck up a conversation."

Why didn't that surprise me?

"Got him to come over to the clubhouse and play pool with the boys a few times, and it seemed like he was just startin' to come out of his shell...goin' on the trip and all. What a shame that happened to him." She looked down, shaking her head from side to side.

"So, are you comin' then?" she asked, jerking her head up.

"Well, I'm not sure. Can I get back to you on that?"

"What *else* have you got to do?" she persisted.

"Well, my daughter said we were getting together this weekend, and I'm not sure what day. But, Sylvia, thank you so much for asking me."

She cracked her gum again, digesting that information.

"How about I pick you up tomorrow and you can come over and meet the girls? I'll make lunch. It's a shame you sittin' here all by yourself all day."

Oh, geez. I sure didn't want to be rude. I guess it wouldn't hurt to have some new friends in the neighborhood.

"That sounds very nice; I guess I can come over for a little while. What can I bring?"

Her face glowed with satisfaction. "Just yourself, darlin'. I'll pick you up at eleven, nothin' fancy."

She turned to leave and stopped to look at my sketchpad.

"What are you workin' on here?" she asked as she turned her head to get a better angle.

"Oh, just something I started today after my walk. I was just adding the finishing details."

"Mighty fine work, Miss Ellen, if I do say so myself!"

Sylvia started toward the door again, hesitated, and turned around, giving me an impulsive hug. I caught the sweet scent of her citrus cologne as she gave me a light squeeze.

"Yep, we're goin' to be best of friends, Miss Ellen!" Then she abruptly turned on her heel and flip-flopped up the sidewalk.

I walked over to the door and peered through the screen as she climbed into a tricked out, hot pink golf cart. No wonder I didn't hear her pull in the driveway. She gave me a big smile, tooted her bicycle horn with an "oooogaaaa," and silently pulled the cart onto a wide dirt path that disappeared behind the orange grove.

I stood there dumbfounded. A tiny green lizard climbing up the screen caught my eye. I watched him scurry across the screen and exit through a teeny space at the bottom of the door. What on earth did I just agree to?

The next morning, I washed out the green plastic basket that my strawberries were in and filled it with lemons from Hal's tree, thinking that Sylvia might enjoy them. I used the colored pencils that I had bought yesterday to fashion a little note card, and just as I was placing it in the basket, I heard Sylvia hollering from the porch.

"Miss Ellen, are you ready?"

A few minutes later I was seated next to Sylvia, bumping along in the golf cart down a dirt path through the trees. She explained that the orange grove and Lakeside, where she lived, were both owned by the same company, so we weren't trespassing.

When we emerged from the grove, we were right at the entrance to Lakeside, landmarked by a larger than life American flag at the top of a huge pole, which at the moment was gently billowing in the breeze. I could hear the fabric rustling above us as Sylvia expertly maneuvered the cart onto the pavement, punched a series of numbers into the security system, and continued driving through the open gate onto Marybelle Lane.

"My street is right around the corner, but I'll take you on a quick tour before we stop." She pointed with her finger, which I noticed was painted crimson today, indicating all the important features of Lakeside.

It really was quite a nice place, not at all what I expected. There was a tan brick clubhouse with a screened-in porch. I could see perhaps a dozen or so wooden rockers lined up inside. An Olympic-sized pool was adjacent to the porch, along with shuffleboard courts and a horseshoe pit.

She made a sharp right onto Lookout Point, and I could see Lake Juliet! There was a large fishing pier and at least a dozen boats moored at the dock. A second clubhouse sat next to another swimming pool, this pool a little smaller, but shaped in a figure eight.

"This one has a hot tub," Sylvia boasted. "And that's the clubhouse where the boys play pool and we have our meetings."

All the homes were very well-maintained, and each one had some sort of decorative sign out front telling the name of the occupant and where they were from, mostly north of the Mason-Dixon line. They really *weren't* my idea of trailers, but more modular homes, just like Sylvia had said.

"We get lots of snowbirds here. Folks come from up north to spend the winter then fly away come summer."

It seemed that Sylvia knew all the residents of Lakeside. She called out greetings to everyone we passed.

I admired how all the driveways seemed to be stenciled with different patterns and colors, and that each home was landscaped beautifully with palm trees, shrubs, and flowers. We swung around the office building and rounded the corner to put us back on Marybelle.

Sylvia slowed down and turned into a tidy pink-sided home, the driveway stenciled in light pink palm fronds on which several other golf carts were parked.

"Looks like the gang's all here!" Sylvia said, smiling.

She hopped out of the cart, skirting the terra cotta pots full of brilliant pink snapdragons, and came around to my side, grabbing the basket of lemons from the storage compartment as she rounded the back of the cart.

"That was so sweet of you, Miss Ellen; we'll put these to

good use!"

She led me up four concrete steps, past a brass wind chime hanging from the sloped side of the carport roof, and opened the screen door to the front room. My first impression was of how spacious her home felt. Even with the living room full of women staring at me, it didn't feel crowded.

"Hi, everyone! This is my new friend, Ellen!"

"Hello, everyone," I said as introductions were made.

The most surprising was Sophia.

"This is my sister, Sophia. We live here together," Sylvia explained.

I extended my hand, and she gripped it firmly.

"Glad to meet 'cha," Sophia said, pumping my hand. "We're twins, ya know."

My mouth must have been hanging open, because Sylvia piped up, "Twins don't have to be identical!"

The only thing remotely "twin-like" was their identical light blue eyes. Sylvia's wardrobe was eccentric, and today she was sporting cherry-red walking shorts and a royal blue tank top covered in a silver sequin design. Sophia was wearing a drab, blue polyester pants suit. Sylvia's feet were tucked into silver ballet shoes, while Sophia was wearing sensible, thick-soled, white sneakers. Today Sylvia's hair tints were gone, but she had it all spiked up with gel and was wearing a red visor that coordinated with her shorts. Sophia's hair was short and gray and appeared to have been "set" at the beauty parlor.

We left the women chatting, probably about me, while Sylvia gave me a tour. I was surprised to see that it was a three-bedroom, one for Sylvia and one for Sophia; I gasped when I walked into the third. It was wall to wall Christmas! Long tables lined each wall, covered in the most authentic looking fake snow

I've ever seen. There must have been hundreds of miniature ceramic houses, stores, and churches all set up to look like a tiny town. I moved in for a closer inspection. It was a village from England, complete with taverns, fish and chip establishments, and chapels. The town was embellished with little townspeople decorating tiny Christmas trees, roasting chestnuts, and walking dogs. I recognized some of the buildings from stories that I've read...

"It's a Dickens village!" I exclaimed.

Sylvia was grinning ear to ear at my delight.

"We've been collecting village pieces for years and years! Finally it just got to be too much to put it up and take it down every year, so we decided to just put it up and leave it up. Pretty, isn't it? Wait until you see it at night with all the little houses lit up."

I turned to look her in the eye. "Sylvia, it's just magnificent!" I had never seen a display done with such painstaking detail, not even in the department store windows in Pittsburgh. I would have loved to stay and scrutinize it a little more, but I didn't want to appear rude to the other guests. I would definitely have to come back!

Sylvia served scrumptious chicken salad sandwiches, fresh fruit salad, and iced tea in tall glasses, each embellished with a slice of a lemon from Hal's tree.

"Would you like another piece of cake, dear?" Sophia asked me.

"Oh, I'd love one, but I've been trying to cut back on desserts; they're my downfall!" The cake *was* really yummy. It was some kind of pineapple angel food garnished with fresh strawberries.

Choosing to ignore my answer, Sophia plopped another piece of cake on my plate.

"This cake isn't bad for you. It's low fat, don't worry! Sylvia eats it all the time, and look at her."

I looked at Sylvia, and she rolled her eyes at me. "Just humor her and eat it, dear."

"I saw that!" Sophia chided. "All you do is add one can of crushed pineapple, including the liquid, to a box of angel food cake mix, and bake. What's so bad about that?"

I was amazed at that recipe; only two ingredients? In fact, it had been an amazing afternoon. As reluctant as I was at first to visit with Sylvia today, I was so very glad that I did.

When Sylvia dropped me off back at my house, which astonishingly is how I have come to think of it over the last several days, she invited herself over for a visit the following day. I had to smile at her tenacity, but I really had enjoyed her company today, and after I waved goodbye and watched until the pink golf cart had been gobbled up by the orange grove, I actually felt her absence. She kind of reminded me of what Abbey might be like thirty years from now. I shook my head and couldn't help smiling at that thought.

On Saturday, I drove over to help Sylvia get ready for the prom. I was going to dinner with Casey, but strangely enough I had gotten caught up in the excitement of the event after spending so much time in Sylvia's company this week. Besides, I was just plain curious. I pulled in under the carport and made my way up the steps.

"Come in, dear!"

It was Sophia who answered my knock. She was sort of stuffed into an aqua, off the shoulder number that fit snugly across her bosom, then billowed out with mountains of tulle. I could see beads of sweat already forming on her brow.

"Hi, Sophia! My, don't you look fancy!" I closed the

screen door behind me, and as I turned, Sophia grabbed my hand and led me to her room.

"Could you please zip me up all the way? I've been struggling with this dang zipper for fifteen minutes! There must be some sort of problem with it. Can you take a look?"

I suppressed a giggle as I surveyed the situation. Apparently, the "problem" was about an inch of compressed flesh.

"Here, let's try this," I said as I fastened the eye hook at the top. "Now, push your shoulders back and hold your breath a moment...there!"

Sophia turned to admire herself in front of the mirror.

"Damn!" we heard Sylvia's voice from the other room.

I made my way down the hallway to her bedroom door, leaving Sophia to squeeze her feet into her aqua pumps on her own accord. My hand flew to my mouth, "Oh, Sylvia! You look beautiful!"

She had gone for the Audrey Hepburn look and had achieved it magnificently! I was accustomed to the flamboyant, flashy Sylvia, but today she had toned it down about a dozen notches.

Her slim figure was poured into a simple, floor-length sheath of Caribbean blue, accentuating the brilliance of her blue eyes. She had teased her white hair into a bouffant style and had expertly applied her makeup with a light hand. A single strand of pearls adorned her throat, with tiny matching pearls on her ear lobes. She looked stunning!

"I just can't find the right *ring*!" she whined, creasing her brow as she rummaged through a jewelry box that must have housed a couple hundred of them. This is the first time I had ever seen her hands without bling. "I just want to wear *one* tonight, but it has to be the *perfect* one." Sylvia was a person who paid close attention to detail, and I knew this night meant a lot to her.

A light bulb went off in my head. "Sylvia, I may have the answer! I'll be right back."

In record time, I drove home, ran to the bedroom and rummaged around in my travel jewelry bag for the blue sapphire, my prize purchase from the home shopping channel, and hopped back in the car. Sylvia would love it!

Minutes later, I could feel the beads of sweat on my own brow as I took the steps two at a time and barged through her front door. I slipped the ring on her finger, and *magic*! It looked just like it had on TV. Why couldn't *I* pull it off? On my hand it looked utterly gaudy, but on Sylvia's, it looked absolutely elegant! She was happy as a clam, and kept holding out her hand to inspect it.

"Oh, Ellen, thank you so much! I'll take very good care of it for you!"

"Sylvia, consider it a gift. It was *meant* for you to wear, not me."

"I insist," I added when she opened her mouth to protest.

I chauffeured the ladies down to the clubhouse for the promenade. They had made plans with one of the men to bring them home so they wouldn't have to drive in their gowns.

The promenade, which consisted of a walk down the sidewalk in front of the clubhouse, was a spectacle, to say the least! Some of the men, who still *had* hair, had fashioned it into pompadours and slicked it back into ducktails, and a few who weren't as fortunate, or didn't have a knack for using hair gel, were sporting fedoras angled low over their foreheads.

"Oh, my! Herb looks like Humphry Bogart in his hat!" Sophia exclaimed as I pulled into the parking space.

Sylvia had feigned disinterest, but I caught the blush on

her cheek as he opened the car door for her.

I pulled out my camera like a proud parent and snapped lots of pictures. The promenade was a kaleidoscope of chiffon, silk, and polyester, but no one could compare to Sylvia as she turned and waved goodbye before slipping through the clubhouse door.

I felt a little melancholy as I drove over to Casey's. My thoughts turned to Hal, and I wondered if he would have gone to the prom with Sylvia had he not broken his hip. The residents of Lakeside really had a sense of community and truly enjoyed each other's company. It was nice to see that. I guess I was still feeling a little uprooted.

Casey and Chris were waiting for me by the pool. We had decided to go out to dinner for a change.

"Mom! You look great! Look how tan you are!" Casey exclaimed as we hugged.

I pulled out my camera and was showing her the prom pictures when Brooklyn appeared.

"Why, hello Ellen!" he called out. "Casey, Chris..."

He joined our little circle and shook hands with Chris, flashing his brilliant smile my way.

"Are you back for another weekend, Ellen?" he asked me.

"No, just dinner this time," I replied as I put my camera back in my purse.

"I was just going to dinner myself," he explained. Dressed in khaki pants and a black shirt that hugged his body, he looked very fetching.

Casey elbowed me gently and raised her eyebrows when I looked at her.

Call me crazy, or call me a bit jealous that my friends, who were at least twenty years my senior, were out having a good time socializing, but I decided to do it.

"Would you like to join us for dinner?" I casually asked him.

"Well, now, that depends…if you let me treat, I'd be happy to join you!"

My eyes opened wide. "Brooklyn, that would be entirely too much!"

"Small price to pay for an evening of being in the company of such beautiful women."

Chris put his arm around Casey and good-naturedly cleared his throat.

Brooklyn flashed him another smile, then looked in my direction. "Ah, Chris, I think this one here will be more than I can handle!"

Then he followed Chris's cue and put his arm around me. I felt a few butterflies flutter in my belly.

At Brooklyn's suggestion– especially since he was paying– we decided on dining at a steakhouse on International Boulevard. We piled into his mint condition, midnight black Lincoln Continental. I felt like it was a limo taking *me* to the prom!

The conversation in the car was light and humorous as Brooklyn expertly maneuvered us down the tourist-clogged boulevard. Jack would have been cursing the traffic and muttering obscenities under his breath.

We had a round of pre-dinner cocktails in the lounge, then we were led to a corner table with a cream colored linen tablecloth and a candle glowing in a faceted, garnet red holder.

I placed the linen napkin on my lap and opened the menu. I felt someone kick my foot under the table and looked up to see Casey peeping at me over the top of her menu. Her lips made a silent "Wow." I lowered my eyes and looked at the prices…holy cow!

Dinner was fabulous, and Brooklyn could not be swayed from his offer of picking up the check. I liked Brooklyn. He was handsome and interesting, and I knew he was trying to impress me, but I did feel a bit uncomfortable with him spending so much.

We returned to the lounge after dinner for dancing. They had a live band playing cover music of the soft, adult contemporary variety. I was enjoying myself immensely, although Brooklyn held me a little closer and a little more familiarly with each slow dance. At first, it just felt strange to be in the arms of another man, but by the end of the evening I was getting used to it, and the butterflies had calmed down a little.

Brooklyn held my hand as we all walked back to the car in the humid, sultry night air, I have to admit that it felt a little awkward to me, like holding the hand of a stranger, which he almost still was.

I had intended on just having dinner with Casey and then driving back to Lake Juliet, but it was already past midnight, and I was a little nervous about making the drive alone so late.

"Just stay at my place tonight, Mom," Casey offered. "Then you can take your time driving home in the morning."

I weighed the decision. I didn't want to put Casey out, but I really didn't feel like driving almost an hour. This was a late night for me.

"Okay, only if I sleep on the couch," I replied, and Casey rolled her eyes at me.

Once we drove away from the bright lights of the still bustling International Boulevard, we were subdued by the darkness of the car, lulled into a state of relaxation, and conversation was minimal. Brooklyn covered my hand with his, moving his thumb rhythmically, all the while keeping his eyes on the road. I rested my head back against the leather seat, feeling the cool air from the vent on my face, and stared out into the darkness.

Brooklyn walked up the staircase to Casey's apartment with me. Casey had decided to stop at Chris's apartment for a while before coming home, so she unlocked her door for me before going across the hall. She gave Brooklyn a little hug, and Chris shook his hand.

"Thanks for dinner, man," Chris said. "Next time it's on us."

"Yes, thank you, Brooklyn. That was very nice of you! Don't wait up for me Mom," Casey added, giving me a wink.

And then they were in Chris's apartment and the door clicked shut…which left me in the hallway with Brooklyn, feeling very uncomfortable. I took a deep breath and turned around. Brooklyn took me in his arms and kissed me quickly, taking my breath away.

Still holding me close, he smiled, "That was so you wouldn't get away from me this time."

And I remembered the peck on the cheek I gave him last week.

He held the back of my head softly but firmly, and came in for another, this time slower and gentler, probing me to reciprocate. I was still and frozen, taking in all the new feelings of him. His muscles were hard as my hands wrapped around his back, and I could feel *his* warm hands on my bare back. *How did he get his hands under my shirt?*

I couldn't think, only feel. His lips were on mine, and he was gently pushing me inside Casey's apartment, closing the door with his foot. His hand was on my belly, riding up. I covered his hand with mine and pushed it down. He moved his lips from my mouth, trailing down the side of my neck, planting flaming hot kisses all the way to my shoulder.

Carnal instincts took over, and I released his hand, pulling his face to mine and giving him the return kisses he had been wanting, suddenly craving them myself. He was confident and experienced and had me under his spell...until I felt his hand on my breast.

I pushed away and inhaled deeply.

"Brooklyn, I'm not ready for this," I said as I ran my hands through my hair with trembling fingers.

He just stood there looking at me for a moment, disappointment registering on his face; then he gave me a quick hug and set me free.

"I thought maybe you'd be saying that," he stated simply.

"I'm sorry," I said as I put my hand on the doorknob.

His hand covered mine. "I said I was patient, Ellen, but I also said I was persistent."

"Thank you so much for dinner. That was very generous of you. I really had a great time dancing, but I think we need to call it a night," I managed to blubber as I turned the knob and opened the door a crack.

He put his finger under my chin and tipped my head up, planting a single kiss on my lips.

"Until next time," he said as he walked out the door, shutting it behind him.

CHAPTER TWENTY THREE

I stood there a moment, trying to collect myself and waiting for the trembling to stop. At least I didn't have a panic attack, but I needed a cool shower!

Afterward, I borrowed one of Casey's nightshirts and snuggled up on the couch, wrapped in a fuzzy, blue blanket to ward of the chill of the air conditioner. I had shocked myself by what I had done with Brooklyn! I'd only known the man a week, and already he had touched me where only one man had ever touched me before. There wasn't a doubt in my mind that if I wouldn't have stopped him when he was trying to get friendly with the girls, he would have made himself right at home with the rest of me. I guess now I knew the answer to how the dating game is played at this stage of my life.

But I wasn't ready to get intimate with Brooklyn, or anyone else for that matter. I *liked* him, but I didn't have real feelings for him. Yes, I could see how things could get out of hand. It felt so good to be kissed and held like that again…but something was missing, and I knew that. It made me feel a little embarrassed that I had let things get so out of control. I never should have let him into Casey's apartment.

I heard Casey come in later, but I pretended to be asleep. I didn't want to discuss this with her tonight, or maybe *ever*! How much should parents tell their children about their love life?

Had I really only been here a week? It was hard to comprehend that. So much had changed, and I'd met so many people…had so many new experiences…ha! That's for sure!

I slept fitfully and woke up feeling completely unrested. I wasn't able to fit into Casey's shorts, but for comfort's sake, I did borrow a tank top, in lieu of my silk button down, to wear home with my dress pants. I was happy that she didn't push me for details about my time alone with Brooklyn, but she was gushing over our dinner at the restaurant.

"He must be loaded, Mom! The check for dinner was probably over three hundred dollars!" she said with a mouthful of bagel.

I shrugged my shoulders. I didn't need to have someone spend money on me to win my affection.

"Looks like he really likes you! What do you think?" she asked me.

"I don't know, sweetie. It's all very strange and a little premature of me to think I could have feelings for someone. It might be nice to have someone to go places with and have fun, but I don't think I want to get serious with anyone yet. I *did* have a really good time last night though." I scraped the crumbs off the tabletop with my hand and threw them in the trash, offering her a tiny smile.

Casey walked me down to my car, and I scurried through the pool area.

"What's the rush?" she asked me.

I just didn't want to run into Brooklyn. I wasn't in the mood to deal with him right now; I needed to think about this situation a little on my own.

"Was I rushing?" I answered as I slowed down my steps a bit. My car was in sight, so I felt safe now.

I gave Casey a hug, started the engine, and found my way back to I-4.

When I turned into the driveway, Sylvia's golf cart was parked next to the house, and she was sitting on the front step waiting for me.

I put the car in park, closed my eyes, and sighed. Then I grabbed my purse and went to face the music.

"Just where were *you* all night, missy?" Sylvia asked with what I assume was mock sincerity.

"Gee, Sylvia, what happened to hello?"

"Hello. So, where were you?" she persisted.

Instead of being annoyed, it made me laugh. She looked so adorable sitting on the step with her arms crossed in front of her and her chin jutting out, as if she were accusing me of being on an adventure and forgetting to include her. Today's tank top and visor were sky blue, and her eyes looked fierce beneath the brim.

I took a seat on the step beside her, putting my elbows on my knees and my chin in my hands.

"Oh Sylvia, why is life so complicated?" I asked with a sigh.

Her expression softened, and she rubbed her hand across my back.

"Sounds like you need a heart to heart. Let's go inside where it's cooler and chat."

I must have "chatted" for a couple of hours straight. It was the quietest I've seen Sylvia since we've met! She was an unexpectedly good listener, and once I started telling my story, the whole sordid thing came out. All about Jack, the house, and my panic attacks. I even told her what happened with Brooklyn. Aside from a few "uh-huhs" and "oh my's" she let me ramble on, and when a few tears found their way down my cheeks, she pulled a travel pack of pink Kleenex out of her fanny pack and offered them to me.

This week had been a surreal experience, but in a good way. I had stepped outside of my life, and aside from a phone call or two from Adam, had distanced myself completely from home. I had enjoyed myself, tried new things, and met new people. I guess that was the reason I had come. But it felt good to share my life with Sylvia. She had rapidly become a close friend, and now a confidant. I had thought that I didn't want anyone here to know about my personal life, but I found that even though I still didn't want my issues broadcast all around Lake Juliet, I needed someone to know. I still had the need to talk about things with someone I trusted.

"Ellen, you've had a rough time of it, dear, and it takes a lot of courage to tell somebody all those things about yourself. I'll tell you my story some day, but let me tell you this much now…I made up my mind long ago that every day the good Lord gives me, I am goin' to choose to be happy and make the best out of it that I can. People can either rest on their laurels and go nowhere, or they can make things happen. I choose to make things happen…in case you didn't pick up on that," she finished with a grin.

"By the way, I won prom queen last night."

I sighed and smiled. Sylvia was just the comic relief I needed.

"That's wonderful!"

"Well, it was luck of the draw. We just put our names in Herb's gray felt fedora, actually. Nobody voted or anything. But I got a plastic crown and a $25 gift card for the Gator Buffet!"

"Well, that sounds exciting!" I answered, still smiling.

"Hey, I have an idea! Let's go bike ridin' later on; the exercise will clear your mind. There's a bike in the garage you can use. I know, because I saw Hal use it. You can ride on over and we'll ride around Lakeside. I'll pack us some sandwiches and we can eat dinner on the dock. Tuna okay?"

"Sounds wonderful."

"Come over around three, that way you'll be back here before it gets dark."

After Sylvia left, I sat on the chaise and picked up my sketchpad, but after two hours, the charcoal pencil still hadn't made a stroke on the paper. I sat and stared at the lake, and I think I must have dozed off for a bit, because when my cell phone rang, I jumped.

The caller ID revealed that it was Brooklyn, and I remembered the night we had punched each other's numbers into our cells. How strange that I had never had the desire to call him, and I didn't want to talk to him now either, so I just let it ring. Figured I'd listen to his message, then decide if I wanted to call him back.

I waited for the "beep" signaling that I had a voice mail, but it never came. He didn't leave a message, and that kind of annoyed me. Sylvia was right. I needed some exercise to clear my mind.

She was also right about the bike. In fact, there were two. I wheeled out the one that must have belonged to Louise and pumped air in the tires with a hand pump that I found on the metal shelf next to the bikes.

I hadn't ridden in a while; the last time was a few summers ago when we went as a family to Presque Isle on Lake Erie and rented bicycles to ride on the trail around the shore...back when everything seemed perfect.

Hopping up on the narrow seat, I took a test spin around the driveway, and once I had my balance, turned onto the dirt path through the orange grove. I arrived promptly at three to find Sylvia and Sophia waiting for me, their bikes parked under the carport.

We rode leisurely around the streets first, and this time I was able to shout greetings to a few of the women that I met that first day at Sylvia's; then we stopped back at her house to pick up the picnic basket.

By the time I was biting into my tuna on wheat, I was feeling a lot better.

Someone with great foresight had placed a picnic table at the edge of the pier, and the three of us sat there in compatible silence, watching a few men fishing and an occasional bird do a flyby looking for a handout.

"What *is* that noise?" Sylvia said, looking around.

"That faint beeping? I hear it too," I said.

Sophia had wandered over to inspect a catfish that one of the men had just reeled in.

Sylvia pulled out her cell. "It's not my phone; is it yours?"

"Nope."

She swung her legs over the bench and stood up, walking slowly around the pier.

"That's a mighty fine catch! Do you like catfish, Ellen?" Sophia asked me, reclaiming her seat on the other side of the table.

The beeping sounded a little louder now. "Can't say that I've ever eaten it. Is it good?"

Sylvia had walked the immediate perimeter of the dock and returned to the table. She cocked her head and walked slowly toward Sophia.

"Catfish is delightful! You should try it, Ellen. Sylvia has a wonderful—*hey*! What are you doing?"

Sylvia had put her head up against Sophia's chest.

"Sophia, that's *you* beeping!" she exclaimed.

"I know; do you think I'm *deaf*?" Sophia addressed Sylvia indignantly.

Sylvia backed away and spread her arms out, turning her palms up, shouting for emphasis, *"Why are you beeping?"*

"It's my pacemaker! The battery's low," Sophia answered calmly.

My hand flew to my mouth.

Sylvia exhaled loudly and started hurriedly throwing things back in the picnic basket. "Sophia, don't you think we should go get that fixed, honey?"

"We're going tomorrow, my appointment is at eight in the morning...remember, I told you?"

This time Sylvia was indignant, and put her hands on her hips.

"You did *not* tell me!"

"I called the doctor this morning, when I first heard myself beep. He said it's just a warning that the battery in my pacemaker is low. It's no big deal. He scheduled me to come in to his office at Lakeland Memorial tomorrow morning for a change out. I *know* I told you this morning."

"I wasn't even *home* this morning! I was over at Ellen's."

"Oh... maybe I told Kathy then."

Sylvia made the sign of the cross on her chest and sat back down on the bench next to me.

I had agreed to accompany them to Sophia's appointment in Lakeland. Sylvia had suggested that I come along to keep her company, and we could browse through some antique shops while her sister was getting her change out. Apparently this was an outpatient deal. Sometimes I just have a hard time wrapping my brain around the fact that medical science has come so far.

Sylvia pulled up bright and early in her inferno red PT Cruiser. Sophia was already tucked into the back seat, so I slid into the front next to Sylvia. It was a convertible model, but we were not riding open air this morning.

After Sophia was admitted, we did some window shopping at an adorable little shop not far from Lakeland Memorial. There were so many things I would have loved to buy, but two things held me back from buying. Number one: I had no money. Number two: I had no home. I was feeling the need for a cupcake.

When we picked Sophia up, she appeared to be totally recharged.

"Hey! There's a Gator Buffet!" Sophia exclaimed, leaning into the front seat and thrusting her pointer finger between Sylvia and me. "Let's stop and use your gift card! I'm starving!"

Minutes later, I was standing at the salad bar behind Sophia, waiting for her to finish with the salad dressing. My chilled plate was heaped with green leaf spinach, diced carrots, black olives, cherry tomatoes, garbanzo beans, and grated cheddar cheese. I was wrestling with myself about whether to add a spoonful of bacon bits or not, and just as I decided that one little spoonful couldn't be *too* bad for you, Sophia turned to me with a big smile on her face.

"You'll have to try this one," she said as she replaced the white plastic ladle into a container, "It says local, so they must make it themselves right here."

Sophia moved on to the bread basket, and I looked at the dressing containers, with Sylvia peering curiously over my shoulder. Ranch, French, Italian, bleu cheese, and lo cal house.

I looked at Sylvia and burst out laughing. She shook her head and said, "Just let it go, dear."

We made our way over to the dessert table after we finished our soup and salad. It had been taunting me all through my meal, beckoning me to come and partake of its goodness. There was cake calling my name, and it had been deafening. It seemed so long since I've allowed myself a big piece of double-layered heaven! I figured it was my reward for putting back the bacon bits.

I chose a colossal piece of chocolate on chocolate, a PMS dream come true. I gave myself points for being conscientious enough to cut it in two and wrap half in a paper napkin to slip into my purse for later consumption.

Then I took that plastic fork in hand and dug in. Putting a bite in my mouth, I closed my eyes, letting the velvety, moist chocolate cake and satiny, smooth fudge icing massage my taste buds into a frenzy.

I opened my eyes and found Sylvia and Sophia staring at me.

"What?" I exclaimed, shoveling in another bite.

"You know, Ellen, you should get out more," Sylvia suggested.

Once every crumb of cake was gone from my plate, Sylvia cashed in her gift card and we piled back into the Cruiser. This time she put down the convertible top. She pulled out a canvas bag from her trunk that contained a rainbow of plastic visors and held it open for Sophia to make her choice. Then she offered one to me.

"I think I'll just go au natural," I replied, feeling brave.

Sylvia huffed and returned the bag to the trunk.

"You'll be sorry."

I felt giddy with delight as the wind tousled my hair and whipped it against my face—it was almost a disappointment when we slowed down to turn into Hal's driveway.

"Sylvia, that was amazing!" I exclaimed.

As we turned the bend in the driveway, we almost ran into a rusted old pickup truck that was parked right in the center.

"What the heck!" I murmured.

There were six or seven men standing under the oak tree, all holding long poles with hooks on the end, reaching up into the branches.

"They're harvesting the Spanish moss," Sylvia said simply.

A tall, slim man with a shirtless tanned torso approached the Cruiser. He rattled off about forty seconds worth of Spanish, the only words connecting with my brain being Senor Hal.

Sophia piped up from the back seat, spewing a reply in Spanish right back to him.

Sophia spoke Spanish...who knew?

I looked at Sylvia, who shrugged her shoulders at me, and I turned around to face her sister with a new respect.

"He said that Hal allows them to come and trim the Spanish moss from his trees," Sophia said.

"Do you think that's okay?" I asked no one in particular. Being the caretaker, I felt responsible.

"I think so," Sylvia replied, "The trees need to have the moss trimmed every so often. They're doing Hal a favor, and he's doing them one. They probably travel around to all the neighborhoods. It's a pretty common thing. I don't think they're

Spanish moss robbers or anything." She had a smirk on her face.

The man was still standing there, pole in hand, grinning at us.

"Sophia, could you tell him it's okay then?" I asked.

She addressed him with more unfamiliar words, which sounded like a lot more than, "It's okay."

Then the man laughed and saluted us with two fingers to his brow.

"Gracias."

I turned to look at Sophia. "What did you tell him?"

"That you'd give them all lemonade when they were done. You do have lemonade, don't you?"

Oh, geez.

We sat in the car watching them for a moment.

"Are you sure it doesn't hurt the tree?" I asked. They were reaching up with the hooks, pulling down the moss and tossing it in the back of the pickup.

"It's fine. The moss is an air plant; it pretty much just needs air and moisture to grow, and the moisture from the morning dew is enough to keep it goin', so don't worry, it'll grow back. Some people think it's like a parasite and lives off the tree, but that's not so. It looks pretty hangin' there, but it's good to thin it out from time to time," Sylvia answered.

"I understand how that benefits Hal then, but what do they do with it?"

"Haven't you ever seen the dried moss in craft stores? And it's used to put on top of the soil around container plants. They probably dry it themselves and bag it up, or sell it to someone who does."

"Ohhhh...I know exactly what you're talking about! I guess I never made the connection between the stuff in a plastic bag and this stuff hanging from the trees."

"You learn something new every day, Ellen," Sophia piped up from the back.

I opened the door to jump out and Sylvia put her hand on my arm.

"We're havin' a covered dish dinner tomorrow night at the clubhouse. Why don't you come over?"

I hesitated only a second. "I haven't been to one of those since Casey was in Girl Scouts! I used to bring taco salad, would that be okay?"

"I *love* taco salad!" Sophia chimed in.

"Are you still comin' to water aerobics tomorrow?"

Sylvia had mentioned the class while were were snooping through the shop this morning. It sounded like something I'd like to try.

"Sure, I'll meet you at the pool then?"

"That would be nice, Miss Ellen. Starts at ten."

She removed her hand from my arm, and I stepped out of the Cruiser.

I trudged into the kitchen knowing that I didn't have any lemonade, but I stood an entire minute holding the refrigerator door open, staring at the nearly empty shelves anyway. I decided to offer them the cans of diet soda Casey had left here. It was that or beer, which I'm sure they would have preferred, but I didn't know how to say, "Do you have a designated driver?" in Spanish.

They were just finishing up when I emerged from the house with the drinks. The shirtless man accepted the cans gratefully.

"Gracias," he said with a smile before he hopped in the bed of the truck.

They all waved to me as the pickup backed down the driveway.

"Adios!" I called, giving myself credit for not being completely clueless.

Remembering the empty fridge, I made a quick trip into town to pick up a few necessities and the fixings for taco salad, and on the way home I somehow managed to drive myself onto a street that I hadn't been on before.

I noticed a ceramic studio tucked in between the dry cleaners and the barber shop, and I just had to stop. When I walked through the door I was consumed by the familiar scents and sights of a working studio, and an immediate wave of nostalgia ripped through my body. My fingers flew to my necklace, and I missed Abbey with an overwhelming sense of urgency. I needed to hear her voice and see her smile. I needed a hug badly.

A gray-haired woman wearing denim shorts and a peach smock emerged from a back room where a class was apparently in session, and approached me with a smile on her face.

"May I help you, dear?" she asked.

"I think I might buy some bisque to take home and paint," I surprised myself by answering. "May I bring it back to have it fired?"

"Absolutely," she replied.

I picked out several items that I thought Sylvia and

Sophia might like, and the woman packed them carefully in a small cardboard box, along with the paints and brushes I had chosen.

Tucking my wallet back into my purse, I carried the box out to the car, feeling a little squeamish at the sight of the nearly negative balance in my checkbook. I hadn't received payment from Hal yet, but I didn't want to ask him for it. I was fortunate enough to just be living in his house!

I set up a workspace on the table on the back porch and pushed the speed dial for Abbey on my cell.

"Ellen! I was just thinking about you!" she answered on the second ring.

My eyes were stinging with tears at the familiar sound of her voice, the ceramic plate in front of me swimming in my vision.

"I miss you, Abbey."

"Do you know how lucky you are right now? We're expecting the snowstorm of the decade this week! It's already started and the grocery stores are all sold out of toilet paper and milk already!"

I laughed out loud! It was common knowledge that for some unknown reason, whenever a snowstorm was predicted, people flocked to the grocery stores in groves, stocking up on things we perceived as necessities…like we'd be stranded for months or something without toilet paper. We all poked fun at ourselves, but we all did it just the same.

"Schools closed early today, and I was just about to close up the shop and go home myself. No one will be out in this weather unless they have to be. So how is it in sunny Florida?"

"Sunny," I giggled.

"Smart shit!" and she laughed with me. "How's the love

life?"

I told her a condensed version of my "date" with Brooklyn.

"Oh for Pete's sake, Ellen. What do you expect from a guy with a girl's name?"

Now the tears in my eyes were from laughing. Abbey really put things into perspective.

"Believe me, Abbey, there is nothing feminine about Brooklyn! He's rock solid muscle."

"So, did he tell you how much he cares for you, or was he just trying to get in your pants?"

"Well, I think at some point in our relationship he must have told me that he likes me!" I honestly couldn't remember any verbal sharing of emotion, only physical. "He gives me lots of compliments though."

"Well, at least that's something. Maybe he's just your transition man."

"Maybe; I don't know if I want to spend time alone with him again though. He keeps telling me that he's persistent, but I don't really know what his goal is."

"Ellen, *I* know what his goal is, and I don't even *know* him!" she exclaimed.

My thoughts turned to Jack, and I wondered if he was still with Jessica.

"Have you run into Jack at all?" I had to ask.

"Nope, not since the supermarket that day with you."

I guess since he moved to Cranberry he wouldn't have much of a reason to be in Jeannette.

"I was just wondering how it's going with his new relationship. I'm curious…but I don't really care."

I heard Abbey sigh from nearly a thousand miles away.

"Ellen, it's okay to still care. You didn't leave your heart in Pennsylvania, you know."

"I know. I guess what I mean is that, well, since I've been here, it's been like I've stepped out of my life. I really haven't been thinking much of back home at all. Do you think I'm in denial?"

"Naw, I think you're just getting on with your life the best way you know how. You'll have to deal with things again soon enough. Enjoy your time away."

"Thanks, Abbey."

I had been gently nudged back into reality though.

"I think I should give Adam a call when we hang up."

"I'd better get going. I'm looking out the window and Route 30 is completely snow covered and the cars are just creeping along."

"Well, be careful."

"I love you, Ellen."

Here come the tears again. Will there ever be a day when I don't cry for some reason? It felt so good to hear those three words. I think everyone needs to hear them from someone every day.

"I love you, too," I squeezed in before we disconnected.

I immediately called Adam, and he didn't answer until the tenth ring.

"Hey, Mom!"

I smiled just hearing his voice.

"Hi, there! I hear that you're in for a blizzard!"

"Yep, looks like a doozy! Cooper and I are all tucked in though, so don't worry. I stopped for food yesterday, so we're well prepared. Hold on a sec."

I could hear a female voice talking in the background.

"I'm back. Mya is staying here with me. We figured if we're stranded, it may as well be together."

Well, there's logic for you.

"Have you checked on my house lately?" I asked.

"Day before yesterday. All is well. Looks like a few people have signed the little log book on the kitchen table, so it's getting some traffic. They were supposed to have an open house this Sunday, but I bet they cancel it because of the weather."

"Good, thanks for stopping by. Have you talked to your dad lately?"

"No, not at all since you left, Mom. I've been really busy with the cat lady house. Oh, guess what? I may have a buyer! Do you remember Mark Hudson? His cousin is looking for a house here because of a job transfer, so they've looked at it twice already! I still have a bit of work to do on it, but it should be done in a couple weeks."

"Adam, I'm so excited for you! Congratulations!"

"Thanks! Hey, is it okay if I call you back later? Mya is putting logs in the fireplace, so I think that's my hint to get a fire going."

"How about I call you in the morning to see how much snow you got?"

"Talk to you then. Love you," he said.

"Love you too, sweetie." I replied those magical words again.

I was still feeling a bit melancholy. In my mind's eye, I had a visual of my house in Jeannette, with the snow battering against the window panes and the wind whipping through the tree branches in the back yard. The snow would pile on the boughs of the pines and along the window ledge of the bay window in the dining room. It made me feel sad to think of it sitting empty, so void of life, with no one to take care of it. No one to turn up the furnace and switch on the lights to make it cozy and warm on a cold, dark January night. No happy chatter of people, no aromas of dinner being made. Jack would tell me that I was being silly because a house is nothing more than an inanimate object. But I felt bad for it anyway.

Jack. I really wanted to hear Jack's voice, to make sure that he was safe and tucked in from the storm, too. Abbey had been right. I can say that I don't care until I'm blue in the face, but the fact of the matter is, I still do. And I don't doubt that I always will, to some degree.

I was so tempted to just call his number and hang up after he said "Hello," just to hear his voice. I could call from the house phone and he wouldn't even know it was me.

I shook my head to clear the thought. Calling Jack is *not* what I need to be doing!

The daylight was turning to dusk, so I picked up all of my ceramics from the table on the porch and set up camp on the kitchen table instead. I grabbed a cupful of cracked corn and walked quickly down to the dock.

"Dora!" I called as I rattled the corn in the cup.

A moment later, she appeared from the tall grasses on the shore and sauntered down the wooden planks, making short work of the corn. Parking herself next to my feet, we sat together, watching the sun set in brilliant crimson glory.

CHAPTER TWENTY FOUR

I woke up this morning to the sun streaming through the twin windows in my room, and my cell phone ringing. It had been Adam. I crawled out of bed and took the phone to the window seat, cradling it against my shoulder as I opened the window to let in the fresh morning air.

"Mom, you are *not* going to believe how much snow we have!" Adam had said. "There's eight inches already, and it's not supposed to stop until this evening. The temperature is fifteen degrees, with the wind chill below zero!"

Now, an hour later, I marveled at the fact that I was here, floating in the pool on my inflatable throne, the color of a blue raspberry Popsicle. Instead of drifting snow, I was watching white, billowy clouds drift aimlessly across a sky almost as blue as my raft. A gentle breeze rustled the palm trees beside the pool and casually nudged me along the top of the water toward the deep end. I thought about how excited I had been to see my first palm tree, and now I almost took them for granted. I was getting spoiled!

I closed my eyes and conjured up a mental picture of what it would look like back home today. I would have put on my black down parka, leather gloves, and the cherry-red scarf that I had crocheted in a class with Abbey. I would have had to warm up the car, brush off the snow, and scrape the ice from the windshield…all before I could have pulled out of the driveway to maneuver the treacherous roads, if the roads were even navigable. The way Adam described it, not too many people would be going anywhere today.

Not that Pennsylvania winters are all bad. It's great if you're into winter sports, and I have tons of great memories of sled riding and building snowmen with the kids. I can hold my own in a snowball fight, and it's hard to beat curling up nice and cozy by the fireplace, with a good book and a cup of tea when the winter wind is howling outside. It's just all about choices.

I opened my eyes and peered up at the mockingbird perched on top of the clubhouse roof, who was serenading me with his full repertoire of songs. The sun was warm on my skin and penetrated my whole body like an elixir. Yes, this is a good place to be on a winter's day…a good choice.

Since I had been up early, I had time to make a quick trip to town and drop off my painted ceramics to be fired. I was anxious to give them to the girls. Then I drove back home, changed into my swimsuit, and bicycled over to Lakeside in time for water aerobics. Not a bad morning.

The clubhouse screen door slammed, and I heard the ladies chatter as they chose their pool noodles and set up camp with their sunscreen and beach towels.

"Hey, Ellen, are you sleeping? Shake a leg!" I heard Sylvia call.

"On my way!" I answered, and rolled off the raft and into the cool water. I swam the length of the pool back to the shallow end, where the group was already assembling. After choosing a tangerine pool noodle from the bin, I took a place in line beside Sylvia.

I'm sure I've met most of the women before, because they all called out a greeting to me. However, it was difficult to tell who they were because they all had their little bathing caps on. The pool was a sea of head latex. Sylvia's was hot pink, of course, with little silver sequins dangling all over it. I was very glad to have my sunglasses on.

All of a sudden, the Beach Boys "Wouldn't It Be Nice" started playing through the speakers, and we all looked up to see, Charlotte, the water aerobics instructor, walking out of the clubhouse door.

Abbey would have peed herself. I don't know what I

expected, but Charlotte wasn't it. She was probably in her mid-seventies, which is no big deal, but her bathing cap fit so tightly around her face, it scrunched all of her wrinkles together like a shar pei, and pushed her mouth into a puckered little pout, like a botox session gone bad. She was probably about fifty pounds overweight, carrying some of it in the flabby rings around her belly, but most of it in her enormous boobs, which hung and swung as she sashayed into the pool. As soon as she hit the water they took on a life of their own, and floated up in front of her like gargantuan, wrinkly life preservers. I just couldn't take my eyes off of them.

Sylvia clunked me on the head with her pool noodle.

"Didn't your mother teach you that it's impolite to stare?" she whispered to me. I clamped my mouth shut and looked over at her, feeling embarrassed. She smiled and winked.

"Let's get started, ladies," Charlotte began.

Everyone began following her lead, doing the warm-up routine to some pretty mellow music. I was beginning to think I would have burned more calories staying home and chasing tree frogs. All of a sudden, the pace really changed when "Pump Up the Jam" blared over the loud speakers. I thought Charlotte's boobs were going to cause a tidal wave.

It actually turned out to be a pretty good workout once we got going, and I was glad that I came. During the cool down, we heard the drone of a lawnmower competing with "When You Wish Upon A Star."

Herb motored by on his green John Deer riding mower. He was wearing a coffee colored safari hat, neon green tee shirt with the sleeves cut off, faded jeans, and scuffed work boots, and he looked very fetching.

"Good morning, ladies!" he shouted. As he drove by, he waved and adjusted his aviator sunglasses. Everyone yelled back assorted greetings, and I swear the temperature in the pool heated up ten degrees. Apparently Herb was the lady's man of Lake

Juliet.

After promising Sylvia that I'd be back later for the covered dish dinner, I hopped on the bike for the short ride home. I slowly pedaled along the road, enjoying the breeze in my wet hair. It was considerably warmer than it had been on my way to water aerobics, and I was glad that I had left my wet swimsuit on under my shorts. It certainly made me feel much cooler. I was planning on just hopping in the shower as soon as I got home.

As I rounded the corner into the driveway, I saw a Harley parked next to the house that definitely wasn't there when I left this morning. Looks like I have a visitor.

I parked the Schwin next to the Harley, feeling a little annoyed. I wasn't in the mood for company, and whoever it was better speak English! As I hopped off, jabbing at the kickstand, I scraped the heck out of my big toe. "Shit!" The million times I have told my kids never to ride a bike with flip flops came back to haunt me.

So it was while I was jumping up and down on one foot watching the blood dripping from my toe, shouting expletives, with windblown, wet hair, no makeup, and wearing only a swimsuit and wet shorts that looked like I had peed myself in them, that I saw him sitting on my front porch drinking a beer and grinning.

Who the hell is he, and how did he get one of my beers? Actually, I didn't give a damn. He was gorgeous! In about two seconds, I took in his brown leather cowboy boots, snug-fitting jeans, and pale blue tee shirt stretched across his chest, with rolled up sleeves showing off his muscular arms. He may have been drinking a single can of beer, but I think he was in possession of a six pack under that shirt. His short, cropped hair was sandy brown with shots of distinguished gray in all the right places, which in my estimation, put him in the over-forty category. His tan accentuated those baby blue eyes that were full of amusement as they looked directly at me.

What am I thinking? There is a strange man on my porch,

who obviously broke into my house *and* my refrigerator, and instead of thinking danger, I'm thinking eye candy! I stopped jumping and took my stand at the foot of the stairs. Maybe Jack had been right and I *do* need crazy pills!

I cleared my throat. "May I help you?" I asked in what I hoped was a serious tone.

He slowly rose from the wooden rocker and came down the steps toward me. "You're Ellen?"

Okay, now what did I tell my kids a million times about talking to strangers? I didn't even have my cell phone on me to call for help, or my car keys in my hand to jab up his nose. I needed to take a refresher course in Mom-101. I decided to go with the bluff.

"My boyfriend will be here any second. He's riding right behind me."

"Oh, I see. *Are* you Ellen Stern?"

Now I was more curious than cautious. How did he know *my* name?

"Yes, I am. Who are you?" I answered boldly.

"I'm Nick... Hal's son."

It wasn't registering.

"Hal...the guy who owns this place?" and he held out his hand for me to shake. "Nice to finally meet you, Ellen," he said in a southern drawl as smooth as honey.

I took his hand, and it felt like electric currents zinged through me. My mouth went dry and I couldn't swallow. My heart was pounding, but not in a panic attack mode. I felt like I was sixteen and working the soda fountain at Isaly's. What is *wrong* with me?

"Nice to meet you, too," I squeaked out. *How lame!*

"Your daughter, Casey, was to call you this morning and tell you that I was stopping by. I can see that I startled you, and I apologize for letting myself in and helping myself to a drink. It's been a long, hot ride," he said as he gestured towards the Harley.

I started to come back down to Earth, and I picked up my brain on the way.

"I didn't have my cell with me this morning, so she wouldn't have been able to reach me."

"If it makes you feel better, I'll wait out here while you go inside and give her a call, and get yourself a Band-Aid. I'll be down by the dock." And with that, he sauntered off around the back of the house.

Standing there in a stupor, I watched him make his way through the backyard, strolling leisurely along the wooden planks to the end of the dock. He took a seat on one of the wooden benches and slouched down, crossing his legs at the ankles. Resting his head on the back of the bench, he tipped his face to the sun, a picture of total relaxation.

Huh. I, on the other hand, packed up my bundle of nerves and went in to talk to that daughter of mine, slamming the screen door on my way in. I marched over to the table in the kitchen where I had sat having my tea this morning, and spied my cell phone.

One missed call from Casey...imagine that. I retrieved the message, and tapped my foot while I held the phone to my ear.

"Hey, Mom! Just wanted to let you know that Chris's dad, Nick, may stop by sometime today to check on some things at the house. I forgot to call and tell you last night. Gotta get back to work. Talk to you tonight. Love you."

I sighed. Okay, he is for real, and I made a great first

impression. I separated two of the slats in the plantation shutters and peeked out at him. He was still in the same position.

I ran up the stairs to the bathroom and jumped in the shower. Exactly eight minutes later, I was dressed and putting a Band-Aid on my big toe. I've acquired a pretty nice tan since I've been here, so I only needed a bit of mascara to look human again, but I added a touch of lip gloss anyway. My reflection in the mirror stared back, mocking me. I didn't want him to think I tried *too* hard, so I smudged off the gloss.

I finger styled my new haircut and it still looked terrific. Casey was right…Emilio *was* magic! Then I reapplied the gloss…what the hell. After taking a quick satisfying glance in the mirror, I ran back downstairs, grabbed two cold ones out of the fridge, and practically skipped out of the back porch door.

Then I stopped in my tracks. What am I doing? Besides acting like a sixteen year old, that is. My divorce isn't even finalized yet, and I'm going gaga over men! Hadn't I learned my lesson with Brooklyn? And Chris's dad to boot. Oh my. Come to think of it, I bet Chris has a *mom* too! I hadn't even thought to check for a wedding band. Of course, why would I? Oh, for Pete's sake.

I began walking purposefully toward the dock, stifling my inner dialogue before analysis paralysis set in. There's nothing wrong with offering him another beer…he'd said that he was thirsty, and I would do that for any guest. Besides, it could count as my nice thing to do today…I've been slacking on that lately.

"Nick?" I said as I stood beside him.

He didn't open his eyes. "You're standing in my sun," he said.

I touched the cold beer can to his cheek, and he opened one eye briefly and took it from me. He popped open the can with his eyes still shut, drained about half of it, then sat up.

"Thanks, Ellen. I guess this means that you talked to

Casey," he said as he tipped the beer can toward me.

"No, but she left me a voicemail telling me that you were coming. Sorry about before, but a girl can't be too careful these days."

"You're right, of course. You *should* be alarmed to find a strange man sitting on your porch, even if your boyfriend *was* riding right behind you." And he winked.

What? Oh, my dim-witted bluff. I wondered if he could tell that I was blushing, or if I just looked sunburned.

"Yeah, well..." and my voice trailed off. I didn't know where to go with that.

He looked down at my feet. "How's your toe? Those kickstands can give a mean bite."

"It's fine, although I'll wear my sneakers to bicycle from now on."

He smiled, and my heart actually skipped a beat. I smiled right back and sat down on the other bench, facing him.

"I guess you're wondering why I'm here."

He drained the rest of the beer from the can, set it down on one of the planks, and flattened it with his foot. Then he stared past me, out over the lake.

"Dad won't be able to come home until he can maneuver around on his own. I want to make the house more accessible to him, so his stint at the rehab center will be as short as possible. The sooner we can bring him home, the better. Although he's not a complainer, I know he hates it there."

I felt a pang of guilt as the thought passed through my head that when Hal comes home, they won't be needing me to house sit anymore, and I would have to leave. I've really fallen for this place, and although I wished Hal a speedy recovery, I was dreading the day that I would have to leave it behind.

"I see. What did you have in mind?" I asked.

"Well, they're estimating his recovery time at three to four months, but if I know my dad, he'll want to be out of there sooner. So that doesn't give us much time. I'd like to move his bedroom from upstairs to downstairs, and give the kitchen and bathrooms a remodel. Make it easier to move around in, just in case he needs a walker or...." He continued to stare out over the water and cleared his throat. "Or a wheelchair. Sorry, it's just hard to see him down. He's always been such a strong man, ya know?"

I could sense the love and respect that he felt for his father, and I wish that Adam and Jack shared that father and son bond. I remained quiet, to give him time to collect his thoughts. A gull flew by, dove down into the lake to scoop up a fish, then continued on its way.

He tore his gaze away from the water and looked at me for the first time since we began our conversation.

"Casey mentioned that you have a knack for decorating, and I was wondering if I could hire you to help me?"

Wow. I mentally pinched myself.

"Absolutely! I'll do anything I can to help. You don't have to pay me though; I'm already getting paid just for staying here," I said.

"Which reminds me," he said as he reached into his pocket and pulled out a money clip, "we owe you for your first week." He pulled out five crisp one hundred dollar bills and offered them to me.

"Dad thought cash would be best."

We had never really discussed how much I was going to be paid. Before I arrived, I guess I had figured anything is better

335

than nothing, and now that I'm here, I almost feel like I should be paying *him* to let me stay here!

"Oh my," I said as I accepted the money. "Nick, this is too generous! This should cover the whole month, not just one week."

He held up his hand in protest.

"Ellen, what you're doing for Dad is priceless. He's so relieved to have you looking out for things here; that's one less thing he has to worry about. This place means everything to him. Especially since Mom passed away, it's been what's kept him going."

Not knowing what to say, I simply nodded.

"I'd like to involve Dad in making the decisions on the renovations…give him something to really look forward to," he continued.

"It sounds like fun," I said. "It will be good for me to have something to really look forward to as well."

Mental head slap. *Did I say that out loud?*

He focused on my face a moment, but didn't say anything.

"Shall we go inside and take a look?" I asked.

We poked around the house, and he shared antidotes about growing up here. I felt a little awkward when we reached the bedroom where I've been sleeping. It's not every day that I have a man whom I've only met an hour ago standing in my bedroom.

We continued walking through the house and concluded our tour out on the back screened-in porch. I felt completely at ease with him, like I had known him for years. He told me that he owns a construction company in Memphis, and due to some personal issues, hadn't been getting down to visit Hal as much as he should; he's been depending on Chris to shoulder most of that responsibility and give him reports on Hal's progress. Sounded like he had a bit of the guilt thing going on.

He was planning to assemble a crew and have them come down to do the work once we had a plan. I felt a little pang of disappointment that he lived so far away.

We spent the whole afternoon discussing our ideas, looking online for products, and making a budget. It was so refreshing to have someone ask for my opinion and actually value it. Quite empowering, actually.

Nick explained that once he had grown up and moved out, his parents decided to fulfill a lifelong dream of converting the house to a bed and breakfast. Apparently they ran it very successfully until his mother became ill. Since she passed, his dad has been living here alone, and not taking in boarders.

"So, how did your dad break his hip, anyway?" I asked, feeling very negligent for never asking that question before.

He smiled. "Mom and Dad were roller coaster freaks…ever since they were first dating. They belonged to a club called "The High Rollers," and every year they all went to try out a new coaster somewhere. This year, Dad finally decided to go with the club again, for the first time by himself."

"Wow! In his seventies and still loves to ride coasters? That's amazing!" I had personally given up on them when I was in my thirties. "I can understand how all that rattling could have fractured his hip. Some of those are just brutal," I said.

He laughed, and his eyes sparkled. "No, he accomplished that just fine. He really loved it! But when they got off the coaster, the little kid walking in front of him lost his lunch, so to speak, and Dad slipped on it and down he went!"

I looked at him to see if he was serious. After a moment of shock, I started to giggle. Then it turned into a real belly splitter, and Nick joined in. We both laughed until we had tears rolling down our cheeks.

"Oh, that felt good!" he said. "I couldn't tell you the last time I laughed like that!"

Abbey and I had always laughed like that, but it had been quite a while for me too.

"Yes, it did feel good, but at your dad's expense."

"Oh, if you think that was funny, you should hear *him* tell it! I'm surprised that he didn't already! He milks it for all it's worth. He's so proud that he could handle the Z-Twist, and an eight-year-old couldn't."

I caught his eye, and we both started another fit of laughter.

Sylvia chose that moment to butt in. "Hey Syl!" I said, still laughing as I answered my cell phone.

"Well, howdy to you too. What's so funny?"

"I'll explain later. What's up?"

"It's time for dinner, that's what's up. I'm savin' you a seat by me, but you know how popular I am, being the prom queen and all. I can't hold it forever!"

I smiled. "Sylvia, I have an unexpected guest. I don't know if I can make the dinner after all."

"You'd better come! Sophia's been looking forward to your taco salad all day. Bring your guest along, we have plenty."

"Hold on a moment then," I said. I looked over at Nick, who was getting the drift of the conversation and already cleaning up our stack of papers.

"Nick, I'm sorry, but I have dinner plans with my friends

over at Lakeside Estates. It's a covered dish dinner, and you're invited if you don't already have plans." I figured there wasn't a prayer that he would accept the invitation. Normally, I would have never even asked him, but this had turned out to be a not so normal kind of day.

He looked at me with a grin.

"Well…I don't have a covered dish, but I *am* hungry! I'll tag along if you're sure you don't mind. I've already intruded on your day; I don't want to ruin your evening too," he said.

I crinkled up my nose at him. "Sylvia, we'll be right over. Save two seats." I could just imagine the jaws dropping when I walked in with Nick. We may have to retrieve a few pair of dentures.

Nick went out to the bike and brought in a small leather bag, then went into the downstairs bathroom to freshen up. I tossed the ingredients for the taco salad together in a large plastic bowl. I would add the dressing when we got there so it wouldn't get soggy. I sealed the lid and took out two plates and silverware. Then I ran upstairs to get ready myself.

A few minutes later, I returned to the kitchen and sucked in my breath. Nick had changed his shirt to a white polo and had combed his hair. *Hot damn!* Oh my, I'm turning into my daughter.

He looked me over and seemed to smile in approval. I was very glad that I was able to fit into my jeans again.

"Do you want to ride over on the Harley?" he asked.

I'd never been on a motorcycle in my life. They scare the hell out of me.

"Uh, I would, but I have to take the salad and our utensils. I can drive Hal's Subaru.

"No problem with the salad. It'll fit in the compartment

on my bike. We can just drive through the orange grove and won't even have to go on the street."

Oh, my. "Okay, then. I've never been on one, and I'm not so sure that I want to," I admitted. What if it scared me into a panic attack?

He looked at me with those baby blues, and said, "Trust me." And strangely enough, I did.

I ran back upstairs and put on my sneakers. I wasn't taking any chances after my incident this morning. After he secured the food, he helped me with the helmet. "I always carry a spare," he said.

He told me to just hang on and lean with him.

My heart jumped in my throat when the engine rumbled to life, and I wanted to jump off immediately. My fight or flight was kicking in, and I really wanted to choose flight. Instead, I put my arms around his middle, closed my eyes, and hung on for dear life.

He was taking it slow, and about twenty seconds into the ride, I opened my eyes. I wouldn't say that I relaxed, but I think my nails probably stopped digging into his flesh at that point. It was an intimate feeling being so close to him. I could smell the fabric softener scent on his shirt and feel the heat radiating from his body.

All too soon for my taste, we popped out of the grove and made the turn into Lakeside. As we pulled up to the clubhouse, several faces were plastered up against the glass looking out at us.

Nick helped me off the bike. "See, it wasn't so bad, was it?"

I handed him the helmet, noticing my hand shaking a bit. "No, although driving through an orange grove is one thing. Driving on I-4 would be another."

He laughed and handed me the taco salad. "Well, I'm proud of you for trying. I know you were scared."

He was *proud* of me? How many times had Jack ever said that to me? Uh....never?

I tilted my head and smiled. "Thanks! You're a nice guy, ya know that?" *You're a nice guy...how corny can I get?*

"Not everyone shares your sentiments," he said. "Let's get inside before someone has a stroke trying to see you through the window."

I learned a lot about Nick during that dinner. Sylvia has a knack of asking personal questions and getting away with it.

Sylvia met her match though, when she asked about how his wife liked him traveling to Florida on a motorcycle. He dodged her question as skillfully as she had asked it. He did say, however, that he had moved from Florida to Memphis originally because his wife wanted to be near her family. So he started his business there, and it became so successful, he just planted his roots in Memphis.

I could tell that he had impressed Sylvia, and that was a major accomplishment. While he played an after-dinner game of pool with Herb and the guys, I helped the ladies clean up. Sylvia grabbed my arm and pulled me aside.

"Ellen, he's a real looker, and sweet as molasses, but be careful you don't get too attached. That wedding band is screamin' danger, honey."

I rolled my eyes, assured her that I would be fine, and went to see if he was ready to leave.

I heard the Harley rev to life, and I plastered my own face to the window just in time to see Sophia wearing the helmet and holding on to Nick. She waved as they turned out of the clubhouse parking lot and rode down the street toward the lake, her baggy, yellow tee shirt flapping in the wind.

"Don't that beat all!" Sylvia said at my shoulder. "I was givin' the wrong girl a lecture!"

Herb chuckled. "Sophia told Nick that she's always wanted to see what it's like to be a biker chick, and Nick was nice enough to give her a crack at it. He's a good man, just like his dad."

"Uh huh," Sylvia replied.

The three of us waited outside for them to return, sitting side by side on the benches next to the shuffleboard court. In about five minutes, we heard the drone of the bike approaching.

"Whew-wee!" Sophia said as she slid off the seat into Nick's arms. "That was just something! Thank you, Nicky!" And she gave him a kiss on the cheek.

Nick blushed and handed the helmet to me. "Looks like we're ready to roll! Thank you so much for an enjoyable evening. I'm sure I'll be seeing y'all again since I'll be around checking on my dad's place. We'll have a party when it's done...Dad would enjoy that."

So he *would* be coming around! I smiled from the inside out.

Everyone said their goodbyes, and I hopped on the bike like I'd been doing it forever. Then off we sped back through the orange grove.

He cut the engine after he pulled into the same spot that he had this morning, but neither one of us moved for a few moments. Then I slowly got off and waited for him to dismount. I handed him the helmet, and he looked at me with the grin that was becoming strangely familiar.

"Sophia gave me a kiss on the cheek after her ride. All I get from you is my helmet back?"

I gave him a little shove on the arm, and stood back a few steps. Were we *flirting*?

He slung his thumbs in his front jean pockets and stood next to his Harley, facing me. My heart was pounding again. I'd been holding on tightly to him all the way home and it had felt so good. *Damn.*

"Well, I'd better get a move on. Ellen, thank you so much for helping me out with this project. I can't tell you how much that means to me," he said in a low voice.

I folded my arms across my chest and hugged myself close to keep from trembling…and from touching him again. "I'm happy to help. I can't wait to get started…really. I think I'll go see your dad tomorrow and get his opinion on some of our ideas."

Nick laughed a deep belly laugh. "Good Lord, girl, you are something!"

I smiled in return and swatted at a mosquito hovering around my face.

"We'd better get you inside before they eat you alive. I'll walk with you until you turn some lights on."

It had been dusk when we pulled out of the parking lot at Lakeside, but it was almost completely dark now. What a gentleman. He walked with me through the kitchen into the living room, as we turned on lights along the way. It was kind of a nice feeling having someone look out for me, if only for a moment.

"If you do see Dad tomorrow, let me know how it goes," he said as he walked back toward the kitchen door. "I need to head back to Memphis."

"Absolutely. I'll call tomorrow evening if I won't be interrupting anything."

"Hmph," he blurted out. "Not much chance of that. Call any time." He turned at the door, and with one hand on the handle, he gently put the other one on my shoulder and gave it a gentle squeeze. "Talk to you tomorrow, then."

And before I could reply, or breathe, he jogged down the steps to his Harley. I stood inside the screen door and watched him bring the engine loudly to life. Then, with a wave of his hand, he was gone.

I stood listening until I couldn't hear the sound of him anymore, watching the mosquitoes hurling themselves at the porch light. I slowly shut the main door and clicked the deadbolt, still feeling the heat from his hand on my shoulder.

I was smiling. The smile turned into a grin. The grin turned into laughter, and in a burst of energy I danced and skipped around the kitchen until I collapsed with a sigh on one of the chairs. I just could *not* get that smile wiped off my face.

My, it felt so good...just to *feel* again! I had never understood those people who say "I'd rather hurt than feel nothing at all" but I was beginning to understand. Although I would never prefer the pain I felt in the first few days after Jack left, it did feel pretty wonderful at this moment to be completely happy and laugh instead of feeling numb. I haven't felt this good in a long, long time.

Still smiling, I picked up my cell and punched in Casey's number. She answered on the third ring.

"Hey, Mom."

"Hi, honey. Um, I got your voicemail a little late today," and I started to giggle again.

"What's so funny about that? Why are you laughing? Are you okay?"

"Oh, I don't know. I'm just happy!"

"Mom," she said, "It's so nice to hear you say that. What's making you so happy?"

Nick.

"Well, I started out the day at water aerobics with Sylvia and the girls, then I came home to find a mystery man on my porch drinking my beer."

"Chris's dad?" she asked.

"Yes, and I hadn't got your message yet!"

"I'm so sorry, Mom. I just found out about it yesterday afternoon, and I had dinner with clients last night and forgot to call you."

"It's okay, sweetie, it all worked out. In fact, that's why I'm so happy."

She was silent for a moment. "Because of Chris's dad?"

Yes.

"Because I'm so excited to help with the remodel project. I can't wait to get started!"

"Oh," she said, sounding relieved. "I thought you meant something else."

Be careful, Ellen.

"Nick wants to involve Hal as much as possible, so I'm thinking of coming over your way tomorrow and spending some time with him at the nursing home."

"That sounds nice. Do you want to come to my place afterwards and have dinner? Chris can do something on the grill for us again."

"Sure, I'll bring dessert."

Now it was Casey's turn to laugh. "Let me guess…cake?"

I laughed along with her. "I'll have you know that I've changed my ways, girl!"

"Around six, then," she said.

CHAPTER TWENTY FIVE

I sat up for hours, sketching floor plans and getting ideas online. Deciding to call Adam in the morning and pick his brain a bit, I felt exhilarated and couldn't believe it when I looked at the clock and found it after midnight.

Later, as I tried to drift off to sleep, it was hard to quiet down my brain. Pictures of flooring, paint swatches, and lighting kept running amok in my thoughts. Kind of like when you drive all day on vacation, then close your eyes at night and you can still see the pavement in front of you. And in between all the remodeling visions, freeze frames of Nick squeezed their way in.

I thought of Jack and his slut…I mean girlfriend. Is this how things start? Just an innocent ride on a Harley or in a G35 Coup, and the next thing you know, you're a home wrecker? I tossed that thought in the recycle bin for another day's pondering and finally fell asleep.

The next day, Hal and I had a wonderful time planning the renovation. He was in therapy when I called early in the morning, but the attendant assured me that my visit would be more than welcome in the afternoon.

When I arrived, he was in the rec room sitting in a chair at the table. He greeted me with a big smile and a hearty hello, and I bent down and kissed his cheek.

"You'd better watch that kind of stuff around here. The other guys are gonna get ideas about us," he said with a wink.

He looked so much healthier than the last time I saw him. He had been in the wheelchair then, and there had been a sadness about him.

"Looks like you're getting your tan back, Hal," I said.

"I've been spending my afternoons wheeling around the flower garden out back. Flowers and sun are good for the soul. How are my hibiscus doing?"

I pulled out my camera and showed him some pictures I had snapped for him. The salmon hibiscus, the tree full of bright yellow lemons, and one of Dora, which made him laugh. I flipped back one photo too far. It was the one of Sylvia at the prom.

"Who's this lovely lady?" he asked holding the camera closer.

"That's Sylvia! She said she knows you."

"Oh my! That's Sylvia?" he said as he leaned in toward the camera. "She looks beautiful! Please don't tell her that I didn't recognize her, she'll have me pegged for Alzheimer's! It's just that the last time I saw her, she had pink and blue hair...."

"Your secret is safe with me," I smiled as I replaced the camera in my purse. "Sylvia and I have become good friends."

"Sylvia is blessed with a real personality, that's a sure thing. What a firecracker!" he said.

"If there's a table back in the flower garden, I wouldn't mind sitting there with you this afternoon," I told him. I would always choose to be outside rather than in.

He grinned his approval, and Lindsey came to assist us in getting Hal back into the wheelchair. We pulled his chair right up to an umbrella table next to a huge azalea full of pale pink blossoms. I could see the spark in his eye and sensed his anticipation when I opened my satchel full of notes and sketches.

We spent a few hours poring over them and probably would have spent a few hours more, but Lindsey came to collect Hal for dinner.

I promised to call him every day and to stop back and visit next weekend. Before she wheeled him toward the dining room, he took my hand and gently kissed it.

"Thank you so much, Ellen…for everything."

It was only four-thirty, so I stopped by a local home improvement store and poked around a bit, picking up some paint swatches and tile samples. I pulled into Casey's parking lot at exactly six.

It was so good to spend the evening with Casey. She looked absolutely radiant, and I sensed a new maturity about her. Chris didn't disappoint. He made us turkey burgers that were amazing! Casey's contribution was a spinach salad and huge baked potatoes.

For dessert, I pulled out a pineapple angel food cake that I had made with Sylvia's recipe, and served it with fresh strawberries, blueberries, and a dollop of low fat whipped cream that I had kept in a cooler in my car.

Casey raised an eyebrow when she saw a cake, but was highly impressed with the ingredients. Score one for Mom.

We sat poolside after dinner, and in the glow of the tiki torches, talked about Casey's job, the boat Chris would like to buy, and of course the renovation project. I watched Chris put his arm around Casey's shoulders and nuzzle her neck with a kiss as they sat side by side on the chaise.

I thought of Nick then, not Brooklyn or Jack, and about how much I would like him to do that to me. Shame on me! Time for me to take my perverted thoughts home. Casey would certainly disapprove of me for thinking those kinds of thoughts about Chris's dad. And what would Chris think? No more burgers for me, that's what. Besides, there had been no sign of Brooklyn tonight, and I didn't want to push my luck.

I faked a yawn. "I'm going to head on home now. I was up late last night sketching, and it's catching up with me. Thanks for dinner and a great evening."

"You can come over any time, Mom. It's so good to see you happy. There's something different about you tonight…in a good way, I mean."

Yes, I met Nick.

"Must be my excitement about the project. It's what I've always dreamed of doing."

I thought of something that Dr. Burke had told me back in Pennsylvania. She had said, "Happiness is a choice, not a response. You can choose to be happy." And from now on in my life, I am choosing to be happy.

Once I got home, I changed into my pajamas and crawled into bed. I'd promised to call Nick if I went to see his dad today, but it was way too late to interrupt his evening now. I can't imagine his wife would appreciate that.

Just as I was drifting off to sleep, my cell phone rang. I jumped and quickly reached over to read the screen. My experience is that if someone calls late, something's wrong.

In this case, I couldn't have been more wrong.

I slid open my phone.

"Hello, Ellen?" a deep voice said.

"Hi, Nick," I said, his now familiar drawl making my heart thump as I lay there in the dark.

"I hope it's not too late to call. I didn't wake you, did I?" he asked.

I looked at the red glowing numbers on the alarm clock...ten-thirty. "No, I wasn't sleeping. It's fine."

It's FINE? Geez, Louise, it's FABULOUS!

There is something very intimate about talking to a man when you're lying in bed at night. It could be the cable guy calling, and it would *still* seem forbidden to talk to him while you are naked in the dark, under the satin sheets on your bed.

Who am I kidding? I was wearing a Tweety Bird nightshirt under cotton sheets, but it *was* dark. And it *was* Nick. And more than likely, it was forbidden. I had a visual of him sitting on the dock, ankles crossed, with his head tipped to the sun. Oh my.

"I talked to Dad earlier, and he was so enthusiastic about his visit with you. I kept waiting for you to call me about it...and you never did. So I just couldn't wait anymore," he said.

Wow.

"I'm sorry. I went to have dinner with Casey and Chris, then I figured it was too late to call. I didn't want to disturb you and...well, are you back in Memphis?"

"Yes, busy day. Trying to catch up on things since I've been gone. So, tell me how my son is doing and then what you and Dad decided today."

I told him about the magnificent burgers that Chris had made, and of course he took the bragging rights of having taught him everything he knows about grilling. Then I gave him the condensed version of my visit with Hal.

"He's really an amazing man," I said. "He jumped right in and made some changes to our ideas, and I think you'll be really happy with them. I'll send you a fax tomorrow. He already looks better than the last time I saw him."

Nick said he would start ordering some of the items and let me know the delivery schedule.

"When things start to arrive, I would like them to go in the carriage house. Then we can take things in as we need them," he said.

The carriage house was huge, with a second story, originally intended for a guest house. It was located off to the left of the driveway, set away from the house behind a wall of shrubs. Although, since it was locked, I hadn't been inside yet.

"Nick, do you know where the key is?"

"I'll find out from Dad. It's really a cool building, I think you'll like it."

Once we had covered the renovation update, we talked about everything under the sun. Except personal relationships, that is. We made each other laugh. He teased me mercilessly about our first meeting and my run in with the kickstand. And I gave it right back to him, teasing him about converting Sophia into a biker chick.

The conversation was easy, and one topic flowed seamlessly into the next. I was still lying in the dark, but had propped myself up on the pillows. My cell phone chirped a low battery warning, and I looked over at the alarm clock.

It was almost twelve-thirty! We'd been talking for two hours, and it seemed like only minutes.

"Nick, have you looked at the time? I think I'd better let you go," I said.

"Wow! I didn't realize it was so late. Sorry if I kept you up past your bedtime."

"You're the one who probably has to get up early tomorrow. I can sleep the day away if I want to. House sitting doesn't require me to punch a time clock, so time is irrelevant."

He laughed a deep laugh. "Well, we'll just have to give you a harder job then. Just wait until the remodel begins! It will be so noisy you won't be able to sleep much past sun up. We start early in the construction field." And I could feel his smile through the phone.

I yawned for real.

"I'll let you get to bed. It's been great talking to you again, Ellen."

I didn't want to confess that I had already been in bed for the past two hours.

"It's been nice talking to you too, Nick. Goodnight."

We disconnected, and I held the phone in my hand, smiling. I reached over, plugged it into the charger, and let out a sigh. I was getting myself in deep. He was such a nice guy! No harm in a phone call…some of it was business anyway. Then I remembered all the late night phone calls that Jack would get, and a light bulb went on in my head.

I wondered if a woman had been calling him at night, and if he had been having intimate conversations with her while I was asleep in our bed. I wondered about all the text messages he suddenly seemed to get. The ones he didn't check in front of me.

I sighed again. Realizations like this make it easier to let it go and move on with my life. However, I also wondered if Nick had been sneaking *our* phone call tonight. I wondered if his wife had been sleeping peacefully in their bed, while he and I were having a crazy teenaged conversation. I certainly didn't want to be a part of that, but we *did* need to discuss business. I vowed to keep our future conversations business-oriented, and to try to put a damper on my attraction to him.

But I would savor the happy way I feel when I'm around him. I closed my eyes and fell asleep.

The next few weeks flew by. I talked to Nick a couple of nights a week, sometimes into the wee hours of the morning...the conversations always started with business and ended with pleasure. We would begin by discussing crown moldings and end up talking about our favorite restaurants or vacation spots. I kept the promise to myself to just keep it friendly, even though I couldn't wait for the phone to ring each night and grinned ear to ear at the sound of his voice.

The materials had begun arriving and were being stored in the carriage house, as Nick had requested. The first time I ventured inside the building, I was amazed. It *was* cool, and I know Adam would have said that it had great bones. He would love to work his magic with it!

It actually had a winding black iron staircase leading up to what appeared to be a loft space. There were stained glass windows on the upper floor, and glass doors leading out to a small balcony overlooking the lake. There was even a huge stone fireplace on the far wall. Nick said that his parents had planned on renovating it to be an apartment to rent or a honeymoon cottage, but had discarded the idea when his mom got sick.

I went to visit Hal twice a week, and he was improving daily. Lindsey told me that they were planning on introducing him to the walker soon. Nick was right about his dad. He wouldn't be down for long!

Sylvia had gotten into the habit of accompanying me on my trips to see Hal. The first time, she said she had some shopping to do nearby and asked if she could ride over with me. Now she goes to visit without me, and her PT Cruiser is pretty much a permanent fixture at New Hope. Most times when I stop by, I find them happy as clams, sitting on the lanai huddled over a crossword puzzle or poring over travel magazines.

Nick's crew of four men arrived the first week in February. I was exuberant to see the plans that Nick and I had created come to life. We didn't want the place to blatantly scream, "I am a disabled person's home!" We wanted it to be a calm retreat where rooms flowed into one another. Even though the kitchen counter position and arched doorways throughout the first floor had ample room for a wheelchair or walker, the average person wouldn't even notice. We would knock out a wall in the downstairs bedroom that was to be Hal's and planned to have doors opening to a private, ground-level deck that would also give easy access to the backyard, with no steps to maneuver. Even if Hal made a full recovery and didn't need assistance to get around, it was a good investment if he ever wanted to open again as a bed and breakfast.

I had thought that maybe the workers would stay here at the house, but Nick insisted on putting them up at a small hotel in town. Nick was tied up with some business crisis that he didn't expound on, and I didn't feel inclined to pry, so he hadn't come back to Orlando since the first day I met him. Even though we had this amazing compatibility over the phone, I was relieved to think that I'd imagined my intense physical attraction to him.

There had been no offers on my Jeannette home, although Adam had made the sale on his fixer-upper as he had predicted, and a closing date was scheduled near the end of the month. January's weather had been one of Pennsylvania's worst in years, so I can't imagine house hunting was at the top of anyone's itinerary; driving to work and the grocery store probably took precedence.

I was doing so much better mentally! I hardly ever thought of Jack, at least not nearly as much as I used to. I kind of liked the fact that I was making a new life for myself, and of course there were the distractions of dodging Brooklyn and burning up the cell phone line with Nick. I hadn't spoken to Jack at all since I'd left. I wondered sometimes if he even knew or cared that I wasn't in town.

I'd kind of been in a bubble, just getting through each day, not dwelling about the past, and not making any plans for the future…just enjoying the moment. I think I really needed this reprieve from the stress of the last several months; I just couldn't handle any more.

Casey had been busy working, so I hadn't seen much of her lately. It was the beginning of tax season, and she had been recruited to help some of the senior attorneys with their overload of clients, which sometimes meant twelve hour weekdays and pretty much a guaranteed Saturday at the least. The one precious day a week that she did have off was spent doing her own personal errands and spending time with Chris. Since I hadn't been over to visit lately, I haven't had the opportunity to run into Brooklyn, although he had called three times. Two of them I hadn't answered, and he left no voice mail, and the third I did answer, but declined his offer of going to dinner, feigning exhaustion from working on the remodel.

The second week of February brought a cold snap…several days with highs in the fifties. Funny, but if the thermometer hit fifty degrees in Jeannette in February, people would be running around in flip flops and washing their cars!

As it was, I had become acclimated to the steamy temperatures of January in Florida, and I dug out the jeans I had stored in my suitcase, along with the hooded sweatshirt I hadn't seen since the last rest stop in Georgia.

The lake looked angry today, gray and choppy, and the dark clouds that scurried across the sky had already opened up and dropped buckets before moving on.

Even though the temperature was brisk, I adhered to my customary routine of taking my sketch pad down to the pier for an hour or two, only today I brought a travel mug of hot tea instead of iced. Sitting cross-legged on the wooden planks, I was diligently trying to capture the likeness of the new arrivals that had shown up near the pier the other day: a family of otters.

I was flabbergasted that otters would live in this lake, but when I mentioned it to Hal, he excitedly told me that he had seen them from time to time, but not for a few years. I was planning on mounting this sketch and one that I made of Dora as a gift to him, so I wanted it to be good.

The otters have usually been flipping around so quickly that it's been hard for me to get the details down on paper, but today they were cooperating, feasting on a catfish they had plucked from the lake, crunching away, oblivious to my presence.

They were brown and sleek, almost silky looking, and had the cutest little button noses! Their tiny little ears were almost inconspicuous, and the white whiskers that jutted from the sides of their jowls made them look almost grandfatherly.

I was just shading in the smaller otter when my cell phone signaled a call from Casey.

"Hello, stranger!" I answered, smiling. I tucked my pencils and pad back into the satchel for safekeeping and moved up to sit on the bench.

"Hey, Mom, got a minute?" her voice sounded troubled, and I instantly became cautious. Come to think of it, it wasn't like her to call in the middle of a workday.

"What's wrong?" I asked quickly, my hands pausing in mid-air, gripping the stainless steel mug.

"*I'm* fine, don't worry. Chris just got some upsetting news though, and I needed to talk about it."

I expelled a whoosh of air.

"Sure, go ahead."

Setting the mug down, I brought my knees up to my chest and wrapped my arms around them.

"His parents met him for lunch today, and they dropped the divorce bomb."

Silence.

"Mom, are you still there?"

I opened my mouth, but nothing came out.

"*Mom!*"

"Oh...sorry, honey...I'm just really surprised, that's all," I was finally able to verbalize.

Talk about the understatement of the year...I was shocked! Nick had never given me any indication that his marriage was in trouble. We had never discussed our personal relationships at all; it had been like a mutual forbidden boundary. At the moment, my insides were churning. I tipped my head up to look at the unsettled sky.

Please don't let me be the cause of this.

"Did he say what happened?" I asked meekly.

"He said it's a long story, and he'd tell me the whole thing tonight, but apparently his mom has been stepping out on his dad. He found out that she was seeing someone a couple months ago, and he was hoping she would change her mind and come back, but it looks like that's not going to happen. She's moved out."

"Oh, my."

I felt slightly relieved that I hadn't played a part in this turn of events, even though no one but me knew the attraction I felt towards Nick. Regardless, I felt bad for the breakup of their family.

"Chris is pretty upset. His dad stayed after lunch and talked to him alone, and evidently she's done this twice before and come back both times, so that's why he didn't want to worry Chris about their problems, if it was all going to blow over anyway."

"Wow."

Nick is a lot more understanding that I am. As much as I

loved Jack, there is no way I could have kept taking him back if he had numerous affairs.

"So get this…the guy she's with now is one she had the second affair with years ago, and they happened to run into each other and it started up again. I guess when his dad found that out, the shit hit the fan."

"So they're filing for divorce then?" I asked.

"Yep. But there's all kinds of legal stuff going on. She's half-owner in his construction business and there's some kind of money issue, so he's trying to figure out if he has to sell the company or can work something out. I guess they're pretty well off, but the business will be a stumbling block."

Apparently the business crisis Nick had mentioned.

"Can you offer any legal advice?" I asked.

"Don't think I want to get in the middle of this, but I can certainly refer someone in my practice. I feel bad for Chris, Mom. Even though we're older, it's still so hard seeing your parents split up."

"I know, sweetie." My heart went out to her. "Maybe you can be there for Chris since you just went through all this."

"I know, but it's hard reliving it all again so soon."

She sounded so sad.

"You know, Mom, I haven't even talked to Dad in weeks."

"Don't take it personally, honey. Everyone is still getting adjusted," I offered, but I despised him for putting her through this. I didn't expect Jack to keep in touch with me, but Casey and Jack had always been so close, so much more than Jack and Adam were. I know this has been a real blow to her.

"Have to go, Mom, I have a client coming in soon. Thanks for listening."

"Any time, you know that. Let's get together soon! I can even drive in and just meet you for lunch or something."

"That would be nice, I need a hug."

"Me too! Call me when you get a chance and we'll make plans."

I sat for a while after we disconnected, staring out at the lake. I'm ashamed to say that a tiny part of me was happy that Nick would be unattached, but the rest of me was very sympathetic to what he must be going through right now. Remembering what I had felt like those first few days after Jack left was torture. I wondered if Nick had someone strong that could help him get through this like Abbey had helped me.

A few big drops of rain plopped on the wooden planks. I grabbed my art supplies and ran through the grass and into the house.

CHAPTER TWENTY SIX

I declined Hal's offer of keeping the cleaning service that maintained the home for him; the least I could do was to clean up after myself.

The construction workers had left for the day, and the house was blessedly quiet. I had put a pot of wedding soup on to simmer earlier, and the aroma was drifting through the house, making it feel cozy on this rare gloomy day. I called Sylvia with the intention of inviting her and Sophia over for dinner, but a special meeting of the Lakeside Community Association had been called, and both being officers, they were mandated to attend. So I figured I may as well get my cleaning done.

I had already dusted all the rooms upstairs; with all the plaster and sawdust, it was a daily chore. My dirty sheets were in a clothes basket beside the bed, and I put on the clean, fitted one, tugging the elastic corners over the mattress and smoothing the wrinkles out with my hand. As I flipped the top sheet in the air and snapped it with a crack, something out the window caught my eye.

Someone was walking down the pier. I let the sheet float down on the bed and went to the bay window for a closer look. It was Nick!

My heart started to hammer in my chest. I practically pressed my nose up against the glass to get a better view. He walked purposefully down to the end of the pier, then just stood there looking up at the sky. The wind had picked up and was tousling his hair and flapping at the tails of his denim shirt. I held my breath.

Then I watched, transfixed, as he appeared to pull something from his finger and hurl it into the lake. Then he sat on the bench with his head in his hands.

Did he just chuck his wedding band?

Instinctively, I wanted to run out to him, to hold him and tell him everything would be okay.

Just then the skies opened up once again, and out of the heavy gray clouds, huge drops flung themselves to the ground, pelting against the glass; I saw Nick stand up and start walking slowly toward the house. I quickly ducked down from the window. With the light on in my bedroom, he would certainly have seen me standing there watching him.

I ran down the steps and arrived at the front door just as Nick appeared.

He was soaked, his wet hair plastered against his head and his denim shirt hanging heavy on his frame.

I opened the door before he had a chance to knock, and he stepped onto the front porch, creating his own puddle.

"Sorry to barge in on you like this…" he started.

"Nonsense! You know you're welcome anytime! Come on in and get dried off. Do you have any dry clothes with you?" I said as I closed the door behind us and bustled him into the kitchen, all the time my heart pounding. I stole a glance at his left hand, and saw a band of white skin on his ring finger.

"I do, but they're in the saddle bag on the bike. I pulled it into the garage because it looked like it could rain. Wow, does it smell *good* in here!"

"Italian wedding soup."

I kind of wished I had made chicken noodle. It wasn't a great day to be reminded of weddings.

A drop of water dripped from the tip of his nose, and he shivered.

"You're not getting sick on my watch," I teased. "You

march upstairs and get a hot shower and find something in Hal's closet to put on, then we'll put your things in the dryer." I gave him a little shove on the back, and had to step back from the shock of touching him.

He pursed his lips and appeared to be wrestling with the thought, but apparently finding no good argument against it, took my advice and headed for the stairway, pausing with one hand on the wooden banister and the other giving me a military salute.

"I assume you'll stay for dinner?" I hollered after him.

"If that's an invitation, then I accept ..." I heard the reply even though he was already out of sight.

I could hear him rummaging around upstairs, then the squeak of the shower handle being turned. I sighed and returned to the kitchen, humming. Wasn't life just quirky?

By the time I set the table and warmed up the loaf of Italian bread that I had bought on a whim from the bakery in town, I could hear Nick coming down the stairs.

He paused in the kitchen doorway wearing a pair of gray sweatpants that were about five inches too short and a lime green tee shirt that sported a picture of a roller coaster, with "High Rollers" written across the front. His feet were bare, and his hair was wet and neatly combed. I turned from the stove with ladle in hand, pausing over an empty bowl, and smiled at him.

He shrugged his shoulders and gave me a half-smile that didn't quite reach his eyes. The sparkle that I remembered so well was missing. Although I could tell he was trying to conceal it, he had a look of resigned sadness about him.

"Soup's on!" I said, trying to sound upbeat. After all, he didn't know that I was aware of his situation.

"Let me put these in the dryer and I'll be right with you," he said as he disappeared down the hallway. I could hear him thumping down the wooden stairs to the basement, and the smell

363

of my citrus shampoo followed him.

Oh, geez, he used *my* bathroom? Something about that seemed very personal, and something about *that* pleased me.

I placed the steaming bowls on the new table and filled two glasses with ice water, adding a wedge of lemon to each.

"Thanks so much for dinner," Nick said as he entered the room. "Are you sure I'm not imposing?"

"It's just me for dinner, I'm so happy that you're here," I replied honestly.

As we took our seats, Nick let out a sigh.

"I apologize in advance for not being good company though. I've had a killer of a day," he said as he took his thumb and index finger and massaged his forehead for a moment.

I nodded. "Warning heeded…how about we just enjoy our food, leave the bad stuff behind us, and put a nice ending on the day."

He looked up and tried out his smile again, this time almost succeeding.

"So, what do you think of the improvements so far?" I asked as I buttered a piece of bread.

He looked around the room as if seeing it for the first time.

"I'm sorry, Ellen, I was so preoccupied I didn't even notice." He pushed back in his chair. "This is the new table we picked out. It's perfect isn't it?"

"Yes, it is, and I'll give you the grand tour after we're done eating. It's really coming along."

"I'm glad we decided on putting the laundry room on this

level. It's something that should've been done a long time ago. I didn't remember how steep those basement steps were until I just went down there! Most homes in Florida don't even have basements, you know. Hey, how long until the new washer and dryer are delivered?"

"Guess what? They came yesterday! They're in the garage. I'm surprised you didn't see the boxes when you parked your bike."

"Wow, I really *am* out of it," Nick set his spoon down in his empty bowl with a soft clank. "Ellen, you're doing a great job with all this. I'm so impressed with your ideas and your follow-through. I don't know how in the world you got them delivered already...I thought there was an eight week wait! And by the way, your soup was amazing! Just what the doctor ordered. I feel so much better about everything already!"

I was glowing inside; his compliments meant so much to me!

After I declined his offer to help clean up, he disappeared into the den. Working in hyper-speed, I had the kitchen spic-and-span within minutes, then was very proud to show Nick what had been accomplished in the house.

Our tour ended in the den, where he had turned on the gas fireplace while I had been on kitchen duty. It was a perfect complement to this unusually chilly night. He had helped himself to a bottle of Hal's wine, and it appeared that he had already downed a glass.

"Would you like some wine, Ellen?"

He refilled his glass and held the bottle poised over the empty one on the coffee table.

"Sure, why not?" I said, watching him fill the crystal goblet with red liquid. We both took a seat on the couch.

A bolt of lightning flashed so sharply that it made me

jump, followed seconds later by a clap of thunder, so intense that it vibrated the windows in the house.

A worried look crossed his face.

"I don't know what I was thinking, riding my bike over here. I should have just gone back to my hotel room after visiting Dad."

I knew that the last time he was here visiting Hal he had stayed at a hotel conveniently close to New Hope. I assumed that's the place he was referring to now.

"Maybe I could borrow Dad's Subaru for the night and bring it back tomorrow?"

"Or maybe you could just spend the night here."

Did I just say that?

I hastily took another sip of wine and blubbered on, "I mean, there are certainly enough rooms, and after all, it *is* your dad's house. This storm is crazy, and why chance driving on I-4 in weather like this?"

Through the sliding glass doors, we saw another bolt of lightning pierce the lake, illuminating the whole backyard like a moment of daylight, then a tremendous boom of thunder ricocheted off the house.

"Ellen, thanks for the offer, but I don't know if that would be a wise thing for me to do."

"Why not?" I asked, feeling courageous. Or was it fear? I really didn't want to spend the night alone in this kind of weather anyway.

His mouth was set in a grim line, and he sat motionless for a moment, then shook his head as if clearing cobwebs from his mind.

"Of course it would be fine– I think I *will* stay…in Dad's room. In fact, it would be nice, actually. Coming here…coming home…always relaxes me. That's why I came today. I pulled out of the parking lot at New Hope and the bike just seemed to come here on its own. I think I just needed to keep moving– I wanted to drive and drive– and this is where I ended up. To be honest, Ellen, in the funk that I was in, I forgot you were staying here."

"Well, thanks for sharing that little morsel. *I* see how it is!" I replied, turning my head away in mock horror.

He put his index finger under my chin, turning my head to face him, and the jolt of electricity I felt at his touch equally matched that of the storm outside. What *is* it with this guy?

"Maybe that wasn't exactly true. Maybe my subconscious knew you were here, and that *is* why I came."

He removed his finger, and I felt the void of his touch. "I know that you're very easy for me to talk to. I've really enjoyed our phone conversations. I feel like I know you so well, and this is really only the second time we've met in person. I just can't believe that!"

I was getting all shaky inside.

"Anyway, we've never talked about our personal relationships, and being a married man, I felt that it might be stepping over my boundaries to discuss that part of my life with you and to ask you about your situation…but it seems that things have changed."

He took a deep breath, and I held mine.

"I'm getting a divorce."

I didn't know whether to lie and pretend that I didn't know or to tell him that Casey had already told me. Maybe I'd just sidestep the issue.

"I'm so sorry to hear that, Nick."

I impulsively put my hand on top of his and felt the physical connection once again. "If you want to talk about it, I'm a good listener."

"I know you are, Ellen, I could tell that right away about you. I don't want to dump on you though. I'm a man…I'm supposed to be able to handle this."

"What the heck difference does *that* make? Why don't I tell you a little about what happened to me, and then you can tell me your story. That way we'll dump on each other and neither one of us will feel guilty, okay?"

The rain was pelting mercilessly against the glass, and the lights flickered. Nick turned his hand over and clasped mine in a warm grip.

"You first," he said, leaning his head back on the couch and settling in, as if it was story time at the library.

I began my tale with the day I came home and found Jack packing his suitcases and ended it with Casey suggesting this job, of course not going into *all* the personal details and skirting some of the more painful issues, but I *did* tell him about my panic attacks. It made me feel upset to relive all those feelings, and I could feel myself trembling inside just from the sheer agony of talking about it again.

He was quiet for a bit after I finished and watched as I wiped a stray tear from my cheek, all the while still holding my hand.

"I'm sorry, Ellen…I should have been more sensitive to your situation. I really had no idea! I'm so sorry I upset you by having you tell me these things. Let me say though, Jack is an ass!"

I had to smile at that.

"Come here," he said as he pulled me close into a hug.

I rested my head against his shoulder, feeling his warm breath at my ear. It felt so good to be in his arms! He gently stroked the back of my head, repeatedly letting his hand slide to the tips of my hair. I was in a total state of contentment and relaxation. The inner shaking was gone, but in its place was a physical longing…and that was very dangerous.

Coming to my senses, I pushed gently away.

"Now it's your turn," I said as I mimicked him by resting my head against the back of the couch and propping my feet up on the coffee table.

Nick poured himself another glass of wine and put what was left of the bottle into my glass. He stood up and walked to the glass doors, looking out into the black night. The storm was still raging, and I was really glad that he was here with me. Since I've been in Florida, I've witnessed the kind of storms that come in the afternoon, and an hour later the sun is shining. This one was a tad more extreme, to say the least.

"J-Rae and I married when we were really young. We were crazy kids in love…at least, I know *I* was in love. Now I'm beginning to question things from way back. I left my family here in Florida to start a business in Memphis so she could be near her family," he began, still facing the door.

"We started the construction company together. I got the jobs and took care of the hands-on construction, and she managed the office: doing the payroll, taking care of the accounting, stuff like that."

"Even when we had Chris, she would have her parents watch him so she could come and work with me. I admired her dedication to our business. She really was good at keeping things moving along at a profitable clip. The business grew and so did the profits."

"We had a great house, nice cars, and went on terrific vacations. About the time when Chris was in elementary school, we had so many jobs going that it was impossible for the men to come to the office to get their pay, so she would deliver the paychecks to the job foreman on-site so he could distribute them to the men."

"One Friday afternoon, I stopped by one of the job sites for an inspection, and I couldn't find the foreman. The crew told me that he was in the job trailer getting their paychecks, so I went to the trailer, but the door was locked. I could hear scrambling inside, and the foreman finally answered the door, still tucking in his shirt."

My heart went out to him. "Oh, Nick, how awful!"

He continued as if he hadn't heard me, immersed in his memories.

"Needless to say, that was the foreman's last paycheck from me. J-Rae thought it was no big deal and said it 'just happened,' no emotional ties. I tried to put it out of my mind, I really did, but once someone betrays your trust, it's really hard to get it back."

"The years went by though and on the surface things pretty much got back to normal between us. Once Chris was in high school, she decided that since she enjoyed the financial aspect of our business so much, she would try to have a side business of her own. I thought that would be fine. I was even *proud* of her! She comes off as being a bit of a ditz, but she's very smart and knows how to manipulate people to get what she wants."

"So, she started getting into real estate investments and was doing quite well for herself. I didn't really understand all that mumbo jumbo, but she loved it and seemed happy. Then she started going away for weekends to different 'training sessions,' and that's when I noticed things starting to change."

Nick walked back and picked up the wine bottle, forgetting that it was empty, then put it back down on the table. He walked over to the cabinet, chose another bottle, and wordlessly refilled our glasses.

"After returning from one of her weekends away, she sat me down and told me that she was seeing someone else and that she wanted to leave me. I was devastated and pleaded with her to stay, for the sake of our son, if nothing else. Chris was almost ready to graduate, I didn't want to ruin his last years at home...and I still loved her, ya know?"

He reclaimed his seat on the couch, tipping his head back and putting up his feet to mirror mine, and continued.

"Turns out the guy was married, too, and he didn't want to leave his wife, so they broke it off and she stayed with me after all. Things were as good as could be expected. Then lately she started going away on the trips again and being very secretive about her phone calls. Then I happened to be looking over the financial books for our company, and for the first time ever, we were showing a loss! I couldn't *believe* it! When I confronted her about it, well, that was the beginning of the end."

Another crack of lightning and rumble of thunder. The lights flickered again and then went out, the fireplace becoming the only illumination in the room.

"Damn," Nick said.

I drained my glass and put it on the table, once again leaning back on the couch, and once again glad that I wasn't alone in the house. With Nick here beside me, it felt cozy and safe. The wine was making me drowsy, and I put my hand to my mouth to cover a yawn.

"So what happened with your business?" I asked.

"I'm still investigating that. I suspect that somehow she was filtering money from our company and putting it into her own. Of course J-Rae denies any wrongdoing. Said she just took her share of a divorce settlement up front instead of going through all the red tape. She reconciled with the bastard that she had been with before, and they're probably off spending my

371

hard-earned profits right now."

"Bad enough that she doesn't love me anymore, but did she have to try to ruin me financially as well? And it's my fault because I trusted her."

"It's not your fault for trusting your wife, Nick; that's what a marriage is supposed to be built on. I think once that trust is gone, though, the foundation is cracked, and it's a very rare couple that can hold a marriage together after that. Sounds to me like you gave her the benefit of the doubt more times than she deserved; as they say: three strikes, you're out!"

He looked over at me, and it looked like he was trying to smile.

"For what it's worth, Nick…J-Rae is an ass," I said smugly.

His face broke into the real deal and he actually laughed. But what happened next was no laughing matter.

CHAPTER TWENTY SEVEN

"Thanks, Ellen, for putting that into perspective," he said still smiling. "It's hysterical to hear something like that coming out of your mouth!"

He leaned over, put both hands on my cheeks, and gave me a quick spontaneous kiss.

My eyes opened wide, and I saw his face turn serious just before I closed my eyes and leaned toward him again. This time I kissed him gently and slowly. Nothing touched but our lips, but I somehow felt like my whole body was consumed by desire. It felt perfect, just as I had imagined it would. Even though this was only our second meeting in person, I felt that I knew *exactly* the kind of man he was from all of our phone conversations. Plus, I knew his dad, I knew his son; they all appeared to be fine men…overloaded with integrity. But nothing so analytical was going through my head at the moment. It was raw emotion and the physical need to be close to him.

He pulled away and looked me in the eye for a second. I nodded slowly, then he pulled me to him and hugged me tightly. We both seemed to be released from our emotional stupor; now that we had confessed our past secrets, we felt free to live in the moment.

"Ellen…" he began, but when I slowly brushed my cheek against his, he captured my lips in another kiss, this time deeper and with urgency. Our hands were moving over each other, and when I felt his hand under my shirt, I did not flinch, but welcomed the sensation…and all the sensations that came after that.

Later, when we found ourselves lying on the floor in front of the fire, I was completely at ease, and I knew for a fact that I loved this man beside me. Crazy, I know, but true. He was the only man that I had shared myself fully with besides Jack. It didn't matter to me that I had just met him. I felt like I had known him in my heart my whole life.

I closed my eyes as Nick grabbed a blanket from the couch and put it over us, and I blissfully fell asleep in his arms, with the sound of the rain still pelting against the windows.

I pulled the blanket up snugly around my chin and rolled over to face the window. I blinked my eyes open and squinted into the bright sunlight filtering through the glass.

Wow, morning already, and last night's storm was a thing of the past...and so was my wonderful dream. I lay there on the floor, eyeing the two empty wine glasses, trying to decipher what was real and what *surely* couldn't have happened.

I heard a rap on the back door and Sylvia's voice calling me.

"Ellen! You in there?"

Oh, geez.

I tossed back the blanket and stood up, tying to smooth the wrinkles in my clothes, and made it to the door just as Sylvia was pounding again. I clicked the lock and slid it quickly open.

"Good morning!" I greeted her, still smoothing my hair. I hadn't looked in the mirror, but how bad could it be?

"You okay?" Sylvia asked, slowly taking in my appearance.

"Sure, why wouldn't I be?" my gravelly voice giving away that those were the first words I'd spoken this morning.

"Oh, I don't know...just that we had a humdinger of a storm last night and lost power and phones for most of the night…and I tried your cell phone, but you didn't answer…and I thought maybe you were scared over here by yourself…but then again, maybe you weren't by yourself after all."

I opened my mouth to speak, but to my dread, nothing came out.

Sylvia cracked her gum in the silence.

I saw a movement behind her, and my eyes focused on Nick down by the shoreline, picking up branches that had fallen during the storm. My face felt warm and flushed. I saw Sylvia follow my gaze and she cracked her gum again.

"Like I said, maybe you weren't alone," she repeated.

"Actually, no, I wasn't. Nick stopped by to check on the construction progress and the storm came and he was on his bike and couldn't leave." I was talking fast, even for a Northerner.

Sylvia blinked, and while she stood in the doorway digesting that information, the aroma of coffee drifted out to us.

"Sure could use a cup of coffee. I have some news to tell you," Sylvia said.

"Come on in. What's up?" I replied, turning toward the kitchen.

We passed through the den on our way to the kitchen, and I knew without even looking behind me that she did not miss the two wine glasses and the blanket still on the floor.

Nick had started the coffee brewing and thankfully made a whole pot. There was also a white crinkly bag of donuts on the table as well. What the heck time did the man wake up? I felt very sheepish for sleeping in. I peeked inside the bag. Oh, my favorite! Jelly-filled and covered with powdered sugar!

I filled two mugs with the steaming brew, settled Sylvia at

the table with the donut bag, and excused myself to freshen up. I dashed into the first floor powder room, which was still under renovation, but at least it had fixtures. One look in the mirror confirmed that I was a total mess. I splashed some warm water on my face and dabbed under my eyes with a tissue to remove some of the mascara smudges. Then I finger combed my hair and pinched my cheeks to give them some color. I really wanted a shower and a clean change of clothes, but Sylvia was chomping at the bit to share her news with me.

My mind was still churning, trying to come to terms with the events of last evening. I threw away my mascara-smudged tissue, and as my eyes focused on the trash can, a tiny, square foil wrapper caught my eye. So it wasn't a dream– Nick and I had made love.

I stared at my reflection in the mirror, and even though I saw the same face that had stared back at me for fifty years, I realized in that instant that inside I was becoming a new person. A woman who is beginning to find out who she really is and actually likes herself. A woman who is intimate with a man she has only known a month! Huh. Imagine that. Instead of feeling embarrassed or ashamed, though, I felt exuberant!

I wanted nothing more than to run down to the lake and throw myself into Nick's arms and hold him tight, but first I had to deal with Sylvia.

I made my way back to the kitchen and presented myself once again for her scrutiny. To my surprise, Nick had joined our coffee klatch and the two of them were in a heated discussion. Sylvia had spread a newspaper open on the table and was pointing to an article with her flamingo pink nail.

"We aren't just goin' to stand by and let this happen to us! No sir-ee!" Sylvia appeared to be uncharacteristically rattled.

Nick picked up the paper, along with a pair of reading glasses, and began to scan the article. He caught my eye for a brief second before he lowered his head to the page, and gave me a smile that I felt all the way through my body.

"What's going on?" I asked as I casually added sugar and cream to my coffee and picked a donut out of the bag. It was so hard to appear normal when I felt like a hundred butterflies were doing the electric slide in my belly.

"Someone is trying to pull the wool over our eyes, and we're just not goin' to stand for that!" Sylvia said, slapping her hand on the table.

"Okay, Syl, calm down and start at the beginning," I said as I put my hand gently on top of hers. "Whatever it is, we'll work through it together."

Nick had finished reading the article, and I watched as he put one spoonful of sugar and two glugs of cream into his coffee and swirled it together.

"Ellen, I think Sylvia has a major concern here, but we might be able to help. Go ahead, Sylvia, start at the beginning."

I was totally perplexed by this point, and I gave her hand a little squeeze of encouragement.

"Well, Sophia was reading her financial newspaper yesterday and stumbled on a tiny announcement that the owners of Lakeside Estates are considering sellin' the property, and that Shoresale Investments is the company interested in purchasing it. It was only by chance that she even saw the article. It was right next to the overstock sale ad for Boscanes...we've been looking for new furniture. Anyway, we called a meetin' of the Lakeside Community Association...all of us on the committee are residents there, ya know, and we look out for the well-being of the community."

I took a sip of my coffee, my donut all but forgotten, as I listened to Sylvia's story.

"First of all, we were shocked to hear that Lakeside Estates was even up for sale...that had never been mentioned to us, and when we saw that Shoresale Investments might gobble it up, we were furious."

"What's so bad about Shoresale?" I asked as I took another sip of coffee.

This time Nick spoke. "Isn't that the company that's buying up all the orange groves down the road and building all those high-end houses?"

"Yep, they're the vultures all right!" Sylvia exclaimed, jumping up from her chair. She began to pace around the kitchen, her hot pink flip flops flapping against the tile. "They bought up two mobile home parks dirt cheap over on Lake Pete too. Gave the residents two months to move out, then built those mansions and made mega-bucks. They tell the sellers that they'll give the residents a fair shake, and then before the ink is dried on the sales agreement, they boot them out on their kazeezers. We know some people who lived over there and that's just the way it went down. If they buy Lakeside Estates, we'll all have to move."

And with that she plunked back down in her chair and shoved the newspaper toward me.

"Sylvia, are you sure about all this?" I asked as I scanned the article.

"Sure as shoot'n, Miss Ellen. We have to put a stop to this."

"Let me talk to Dad. He knows everyone in this area and is very knowledgeable about real estate, Sylvia," Nick offered.

"Well, that would be dandy, honey. I think I'll go over that way this mornin' and talk to him myself."

And with that she picked up her paper and her donut and headed toward the door.

"Thanks for listening, and for the idea to talk to Hal. If anyone has a good head on his shoulders, it's Hal!"

"I could ask Casey to look into it, too," I suggested.

She opened the sliding door to exit the way she came in, and turned to look at us over her shoulder.

"Ellen, just because I'm riled up this mornin' doesn't mean you're off the hook. I'll talk to *you* later!" She wagged her finger at me, then slid the door closed and disappeared around the back of the house, the silence of her absence filling the whole room.

I felt the heat radiate from my inner core, igniting every inch of my body to reach my outer extremities, I'm sure coloring my face beet red. Of course she wasn't aware that Nick was getting a divorce.

Almost afraid to see Nick's reaction, I waited a few moments before I had the courage to glance his way. When I did, I found him looking at me, studying my face with his gentle blue eyes and a smile that was almost shy. He was leaning back in his chair, his hands turning his coffee cup slowly in a circle.

I found myself smiling in return, my nervousness gone. I broke off a small piece of donut and popped it into my mouth without taking my eyes from his. He reached over and ran his thumb across my lips.

"Had a little powdered sugar there," he explained. Then he leaned over and gently kissed me. "I missed a spot."

I was breathless and hungry for more– kisses, not donuts. But he pulled back and resumed his laid-back posture, raising the mug to his own lips and taking a long sip. And when he put the cup back down, his eyes were troubled.

"Ellen, *about* last night...." he began.

Oh, no! I knew I did not want to hear the end of any sentence that began that way.

"Nick, last night was wonderful," I interrupted.

His eyes jerked up to mine, searching.

"You aren't upset with me?" he asked.

"Why would I be upset with you? We were two consenting adults," I replied, narrowing my eyes.

"Well, I show up unexpectedly, soaking wet on your doorstep, and spill out my broken-hearted sob story. We drink some wine, the lights go out…and…well…I thought maybe you felt that I took advantage of you and the situation."

Actually, I hadn't had time to even consider that scenario. I was still basking in the joy of receiving so much pleasure.

"Well, *were* you?" I asked point blank, surprising myself.

He didn't reply right away, and I pushed my chair back, loudly scraping it against the floor. The warm, fuzzy feeling was instantly replaced by embarrassment and hurt. So he *did* take advantage of me. First I let Brooklyn get personal with me, and now I actually got intimate with Nick. What is *wrong* with me? I was morphing into one of those women that Abbey and I used to roll our eyes at. The ones who sit at wine and cheese night and compare notes about all the men they've slept with and act like they have nothing better to do than find a man. We used to wonder why they just couldn't be themselves for a while without being in a relationship. Now I was finding out.

I turned my back to the table and rinsed my mug in the sink. Before I could turn back around, Nick's warm arms circled me from behind and turned me to face him. Tears were stinging my eyes, and I was really trying not to let them overflow. However, when he put his finger under my chin and gently forced me to look him in the eye, they defied me and spilled out onto my cheeks.

"Oh, Ellen…I'm so sorry," he said as he pulled me close. He smelled of fresh air and fabric softener and coffee.

I gave a tiny shrug, not trusting my voice.

He pushed me away just far enough to look in my eyes again.

"Ellen, I'm not sorry it *happened*...I guess I'm just sorry it happened under those circumstances. I don't want you to ever think that I'm making love to you because I can't be with someone else. I want you to know that when I'm with you...well, I'm totally with *you*. I'm so mixed up right now. I'm raw with hurt inside over what just happened in my marriage. I've got a lot of anger and confusion, and just stuff I need to work out. I've been feeling very lonely for a while now, and I can't tell you how much talking to you on the phone has helped me through these past weeks."

I nodded, still not able to talk.

"And when I saw you in person yesterday, all these feelings for you hit me like a load of bricks, and I just wanted to be with you. I just couldn't get enough of you."

"So what exactly are you trying to say, Nick?" I had found my voice, and my exasperation was reflected in my tone.

He expelled a heavy sigh, gave me another quick hug, then pushed me away again to face him.

"What I'm having such a hard time saying is that I have real feelings for you, Ellen. I have from the very first moment I saw you jumping up and down with a bloody toe, and the more I get to know you, the more I've come to like you, to feel close to you. I love your humor and kind ways, I respect your knowledge and creativity. Now that I know what you are overcoming after your marriage, I have admiration for your courage and confidence."

Was he talking about me, or was there another Ellen in the room?

"I just have to get my shit together before I can commit to any kind of serious relationship. I don't want to lead you on to think that I can do something that I'm not ready to do, that's all."

"Nick, if anyone understands how you're feeling right now, it's me. I'm still coming to terms with my *own* feelings. Even though I'm not devastated daily about Jack leaving, I'm still hurt and still think about him. I don't expect a committed relationship from you right now. I'm not really ready either. And I don't want you to think that I sleep around. You are the *only* man I've ever been with besides Jack."

He had been watching me intently as I spoke, and I could see the relief in his eyes.

"So, how do you want to handle it from here?" he asked.

I shrugged, and he pulled me close into a hug.

"I can't deny that I have feelings for you, Nick; I wouldn't have let that happen last night if I didn't," I breathed into his ear.

"Ellen," he began as he stroked my hair, "How lucky can a man be?"

I smiled and pushed *him* away this time. "Well, if you play your cards right, maybe you *will* get lucky again."

He threw his head back and laughed loudly, and I ducked out of his embrace and dashed through the living room and up the stairs with Nick hot on my trail. He tackled me on my bed, and we both collapsed on the mattress, breathless.

Today was much brighter than yesterday, and much warmer. After showering, I slathered on my usual sunscreen, and took some extra time with my hair and makeup. I hiked up a pair of denim walking shorts and yanked a black and white print tank top over my head, finishing off by sliding my feet into a pair of black sandals.

Taking a deep breath, I looked in the mirror and gave myself a quick once-over. I saw a vastly different reflection than the one that had greeted me in Jeannette on that fateful day that Jack had left.

The dark under eye circles, puffy lids, and pale skin had been replaced by well-rested, clear eyes, and just enough tan for a healthy glow. Instead of the inch or so of gray roots, my color and highlights have held up quite nicely. In fact, I now have some natural highlights from the sun. Note to self though: ask Casey soon about a hair stylist. The smile that I used to force was now pretty much a permanent fixture and came easily and naturally. Oh, I've certainly had my sad moments since I've been here, but for the most part I think I'm healing quite nicely. The good days way out number the not so good ones.

This one in particular has turned into one of the best days! I know most of the glow on my face today is because of Nick. After we snuggled and kissed on my bed this morning, we both decided that we should put the brakes on being more intimate for a little while to give him time to come to terms with his situation, and for us to get to know each other better. Dr. Burke would have been proud! I still find it hard to believe that last night actually happened at all, but it did, and I'm determined to embrace it, not feel guilty about it.

So…we are dating. Well, sort of, I guess. We also came to the conclusion that it might not be in anyone's best interest to make that a well-known fact. I'm not sure how Casey would feel about me dating Chris's dad, and I'm very sure that Chris wouldn't appreciate me getting chummy with Nick when he hasn't even adjusted to his parents' break-up yet. Heck, he just found out yesterday at lunch!

Even though Nick probably isn't totally aware of it, he has a lot of healing to do yet. I can vouch for that. At least I'm a few steps ahead of him in that game.

So complicated. Although as much as I was in a fog about

the end of my relationship with Jack, I feel that I have total clarity on this one beginning with Nick. I have real feelings for him, and I'm prepared to be patient and enjoy every step of the way and hopefully it will have a happy ending.

But for now, Nick was waiting for me downstairs. He was taking me to an early dinner at a place in town that is one of his favorites.

I bounced down the steps and found Nick in the sitting room, hovering over my sketches. He looked up as I entered the room.

"Ellen, did *you* do these?"

I came to stand beside him and looked down at my work, shaking my head up and down.

"They're amazing. *You're* amazing!"

I always wondered what people meant when they said that they swelled with pride. Now I know. I was so pleased that it felt like my insides were going to burst.

"Thanks! I hadn't touched a charcoal pencil in forever, but it's coming back to me. I'm going to give the otters and the one of Dora to your dad," I said as I held them up for his inspection.

Geez, were his eyes misting over?

"Ellen, I just can't believe you. J-Rae and Dad never really got along; she thinks of him as a persnickety, crazy, old man, and he's always just tolerated her to keep peace in the family, but you've only known him a short time, and you're making him such a wonderful gift from the heart. I'm overwhelmed!"

"Nick, I just *love* your dad! He's a gentleman, and is so kind and generous, and what a sense of humor! He made me feel welcome right from the start, and to give me the opportunity to have this job, well, *I'm* overwhelmed with that!"

"He loves you too. He told me so," Nick said quietly as he carefully placed my drawings back on the table.

"I think he may be falling *in* love with someone else though," I said carefully.

"Sylvia?" Nick asked smiling.

"You noticed too?"

"Hard not to! She's been visiting him all the time, and he talks about her every time I call him. It's always, "Guess what color Sylvia had her hair today?" or, "Sylvia wants to join the High Rollers!" or "Sylvia snuck in a cheeseburger from Big Al's for me!"

"Are you okay with that?" I asked, curious to know if he could accept his father being with someone else after his mom's passing.

"I think it's great! Really. He and Mom had the perfect marriage, and it's been three years now. I want him to live the rest of his life being happy, and I know he's been lonely."

"That's really sweet of you to say, Nick. I know he'll be looking for your approval, and I'm so happy that you feel the way you do. And I think Sylvia will be a good partner for him. She's just so full of life, and she has a heart of gold."

"Well, tomorrow *is* Valentine's Day…" Nick said as he opened the front door for me, then made sure it was locked behind us. "Maybe love is in the air."

I had completely forgotten about Valentine's Day. Huh.

Nick handed me a helmet, and we both mounted the bike and took off down the road towards town.

CHAPTER TWENTY EIGHT

Joe's was a small mom and pop restaurant tucked in between the strip mall and the dry cleaner's on Cypress Street. We walked under the wine colored canvas awning, past the plate glass windows lining the front of the building, and as Nick held the glass paneled door open for me, the wonderful aroma of spaghetti sauce was almost too much to bear.

"Oh my gosh, Nick, it just smells *delicious* in here!" I exclaimed as my belly started rumbling. I hadn't eaten anything since the jelly donut I splurged on this morning.

The place was on the small side, and there was only one other family dining. Nick told me that if you wait until later in the day though, people would be waiting on the sidewalk outside to get a table.

"Nicky! Nicky!"

A man with short gray hair balding from the forehead and dark bushy eyebrows came quickly out of the kitchen, wiping his hands on his black apron. He was wearing black pants held up by suspenders over a crisply starched, short-sleeved white dress shirt, rolled up to expose his muscular forearms. He pushed his gold wire-framed glasses up on his nose and extended his right hand to Nick, pumping it up and down and simultaneously patting him on the back with his left.

"It's a-been-a long time no see, eh?" he said as he looked up into Nick's face. Nick was about a head taller.

"Who have-a we here?" he said, looking at me with a smile.

I immediately loved this man.

"This is my friend, Ellen. She's taking care of Dad's place while he's in the nursing home. Ellen, this is Ernest. He and his wife own the restaurant."

Ernest gave me a warm smile that lit up his whole face, and he started pumping my hand with the same exuberance.

"I can't wait to try your food…it smells wonderful in here, and Nick told me that you have the best homemade spaghetti!" I told him.

He blushed a little and led us to a booth back in the corner. The tabletop was white Formica and the benches were sunshine yellow, made of the same material. Salt and pepper shakers kept company with clear glass containers of crushed red pepper and white plastic napkin holders on each table.

"You have-a seat-a here. Two spaghetti's? How many meat-a-balls do you want?" Ernest looked at us expectantly. And I looked at Nick raising my eyebrows.

"Give us each three, please!" Nick replied.

"Three?" I looked at Nick with my eyes wide.

"Ellen, I've seen you eat."

Ernest shuffled back to the kitchen, his black Reeboks not making a sound.

The door had hardly closed when it opened again, and this time a robust woman came out, with the same gray hair as Ernest, only hers was caught behind her head in a twist and covered by a hair net. She was also wearing a black apron, covering a mid-calf black skirt and a white button-down blouse.

Her already rosy cheeks seemed to gain more color with every step she took towards us.

"Nicky! How are you?"

Nick stood and embraced her, and they rocked back and forth a moment.

"How is that father of yours?"

Nick explained briefly that Hal was doing fine, then he introduced me.

"Ellen, this is Josephine, Ernest's wife, and the best noodle maker in the world!"

She patted him on the cheek then bent over the table to shake my hand.

"Nice to meet you, Ellen. This boy knows that flattery will get him everywhere, or at least an extra meatball!"

Ernest brought out a red plastic basket filled with warm bread and a bottle of red wine with four glasses, which he filled, handing one to each of us.

"To old friends and–a new friends!" Ernest toasted, and we all clunked our glasses and took a sip.

"This is a new batch...good, no?" Ernest asked.

We all agreed exuberantly.

"Ernest makes his own wine." Nick told me after they both went back in the kitchen to prepare our food.

"Nick, they seem so nice! How did you get to be such good friends?"

"I worked here after school bussing tables and helping clean the kitchen. They're good people."

"Why do they call it Joe's if his name is Ernest?"

"Well, *her* name is Josephine...Joe for short."

Turns out that "Joe" *is* the best pasta maker in the world, or at least makes the best that I've ever tasted! Our white china plates had come heaped with pasta, delectable red sauce, and meatballs. Josephine was true to her word, and gave Nick four. I leaned back on the bench with my hand on my stomach.

"Wow! That was amazing!"

Nick smiled at me, and we both turned our heads as the door to the kitchen opened once again.

I looked quickly at Nick, who was now grinning from ear to ear, and then back to Ernest who was sauntering towards our table, playing of all things, the accordion!

I had never seen one played in person, only on the Lawrence Welk show that I watched with my parents when I was a kid. I sat mesmerized as he held the box-shaped instrument, the fingers of his right hand nimbly moving up and down the keyboard, while his left hand opened and closed the bellows to make a truly delightful sound.

He was like a one-man band, and after studying his moves, I could tell that he was playing the melody on the piano-like keys and playing the chords by covering the valves with his left hand, all the while pumping it in and out and crooning in a way that would have given Dean Martin a run for his money!

I found myself humming along. His music literally gave me goose bumps! The last song was "Volare," to which Nick and I stood and clapped the rhythm along with him.

I couldn't control the happiness that I felt. I reached up and gave Nick the biggest hug!

"Ernest, that was just *incredible!* Thank you so very, *very* much!" I said as I looked him in the eye and put both of my hands on my chest.

We said our goodbyes, exchanged our hugs, and after promising to come back soon and accepting a takeout order of spaghetti and meatballs to take to Hal, we hopped on the bike and headed home.

I was on such an incredible high from the good food and amazing music, and the fact that I had shared them with Nick made them all the more memorable.

"Nick, I can't thank you enough for dinner. I had such a wonderful time!" I said as I handed my helmet to him and he tucked it away in the compartment on his bike. I knew that he needed to leave soon. He was going to stop in and see Hal, then spend the night at the hotel and leave for Memphis in the morning, so I was going to pack Hal's spaghetti in some ice to keep it cool for the ride to New Hope.

We walked arm in arm across the driveway, both of us singing, *"Volare, oh oh oh oh...no wonder my happy heart sings...your love has given me wings..."* And at that moment I felt like my heart *did* have wings!

Nick rummaged around and found a small cooler that would fit on the bike, and as I moved to the freezer to get the ice, I noticed that my cell phone, sitting on the table where I had left it, had a missed call.

While Nick completed the packaging, I picked up my phone and saw that the missed call was from Annee Slater, and I began to listen to her voice mail.

"What's wrong?" Nick said as he quickly came to my side. "Your face just turned white as a ghost!"

He grabbed my free hand as I held the phone next to my ear. Slowly I looked up at him and put the phone back on the table.

"We have an offer on the house."

I thought I was okay with this. I thought I was over this. I thought, well, I thought I would be happy when it was sold so we could get some closure. I thought wrong.

It felt like someone had sucker punched me in the

stomach.

Nick pulled me close, holding me tight and stroking the back of my head. I didn't want to cry right now. Maybe later, but not now in front of Nick.

"I'm okay," I said as Nick released me. "Just came as a shock, ya know?"

"I can imagine, Ellen. I know how I'm going to feel when I have to sell my house in Memphis."

I busied myself by moving over to the counter and putting the spaghetti in the cooler.

"I know that you have to get going; I'll be fine. Be careful driving, okay?"

Nick looked at me a moment with a frown on his face, then put his hands on top of mine, stilling them from their frantic motions.

"I'm sorry you have to go through this, Ellen."

"Me, too!" I tried to laugh and make light of it.

"Well, I hate to leave you under these circumstances, but I really need to get going."

"Call me when you get a chance. Do you think you'll be coming back soon?" I asked, maybe a little too hopefully.

"Not sure if I'll be back before Dad's birthday, and that's in two weeks. Just so many details to figure out. I'll call you though, and you can call me anytime…please."

I handed him the cooler and we walked side by side out to the bike. He loaded up and turned to look me in the eye.

"I'm going to miss you," he said as he pulled me close.

"I'm going to miss you, too."

He bent his head and kissed me gently, then hopped on his Harley and fastened his helmet.

"I love you," almost came out of my mouth, because it was true, but I caught myself just in time and touched my fingers to my lips and blew a kiss his way.

He smiled and winked, then he was rumbling down the driveway.

I crossed my arms in front of my chest and gave myself a hug as I stood listening to the sound of Nick fading away, then I walked slowly back into the house. The construction crew had been here for a short time this afternoon, going over the plans with Nick. Everything was moving along quite nicely and really should be completed in a few weeks.

I've really been enjoying watching it all come together, and I was very excited for Hal to see all the improvements. I've been taking pictures and showing them to him on my laptop, and it seems that Hal has been improving as quickly as his home. Before too long he would be zooming around the new kitchen with his walker, chasing Sylvia into the new bedroom. Now that was a visual!

The faint scent of Joe's spaghetti still lingered in the air as I grabbed my cell phone off the kitchen table. I had dropped it there like a hot potato after hearing Annee's message. I meandered through the house and out the back porch door, making my way down to my favorite spot on the pier. Dora came up to join me, and I tossed her a handful of corn and plunked down on the bench.

The days were slowly getting longer, so I figured I had time to make my call before darkness consumed the lake, and before I chickened out. Taking a deep breath, I pushed the button for return call.

Her receptionist answered, and in a moment Annee's

clear voice greeted me.

"Mrs. Stern, how are you?"

"I'm magnificent, really..." I answered.

"Wonderful! You picked a great time to leave. This winter has been one of the worst ever! I would give anything to be in Florida with you!" she gushed. "I have equally wonderful news for you. We have a nice offer on your house!"

"Oh."

"I'm glad you called back before I left the office; I wanted to go over the particulars as soon as possible because we need to respond to the potential buyer within twenty-four hours."

My heart lurched in my chest. There would be no lollygagging on this decision.

Annee started spewing out legal mumbo jumbo, explaining the details of the proposal as I sat dazed with my eyes focused on the horizon.

"So, all that said and done, in layman's terms, they have offered you fifteen thousand dollars below asking price and are requesting that you pay closing costs. Not really a bad offer in this economy, especially at this time of year. What do you think, Mrs. Stern?"

Now that she had come up for air, I knew that I had to fill the empty air space with a response. The only one I could think of involved saying his name.

"What does Jack want to do?"

Annee sighed. "Why don't you tell me what you think first, then we'll get into that."

"Well, it seems when I watch all the TV shows, the seller usually counters with an offer. Do you think that's worth a try? I know we don't have a tremendous amount of equity left in the house, so every little bit would help."

"I'm glad to hear you say that, Mrs. Stern. That would be my advice to you. I heard from Jack's camp today, and Jack is willing to take their offer and call it a day."

I started fuming. Of course he would say that! He just wants to unload the burden. He already has his new house, whereas I have nothing.

"So, now what?" I asked.

"I think a good counter offer would be to split the difference in half. Let's ask for seventy-five hundred under asking price."

"I'm agreeable to that, but what about Jack?" My feet were tapping double time on the wooden planks. I hadn't felt this nervous in a long time.

"I think your request is reasonable, and I think his attorney will agree with that. Let me give them a call and I'll get right back to you. Keep your fingers crossed!"

The sun was low on the horizon, hiding behind a wispy, soft layer of clouds, promising a spectacular sunset. However, with every degree that the sun dipped lower, so did my spirits. Dora was munching happily on her treat, oblivious to my dilemma. Within five minutes though, my cell phone rang, and I immediately put it to my ear.

"Hello?" I anxiously answered, expecting the worst from Annee.

"Hey, Ellen," said a voice that was definitely not Annee's. Just the sound of it and that familiar greeting sent a flash of heat all through my body.

"Hey, Jack," I replied as my hand held a death grip on the phone.

"So, looks like we have an offer on the house," he said matter-of-factly.

Play it cool, Ellen.

"So I hear," I replied, trying to hide the quiver in my voice. I figured the fewer words, the better.

"It's a damn good offer, and the only one we've received in almost six weeks. I think we should take it."

Now what? This was why the attorneys were to handle everything. I did *not* want to have this conversation with him.

"My attorney will give you my answer. I just spoke to her."

"Cut the crap, Ellen. I know you want to counter; I just got off the phone with *my* attorney! Listen, *you're* not the one paying the mortgage. I need this house to sell!"

I was trembling inside and out.

"Jack, I'm *not* going to argue with you. Give your answer to my attorney." I was prepared to disconnect right then and there.

The line was quiet for a couple seconds, and I could sense him regrouping.

"How about you meet me for a drink? I can be at the Backyard Grille in forty-five minutes," he said in a softer voice. "We can discuss this face to face."

I almost laughed out loud! He had no idea where I was, and that thrilled me to pieces. Immediately my trembling stopped.

"No thanks, Jack. I really want to counter offer at least once," I said firmly.

"What's the matter, are you too good to have a drink with me now?"

I bet he had already had a few this evening, and I found his comment unworthy of a reply.

After a couple more seconds of silence, he tried another tactic.

"Well, if we lose this sale, it'll be *you* paying next month's mortgage!"

As the sun dipped below the horizon, the heavens had turned to crimson, laced with deep orange and dark gray. It appeared as if the sky had been on fire, and all that remained were glowing embers. In stark contrast, the palm trees were silhouetted black against the brilliant hues, and a soft, rosy glow reflected on the windows of the homes lining the lake's shore, almost convincing one to believe they were made of gold. I inhaled deeply, practically drawing the tranquility of my surroundings into my body.

"Jack, we are going to counter their offer, and they are going to accept it. Goodnight."

And with that I smiled, hung up the phone, and walked slowly back to the house. I made a cup of tea and sat in the den framing the sketches that I had made for Hal, using a forest green matte and a black, gallery style frame for each, remembering the way Nick had been emotionally moved by them this afternoon. I thought of the intimacy that we had shared last night…and then I thought of it some more. I wanted to pick up the phone and talk to him, to reconnect, but I knew that he was probably still visiting with Hal.

Then thoughts of Jack tried to push their way in; he could still exasperate me in the expanse of two measly sentences. In another time and place our conversation would have devastated me. Now that I was out of the box looking in, I realized how manipulative he could be, and I felt a burst of energy just knowing that I didn't have to deal with it anymore…at least not face to face and not on a daily basis.

Just as I pushed down the last tab on the back of the frame for the Dora sketch, my phone rang, making me jump.

This time I looked to see who was calling before I answered. It *was* Annee.

"Hi, Annee!" I felt so much better about *this* phone call.

"Mrs. Stern, I have very good news for you. Are you sitting down?"

I sat down on the soft, brown leather sofa. "Yes, I'm sitting."

"You just sold your house! Congratulations!" Annee sounded elated.

I, on the other hand, felt…I didn't really know what I was feeling. I was relieved to have this part of my ordeal finalized, but it still made me sad.

"Wow." That was about all I could muster.

"I don't know why Jack had a change of heart, but he approved the counter offer and his attorney called me back shortly after I talked to you. We presented the buyers with your offer, and they accepted! So seventy-five hundred dollars under selling price. Job well done, Mrs. Stern!"

"So, now what happens?"

"I'm going to overnight some documents for you to sign. I'd like to send them to Casey's office, and she can walk you through the signature process. Can you get there tomorrow?"

"Sure, as long as she's available…it's Valentine's Day, you know."

Why I expected the world to stop on Valentine's Day, I don't know.

"And it *is* Saturday...do you want to check with her and let me know? I'll be here at the office another half an hour," Annee said.

"I'll do that and get right back to you."

Casey was exuberant when I told her the news.

"Mom, that's awesome! And I'm so proud of you for deciding on making a counter offer! How about I call Annee and set everything up as far as getting the paperwork. I'd like to look everything over before you sign anyway. I've been working every Saturday during income tax season, so no problem with me being in the office."

"That would be great, Casey. Annee said she'll be at the office for another half an hour, so could you call her right away?"

Casey laughed. "I'll call right now."

I dilly-dallied around the house, walking to each window and looking out into the darkness, straightening up a pile of mail, thinking about Nick, thinking about the house, and, sadly but truly, thinking about Jack. My thoughts were jumping around like popcorn in a popper, and I felt that any minute my head was going to explode like a silver foiled Jiffy Pop.

I greedily answered the phone when I heard Casey's ring tone.

"It's all set, Mom. I should have everything here first thing in the morning. Why don't you just come to my place early, and you can ride to the office with me."

"Sounds like a plan. Casey, thanks so much for all your help."

I was pacing back and forth across the kitchen floor.

"No problem, Mom. I have an idea! Why don't you just plan on staying over this way for the afternoon? I would like to treat you to a celebratory lunch."

Oh, that did sound nice; I could use some one-on-one time with my daughter.

"Sure, that sounds fabulous! I have to tell you about this wonderful little Italian place that—"

And I stopped just before I said his name. I am *not* going to be good at this.

"That I heard about," I hurriedly interjected.

"You can tell me all about it tomorrow then. I'll call you in the morning."

We disconnected, and I stood for a moment looking at the phone. Punching in Adam's speed dial, I listened to it ring as I gravitated to my favorite nesting spot in the den. As I snuggled deep into chocolate brown leather, I heard Adam's voice answer the phone, and I immediately smiled.

"Hey, kiddo!"

"Hi, Mom!" Adam replied jubilantly. "How's the tan coming along?

It felt so good to hear his voice! I really missed him.

"Everything is going great, sweetheart. Guess what? We sold the house tonight!"

I realized that I was actually happy to tell him that, so I *must* be okay with it…right?

"Great news, Mom!" he said excitedly. "When's the closing?"

"You know, I don't even know that! Annee Slater is sending the documents to Casey; they'll be here in the morning for me to sign, so I guess all that will be in there."

"Well, that's really good news. I know how excited you must be."

"Yes and no, honey. I still can't believe we're selling it, and when I think of someone else living in it, I kind of get misty-eyed."

"Ah, you'll find something you like better, something that suits just *you*. Maybe we can look for a fixer-upper, and I can make it just the way you want it."

He was being really sweet, and maybe that might not be a bad idea. I was thinking of an apartment or townhouse rental, but I don't think I would be happy if I didn't have a yard of my own.

"Now that the house is sold, you won't have to check on it all the time. Oh, I guess we'll have to get the rest of the furniture out now."

"No problem, Mom, there's not much there anyway, just the few things we used for staging. Mya and I can take care of that in one afternoon. I'll just store it in my garage until you come back."

"Sounds like a plan. Adam, thank you so much for all your help with this. I couldn't have done it without you. There's no way I would have come to Florida if you weren't keeping an eye on the house."

I felt tears stinging my eyes. I really missed Adam!

"So, how is everything down in the sunshine state? How's the reno going?"

I filled him in on the progress we'd made, and I could sense his excitement over the phone.

"Mom, you are so lucky to be living in such an amazing property. The pictures you've been sending are over the top! I'd love to see it in person!"

An idea was brewing in my overloaded brain.

"Well, why don't you just hop on a plane and come down?" I asked.

A pause on the other end of the line told me that he was actually considering it.

"Seriously, Adam, can you get away for a few days? Maybe even a long weekend?"

"Well…there's really no concrete reason why I *couldn't…"*

My idea was gaining momentum.

"You can even call it a business expense. You can check out the construction and be my consultant! Maybe Nick can come while you're here and you can talk about construction stuff. I bet he'd like that."

"You're making it very hard to say no, Mom! Who's Nick?"

Oops.

"Hal's son…Chris's dad…you know, I've been telling you that we're working on the house together?"

"Oh, yeah, just the way you said it made me think it was someone else you were talking about."

My feelings were evident just in the way I said his name?

"Actually, after this winter, it wouldn't take much to twist my arm on escaping to a warmer climate. There might be one little catch though.

My heart sank. "What?"

"I'd like to bring Mya with me; would that be okay?"

My heart smiled again.

"Of course, Adam! I'd love to have her, too!" I talked as if I owned the place, but I don't think Hal would mind me having my family visit. I would confirm with him though, just to be on the safe side.

"By the way, what are you giving her for Valentine's Day?" I asked, still smiling.

"Ah, wouldn't you like to know? I'll tell you tomorrow after I give it to her. I'm sure she'll be equally excited about a trip to Florida though!"

Someone was beeping in on our call, and a quick look at the screen told me that it was Nick.

"Well, I'll talk to you tomorrow then, sweetie! Good night and I love you!"

"Wow, you gave up easy. Catch you tomorrow. G'night, Mom, love you too."

I greedily pushed the answer button.

"Nick?" I said, my heart pounding.

"Hi, Ellie."

He had called me that nickname a few times while he was here, and I was actually growing fond of it. No one had ever called me that before, and it made me feel special.

"I won't keep you long, but I had to hear your voice and make sure you were okay. You seemed so sad when I left, and I regretted not staying longer until you called your attorney back."

I extracted myself from the soft leather and made my way up to the bedroom, tossing myself on the mattress and looking up at the ceiling, a smile cemented on my face.

"Thank you so much for calling me; I was missing you."

"I miss you too, Ellie," he said softly.

"Well, so much has happened since you left."

I told him all that had transpired since he sped down the driveway, finishing with my invitation to Adam.

"Do you think Hal will mind them coming to visit?"

"Are you kidding? He'll be ecstatic! He loves to share his place, and he'll be happy to meet Adam, I'm sure. I have some good news too, and maybe we can coordinate it with Adam's visit."

I was really curious, and I rolled over on my belly, propping myself up on my elbows.

"What's your exciting news?"

"When I visited with Dad tonight, they said he was doing so well that in another week or so he can come home on a field trip, and if we have the first floor bedroom and bathroom finished, he can spend the night."

I sat up straight.

"That *is* exciting news! How wonderful, Nick! Does Hal know? Do you think we'll be done by then? Will he be in a wheelchair or walker?"

Nick was laughing. "One question at a time! Yes, yes, and not sure!" he answered quickly.

Now I laughed because I couldn't remember the order in which I asked the questions!

"So…Hal *does* know, you *do* think we'll be done, and you're not sure about the wheelchair."

"You're good, and not just your memory," Nick said in a tone that revealed his thoughts were not on the moment, but on last night.

I'm sure I was blushing; my face felt hot.

"Nick, last night was so special," I said, making the understatement of the year.

He sighed on the other end of the line, and then I heard a yawn.

"Okay, buster, you'd better get some sleep. I don't want to have to worry about you falling asleep driving tomorrow."

"I'll be fine, Ellie, but it makes me feel good that you're concerned. So, you're feeling good about everything now?" he asked as he stifled another yawn.

"Nick, my head is spinning! So much has happened in the last twenty-four hours…I think I just need time to digest it all."

"I doubt if I'll be back before Dad's birthday, so I'm going to count on you to keep a fire lit under our workers to get the job done in two weeks. I want them to concentrate on that downstairs bathroom. They should install the ceramic tile in the next day or so, and get the painting done so you can go and pick out the accessories."

"Then they need to finish the ramp for the new entry; that will make it easier for him, even if he's not in a wheelchair. And have them move Dad's furniture down to his new bedroom; the painting is done there, so you can decorate that while they're working on the bathroom."

I saluted the phone. "Aye, aye captain!"

There was silence on the other end of the line.

"I'm kidding, Nick."

"Oh, I wasn't sure. I thought maybe I was coming across as too bossy."

"Oh, my gosh, I'm so excited to do all of those things! Don't worry, we'll have it all done in two weeks, and I'll have the extra incentive of knowing that I'll be seeing you then, too."

"Well, I'll let you go," he said reluctantly.

"Good night, Nick, and drive carefully tomorrow. Call me when you get in. And I hope everything goes smoothly for you back in Memphis."

"To be honest, Ellie, I wish I didn't have to go back and face it all, but I know that the sooner I do, the sooner it will all be over."

My emotional barometer just did a nosedive; with all the good things happening, I'd almost forgotten what was really going on in his life. Shame on me.

"You'll be fine, Nick, just take it one day at a time," offering him some good advice that I'd been given.

After we hung up I got ready for bed. It had been quite the eventful evening! As I lay there cuddled under the sheets, the moon sent a soft glow through the windows, casting shadows across the bed.

I felt exhausted, mentally and physically. So many thoughts were going through my head. I set my cell phone alarm and began to get drowsy as I replayed last night over and over again in my mind; I smiled as I thought that I would have to remember to empty that bathroom trash can and get rid of the evidence before Sylvia came back to visit. Oh, Sylvia! I had completely forgotten her dilemma! Shame on me again! Was I still being so consumed by my own life that I couldn't reach out to others?

Before I fell asleep, I made a mental note to stop by and see Sylvia.

CHAPTER TWENTY NINE

I pulled into Casey's parking lot precisely at nine; the plan was to leave the Subaru here and ride to the office with her. Beeping the car locked, I slipped the keys back into my purse and made my way down the palm-lined path toward the courtyard. I spied Casey leaning over her balcony railing talking to someone below. Oh, it was Brooklyn!

They both turned to look at me as I stood there debating whether to proceed forward or turn and run like the wind.

"Mom! You're on time!"

Was she insinuating that I'm usually late?

"I'll be right down! Let me grab my purse," Casey shouted. I saw her disappear and heard the thunk of the sliding glass door closing.

I sighed.

"Ellen! You look *beautiful* this morning!"

I had almost forgotten what a charmer he was. And even though I knew he would probably say those words to every woman he saw this morning, it still was nice to hear.

I heard Casey's heels clicking down the steps, and I smiled in relief.

Brooklyn must have mistaken that my smile was intended for him. He closed the distance between us in several quick strides and grabbed me in an enormous hug. His freshly applied cologne was so strong that it was almost suffocating, and I struggled to pry myself from his embrace. But before I knew it, his lips were on mine! He *was* a good kisser, I'll give him that…but I felt no emotion for him. He held me in a five second lip lock, and when he released me I stood breathless and shocked! What *is* it with this man that makes him think he has free reign over my body?

I put the back of my hand to my lips as he told me, "Happy Valentine's Day, sweetheart!"

Just then Casey turned the corner and said, "Hi, Mr. Blackwell!"

I had a sinking feeling in my stomach, and as Brooklyn put his arm around my shoulder, we both turned to look behind us.

Nick was standing there with a look of total disbelief on his face.

I couldn't speak, I couldn't move; I just stood there with my mouth open and Brooklyn's arm possessively around my shoulder.

Nick's face had gone pale and his expression looked like he was trying to make the same decision that I was a few moments earlier: to proceed forward or run like the wind. To his credit, and my chagrin, he proceeded forward.

Clearing his throat and keeping his hands occupied by rolling and unrolling the papers he was carrying, he began to slowly walk toward us.

Casey had reached our eclectic little group by now and reached up to give Nick a hug.

"Nice to see you again! Chris said you were stopping by this morning," I heard Casey tell him as she wrapped her arms around his neck.

This might have been useful information to me; thanks so much for sharing, daughter.

Nick looked over Casey's shoulder but didn't meet my eye.

As Casey released him, I felt Brooklyn's arm drop from his dominant hold on me as he extended his right hand to Nick.

"Nick, good to see you again! How's the construction business going?" Brooklyn asked, all smiles.

Nick hesitated for a moment, and I was almost afraid he wasn't going to shake Brooklyn's hand, but the pause was so minute I'm sure I was the only one who noticed.

Nick shifted the papers to his left hand and briefly pumped Brooklyn's with his right.

"Oh, having its ups and downs like most businesses these days," Nick replied carefully.

I was still standing there, rooted to the spot, watching this ridiculous exchange of pleasantries like I was a bystander instead of a participant.

To my horror, Nick extended his right hand to me.

"Nice to see *you* this morning, Ellen. What a *surprise!*" Nick said as his blue eyes leveled on mine.

I reached out and put my hand in his, his touch waking me from this surreal experience and bringing me immediately back to reality. I had to say something, but I couldn't say the things I wanted to…needed to.

Our hands held maybe a moment too long, but then again, maybe no one but me noticed.

"I'm a bit surprised to be here myself, actually. We accepted the offer on my house back home last night, and the papers are being sent to Casey's office this morning. I'm going in to work with her to sign them," I said softly, even though he already knew.

"Well, that's cause for celebration! I'm also very close to closing a wonderful property deal myself. I would like to take you out to lunch to celebrate. All of you, that is." Brooklyn said exuberantly, replacing his arm around me and giving my shoulder a squeeze.

I wanted to vaporize.

"Thanks, Brooklyn, but Casey and I have already made our plans for the day," I quickly replied as I bent down to fix the strap on my shoe that really didn't need fixing at all. When I straightened, I took a step away from Brooklyn, hoping to deflect another of his attempts to touch me. "In fact, we'd better be on our way."

"I need to be on my way, too," Nick said as he took a step away from our group, "I just stopped by to give these documents to Chris, then I'm heading back to Memphis. Nice to see y'all."

And with that, he gave us a little wave and disappeared around the corner. I could hear him clomping up the steps that Casey had just descended. He hadn't even looked at me when he left. Did he really think that I *wanted* to be with Brooklyn?

"Well, happy Valentine's Day, ladies. Ellen, do you have plans for dinner this evening?" Brooklyn asked hopefully.

"I do, actually. Happy Valentine's Day to you, too," I said as I started towards the parking lot.

"See you later, Brooklyn," Casey said as she fell into step beside me.

"What plans do you have for dinner, Mom?" Casey asked.

"I plan to *eat* it," I replied curtly.

I guess Casey knew by my tone to let it go, because she

didn't question me any further about Brooklyn. However, it seemed that she wanted to talk about Nick.

"Chris's dad looked a little sad or something, didn't he?" she asked as she looked back over her shoulder to pull out of the parking space.

I didn't answer until she had maneuvered onto the highway.

"Maybe," I said simply. My mind was too preoccupied with fluctuating between mentally berating myself and cursing Brooklyn to vocalize a coherent response. If Brooklyn wouldn't have been there, Nick wouldn't be upset right now and I could have...could have what? I could have given him a knowing smile, a wink—something to seal our conspiracy.

"Well, usually he has lots to say and is very friendly. I think he's taking his divorce stuff really hard. Chris said that his dad really loved his mom and was just crushed by her leaving for good. You talk to him about fixing up the house, Mom; did he say anything to you about it?" Casey asked as we stopped at a traffic light.

I mentally sighed.

"He stopped over to check on the house and told me they were getting divorced," I replied, not wanting to lie to Casey.

"Well, is it the same for you as it is for me? I want to help Chris through this, but I really don't want to think about you and Dad splitting. I'm just starting to accept it myself. Were you able to talk to Mr. Blackwell about it?"

I reached over and put my hand on her arm as she stepped on the gas and made a right onto Orange Blossom Avenue.

"I'm sorry, sweetie. We talked a bit, and you're right, it's hard to bring those memories to the forefront again just when we've finally started to put them behind us. But after I cried a bit, I found that I did feel better talking about it."

411

"You cried in front of Mr. Blackwell? How did he take it?"

I remembered him holding me close and feeling his warm breath in my hair, and what happened afterward.

"Oh, he felt bad at first because he saw that talking about it made me sad, but then he told me a little about his breakup, and I think it made him feel a little better. It helps to relate to someone who's going through the same thing as you are. Helps you to know that you aren't alone," I replied. Although right now he was probably going through hell all over again after seeing me with Brooklyn.

The parking attendant gave Casey a wave as we pulled into the lot where she had her parking lease, then she slid her car effortlessly into an empty space and cut the engine.

We rode the glass enclosed elevator to the fifth floor and stepped out into the hushed quiet of an office building on Saturday. I was highly impressed with the gallery style art work on display in the reception area that was situated behind modern, yet comfy looking chairs.

Casey slid her thumb over a silver pad, which read her fingerprint and granted us entrance through large glass doors with huge brass handles. Everything looked sleek and modern, but felt welcoming instead of cold and sterile. Not easy to pull off, and I admired the designer who came up with this concept.

Casey's heels clicked on the shiny, gray marble as we made our way down the hallway to her office. A silver plated sign on the door read "Casey Stern" and my eyes got misty.

"Casey, I'm so very proud of you! Look at this place! It's like something in a futuristic movie! I can't believe that you get to work here every day!" I stammered.

"Mom, are you *crying*?" she turned to look at me. "Ah, it's okay, come here."

She held me in a bear hug, rubbing her hand across my back just as I have done for her hundreds of times before, this gesture bringing actual tears.

"I'm just happy and proud, Casey," I managed to say as she handed me a box of tissues from her desk.

"Well, thanks; I couldn't have made it without your support, you know that. I'm proud of you, too," she said, and took a seat behind a polished cherry desk. She stretched behind her and pulled a large, white envelope from her inbox on the credenza. "Looks like your papers have arrived."

She scanned through them quickly, then I read them over carefully while she finished some other work that was waiting for her attention. When I finished reading, I leaned back in my chair, folding my hands on top of the papers on my lap.

"Everything look okay to you?" I asked Casey.

"Looks perfect, Mom. All you have to do is sign where Annee put the little arrow stickers that say 'sign here'." She laughed as she handed me a silver pen bearing her firm's logo. "Let me buzz Lauren and see if she can come notarize them for us."

Lauren was the secretary who helped several of the attorneys on the floor and apparently had been drafted for Saturday work as well. She appeared within minutes, and with her as my witness, I signed on the blank lines beside my printed name, and under the places where Jack's signature was already scrawled in his bold, illegible handwriting. It made me nauseated to see his signature again, but I had indulged myself in gently running my finger over it, like somehow touching the same paper that he had touched less than twenty-four hours ago might be significant. But it didn't make me feel better, just weird.

I watched as Lauren put her own neat signature on the notary line and stamped it with her official seal.

"I'll make you a copy if you'd like," she addressed Casey.

"That would be great, and then if you could get the original overnighted to this address I would really appreciate it," Casey replied as she handed Lauren the address of Annee's firm.

When Lauren had left the room, I looked over at Casey and our eyes locked.

"Well, I guess that's it then. Done deal," I told her.

"You did good, Mom. It was the right thing to do. You'll be happier in the long run. And just think, now you'll have some money to buy your own place. And this should help the divorce settlement along too, right?"

"Yes, that would be true," I replied slowly. "I guess I should've been calling Annee more often to see how all that's going."

"Well, I'm sure she'll be calling you in the next few days to give you information about the house. They'll have to schedule an inspection and all that. She'll want to keep you well informed. You can ask her what she dug up next time she calls."

Lauren appeared with my copy of the sales agreement and quietly disappeared back to her own office. Casey inserted the papers into a manila envelope and handed it to me, with a smile on her face.

I took a deep breath, accepted the envelope, and returned her smile.

"Let's blow this joint! Selling my parent's house always makes me hungry. Let's go eat lunch!" Casey said with a laugh.

She treated me to a delicious lunch at a Mexican place just down the street, and within walking distance of her office. We strolled down the sidewalk arm in arm, window shopping along the way.

Between bites of soft tacos and sips of strawberry margaritas, I filled her in on the happenings of the week. Adam's pending visit, our rush to get the construction done in two weeks for Hal's field trip home, and Sylvia's situation with Lakeside.

"Wow, lots of news, Mom," Casey said as she dipped a nacho chip in salsa. "I've actually heard about that company, Shoresale. Apparently they've done some shady deals, and she's right about them buying up places where seniors live and making them move out. I think our firm may have represented someone filing a claim against them. I'll have to check on that for you. Maybe something will jump out that will help your friend."

She also promised to call Adam and help persuade him to come down for a visit.

"I can't wait to show him my place; he's going to love it!" Casey said. "And he's going to be so jealous!" she added.

We walked to her car and talked nonstop all the way back to her apartment. It sure felt good to spend the afternoon with her! Just like old times…only different, because now she wasn't just my daughter, but my friend as well.

"So, what are you and Chris doing for Valentine's Day?" I teased her, as I slammed the passenger door shut and walked around the front of the car to meet her.

She shrugged. "I dunno…he said it's a secret."

"Huh…sounds like what Adam said when I asked him what he got for Mya," I told her with a grin.

"Probably means that neither one of them has bought a gift yet!" Casey laughed.

We hugged goodbye, and while I waited for the air conditioner to cool off the car, I watched her walk back down the path toward the courtyard.

The drive home went quickly; I had so many things to

think about, and before I knew it I was pulling into the familiar driveway of this place I now call home. I love everything about this house– I love the lake, I love the friends I've made here. It was going to be very hard to leave when the time came.

I guess I did have a feeling of relief since the house had sold. One less tie to my past.

I mentally clicked off the things I wanted to accomplish this afternoon: make a checklist of the jobs to be completed for Hal's homecoming visit, talk to Sylvia, and most importantly, talk to Nick.

I knew that Nick would still be driving, and I didn't want to say what I had to say in a voicemail, so I decided to wait to call him. And I could make a list any old time. I needed to talk to Sylvia.

I jogged up the steps to my bedroom to change into shorts and a tank top, and no sooner had I reached the top landing when the front doorbell rang. Who the heck could that be?

Jogging back down the steps, I could see a florist van parked in the driveway, and a man was standing at the front door with a flower arrangement in his hand.

Oh my gosh! Who sent me flowers? Maybe it was a mistake.

I opened the door, half expecting him to ask for someone else, but when he asked, "Ellen Stern?" my heart did a little flutter. I signed the receipt on his clipboard and accepted the beautiful crystal vase of red roses and baby's breath.

I don't think there's a woman alive who doesn't like getting flowers, but the memory of the Thanksgiving flower arrangement that Jack had sent me intruded to cloud this moment of happiness.

Certainly they couldn't be from Jack. He didn't even know that I wasn't back home in Jeannette.

I took them to the kitchen, put the vase carefully on the table, and took the tiny envelope out of the clear plastic prongs.

My hands were shaking as I pulled out the miniature card and read the handwritten message:

"Ellie, Happy Valentine's Day! Sorry I couldn't be with you, but you are with me in my heart. Thank you for being you. Nick."

I read and re-read it several times, tears plopping on my hands. I was sure he wrote this card before he saw me in a lip lock with Brooklyn this morning, and that made me feel even worse. I ran my fingers over his precise, neat handwriting and felt warm inside just knowing that he had touched this card hours ago…and that I *did* find significant.

I replaced the card in the envelope and laid it on the table, then slowly walked up the steps to change. I carried my camera down with me and snapped a picture of the roses. I would always want to remember this special gift, my first from Nick. Not that I was ever likely to forget this gesture, or get another gift.

I scooped up the card and put it in my shorts pocket, wanting to carry a piece of Nick with me, and headed out the door at a fast clip. I seriously needed to walk and burn off some of this nervous energy and the fried ice cream that I split at lunch with Casey.

Fifteen minutes later, I was regretting not bringing a water bottle with me as I raised my hand and knocked on Sylvia's front door.

Sophia answered, carrying a folded up newspaper in her hand, and…wearing a coat?

"Ellen! So nice to see you! Come on in. Look at you sweating, would you like some iced tea? Of course you would. Come on in, dear!"

I smiled in spite of myself and followed Sophia to the tidy kitchen, watched her fill a tall glass with ice and then pour tea over the cubes, making them crackle.

"Thanks!" I replied, and sipped greedily. "Whoa, Sophia, it's really chilly in here," I said as my damp body shivered in the cool air.

She took a spare sweater that had been draped over a kitchen chair and placed it around my shoulders.

"Sylvia's in a mood, and she's cranked up the air conditioning, dear," Sophia said.

"Is she here?" I asked, placing my empty glass on the table.

"She's in the Christmas room making it snow. She always does that when she's upset," Sophia said as she led the way down the hall.

It was even colder in the hallway, and as I stood in the doorway to the Christmas room, there was Sylvia wearing a bright red fleece sweat suit, kneeling on the floor with an industrial sized sugar shaker full of artificial snow in her hand. She was sprinkling it over a building that appeared to be a new addition to the village and looked up as I entered the room.

"Look what the wind blew in!" Sylvia said simply as she returned to her task.

"Are you angry with me?" I asked bluntly. I couldn't bear her being angry with me.

She turned and looked me right in the eye.

"Why would you think a darn fool thing like that?" she asked, pausing the blizzard.

I shrugged, and she stood up and walked over to me.

"*Concerned* about you? Yes. *Angry*? No. I'm just trying to figure out this mess with Shoresale. They've really got my dander up."

"Oh, I thought that was *snow*!" I teased.

She puckered her mouth, then smiled.

"Feel like a walk?" I asked her. "I really need to burn off some steam, too."

"Okay, let me change into something more suitable."

A few moments later, after Sylvia had changed into camel colored walking shorts and a leopard print tank, and had reset the thermostat, we left Sophia to her newspaper and marched down the street toward the lake. We didn't speak for the first few minutes, enjoying each other's company and letting our bodies work off some misguided tension.

It was just too warm to chug along at a fast pace any longer, so we slowed down to a comfortable stroll as we rounded the corner by the clubhouse. Sylvia jumped right into the conversation with her normal tact.

"So, I guess you're sleeping with him," she said bluntly.

"Oh, Syl, it's so complicated."

I really needed to have this conversation with someone, and I hoped she would condone my behavior and not condemn it.

"I'm listening," she said as we made a left onto Cascade.

"Sylvia, I know you'll think I'm silly, but I really feel that I'm falling in love with him."

"And I suppose he said he loves you too?" she asked.

I was grateful for the shade of the cypress trees lining the road. Our steps were matched as we walked side by side, and I considered my answer.

"Well, he has feelings for me, but we certainly didn't say the "L" word to each other. I know that you warned me about getting involved with a married man, but he's getting a divorce."

I expected her to stop in her tracks or at least tell me that's what all the guys say to get in your pants, but she surprised me.

"I know he is. From what I hear, he's better off without that hussy! He'd be far better off with a woman like you."

Now I stopped in *my* tracks.

She kept walking a few steps, then turned back to look at me.

"Come on, you're breakin' our rhythm," she said as she motioned with a big sweep of her hand, and resumed our pace.

I caught up, matching her step by step, and put my hand on her arm as we walked.

"How do you know about his wife?"

"Hal told me all about it when I went to see him, honey. He's happy that you two are getting cozy, but—"

"You *told* him?" I could feel the heat in my cheeks, and it wasn't because of exertion. How embarrassing to have my love life, or whatever it is, being discussed by other people.

She patted my hand that was still on her arm.

"Ellen, I'm your friend. Hal is your friend. Hal is Nick's father, and I love you like a daughter. It just made sense to tell him, honey."

Tears were stinging my eyes. How could I be upset with her though? I sighed heavily as we rounded the block and returned to the lake.

"Want to sit a bit?" she asked as she pulled two small water bottles out of her fanny pack.

We situated ourselves at the picnic table on the dock, the large canvas umbrella offering some shade, and the slight breeze coming from the lake breathing its coolness over our damp skin.

I took a long swig of the cold water.

"I'm so confused, Sylvia. Nick and I had a plan, and now something's happened that I'm afraid will ruin everything."

As she sat silently sipping her water, I spilled out the story about how my relationship with Nick had progressed, leaving out the more intimate details of course, and I told her about our arrangement to discreetly continue to see each other. She was nodding in what I assumed was approval, and then I told her about the incident with Brooklyn. She slammed her bottle down so hard that the water remaining inside was now splashed all over the table.

"That weasel! If I'm ever in the presence of that man, Brooklyn, I'm going to give him a piece of my mind!" Sylvia was indignant.

I had to smile. I could just picture Sylvia taking on Brooklyn. He wouldn't know what hit him!

"You call Nick tonight and explain. He'll understand."

"I hope so, Sylvia. I really care about him."

"Just take it slow, dear. He's going through a lot right now; give him some time."

"I know. He told me as much. He's not ready for a relationship yet, and honestly I'm not really either, but there's just all this emotion and I don't know what to do with it."

421

We sat for a few minutes staring out at the lake, Sylvia being uncharacteristically quiet.

I looked over and saw her chewing on her bottom lip and absentmindedly twirling the empty water bottle on the table.

"I'm sorry, Syl, I've been monopolizing the whole conversation. You're really upset about this Shoresale deal, aren't you?"

She blinked and stopped the twirling.

"Sure, I am. But that's not what I'm thinking about right now. May I speak to you in confidence, Miss Ellen?" she asked, turning to look at me, the usual spark in her blue eyes replaced with softness.

This time I covered her hand with mine.

"Of course, Sylvia. What is it?"

She paused a moment before answering.

"Well, dear, I understand what you're telling me about how you feel about Nick. Feeling like you are falling in love after such a short time. I feel the same way about Hal."

I smiled a big smile and gave her hand a squeeze.

"Well, I figured as much. I'm not surprised at all! Why, I was just talking to Nick about it last–"

"You *told* Nick?" she interrupted, her eyes wide.

"Sylvia, I am your friend. Nick is your friend. Hal is Nick's dad, and I love you like a mother…it just made sense to tell him!"

I started to laugh, and after a moment, the look of shock on her face was replaced by amusement, and she started laughing too.

"Aren't you just a little smarty pants?" she said with a smirk on her face.

"Seriously, I think it's wonderful, and if you're interested in knowing, Nick thinks it is too," I said.

"Really?" she asked with a hopeful look in her eye. "I was concerned that he might not like the idea of his daddy having a girlfriend."

"I would absolutely not give that a second thought, Syl. Both of us couldn't be happier for you."

"I really do love him, Ellen," and she added almost shyly, "and he told me that he loves me too. At our age, you don't get many second chances."

I reached over and gave her a hug.

"I'm really happy for you, Sylvia."

"This is our little secret for now; I haven't confided in Sophia yet."

After swearing to secrecy, I walked Sylvia home and made my way through the orange grove and down to the dock to try and sort out all of the thoughts swimming around in my head. Sitting on the bench, I leaned back, taking in the warmth of the sun. Before I could even get my mind in gear, a loud squawking in the tall grasses made me sit upright. I put my hand to my brow to shield my eyes from the glare, and out popped Dora, fluttering and flapping and making a huge racket.

I was afraid a gator was after her and nervously eyed the long pole tucked behind the bench. Nick had warned me the first day I met him that there could possibly be gators in the lake, and had showed me the pole in case I found myself trapped on the dock and needed it for protection. I kind of forgot what I was supposed to do with it though.

I leaned forward a bit as Dora made her way towards shore, and out from the grasses, chasing her at full speed, came another duck, its brown feathers flapping as much as Dora's white ones were. Ah ha! Dora has a friend!

Once they hit the sand, she calmed down, gave her buddy a few quacks, and waddled up the wooden planks. I now kept some cracked corn in a tin under the bench, and as I pried off the lid, she eyed me expectantly.

"So, who's your pal?" I asked her as I tossed a handful of kernels in her direction. "Don't be so greedy! Tell him to come up and join us."

As if on cue, she quacked a command, and the other duck slowly waddled up toward us and apprehensively began nibbling the corn that had scattered the farthest.

I shook my head. It appears that even Dora is in love.

CHAPTER THIRTY

I spent the remainder of the day making my list for the workers who would be arriving first thing Monday morning, and another for myself of items to decorate Hal's new bedroom and bath. Now it was after ten, and I was lying in bed alternately looking at my red roses and staring at the blank screen on my cell phone.

My fingers brushed lightly over the numbers, wanting to apply the pressure to make the call go through, but I just couldn't do it. I wanted so badly to set things right, but I didn't want to hear Nick say that our relationship was over when it hadn't really even started yet. Damn Brooklyn.

I finally mustered up the courage, pushed the number, and tapped my fingers on the phone while I listened to it ringing.

"Hello."

I closed my eyes at the sound of his voice.

"Hi, Nick." I answered cautiously.

I didn't know how to start, but Nick helped me out with that.

"Have a nice Valentine's date with your buddy?" he asked.

My eyes snapped open, and I focused on the roses again.

"Nick, you can't honestly think that I'm seeing Brooklyn."

"All I know is what I saw, and you two looked pretty friendly to me," he said bluntly.

"Brooklyn has an uncanny way of showing up when I least expect him to, and taking the liberty of doing things I least expect him to do. I'm so sorry that you had to see him taking advantage of the situation, but honestly, that's all it was."

"So you haven't dated him? Chris told me that he thought you might be, since you all went out to dinner together one time, and it seemed like you liked him."

A small sigh escaped my lips. How do I explain about Brooklyn without making myself seem like a floozy, especially when I probably *was* acting like one.

"Nick, I only went out with Brooklyn that one time, and it wasn't really a date; he invited Casey, Chris, and me out to dinner, that's all. I never really had any feelings for him. It was right after I got here, and I had never been out with anyone before …" I trailed off pitifully, remembering the after dinner groping session.

There was silence on the Memphis end of the line.

"Nick, thank you so much for the beautiful flowers. I love them."

More silence. Why was he being so difficult?

"Talk to me already! *Yell* if you want…just say *something!*" I was getting exasperated.

"Ellen, remember when I told you about walking in on my wife and her *friend* in the job trailer? It's just that all those hurt feelings came back when I saw Brooklyn kissing you. It was like someone punched me in the gut."

My exasperation melted into a puddle of remorse.

"Nick, once again, I am *so* sorry! I understand what you're saying, and I'm sorry to be the cause of your pain. But, really, he just grabbed me and kissed me. It shouldn't have happened, and I won't let it happen again."

"Damn, Ellie, you really messed with my mind! It was not a very good ride back to Memphis when all I had to occupy my time was the flashback of you tangled up with Brooklyn the bridge."

I laughed out loud, and relief flooded through my limbs. He had called me Ellie again!

"Oh, sure…funny, but *not!*" he said with laughter in his voice too. "I know how Brooklyn operates! He can't keep his damn hands to himself or his winky in his pants!"

I was laughing so hard I couldn't speak.

"Since Chris has lived there, I've seen him in action plenty of times; in fact, he even came on to J-Rae at one of the barbeques. It just really bothered me to think that you had fallen for his tactics," he said a little more cautiously.

Finally, I found enough breath to say a few words.

"Oh, maybe at first I was flattered by his attention. You have to remember that I had been married *forever* and this was all new to me. But then I learned…and just so you know, I never saw his winky! Nick, I miss you!" I told him as I held the phone close to my ear, still smiling.

I heard him sigh, then yawn. "I miss you too, Ellie. I've been wound up tighter than a spring all day! It feels good to set things straight between us and relax."

I heard the pop of a can being opened.

"Having some refreshment?" I asked.

"You bet! A beer and then bed. I'm not looking forward to tomorrow's tasks."

"Well, then I'll let you get some rest, and I'll do the same. I brought the roses up to my room so I can see them before I go to sleep and first thing in the morning. Thank you so much. I just love them."

"You are very welcome. I wanted to do something nice for you, and I could tell that you really like flowers."

"I love them. I'll get to work tomorrow getting things going here, so don't worry about anything on this end. Talk to you tomorrow?" I asked hopefully.

"Absolutely. Thank you for doing this. I couldn't handle all of my personal issues here and take care of Dad's issues there too."

"I'm on it. Good night, Nick."

I fell asleep breathing in the sweet scent of roses and holding a warm cell phone in my hand.

Monday morning the work crew arrived bright and early, and I put them right to work on the downstairs bathroom for Hal. By the time I left for town, they were already doing the preliminary work for laying the tile floor.

After a quick stop in a little boutique on Sunset Avenue to pick up a few accessories, I browsed through a big box bedding store and chose the perfect comforter and window treatments: manly, but not overboard on the testosterone, keeping in mind the fact that Sylvia may be having sleepovers.

I did a two mile walk around the lake, grabbed a grilled chicken wrap at a drive-thru, and headed home.

The men were sitting on the back porch eating lunch, and they promised to move Hal's bedroom furniture down for me before they left for the day. A quick glance in the bathroom showed me that the tile was already laid and ready to grout. Not a bad day!

That evening, as Hal's new sheets were tumbling in the dryer downstairs, I sat on the naked mattress looking around the room, trying to decide on the placement of the accessories that I had strewn all over the bed.

I absentmindedly picked up my phone when it rang, and a familiar voice instantly pulled me out of my preoccupation and made my heart beat faster.

"Abbey!" I exclaimed.

"Hey there, girlfriend! I thought you forgot about me!" her voice sounding as clear as if she were sitting on the bed right here with me.

"Never, *ever*, could I do that! How *are* you?" I asked smiling from ear to ear.

"Couldn't be better! Maybe I could be a bit warmer, but all is well. In fact, I may be getting warmer soon. Guess what my wonderful hubby gave me for Valentine's Day?"

"A space heater?" I joked.

"There's the friend I miss! No, silly…he gave me a plane ticket to *Florida*!" she said, practically shouting. "I'm coming to visit you!"

My bottom was bouncing up and down on the bed. "Abbey, that's wonderful! When are you coming?"

"Would next week be okay?" she squealed.

"Yay!!!!" I squealed back at her, and we continued to shout like a couple of school girls who just got asked to the prom.

"That will be just *perfect*! We're going to celebrate Hal's birthday the weekend after this, and we're going to have a big party. You can meet everyone! Can you stay for that?"

"I'll be there from Wednesday to Wednesday, if that's

okay."

"Couldn't be better timing. Oh, guess what? I think Adam is coming down then, too!"

"Oh, Ellen, maybe that'll be too much. Will there be room for everyone?" she asked, sounding deflated.

"It will be so *great* to have all my family together! There's *plenty* of room here! Are you coming alone?"

"Yeah, we were all planning on coming during Natalie's school break, but we've had so many snow days off that they had to make them up, and now she's not getting a break after all. I was so bummed about it, Rick decided that he would stay home with Natalie and take care of the shop since it's still our slow time, and give me the treat of a week with my best friend, whom I miss terribly I might add!"

"Wait until you see this place, Abbey! I have so much to show you and so many people for you to meet! I can't wait!" I said, tugging gently on the cross around my neck. "When I come home, I'm giving Rick the biggest hug ever!"

"He's still recovering from *me* squeezing the daylights out of him! I love that man of mine."

I could hear in her voice that she meant that from the bottom of her heart, and it made me feel so good to know that my best friend was so happy, and still so much in love.

"By the way, Ellen, I hear congrats are in order for you! I rode past your house just for shits and giggles, and I saw a 'Sold' sign in your yard!"

"Yeah, we're still waiting on the home inspection and to set the closing date, but looks like it will be a done deal."

"Are you okay with that?" she asked gently.

"As okay as I'm going to be, I guess," I replied honestly.

I had so many other things on my mind that I had hardly thought about it since signing the papers.

We chatted a few minutes longer, then hung up with the promise of a reunion lingering in the air.

I immediately pushed the speed dial for Adam, and he answered right away.

"Hey, Mom!"

"Hi, sweetie. Guess what? Abbey's coming down to visit next week! Are you still going to come too?"

"Wow, that's exciting news! I haven't bought any tickets yet, if that's what you're asking, but Mya and I should be able to swing it. When should we come?"

"Come for Hal's birthday party the weekend after this."

"Let me get online and see what kind of plane fare I can find, and I'll get back to you. Mom?" he asked with a tone that immediately put me on guard.

"What is it, sweetie?" I answered, sitting up straight.

"I have some exciting news, too, but I want to wait and share it in person. Man, I can't *wait* to see you!"

"Well, now you have me intrigued for sure. Can't you give me a hint?" I asked, relaxing back against the pillows.

"It's good news; well, at least *I* think so. I'll let you know tomorrow about our travel plans."

"Sounds great to me! I love you, Adam, and I can't wait to see you!"

The anticipation of seeing Abbey and Adam sent

inspiration coursing through my veins, and energized me to stay up until the wee hours of the morning hanging pictures and strategically placing the pieces I bought.

Sunrise found me back to work hanging the draperies, and I was already tucking in the new sheets by the time the work crew arrived. I called Sylvia to come over for breakfast to see what she thought of my efforts.

"Ellen, it's magnificent! Hal is just going to love it!" she exclaimed as she stood in the doorway with her coffee mug clutched tightly in her hands. "You are one talented woman! How come you're not doing this for a living?" She eyed me speculatively.

"Well, maybe I will. Do you like the sketches I'm giving Hal for his birthday gift?"

She took a few steps into the room, her flip flops flapping against the new hardwood floor. I had mounted the finished sketches on the wall facing the bed and attached an oversized bow to each.

"Ellen…"

She moved in closer, and for once, she was speechless.

I went over and stood beside her, wrapping my arm around her shoulder and planting a little kiss on her pink frosted hair.

"Thanks, Syl," I said, grinning.

We turned and surveyed the room. I had done the walls in vanilla cream, with a white crown molding. The draperies and comforter sported accents of cream, white, and cornflower blue. The accent pillows splashed varying shades of darker blues with slight touches of cranberry and chocolate brown as they rested in front of the headboard. The gliding rocker placed in the corner had a chocolate brown cushion and was equipped with a pillow that coordinated with the ones on the bed. I had tucked some of

Hal's special personal things around the room, bringing in his personality. All in all it looked fresh, clean, and happy.

"Hal is just going to be overwhelmed! I can't tell you how happy he is to be coming home, if only for a weekend," Sylvia said as we walked back to the kitchen.

She rinsed her cup and placed it in the dishwasher.

"Let's plan a really big shindig! Especially since your friend and son are coming too. Shall we do it Saturday night?"

I agreed wholeheartedly, and an hour later we had umpteen lists of all the things we needed to do to make the party a success.

Leaning back in my chair, I sighed and rubbed the back of my neck.

"This is really fun, Sylvia. Hey, how's it going with your investigation of Shoresale? Any new developments? No pun intended."

"Not really, but in my exasperation, I added a whole new street to my Dickens village! Apparently the people involved are very secretive and don't publicize their names. But Sophia is digging. She even bought herself a new laptop! We have an association meeting scheduled next week to try and come up with a plan though. You can come if you want to."

"Well, we'll see how my schedule goes with all my company arriving; I'd love to help in any way I can, you know that."

The work on the bathroom had been put on hold for a day to allow the tile to set before the grout was applied, so the men were working on the ramp to the rear entrance. Sylvia and I gave them a wave as I walked her to the golf cart.

The next week was a blur as the plans for the party were completed and the work on Hal's bedroom, bath, and ramp were finished. The only construction left to do was to move the laundry to the first floor, and that could wait until after Hal's visit.

Nick and I had fallen into our old routine of nighttime phone conversations. I found myself anxiously awaiting his call each night and eagerly anticipating his return to Lake Juliet. The plan was for him to pick up Hal early Saturday morning, then return him to New Hope on Sunday evening.

I had received a call from Annee, and the home inspection had gone without a hitch. The buyers were anxious to close, so the date had been set for two weeks from Friday. She was sure that everything could be handled without me physically being there, so I was relieved to hear that. I didn't want to meet the people moving in, and I certainly didn't want to sit at a table with Jack.

Wednesday afternoon I found myself sitting in Hal's Subaru parked among the other cars in the waiting area of Orlando airport, my eyes peeled to the sky as one plane after another zoomed over my head on their way to landing. My foot tapped about three beats per second while my hands gripped the steering wheel. Finally, my cell phone rang.

"I'm *here!*" Abbey's voice shouted.

"Yay! I'm on my way!" I shouted back with equal enthusiasm.

I wasted no time starting the engine and shifting into drive. In fewer than five minutes I was parking along the curb next to Abbey, who was jumping up and down on the sidewalk next to her tapestry canvas suitcase.

I gave the door a slam and scurried around the back of the car to Abbey's waiting arms. Oh, it felt *so* good to hug her!

"Ellen, *look* at you!" she exclaimed as she held me at

arm's length. "You're tan, and slim, and …you look so *happy*!"

"I *am* happy, Abbey, and now I'm *really* happy!" I told her as I gave her another hug.

"You'll have to move along, ma'am," an approaching police officer told us in a serious voice.

Abbey and I burst out laughing, and after lugging her bag over the curb and depositing it in the trunk, we jumped into the front seat and buckled up.

I looked over at her and smiled as we pulled away from the airport and hit I–4. She was like a kid taking it all in, and it was a pleasure to experience the excitement all over again through her eyes.

"Ellen! Look at the palm trees!" she exclaimed, pressing her nose to the window. I remembered seeing my first palm tree and having Casey take my picture in front of it. I also remembered her telling me that I would soon be taking them for granted, and she was partially right. I didn't get all that excited about them anymore, but I still loved looking at them. I try really hard not to take *anything* for granted.

"Would you rather have the windows down instead of the air conditioning?" I asked.

"Oh, could we? When I left home this morning, it was below freezing! This is just amazing!"

It was a beautiful day; currently the thermometer in the car showed that the outside temperature was 79 degrees, and there seriously wasn't a cloud in the sky. I pushed a button on the door, and as the windows slowly disappeared, a rush of fresh, warm air flooded the car. Abbey stuck her head out a bit, the wind blowing her ponytail straight back. It reminded me of how Cooper looks when Adam takes him for a ride in his truck, and I laughed out loud. What a joy to have Abbey here!

When we finally passed the orange groves and pulled into

the secluded driveway of Hal's home, Abbey's jaw actually dropped.

"Holy mansion!" she whispered, somewhat subdued.

She stared in awe at her surroundings for a moment, then looked at me.

"*Yeehaw!*" she shouted. "I can't believe I get to stay here for a week! Let's go!"

She scrambled out of the car and did an impromptu dance around the yard.

I shook my head and opened the trunk, pulling out her bag and yanking up the handle as I placed it on the ground. The wheels bumped over the grass as I lugged it behind me, catching up to Abbey as she peered into the front screened porch.

"Oh, here, give me that! Where are my manners?" she exclaimed with chagrin when she saw me with her suitcase. "I'm sorry, Ellen, I'm just overwhelmed by this whole thing!"

She continued to be impressed as I gave her the grand tour, and after much debate, she finally chose the same bedroom that Casey had stayed in, the one with the canopy bed. She sat on the bed, bounced a few times, and fell backward on the mattress. I followed suit, minus the bouncing, and we lay side by side looking up at the canopy as the edges fluttered in the breeze.

"Ellen, this is just surreal! You are the luckiest person in the world to be staying here. Aren't you glad that you took this job?

"I love it here! And I felt at home immediately. It's really weird though, Abbey, like I'm living someone else's life right now…like I've stepped out of my own skin and become someone else."

She turned her head to look at me.

"Well, in essence, you have, kiddo. I can tell just by the short time I've been with you today that you are *not* the same Ellen. You are new and improved! There's just something about you that is different, in a good way, I mean."

She grabbed my hand as she stood up and pulled me with her.

"I'm starving! Got any food in this place?"

Laughing, we walked arm in arm to the kitchen.

CHAPTER THIRTY ONE

After dinner and a swim, we strolled down to the dock and sat side by side on the bench. I popped open my can of beer and took a long swig.

"What the heck is *that*?" Abbey asked, gesturing toward the driveway.

Sylvia's pink golf cart was glittering in the late day sun as she pulled in neatly beside the house.

"Oh, that's Sylvia. You're going to love her!"

I waved at Sylvia, and she made her way down to the dock. She was wearing lime green linen walking shorts with matching flip flops, and a white tank top with identical green polka dots. Her visor of choice today was white, and little wisps of green hair sprung out from under the brim.

"Oh, my Lord!" Abbey whispered as she approached.

"Howdy, Miss Ellen! This must be Abbey! Nice to meet you," Sylvia said as she marched right up to Abbey and extended her hand.

"Nice to meet you too, Sylvia," Abbey said.

I smiled inside and out. It was so nice to have my two best friends finally meet, and I could just imagine what Abbey was going to say after Sylvia left!

We all chatted a few minutes, then Sylvia got down to business.

"Just wonderin' how you're doin' on the list. I have to tell ya, Ellen, I'm getting *real* excited about this weekend...and so is

Hal! I went over to see him today, and he practically had his walker airborne!"

"Don't worry, everything's under control. I thought Abbey and I would go tomorrow and get the groceries, and I think that's about all I have left to do. The construction guys left yesterday– Nick gave them a long break. Everything is ready."

"That's good, then. By the way, we had our association meetin' yesterday about the sale of Lakeside, and Sophia came up with a great idea: *we* want to buy the park!" she said, putting her hands on her hips.

"What?" I exclaimed. "You and Sophia want to buy the park?"

"Well, not just us. We want to form a sort of company so all of the residents can be part-owners."

"That sounds wonderful, if it will work," I replied thoughtfully.

"Of course it can work! You just wait and see!" She was practically bouncing up and down in excitement.

"I can't wait to hear all about it! Did you get any legal advice? Maybe Casey would be able to help you."

"Already called her, Ellen, and she's lookin' into it for us. Well, have to go. I'm planning some special entertainment for the party, and I still have some phone calls to make."

"Sylvia, you're something!" I smiled at her.

"I'll call ya tomorrow," Sylvia said, then she started sniffing the air.

"Smell that?" she asked.

Abbey and I looked at each other and sniffed rather loudly, then we both looked at Sylvia.

"Orange blossoms...they're startin' to bloom. You can't smell that? Wait a few days, it'll be intoxicating! I just love this time of year!"

And with that, she flopped back up to the golf cart, turning to wave just before she disappeared into the grove.

"I repeat, what the heck was that?" Abbey said as she stared at the driveway. "Is she always like that?"

"Of course! That's what makes her so wonderful! You kind of get used to it. She just has so much energy and–"

"But some of her hair was *green!*" Abbey interrupted me.

"And tomorrow it may be pink!" I laughed out loud.

"How does she do that?"

"Haven't a clue...I've never asked her."

I don't think I've ever wanted to know, just accepted it as one of those surprisingly quirky things about Sylvia.

Abbey and I spent the remainder of the evening catching up. Abbey told me how tired she was of shoveling snow and driving on icy roads, and I told her about water aerobics and my rekindled passion for sketching.

"So, do you know when you're coming back?" she asked as we sat snuggled deep in the cushions of our lounge chairs by the pool.

We had strung twinkle lights around the perimeter of the porch in preparation for the party, and they sparkled off the surface of the water. I watched as the light glistened off the ripples made by the filter.

"I don't know. I really just don't *know*. I guess we'll see how Hal does this weekend. I can't see it being any more than another month or so." I stretched out and pointed my toes.

"Do you even *want* to come back?" Abbey put into words the question that had been plaguing my thoughts lately.

I looked over at her and shrugged.

"I'm kind of mixed up at the moment. I don't know where 'home' is. When I go back I guess I'll stay with Adam until I find a place, but I feel really at home here, too. Sometimes I think that I might just like to stay here for a while. I don't know, Abbey. What do you think I should do?"

Her face was shaded in the dim lights, and I couldn't really read her expression.

"It has to be your decision, Ellen. I'll miss you so much if you decide to stay here, but I want you to do what's right for you. Besides Adam, me, and a great job, what do you have to come back for?"

I had to smile. "Well, the job *is* great! I've missed it…and you. And of course I've missed Adam. I'm so excited to see him Friday morning, but I've found that I really do enjoy designing, and maybe it's time for me to make a change."

This was the first time I'd voiced my thoughts out loud, and it was a bit scary. As long as they were in my head they didn't seem real, but now that I've spoken them, the words rang with possibility. I was also thinking of Nick, but I didn't mention him. I didn't want to make it seem like I would be moving here for him.

"Well, I'm proud of you, Ellen. It takes so much courage to make such a huge change in your life. I hate to bring this up, but how are the panic attacks going?"

I took a deep breath, not wanting to jinx myself.

"I haven't had one since I've been here. Had a couple of close calls, but I talked myself out of them. I haven't felt that tired, worthless feeling either. I *want* to get up and start each day, instead of not even wanting to get dressed. I can't believe how bad it was, Abbey. It was such a terrible time in my life. I don't ever want to feel that way again."

"Do you think that's why you don't really want to come back? Are you afraid that they'll start up again?" she asked in her usual candid fashion. That's something that I admired about Abbey and Sylvia. They call it as they see it and aren't afraid to ask the tough questions.

"Maybe deep down in my subconscious, but it's certainly not something I dwell on. I had missed Casey so much, and even though she's busy at work and I don't see her as much as I'd like, it's still comforting to know that she's nearby. But I miss Adam when I'm here. It's like a no-win situation with the kids."

Abbey reached out her hand to me, and I grabbed it and squeezed.

The next morning after an early swim, which Abbey insisted on because she wanted to good-naturedly rub it in to Rick and Natalie when she called them later, and a fresh fruit and cereal breakfast on the porch, I drove us into town to gather the items for the party.

Abbey loved the little shops and the walking trail around the lake, and she adored the grocery store. She made me promise to bring her back before she left.

After we put the groceries away and ate salads that we had bought at the deli, I gave Sylvia a call.

"Hey, Syl, would you like some company this afternoon? I wanted to bring Abbey over to show her your place. She'd really like to see your Dickens village."

"I'll be here for a while, then I'm going over to see Hal for dinner and help him get packed for the weekend. Want me to come over and pick you up in the golf cart? Then we can give her a tour of the whole Lakeside complex."

"Sounds great to me. We'll be waiting outside for you."

Twenty minutes later I was hanging on to the golf cart for dear life as we bumped along through the orange grove. I had let Abbey ride shotgun with Sylvia, and I took the rear seat facing backwards. I would be so happy when we finally hit the pavement at Lakeside.

"Sylvia, it sure feels different riding back here!" I exclaimed.

She tossed me a backward glance, peering at me under the brim of her navy blue visor.

"Sorry, honey, I'll take it slower," she promised.

Halfway through the grove, Abbey turned back to look at me.

"Ellen, do you smell that? I can smell it now, Sylvia! Oh, look at the blossoms!" she exclaimed.

I could smell it, too. What a wonderful scent surrounding us, enveloping us in its sweetness.

Sylvia rode up and down every street at Lakeside, and we waved and called a greeting to everyone who was outside. After a quick stop at the lake, we pulled silently into the carport at Sylvia's home.

"Here we are! Everybody out of the pool!" Sylvia said as she hopped out.

Abbey looked back at me again with a mischievous smile.

We found Sophia at the kitchen table, squinting at her computer screen.

"Guess what?" she called out to us. "I think I might know who the owner of Shoresale is. I have a clue!"

Sylvia hustled over to the table.

"Who?" she asked excitedly.

"Well, I don't rightly know for sure yet. I said I have a *clue*, I haven't solved the mystery! I was talking to Esther, you know, she used to live at Lake Pete before they got the boot. She said the guy's name was like something famous, but she couldn't quite remember what it was."

Sophia clicked off the website she was on, and her screen saver popped up to fill the screen with a picture of bright green plants.

Sylvia looked closely at it for a moment.

"Sophia, honey, you have a picture of marijuana as your *screensaver*?" Sylvia asked accusingly.

Sophia squinted at the picture. "Oh, is *that* what it is? How do *you* know what marijuana looks like?" She narrowed her eyes as she looked back at Sylvia.

"Because it *says* so right in there in the corner!"

Sophia directed her attention to the computer screen again.

"They have a bunch of pictures you can pick from, and I *liked* this one. It made me feel real relaxed. I was thinking we should try to buy some of those plants for our planter outside. I guess we can't do that now, can we?" She sounded so disappointed.

Sylvia turned to face us and shook her head.

"No, I don't think we're going to be able to grow any of those plants unless you want to end up in jail, and I do *not* look good in stripes."

Abbey looked at me, and we both burst out laughing! We just couldn't help it.

After introducing Sophia to Abbey, Sylvia led the way down the hall to the Christmas room. Fortunately, the temperature was not set to the freeze zone today.

Abbey's hand flew to her mouth when she entered the room.

"Holy blizzard! This is something else, Sylvia!" she exclaimed, rushing over to the first table for a closer inspection.

Sylvia had a proud look on her face, and she took her time giving us a tour of the village she had created.

I noticed one structure still in its box beside the table. It was a beautiful stone church.

"Is this a new addition?" I asked, pointing to the box.

Sylvia's face colored slightly. "That's a gift from Hal. It was for Valentine's Day," she said softly.

My eyebrows raised a bit as I pondered whether the chapel was a random choice, or if it carried a hidden meaning. One look as Sylvia's face told me that it was an intentional selection.

She smiled at me and shrugged.

"Speaking of Hal, we should let you get going. Abbey, do you want to walk back?" I asked.

"That would be fine with me, then I can eat more at the

party if I get the exercise out of the way first!"

We walked down the hall, and Sophia called out from the kitchen.

"Nice meeting you, Abbey. See you at the party!"

I slept with the bedroom window open, and when I woke up, the aromatic scent of orange blossoms filled my room. Sylvia had been right, it was intoxicating!

I turned off the air conditioning, and we opened all the windows to let the scent ride on the breeze throughout the house. It was magical!

Abbey and I went back into town, as promised, and we walked a few laps around the lake, then returned home to give the place one final good cleaning. By mid-afternoon we had completed all of our tasks, and my phone rang with a much anticipated call.

"Hi, Mom! We're here!" Adam's voice happily announced.

Casey had wanted to pick them up at the airport and take them back to her place. I think she wanted to show it off and was also anxious for Adam to meet Chris. Abbey and I were going to drive over to Casey's and have dinner, then bring Adam and Mya back home with us.

An hour later, I slammed the door to the Subaru and waited for Abbey by the front of the car.

"This is some place!" Abbey exclaimed as she took in the palm-lined paths and flower-filled planters. "Ellen, it's just so *weird* to see so much green!"

"Don't I know it!" I replied, smiling. "When I first got here, I couldn't get over flowers blooming in the middle of winter!"

The scent of something delicious being grilled tickled my nose as we entered the clearing by the pool, where we found Adam, Mya, Casey, and Chris all reclining on lounge chairs. Adam saw me first and jumped up from his chair, practically running to greet me.

"Mom!" he said as he hugged me tight.

I felt the tears welling up immediately. I knew that I had been missing him, but hadn't realized just how much until I looked into those familiar eyes and felt the strength of his hug.

"Adam, it's *so* good to see you!" I whispered into his shoulder as we still clung to each other.

Abbey had been standing off to the side, and as Adam released me he grabbed her in a hug as well and gave her a peck on the cheek. Then, taking each of our hands he led us over to the rest of the group.

Mya stood up, and I marveled again at how pretty she was.

Hello, Mrs. Stern," she said almost shyly.

I reached over and embraced her. "Mya, I'm so glad that you could come, too!"

After we finished exchanging hugs and greetings, Casey handed us each a glass of champagne.

"Wow, what are we celebrating?" Abbey asked.

Casey, Chris, and Mya all looked at Adam, then so did I as I wondered what was up.

"Mom, Mya and I are getting married!" he said excitedly as he grabbed her hand and presented it to me to see the ring.

A gazillion thoughts ran through my head. I pressed a smile to my face, as they all looked at me expectantly, waiting for my reaction.

I took her hand in mine and admired the sparkling diamond ring.

"Oh my…it's beautiful! Adam and Mya, congratulations!" I managed to say.

Everyone began talking at once. Evidently Casey and Chris had been privy to this information before Abbey and I arrived.

Adam hugged me again and whispered in my ear.

"Don't worry, Mom, everything will be fine."

How can my son possibly be so understanding and mature? How can he be getting *married?* I wasn't sure how I felt about all this. Well, that's not true. Yes, I *was* sure how I felt about it, I just couldn't find the words to describe the jolt I'd felt at those words, but I think being in a state of shock would pretty much cover it. To say that this announcement had taken me totally by surprise would be a gross understatement. I downed my glass of champagne and sat down on the lounge next to Adam.

I always thought that Casey would be the one to get married first; in fact, the shock factor wouldn't have been nearly as intense if she would have told me that Chris had proposed. I could see how in love they were and how close they had become.

I guess I wasn't being fair to Adam and Mya in that respect. I hadn't been home to see their relationship blossom. It just seemed kind of sudden. They'd only known each other, how long? I counted back the months to last summer….

Then it hit me. What a hypocrite I'm being! I was professing my love for Nick after I'd only met him twice, and now I'm passing judgment on *them? Grow up, Ellen.*

And I can't say that they're too young. Jack and I were married when I was only nineteen...but look how that ended up.

And that thought led me to wonder if they had told Jack.

Adam was poking me in the arm with his index finger.

"Mom, I can't believe that you didn't press me for details about Mya's Valentine's Day gift! You were so easy to scam!" he said jokingly. "I'm glad though, because I wanted to tell you in person."

I remembered that phone call. Nick had been beeping in, and I was anxious to talk to him.

"Well, glad I could oblige," I returned the banter. "Is that why you were so easy to talk into making this trip?"

"Yep, why else would I want to leave a foot of snow and freezing temperatures behind?" he said as he put his arm around Mya and pulled her down to sit on his lap.

The champagne was working, or maybe the initial shock was wearing off, but I was actually feeling genuinely *happy* about this now!

"Mya, I am so happy for you! Did you set a date yet?" I asked.

"We haven't picked the date. There are some things I have to go over with my family, and we wanted to talk to you first, but we're hoping for next spring."

"Mya asked me to be her maid of honor!" Casey chirped in as she refilled our glasses with the sparkling liquid.

This time I would sip instead of gulp.

"I propose a toast!" I said as I tipped my glass toward the happy couple. "To Adam and Mya! Congratulations on their

449

engagement, and may they have a happy and healthy life together!"

"Would you be open to a destination wedding?" Abbey asked.

I wondered what she was getting at. Adam and Mya just looked a little uncertain, and Adam shrugged.

"Like where?" he asked.

"I know the *perfect* place!" Abbey squealed. "Hal's house on Lake Juliet! Ellen, could you just see that place all decked out for a wedding? We could rent tents and a gazebo, and have tons of flowers and twinkle lights. It would be *fabulous!*"

Actually, I *could* see it in my imagination, but it wasn't my decision to make, and I turned to Adam.

"Well, it really would be a perfect place for a wedding. It's just lovely. That's a pretty big expense to have everyone fly down though," I said.

"My family all lives out of town and will have to travel anyway. It probably wouldn't matter to them what city they were buying a plane ticket for," Mya said, as the idea picked up momentum.

"You guys...the place would be outrageous! Abbey's right, it could really be done up right!" Casey said excitedly.

I looked over at Chris, who had been sitting quietly through all of this.

"Here we are making plans for a home that's not even ours. We'd have to see what Hal thinks," I told them.

"Oh, Granddad would be pleased, I'm sure," Chris said. "You can talk to him about it this weekend."

Casey bent over and gave him a kiss on the cheek.

"Maybe I should save it for my *own* wedding someday then."

My eyes immediately flew to her left hand. Her ring finger was thankfully still bare.

"And is that anywhere in the near future?" Adam teased.

Casey playfully punched him in the arm.

"Well, dear brother, we shall see."

"Casey, the potatoes are about done," Chris said as he checked the grill. "Do you want me to start the steaks now?"

"Let's do it. I'm starving!" Casey replied. "Abbey, do you want to come up and see my place?"

Casey, Mya, Abbey, and I all trooped up to Casey's condo. While Casey was giving Abbey the tour, Mya and I carried the steaks down to the guys, then went back up for the salad and plates. Mya and Abbey took the second load down, and Casey pulled me aside for a moment.

"Are you okay with this, Mom?" she asked. "Kind of a surprise, huh?"

"Yeah, *really* a surprise, but I'm good with it. I think they make a great couple. How do you feel about it?"

"Oh, yeah," she replied without hesitation. "I don't know Mya that well, but what I know, I like. Adam doesn't make snap decisions; I'm sure he really thought this through and is sure that Mya is the one."

I agreed. Adam was the planner and thinker of the family.

"Oh, I wanted to run something else by you too, but I didn't want to do it in front of Chris," she said in a hushed voice.

"Chris's mom stopped by the other day to see him, and I got to meet her, just for a moment because I was on my way to the office. But, get this…when I was pulling out of my parking space I saw her get in her car, and then Brooklyn got in with her and they left together! Do you think that's who she's seeing?"

Wow, that was a bomb.

"I don't know, Casey."

I thought about Nick telling me that Brooklyn had come on to her at one of the barbeque parties.

"It seems unlikely. Remember that Brooklyn wanted to take us all out for Valentine's Day? Wouldn't you think he would have been spending the day with her if they were a couple?"

"Well, I thought of that, too," Casey said. "But I remembered hearing Chris talking on the phone to his mom on Valentine's Day, and it sounded like she was out of town on business."

"Huh."

I didn't know what else to say.

"Didn't she tell Chris who she was seeing? You would think that would be something she'd share with her son. I know that I would want you to know the person I was with."

As soon as the words were out of my mouth, I could feel myself blushing. I really *was* turning into a hypocrite.

"No, he said that they haven't talked about that at all. Maybe it's different for guys and their moms," Casey said thoughtfully.

"Well, maybe she has her reasons for keeping that relationship to herself," I said, trying to make myself feel better.

"I'm glad I never met Dad's girlfriend. I wasn't ready for that at first…and maybe Chris isn't ready yet either."

This seemed like a good opportunity to broach the subject.

"Do you know if Adam told your dad about being engaged?"

Casey sniffed dramatically. "Highly doubt it. He said he hasn't talked to Dad since right after you left for Florida. Isn't that a shame, because they at least live in the same state! I bet he's never even met Mya. I've only talked to him once, and he was busy at the time and kind of blew me off."

"Oh. Well, as much as I hate to say this, I think he should let your dad know. Getting married is a pretty big deal."

"Have *you* talked to him recently?" she asked me.

"No, not since we had the offer on the house. But that's different! You guys are his kids and will probably always be in his life. I don't necessarily have to be in his life once we're divorced, only when it pertains to you guys."

"Well, aren't you just the diplomat?" she teased me. "I figured you'd want us to tell him to pound salt."

"I'm trying to be nice, but don't push it, because it's not coming easy," I told her earnestly.

After feasting on our steak dinner, we packed the Subaru with Mya and Adam's suitcases and waved goodbye to Casey and Chris.

"See you tomorrow!" I called out before I put up the window.

When we arrived at Lake Juliet, Adam and Mya were as taken with the place as I knew they'd be. It was already dusk when we arrived, so they really couldn't appreciate the beauty of the grounds, but Adam was just enchanted with the house.

"Mom, the pictures didn't do this place justice! Man, you are so lucky to be living here! My place will seem like slumming when you come home," he said as he ran a hand across the granite counter top in the kitchen.

Mya was leaning on the island, her chin propped in her hands.

"Adam, I really think I *could* see our wedding here. What do you think?" she asked him timidly.

"I think we could make it work. You just have to charm the heck out of Hal tomorrow," he replied, planting a kiss on top of her head.

"Yay!" Abbey said, clapping her hands. "I knew I'd find a way to come back here!"

"Assuming you're invited?" Adam teased, giving her a soft punch in the arm.

She took him in a headlock and rubbed his hair with her knuckles. "It was my idea to have it here, kiddo, and don't you forget it!

CHAPTER THIRTY TWO

I assigned the bedroom facing the front of the house to Adam and Mya, leaving Hal's old room for Nick. It practically gave me goose bumps to think of Nick spending the night in the room next to mine.

After the workmen had moved Hal's furniture downstairs, I asked them to bring up a spare single bed that I had seen in the garage. I knew we'd have a houseful this weekend and that it would come in handy, and I knew that Nick wouldn't mind having the no-frills room.

Saturday morning I woke up just as the sun was peeking over the horizon. I stood in front of the bay windows in my room, stretching my hands above my head and taking a deep breath. The mist was rising from the lake, and the birds were trolling for their fresh fish breakfast.

Today was going to be one busy day and I shivered with the excitement of it. I wanted the place to look perfect for Hal. I can't imagine how he'll feel coming home after being gone for so long!

I showered and dressed quickly, noting that Adam and Mya's door was still closed, as was Abbey's. After I started the coffee, I mixed a batch of oatmeal raisin muffins, and while they were baking, I took a stroll outside to cut some flowers. I wanted to make a fresh centerpiece for the dining table.

As I was arranging the flowers in a huge crystal vase, Abbey came up behind me looking fresh and lovely in blue denim walking shorts and a pale pink sleeveless shirt.

"I followed my nose to your muffins. Ellen, I am being spoiled rotten this week…and I love it! Hey, the flowers are lovely. Great job!" she said as she tenderly touched a petal.

Reaching for the folded cornflower blue linen cloth, she flipped it expertly over the dining room table, and as I put the flowers in the center, I heard the unmistakable sound of Nick's arrival. As he cut the engine on the Harley, my hands stilled and I looked up at Abbey.

"What's wrong?" She abruptly put down a handful of silverware and started around the table toward me.

My heart was pounding, and I clutched the linen napkins tightly in my hand. My mouth felt dry as I tried to answer her.

"Uh, Nick's here," I managed.

"Holy contractor with benefits!" Abbey said as she hurried toward the window to check him out.

All I wanted to do was to run out the door and into his arms, but I stayed rooted to the spot, not knowing *what* to do. Of course I had told Abbey that I felt attracted to him, but I didn't want to betray Nick's confidence and tell her *everything* that had happened.

I looked at the flowers, took a deep breath, and practically skipped over to the window to join Abbey.

She was spreading apart two slats of the plantation shutters with her thumb and forefinger and tilting her head sideways.

"My, my, oh my!" Abbey said, then whistled low.

My heart was still pounding, and I couldn't help but smile at the sight of him. He was wearing the faded jeans and worn boots that have become so familiar, and a black tee shirt that was snug across his chest and arms.

"Well, sweetheart, your face is as red as a beet!" Abbey joked, putting her hand on my forehead.

I knew that I was blushing, I could feel the heat radiating

from my cheeks.

Nick was already up to the front porch and entered without knocking. Abbey and I jumped away from the window just as he came through the door, lugging a worn black leather duffle bag. Although we had talked every day since the Brooklyn debacle, this was the first time we had come face to face. Wow.

He paused a beat as he entered the room, then recovered nicely.

"Hello, ladies! We have an exciting day ahead of us! The place looks great, Ellen!" he said all in one breath as he walked toward us and gave me a brief hug, then extended his hand to Abbey.

"You must be the infamous Abbey!" he said clasping her hand gently.

I was still recovering from the hug. This was going to really be a difficult day.

"And you must be the guy I've heard so much about," she said as she accepted his hand in hers.

He raised his eyebrows as he shook Abbey's hand and glanced my way with a smile on his face, but eyes that searched mine. I shook my head 'no' ever so slightly. I *hadn't* told Abbey that we had spent the night together. Nick and I had made a promise to each other to keep that confidential, with the exception of Sylvia, of course, who pretty much knew everything about everything, so she didn't count.

"I'd love to stay, Ellen, but I really have to go pick up Dad. He's already sitting in the lounge waiting with his suitcase! He's called twice already this morning, and he even tried to negotiate a ride over on my bike, but Lindsey would hear nothing of it!"

I laughed out loud because I knew Hal well enough to know that is exactly what he would be doing right now.

457

"Well, get going then! I'll take your bag upstairs. Want a muffin for the road?" I asked moving toward him.

"Thought you'd never ask. They smell delicious!" he replied, leading the way to the kitchen.

While he removed the muffin from its paper wrapper, I searched my purse for the Subaru keys.

"How about some coffee, Nick?" Abbey asked as she poured herself a cup.

"No thanks. I'll have some when we get back though, and I bet Dad will too. He'll want to sit out on the back porch and look at the lake. I'll tell him you're saving him a muffin."

I dangled the keys in front of Nick, and as he took them from me, his hand brushed against mine, and my whole body smiled. It was so very good to see him again.

He leaned forward as if to kiss me and caught himself just in time. Abbey was looking on with unabashed interest, leaning with her rump against the countertop and holding the coffee mug to her lips. Was she concealing a smile?

"I'd better get going, I have to pick up Sylvia on the way. She insisted on coming along to pick him up. See y'all in a little while!" Nick called on his way out the door.

I leaned back against the counter and sighed.

"So, I see you found Romeo at Lake Juliet after all!" Abbey teased. "I can see why you're so smitten with him, he's really hunky!"

I laughed out loud at her choice of words.

"Abbey, you're too much," I said as I pulled myself away from the counter and reached for a mug from the cupboard.

"I know," she replied.

Two hours later, everything was ready, and I was getting antsy.

Standing at the kitchen window, I could see Adam and Mya at the edge of the dock holding hands. They had enjoyed their breakfast on the porch then gone for a walk around the grounds. The morning mist on the lake had disappeared and the water was sparkling blue.

Abbey was curled up on the chaise by the pool enjoying a novel that she had brought with her, a bowl of strawberries and a cup of coffee at her side.

All very tranquil and relaxing…so why did my stomach feel like it was somersaulting over itself? Then I heard the slam of a car door, and my stomach did a front aerial with a side twist.

I flew out the door to the driveway, and Sylvia had already beat Nick out of the car and was monitoring Hal's progress disembarking from the front seat.

"Hal! Welcome home!" I shouted as I ran over to the car.

"Ellen, my girl! Look at this place! It looks like I never left …even better! You might be too good of a house sitter; the house won't want me back!" he joked as he swung his legs out of the car and planted his feet on the ground. "Ah, it feels so good to be home!"

"Now I know you're gonna want that walker, but we promised Lindsey we'd use the wheelchair at first, so don't give me any slack!" Sylvia told him with authority.

Hal smiled broadly, obviously amused.

Nick had collected the wheelchair from the trunk and was pushing it around to Hal when I caught his eye. He smiled, and I flashed back to the first day that I met him and he had been so emotional talking about his dad. Today was not just a milestone for Hal, but for Nick as well.

"Here ya go, Dad, hop on in and we'll try out the new ramp. I had them put in speed bumps, so don't get any ideas." Nick let Hal get himself seated, but stood near enough to help if it was needed.

"I feel like such a burden," Hal said, his smile disappearing.

Sylvia grabbed Hal's hand as Nick began to push him toward the house.

"I don't want to hear any of that talk!" she told him. "You'd do the same for any of us, and this chair will be collecting cobwebs before you can say alligator bite! Soon enough, you'll be walkin' yourself around and beggin' me for a ride in my golf cart!"

I had a visual of Hal and Sylvia racing along through the orange grove in the glittery pink cart, and I laughed out loud. "I'll buy tickets to see that!" I told them.

It also brought a smile back to Hal's face.

Adam and Mya had made their way up through the yard and joined our little caravan, and Abbey, hearing all the commotion, was just coming out the front door.

"Well, look at all my visitors!" Hal said with genuine excitement in his voice.

I introduced Hal to everyone, and they all thanked him profusely for letting them stay.

"Hal, I feel like I'm living in a page of *Better Homes and Gardens* magazine!" Abbey told him as she put a hand on his shoulder.

"Yes, sir, this place is really something!" Adam said as

he shook his hand.

"And we have some exciting news!" I wanted to share with the people I now considered my family. "Adam and Mya just got engaged on Valentine's Day!"

Nick caught my eye, and I felt like he was trying to look into my mind to see if I approved. We just had this uncanny connection that's hard to explain. I smiled at him, and he smiled back at me.

"Well, this is really a weekend of celebrations!" Sylvia said.

"Congratulations! Let's move this party inside and we can hear all the details," Nick said as he started to push.

"Would you look at this!" Hal exclaimed as we rounded the corner of the house. "You can hardly see that a ramp is here. Great job, you two!"

I had to admit that we did do a good job. The tall grasses and shrubs we planted really made the ramp look like part of the garden and not a handicapped space at all. And the terra cotta planters full of pink begonias added a colorful welcome.

We all paraded up the ramp, and while Nick and I gave Hal the tour, the rest of the crew continued the parade out to the back porch.

Hal was ecstatic about the first floor laundry and the kitchen upgrades, but he really became emotional when Nick wheeled him into his new bedroom.

"Oh my…," he said as he looked around the room, taking it all in. "This is just magnificent, Ellen. I know we talked about how things would look, but seeing it in person is just wonderful! How can I ever thank you?"

I leaned over and gave him a hug. Did I feel the wetness of his tears on my cheek?

"Oh, Hal," I said, wiping them away gently with my thumb. "I love you."

I looked up and saw Nick watching our interaction with curiosity.

"By the way, happy birthday to you!" I said as I stepped away from the wall and dramatically gestured with my hands, game show style, toward my sketches.

"Dad, Ellen made those for you," Nick said proudly.

"Really?" he said as he leaned in. "Why, that's Dora, isn't it? Have you made friends with her?"

"Yes, I have a can of cracked corn down on the dock, but now that I think of it, I haven't seen her for a while."

"And the otters…Ellen, you are very talented! How can I ever thank you for all you've done for me? You've made an old man a very happy man," Hal said as he reached out and held my hand.

Abbey had the coffee and muffins set up on the porch table, so we made Hal comfortable in the rocking chair and spent the rest of the morning chatting.

Mya had enchanted the heck out of Hal, so he wholeheartedly agreed to let them use his house for their wedding day. He told them that he would be honored to host such a sacred occasion, and he was so happy to see young people starting out so much in love. I don't know who was more excited about that, Mya or Abbey!

Of course I was excited about it too. I don't think it's fully sunk in with me yet that my son is getting married. It's hard to think of marriages ending at the same time a new one is beginning. Stupid little thoughts kept popping into my mind.

Will I be able to even enjoy the wedding with Jack in such close proximity? How would I feel seeing him dancing with Jessica, providing they are still together of course. Then my mind would flip flop and I would think, *why should I care?* I'm in love with someone else anyway. Then I would feel guilty about that. I should be thinking about what a happy day it will be for Adam and Mya, instead of how I'm going to feel.

I need to take Dr. Burke's advice again and just think of one day at a time, because I'm starting to get overwhelmed with everything. They are all good things, but it sure is a lot to comprehend at one time, and I can feel my emotions riding very close to the surface. I want to enjoy and savor every moment of planning and participating in Adam's wedding, but I feel like I'm being sidetracked by thinking about my own situation. I've always put my kids' and Jack's feelings ahead of my own, but since I've been at Lake Juliet, it's been different.

I don't think I'm being selfish. At least I hope I'm not! But I *have* taken time to get to know myself again, and I've just begun to figure out what I like to do and what I might want to do with my life. I need more time to think about things.

Even though I wouldn't want my life back to the way it was, the whole Jack thing still really kind of ticked me off. Here is our son getting married and we should be celebrating together, my husband and I, laughing and hugging and drinking champagne, toasting ourselves on raising such a fine son, and applauding his choice of such a wonderful woman to be his bride. We should be introduced at the reception as the parents of the groom, and Jack should be whirling me around the dance floor, he in a tux and me in–

"Mom!" Casey interrupted my thoughts, putting her hand on my arm. "You look like you're in another world, are you okay?"

I couldn't tell her that I really *was* in another world, a weird little world in my mind. The reality was that Adam didn't even feel inclined to *tell* Jack that he was getting married, and Jack's reaction would probably be something like, "Don't expect me to pay for anything," anyway. It was always about money with him. Which reminded me that I need to call Annee this week.

"I'm fine…just thinking," I answered, patting her hand.

"Looks like the bingo bus has arrived," Abbey whispered in my ear.

I looked in the driveway, and our guests were starting to arrive. Sophia had driven Sylvia's PT Cruiser, and it was filled to the gills with Hal's friends from Lakeside. Sylvia and I headed up the driveway to greet them, and several more vehicles pulled in before we had a chance to walk back down to the house. I was grateful that I would have to focus on making Hal's birthday party a success instead of having my thoughts racing through idiotic scenarios.

I found Abbey, Casey, and Mya in the kitchen getting the food ready to serve. They had shooed Sylvia away, telling her to keep the guests entertained. At the moment, she was leaning over the grill keeping watch over Nick and Adam as they applied barbecue sauce to the chicken. Chris was handing his grandfather a glass of iced tea and taking care of serving everyone beverages.

We loaded the dining room table with fruit salad, cheesy potatoes, baked beans, grilled asparagus, and lots of other dishes that were brought by some of the guests. Everyone filled a plate and migrated into little groups to eat.

After dinner, I stood at the kitchen window again, surveying the scene, feeling a sense of relief that everyone seemed to be having a good time. Abbey was having an animated conversation with Hal and Sylvia about who knows what. Herb, Sophia, and several of the others had brought a deck of cards and were gathered around the picnic table playing poker. The younger folk were sitting poolside dangling their feet in the water. But where was Nick?

It was so hard not to reach out to him today. I

accidentally-on-purpose found numerous excuses to inconspicuously touch him…to brush against his arm as I walked past…to touch his fingers as I handed him a drink…to meet his gaze across the table…I felt juvenile doing things like that at my age, but I can't explain the overwhelming urge I had to just be near him. Although my thoughts had temporarily been consumed by Jack, they were thoughts of the past, and Nick was right now.

I heard the front door open, then close, and as I turned, I saw Nick coming toward me, wearing a huge smile.

"There's my girl!" he said as he put his arm around my shoulder.

I wanted to turn into his embrace, throw my arms around his neck, and touch my lips to his. Instead I settled for grabbing his hand. At least I knew that wouldn't be visible through the window.

"I was checking on Sylvia's surprise. It's here!" he said excitedly. "Dad is going to love this!"

"Oh, so *you* know? What *is* it?" I asked, feeling a little miffed that Sylvia had let Nick in on the secret and not me.

"You'll find out," Nick teased. "The only reason she told me was because she needed some help with it today, so don't get all bent out of shape," he added as he rubbed his knuckles gently against my head.

"Shall we serve the cake now?" I asked as I removed a double layer sheet cake from the white bakery box.

"Sure, let me help."

Nick opened a box of birthday candles and began spacing them around the edge of the cake.

"How many are we putting on?" he asked.

I took another box out of the bag.

"Let's just use them all!"

"Good grief, we'll be burning down the house! They're going to melt the roller coaster!" he said, but he opened the third box of candles and began pushing them into the chocolate frosting.

Maria's Bakery had done an outstanding job of decorating the cake! I don't know where they found the roller coaster cake topper, but they hadn't even flinched when I requested it. The cake looked amazing, and it was Hal's favorite, yellow cake with chocolate fudge icing.

As Nick placed the last candle, he dipped his finger in the frosting and playfully touched it to my lips, then quickly pulled his hand away.

The sliding door from the porch opened and Casey stepped inside.

"Wow! What a cute cake, Mom!" she exclaimed, coming in for a closer look.

I licked the frosting from my lips and gave Nick a look over Casey's head.

"Yeah, I think he'll like it," I replied as I took a lighter out of the drawer.

"Casey, if you want to help your mom light the candles, I'll go get Dad up to the table and get the group together."

Casey grabbed another lighter and we double-teamed the candles.

"So, looks like you two are getting along," Casey said.

I didn't know if this was a statement or a question that she was expecting an answer to, so I changed the subject.

"I think the party's going great, don't you?" I asked.

"Yep. You really did a nice job on it, Mom. Hal looks really happy. So, what's with him and Sylvia?"

"Oh, I think they've become really good friends," I answered.

"Oh, I think it's a little more than that. They're winking at each other so much, I thought they had nervous ticks!" she said with a little laugh. "It's sweet though."

"Yes, it is," I replied with the taste of chocolate fudge frosting still lingering in my mouth.

The candles were lit, and Casey opened the door and began the singing. As we all joined in, I carried the flaming cake over to the table and placed it in front of Hal. Sylvia sat at his side, and the rest of the group had gathered around the table.

The candle light reflecting on Hal's face revealed a happy tear dampening his cheek. He closed his eyes to make his wish, then made an attempt to blow them all out.

"It's good luck for everyone to help blow out birthday candles," Sylvia said as she saved the day by puckering up her rosy glossed lips and taking out about a third of the candles herself.

Finally, the flames were all extinguished and a round of applause broke out.

"Thank you all so much for being here. I can't tell you how happy I am right now!" he said as he looked around at all the smiling faces.

I cut the cake, and Abbey added a scoop of ice cream to each plate and handed it to Casey to deliver.

Abbey leaned over to whisper in my ear, "Good thing no one was on oxygen. With all those candles we would have all gone up in smoke!"

I started laughing and just couldn't stop. It was a comment only Abbey could get away with without sounding rude…well, with the exception of maybe Sylvia.

"What's so funny, you two?" It was Nick's voice behind me, and his hand reaching over my shoulder for a plate of cake.

I just shook my head, sliced the silver knife through another chunk of cake, and handed it to Abbey on our assembly line.

Abbey and I had just settled ourselves at the table to finally enjoy our dessert, when Nick rounded up Adam and Chris and herded them out the door.

"We'll be right back," Nick hollered over his shoulder as they disappeared into the darkness.

I had been so preoccupied, I hadn't even realized that the sun had set.

A few moments later I saw a flame in the yard down by the lake. Alarmed, I sat up straight and squinted my eyes. Hurriedly putting my plate down on the table, I pushed my chair back to investigate.

"It's okay, dear," Sylvia said, putting her hand on my shoulder and bending down to whisper in my ear. "It's a little bonfire…part of my birthday surprise."

"Oh," I said, sitting back down but keeping my eyes peeled on the flames leaping into the night sky.

"Where's a marshmallow when you need one?" Abbey piped up.

Sylvia had brought a sweater out for Hal, and he grudgingly switched from the chair at the table back to the wheelchair.

"Sylvia, I can use the walker," he was telling her, but she cut him off with a shake of her head.

"I'm not taking a chance on you trippin' over a root or something in the dark. Besides, you'll be more comfortable in this chair," she said as she helped him into his sweater.

Hal was smiling though, clearly excited about the bonfire and thoroughly enjoying her attention.

Casey and Mya had been cleaning up the empty dessert plates, and as Casey dropped mine into the black trash bag, she plopped down in the empty chair beside me.

"So, why the bonfire?" she asked me as she looked out into the yard.

"Part of Sylvia's surprise for Hal. I guess maybe he likes bonfires or something. He seems pretty excited about it," I told her.

I could see Chris lighting tiki torches around the back yard, illuminating Adam and Nick as they put out chairs in a circle near the fire. There were also things that looked like kegs or something, but I couldn't tell exactly what they were from this distance.

Sylvia was next to the door with her hands on the grips of Hal's wheelchair, and the rest of the group had huddled behind them, watching the scene in the backyard with curiosity.

I heard Nick's voice from right outside the door.

"Okay, everyone, come on down and find a seat."

"Here, Sylvia, let me push," Herb said, taking control of Hal's chariot, and we all followed them down to the fire circle.

"Holy percussion, they're bongo drums!" Abbey said as we walked arm in arm through the grass.

And indeed they were! Some were very large, probably as high as my waist, and smaller ones were placed on some of the chairs. It looked like there were enough for everyone.

"Ellen, I have to say that this week has been quite the experience!" Abbey said as we took a seat around the fire.

"Mind if I take this seat?" Nick asked, and he didn't wait for my answer, but sat on the folding chair next to mine.

This night was just getting better and better.

After we all sat down, Sylvia clapped her hands for our attention.

"Welcome to our drum circle in honor of Hal's birthday! Hal told me how much he used to enjoy goin' over to Sarasota and joinin' in their drum circle on the beach, so I wanted to recreate that experience right here at Lake Juliet. You don't have to know how to play; we'll get a beat goin' then everyone can join in. If anyone wants to dance that would be just dandy…except for you, Hal. Sophia, do you want to get us started, dear?"

And without a moment's hesitation, Sophia started pounding away. She had one of the large drums and the sound was mellow and deep. Dum, dum, dum….dum, dum da dum dum…over and over again.

Hal had a large drum too, and joined in with a dum, da, dum, da, dum, dum, da, dum rhythm.

Nick reached down and grabbed the set of bongos near my feet.

"Here, put them between your knees like this."

He spread his legs a bit, then gripped the drums with his knees.

470

"Oh, I don't know how to play drums..." I started.

"Oh, Ellen, *come on!* When will we ever get to do this again?" Abbey said as she followed Nick's instructions and began her own rhythm. "Oh, this is so much fun!"

"Go for it, Mom!" I heard Casey yell from somewhere on the other side of the fire.

Everyone else was already joining in, so even though I felt a little foolish, I stuffed them between my knees and began hitting the pads lightly with my fingertips. Abbey was right, it *was* great fun!

The sound was simply amazing, and as I looked around the circle I thought of how bizarre this was. A group of people whose ages were as many as five decades apart, all gathered together and having a whopper of a good time, playing bongos! Who would ever believe it!

Mya jumped up and pulled Casey with her, showing her how to do a bit of an Indian dance. The moves were simple, and Casey caught on right away. I could see that I was in Mya's line of vision, and I knew that she was coming for me next.

I laughed as she pulled my hand, and I grabbed Abbey's on the way up.

"I'm not doing this alone!" I yelled at Abbey over the seductive rhythm of the drums.

We swayed and gyrated and I laughed so hard I thought that my sides were going to split. Sylvia and Sophia joined our little dancing harem, and before you knew it, all the women were dancing, and it was only the men pounding away on the drums.

The beating finally slowed down, and I fell breathless into my chair and looked over at Nick.

"This is awesome!" I said to him.

"*You* are awesome," he replied.

I felt all warm and tingly inside and looked around to see if anyone else had heard.

Nick rose from his chair and opened a cooler behind him. Grabbing an armful of cans, he went around the circle passing out beer, iced tea, and cola. The drumming had stopped now, and we all sat quietly looking at the flames leaping toward the starlit sky. I leaned back in my chair, sipping my beer and listening to the gentle conversations around me. Something in the fire snapped, and a spark flew up toward the sky leaving a trail of tiny burning embers.

"Rick would have loved this evening," Abbey said softly.

I reached over and grabbed her hand. I knew that she was having a great time but was probably missing her family as well.

"We'll have to do this again when you come back," I promised.

"Ellen, everyone here is so nice," she said. "And the place is so beautiful! I feel like I'm living in a dream right now."

"I've felt that way for the past two months!" I told her honestly.

I looked around the circle and it seemed that everyone's energy was spent. Casey was sitting on Chris's lap with her head on his shoulder, Adam had his arm around Mya and she was grasping his hand in hers, Sylvia and Hal were talking softly between themselves with their heads bent together...and Nick was slouched down in his chair, head tilted up towards the sky and feet crossed at the ankles.

I flashed back to the first day that I met him and he had struck this same pose on the dock, only that day tipping his face to the sun.

"Well, I think I've used up my whole week's energy on

this evening. My body's just had enough of me!" Sophia said. "Whoever's ridin' with me, let's get a move on. I need to hit the sack!"

The others who had come from Lakeside expressed the same sentiment and started getting up and milling around, and the low murmur of conversation replaced the frenzy of the drums.

"Now, none of you have been drinking too much to drive, have you?" Nick asked wisely. "Sophia?"

"Oh, for Pete's sake, Nicky!" she replied with a snort. 'My buzz faded hours ago!"

He laughed and put his arm around her as we all walked up toward the house, the flickering tiki torches lighting the path.

Herb parked Hal inside the porch and Sylvia hovered nearby.

"I'm goin' to ride back home with Sophia," she told us as she gathered her purse, "but I'd like to come back for breakfast."

Abbey elbowed me in the ribs.

"Miss Ellen, thank you so much for planning the party with me," Sylvia said as she hugged me tightly.

"It was fun, Syl, and the drum circle was great! Where did you ever get all the drums?" I asked.

She waved her hand through the air. "Oh, you can pretty much rent anything you want at Larry's Rent-All, Ellen."

She bent down to kiss Hal on the forehead. He grabbed her hand and pressed it against his lips.

"Thank you, Sylvia," he said simply, and she was out the door.

CHAPTER THIRTY THREE

Abbey poured white dishwasher powder in the compartment on the door and closed it with a thump.

She yawned as she pushed the "start" button and the gentle swish of water began.

"I'm beat, Ellen," she told me. "If you don't mind, I think I'll go get a nice hot bath, call Rick, and turn in. I'm not used to having such an active social life!"

I yanked the trash bag out of the kitchen can and gave the tie a firm pull.

"I think I'll be right behind you," I said as I pulled a new white plastic bag from the box and inserted it in the can. "Thanks for helping with everything today. Sorry you had to work on your vacation."

"Are you kidding? I had a blast! Rick is never going to believe that I played bongo drums around a bonfire tonight! I wonder what the weather's like back home."

"I used to wonder that every day, but now I'm so used to it being warm that I forget it's actually cold back home," I told her.

"At least when you come back, it'll be spring," Abbey said as she gave me a quick hug and turned towards the steps.

"Good night, Abbey," I called after her.

I did feel exhausted…but also exhilarated! Everything had gone so well today! It was wonderful to have all my family and friends together, and to have Hal home. And who am I kidding…it made me just plain giddy to have Nick here.

We'd been skirting around each other all day, taking care of the business of having a houseful of guests, yet finding moments to catch each other's eye and share a smile or inconspicuous touch. At least I *hope* we were discreet.

Casey and Chris decided to spend the night here as well, so I had piled blankets and extra pillows on the couch for them. They were still huddled with Adam and Mya down by the fire, which by now had burned down to a pile of glowing embers, and I expected they would talk half the night away.

Nick had taken care of getting Hal ready for bed and tucking him safely in, and then had gone out to load the drums back into the white van in the driveway. Apparently someone would come to pick them up in the morning. From the kitchen window I could see him placing the last one in the back and giving the door a good slam.

Now what? I was a woman on a mission, that's what.

I opened the kitchen door and toted the bulging trash bag outside toward the big metal cans. Just as I had hoped, Nick saw me and beat me to them, prying the lid off of one and relieving me of the heavy bag.

"I would have carried that out for you," he said as he clunked the lid back on.

"I know."

He stared at me for a moment, then grabbed me by the wrist and pulled me toward the back porch. I almost had to run to keep up with him. Opening the screen door quietly, he gently nudged me inside and closed the door without a sound.

We stood deep in the shadows; the only thing I could hear was our breathing. The scent of orange blossoms hung heavy in the damp night air, and the sensual rhythm of the drums was still beating in my mind.

Nick pulled me to him, wrapping his arms around me, and

I was home. I clung to him as if I had been drowning all day, and he was my breath of life. Stepping on tiptoe, I turned my face upward just as his was descending on mine.

Our lips touched and all the passion that I'd been holding back all day broke free. If this were a cartoon, I swear that fireworks would have exploded above our heads.

A sound made me jump, but it hadn't been fireworks at all…it was the screen door.

Quickly, I turned around to see Casey pausing to look in our direction, then continuing on her way into the house as if she hadn't seen a thing, slamming the sliding door with a vengeance.

I faced Nick and slumped against him, resting my head against his chest as his fingers calmly and slowly massaged my back.

"Maybe she didn't see us," he whispered, sensing my defeat. "Hell, *I* can hardly see us."

"No…she saw…I could feel it," I replied in the same hushed tone.

"Well, then, I think the time has come to let our kids know how we feel. We're not doing anything wrong, Ellie."

"I know. I don't think I've ever done anything so *right*! It's just that I don't think Casey will approve of me being with her boyfriend's dad, especially so soon."

Nick sighed heavily.

"I need to go talk to her," I said as I pulled away from him. My emotions were churning; I felt guilty for the first time since I've been with Nick. I felt embarrassed, ashamed, and childish.

"Ellie…" he said, squeezing my hand, "Everything will be fine."

I nodded and made my way to the sliding door. As I opened it and stepped inside, I turned to look at Nick, whom I could see plain as day. Of course she had seen us. Forcing a little smile for him, I closed the door and went in search of Casey.

I found her sitting on my bed staring straight ahead, with tears streaming down her cheeks, and my heart went out to her. She looked up as I entered the room and the vulnerable expression on her face hardened to one of disapproval.

She narrowed her eyes and put her hands out, palms up.

"Mother, what the hell are you doing?" she asked, mincing no words.

Her swift change of demeanor must have triggered mine because I suddenly felt angry. I didn't want to have to defend my actions and be judged by her when she had no idea what I was feeling inside.

"I was kissing Nick, as I'm sure you saw," I replied, matching her tone.

"Yeah, *that* was pretty evident! The question is, '*Why*?' Why, out of all the guys in the world, do you have to hit on Chris's dad? You know that his parents just broke up! Don't you think you're taking advantage of the situation? Chris is hoping they'll get back together. I'm so glad he didn't come up to the house with me. Imagine what he would have thought!" she blurted out.

I sat down on the bed next to her, and as I did, she stood up and put her hands on her hips.

"Casey, I really like Nick. We've been talking a lot on the phone, and we've become very close. I'm *not* hitting on him…" I tried to explain and keep my emotions in check.

"So, this has been going on for a while, then?" she butted

in.

I closed my eyes, inhaled and exhaled slowly.

"Mom, this wasn't going on while he was still *really* married, was it?" she asked accusingly, her index fingers making quotation marks in the air when she said *really*.

My eyes popped open and looked into hers, silently incriminating myself.

"Casey, please calm down," I began.

"Oh, for Pete's sake," she shook her head at me, "I can't believe this."

She turned on her heel and flounced out of the room. I heard her clomp down the stairs as I felt the bottom drop out of my stomach.

I slowly stood up and gravitated toward the window. I could see Casey's shadowy figure walking slowly back to the remains of the bonfire. She took the chair next to Chris and snuggled into his shoulder.

I flopped back down on the bed, feeling exhausted. My brain felt numb, but surprisingly, I didn't cry. I didn't have the energy for even that. I just felt…sad…so very sad. I pulled my pillow out from under the comforter, unceremoniously laid my head on it, and closed my eyes. I didn't want to think about this or anything else; I just wanted to fall into the deep oblivion of sleep.

Somewhere in my dreams, I felt a gentle hand smooth my hair and a soft kiss press against my forehead. The light flutter of a sheet covered my body, and I clenched it in my fists and pulled it up to my chin.

Sunlight pierced through my fog of slumber, and as I

opened my eyes I knew that it was at least after nine. The comforting aroma of coffee and bacon was beckoning me to swing my feet over the side of the bed and venture down to the kitchen. But as I flung the sheet aside, I realized that I was still wearing yesterday's clothes. I closed my eyes again. I needed to set things straight with Casey. I couldn't bear the thought of her being angry with me. My kids are all I have right now, and I can't put my relationship with them in jeopardy, even if it means giving up someone that I care so much about.

Somewhere along the line I had gone from being the victim in my whole divorce scenario to being the bad guy, and that wasn't sitting very well with me.

As I quickly showered and dressed, I wondered if she had told Adam, and what he would think. I certainly didn't want to argue with him today, too. As I padded down the stairs, I was prepared to give up everything I had with Nick if it meant keeping harmony in my little family.

I could hear everyone talking on the back porch, so I passed through the empty kitchen, poured a cup of coffee, and helped myself to some bacon and scrambled eggs that were still warm on the stove.

As I stood by the sliding door trying to decide how to open it without fumbling my breakfast to the floor, Nick jumped up from his seat at the table and came to my rescue.

"Good morning, Ellie!" he said with a huge smile on his face. I smiled in return, but couldn't quite meet his eyes.

Everyone looked up from their place at the table and greeted me with gusto as if this were any normal day. Everyone but Casey, who was noticeably absent.

I sat down between Sylvia and Abbey and took a small sip of my coffee.

"Is Casey still sleeping?" I directed my question to Abbey, who shrugged her shoulders.

479

Chris answered me from across the table.

"No, she had to leave early this morning. She said a client had an emergency and she had to get to the office to take care of it," he said. "I'm hitching a ride back later with Dad and Grandpa."

"Oh," I replied as I stabbed a piece of egg with my fork. I really didn't feel like eating anymore and laid the fork down on my plate.

"We were thinking of going to the beach for the afternoon– are you in?" Abbey asked me excitedly.

All I really wanted to do was go back and crawl back under the covers.

"I'm up for whatever," I heard myself reply.

Abbey eyed me suspiciously.

"Hal said we could take the Subaru," Adam joined in the conversation. "It would just be you, Abbey, Mya and me. Everyone else is hanging here."

My first thought was that it was rude of us to leave Hal on his big weekend home, but then I realized that he might appreciate some time alone with his family, without all the commotion of my added guests.

"Count me in then," I said as I stood and began to gather up the empty plates from the table.

"You just leave 'em all on the counter, Miss Ellen, I'll take it from there," Sylvia instructed. "We can have the leftovers from the party for dinner if y'all are back in time. Hal will be leaving around seven to go back to New Hope."

"We'll be back to see you off, Hal," I said as I patted his back.

"You kids go have a good time today, and you Yankees remember the sunscreen!" he joked.

Once again Nick opened the door for me as I carried in a stack of plates.

"Is everything okay?" he asked once we were alone in the kitchen.

I shrugged as I put my load on the counter.

"Casey's *really* angry with me. I don't think her client had an emergency. She just didn't want to deal with *me* today," and I could feel the tears that had been denied last night threatening to fall.

The sliding door opened again and the rest of the crew piled in, chattering excitedly, so I turned quickly toward the sink and, against Sylvia's request, began rinsing the dishes.

Two hours later, after we had followed Nick's directions, Adam pulled into a parking lot at Cocoa Beach. We had driven east on the B-Line, and the sight of the Atlantic Ocean had lifted even *my* spirits. Abbey and Mya were absolutely ecstatic, whooping and hollering as the Subaru bumped over the sandy soil and came to a halt next to a parking meter.

As I got out of the backseat, I took a deep breath of the salty ocean air, trying to cleanse my mind.

We all grabbed something. You'd think we were staying for a week instead of only a few hours by the amount of stuff we brought.

Sylvia had packed a cooler full of cold drinks and snacks, we had assorted beach chairs, two beach umbrellas– at Hal's insistence, and various totes filled with towels and sunscreen.

Abbey kicked off her flip flops and carried them instead.

"Oh, sand between my toes in February!" she exclaimed.

Of course the beach wasn't crowded, only tourists like us. The water was a little too chilly for the locals this time of year. We stopped to set up camp in the soft sand, right before the line of demarcation where it became hard and wet from the waves. The tide appeared to be on its way out.

Adam grabbed Mya's hand and they ran down to the ocean, not stopping until the water was up to their waists. I heard Mya's happy scream as the first wave crashed over them.

"Let's walk..." Abbey said as she grabbed *my* hand and pulled me toward the water.

We walked along the shoreline in silence for a while, the gentle waves lapping over our ankles before rushing back out to sea. We passed a flock of gulls waiting patiently in the sand for each surge of water to retreat so they could scavenge the goodies it left behind for them. Every so often, Abbey or I would bend over and pick up a shell that caught our eye, then stoop back down to wash it off in the next wave.

The wind was in my hair and I could taste salt on my lips.

I was starting to feel better. Maybe I could just keep walking on the beach forever...did the beach ever end?

"So, are you ready to tell me what's going on?" Abbey stopped walking and moved in closer to be heard over the sound of the waves.

I looked down and watched a piece of seaweed wash over my foot and up in the sand, being left behind. My feet were slowly sinking as the constant movement of water eroded the sand around them.

Lifting my eyes to the horizon, I felt the need to unburden.

"I messed up," I confessed to Abbey.

"In what way?" she replied as she flicked a piece of seaweed from her foot.

I shifted my position, pulling my feet out of my sand shoes and taking a step backwards to fresh sand, only to have it start all over again.

"I've been seeing Nick, and last night Casey saw me kissing him on the porch. She's ticked off big time."

If Abbey was shocked, she didn't show it.

"So, is she upset because she doesn't want you to be with anyone?" she asked.

"No, she didn't mind at all when she thought I was seeing Brooklyn. In fact, she encouraged it. She's upset because she thinks that Chris will be upset. Evidently he's hoping that his parents will get back together, and Casey thinks I am an unsavory roadblock to that happening."

I shifted my feet again.

"So, how serious is it with you and Nick?"

To hell with promises and secrets.

"I slept with him."

She instantly grabbed my arm and turned me to face her. Her eyes were wide and her mouth was open.

I averted her gaze and looked down to my feet.

"Ellen! When? Last night?" she asked in a rush.

I looked back up and met her blue eyes.

"No! Not last night…it was a while ago."

"And you didn't tell me, *why?*" she asked, acting insulted. "That's kind of an important detail to leave out!"

"We decided that it might not be the best news to broadcast. I mean they officially just split up less than a month ago. And…we're not really sure where it's going yet. In Nick's words, he has to get his shit together before he can commit to another relationship."

"And what are *your* words?" she asked

"I love him."

"Oh, Ellen…" she said, taking me in a brief hug. "It's early for you to be seriously involved with someone too, right?"

I shook my head up and down.

"I know. But, Abbey, it's something I never thought would happen. You know me. I would normally *never* do something like that! But it happened, and it was wonderful. I had absolutely no regrets until last night when Casey confronted me."

"So, do you want to take me back to the beginning and tell me all about it now?" she asked as we turned and started walking slowly back toward our camp.

I did want to tell my best friend, and by the time we reached our umbrellas the story was told.

Adam and Mya were walking the beach in the other direction, so we sat down in the chairs under the huge red and white striped umbrella. I reached into the cooler and pulled out two bottles of water. Brushing the sand from my hands, I gave one to Abbey then twisted open the lid on mine and took a long, cool sip.

"So…" I asked her, "What do you think?"

She had listened without making a comment through the whole confession. I looked at her intently while she sipped her water then screwed the cap back on.

"You realize, it's not about what I think, or anyone else for that matter. It's about what *you* think. Ellen, Jack bullied every one of your thoughts for so long, maybe you forget what it's like to think for yourself."

"Yeah, sure, it's easy for *you* to tell me to do what I want, but it's not your daughter who's not speaking to you."

"Well, I didn't *say* to go do whatever you want. I said you have to decide for yourself what you want to do."

That wasn't what I wanted to hear from her.

"But what *do* you think?" I pushed.

"Seriously? If you had called and told me all of this on the telephone, I would have told you to pack your bags and get your horny ass back home!"

I smiled, despite the harsh words.

"But I've met Nick, and I really like him. I can see you two as a couple someday. I think he really suits you and he seems like he's a good man, not to mention the super attractive factor. And you two did make a good plan to just date and cool things down until you both are ready for more…that was really mature of you, Ellen. I really think that he's too fancy of a fish to throw back in. He's a keeper!"

Now I was really smiling.

"So that being said, this whole bunch of trouble is because Casey *thinks* that Chris would be upset? Did anyone think to ask *him*? He seems like a nice guy, too, and I bet he can think a thought through. Maybe he would be okay with it. Might be kind of weird, but at least it would save on visiting two sets of in-laws on a holiday! And you never know, they could break up next week, and then you would have given up Nick for nothing."

She took another swig of water and began to root around in the cooler for something to eat.

"Holy cow, Ellen, you're better than a soap opera!" she exclaimed, pulling out a package of peanut butter crackers.

"I think the only real mistake you made was hiding it," she finished.

"I know, and I feel embarrassed about that. It just seemed right at the time. I only did it to avoid exactly what happened anyway," I admitted.

"How does Adam feel about it?" she asked.

"Haven't told him about it at all," I said as I chose a package of crackers with cheese.

She expelled a deep breath.

"Well, two wrongs don't make a right. Now's your chance," she said, nodding her head toward the water.

Adam and Mya were several yards away and closing in fast.

They plopped down in the chairs under the green and white striped umbrella next to us, and Adam pulled out water and two small bags of chips.

"This is great stuff, Mom!" he said, smiling as he handed Mya her water. "I love the ocean!"

"We found some really nice shells," Mya said as she held up a small plastic sandwich bag that they filled on their walk. "I'm going to put them in a glass jar on the mantle when we get home."

I pulled out the containers of fruit and cheese that Sylvia had thoughtfully provided, and after we had eaten every morsel, including the chocolate chip cookies, Abbey touched Mya on the shoulder.

"I really need to use the ladies room. Want to come with me, Mya?"

"Good idea," Mya said as she stood up and looked at me. "Coming, too?"

Abbey winked at me and nodded toward Adam.

"I'll meet you guys up there in a few minutes," I replied as I put the empty containers back in the cooler.

Adam stood up as if to follow them, and I touched him on the back.

"Honey, can we talk about something for a moment?" I asked him.

He sat back down with a perplexed look on his face.

"Is something wrong?" he asked when he saw my expression.

"Well, I have something to tell you, and I hope you'll be okay with it. Casey's angry with me right now. I think that's why she left this morning. She didn't say anything to you?"

"Nope, last I saw her was at the bonfire last night. She seemed quiet toward the end, but I figured she was just getting tired. What's up?"

"Well...."

This was a lot harder than I thought.

"I really like Nick, and we're sort of dating."

Adam laughed heartily.

"*No kidding*! I knew you liked him even before I got here. You talked about him enough!"

"What?" I asked. "I didn't talk about him *that* much, did I?"

"Only every phone conversation we had! Man, Mom, I'm no dummy!"

Huh.

"So, how do you feel about me dating him?" I asked.

"What's it matter what I think? If you like him, then go for it! You deserve to be with someone who's gonna treat you right, and I really like the guy. I like Chris and Hal, too. So what's the big deal with Casey?"

My insides were jumping for joy!

"She thinks Chris might not like it because he wants his mom and dad to get back together. That's why she left this morning, I think she didn't want to be around me."

Adam whistled low.

"Didn't see that one coming. Well, maybe you just need to tell Chris and see what he thinks. Or have Nick talk to him. If there's no way his parents are getting back together, then I can't see why he'd object to someone as nice as you dating his dad. Don't worry about Casey; she'll come around."

"Did I tell you today how much I love you?" I asked him.

He squinted and kicked a bit of sand at me with his foot.

"Nope, you were too busy being a hussy," he said, and took off running.

I chased him all the way to the restrooms.

CHAPTER THIRTY FOUR

That evening, as we all were gathered around the table enjoying leftovers, I felt more relaxed than I had in days. I hadn't realized how much of an emotional and physical burden it had been to keep my relationship with Nick all bottled up inside me.

We had arrived home from the beach a little sunburned and a lot sandy, sticky from the sunscreen still lingering on our skin. Nick had come out to greet us even before Adam cut the engine. It made me happy to think that he'd been watching and waiting for me.

"I missed you," he had whispered in my ear as we unloaded the beach paraphernalia from the trunk, and I had given him my best smile.

After showering and dressing for dinner, I walked past his room and heard him call out to me.

"Ellie, come here," he had said as he patted the spot next to him on the bed.

I sat down beside him, and he gave me a quick kiss and picked up my hand and held it in his, moving his thumb back and forth across my knuckles.

"I talked to Chris while you were gone. I wanted to set this straight. I don't want to be coming between you and Casey, and I don't want to lose you because somebody got their wires crossed."

I didn't know what to say, so I just sat there with my heart hammering, focusing on the sound of his voice and looking deep into his eyes.

"Chris and I took Dad fishing down at the pier and we all had a good heart to heart talk. Of course Dad already knew about us and he's completely fine with it, but Chris was a little surprised. But, Ellie, he likes you a lot, and I think he'll warm up to the idea. He's not upset about *you,* he's just not liking the idea of me being with *anyone.* "

My stomach did a little flip flop. "So Casey was right," I said softly.

"Well, not entirely," he said, continuing to massage my hand, "After I explained some things about my relationship with his mother, and told him that I have no intention of reconciling with her, he sort of came around. It's a hell of a conversation to have with your kid."

I dropped my eyes to look at our clasped hands, remembering Casey and Adam's reactions when they found out about Jack and me.

"Casey told me that it's hard for kids to handle a divorce, even when they're adults," I admitted.

"I feel like such a screw up," Nick said, releasing my hand and running his through his hair instead.

I knew exactly what he was feeling. I knew firsthand what it felt like to think of yourself as screw up, but I gave it my best shot to try and make him feel better.

"If it's any consolation, as time goes on there are fewer days that you'll feel like a total failure," I said seriously.

He laughed loudly, and my head snapped up.

"Ellie, you're something!" he said as I blushed deeply.

"By the way, Dad put in a good word for you."

Ah, Hal. "He is so sweet, Nick."

"I guess we'd better get down to dinner. I just wanted to tell you that things are going to be okay."

491

I was really glad to hear that he talked to Chris, and I automatically reached up to wrap my arms around his neck.

"I am *so* happy to hear you say that!" I told him as I held him tight. "I talked to Adam too, and I'm pretty sure we have his blessing."

"Now all we have to do is get Casey on board, and we'll be all set," he said.

"Nick, I can't tell you how good it feels to have that burden lifted from my shoulders!"

"No more burdens, let's just see where it takes us, okay?" he said.

We walked down the stairs to dinner, and even though at first I felt a stab of self- consciousness, when Chris looked up and gave me a smile, it vanished.

"You might want to soak those shells in a bit of bleach and water, then you can shine 'em up with a dab of baby oil," Sophia was telling Mya.

Sophia had come over for dinner, and as I helped myself to seconds of the fruit salad, I listened to their conversation with interest.

"Oh, thanks! Maybe I'll do that tonight so they'll have time to dry before I pack them," Mya said as she scraped the bottom of the cheesy potato pan to get the really brown ones.

"Good idea! Right now they reek," Adam told her as he waved his hand in front of his nose.

"Sylvia, any news on the Lakeside purchase?" Nick asked.

"Well, remember Esther told me one of the guys that bought their place had a famous name?" Sophia jumped into the conversation. "Well, she remembered that it has something to do with New York."

I about choked on a piece of watermelon.

Realization hit Sylvia and I at the same time. "*Brooklyn!*" we said simultaneously.

"Well," Sophia said, pursing her lips and looking up to the ceiling, "That could be it."

"Oh, my gosh!" I said, "I can totally see it now. He told me he came over this way sometimes because he owned some property in this area."

"And that would be the Lake Pete site I betcha!" Sylvia interjected excitedly.

"And, Nick, remember that morning when I told him that I sold my house, he said that he was getting close to closing a deal on some property, too. He was really excited about it and even invited us all out to lunch to celebrate!"

"Yeah, he had a real hard on about it," Nick mumbled under his breath, tipping his beer bottle up to finish it off.

I was instantly sorry that I brought up memories of that day, but it was an important piece of the puzzle.

"Well, the orange grove that you see out the window is owned by the Lakeside people as well. I'd sure hate to see that go away," Hal told us. "All that property used to be owned by old man Schaffer, then he sold it years ago when he retired to Key West."

"Well, that Brooklyn is no good from what I hear," Sylvia was indignant. "We'll have to be very sharp to outsmart a weasel like him!"

I remembered what Casey had told me about seeing J-Rae in Brooklyn's car, but I thought this wasn't the most appropriate time to bring that up.

"Who is this Brooklyn character?" Adam asked.

"He owns lots of real estate, and the condo where Casey and I live," Chris told him. "He's kind of full of himself, but he always seemed like an okay guy."

"So, if someone new buys Lakeside, what's so bad about that?" Mya asked.

"Someone has been buyin' up mobile home parks where the seniors live, and then givin' them the boot and buildin' new houses on the land," Sylvia explained.

"Orange groves too," Sophia told her.

"I guess it would be hard to find a new place to live?" Mya asked trying to understand.

I offered my explanation.

"It's not that they couldn't find somewhere else to live, it's just that Lakeside is an exceptional place; it's a really close-knit community. They do all kinds of activities together and go on trips, everyone knows everyone, and they all keep their places so nice. It would just be a shame to ruin something like that in the name of progress and split up the friendships."

"Is there anything you can do about it then?" Adam asked.

"We're tryin' to form our own company of all the residents, then we can try to buy Lakeside instead of a development company gettin' their hands on it. Casey's lookin' into the legalities of it for us." Sylvia said, fuming. "Ellen, can you check with her tomorrow and see how that's comin' along? I don't want to be a pain in the pettuti."

I felt a gagging feeling in my throat. I had forgotten in the momentum of the conversation that Casey was still angry with me, and the realization of it hit me like lightening.

I looked at Sylvia, who was staring back at me, her hair today tinted in pastel blue and pink and wearing a sky blue silk shirt that emphasized her electric blue eyes.

Abbey saved me.

"Sure, maybe we'll take a drive over to see Casey tomorrow after we take Adam and Mya back to the airport. Ellen, you promised me a trip to the outlets anyway."

I smiled my thank you to Abbey.

After dinner, we packed up Hal in the Subaru with a renewed spirit and a determination to return for good in a few weeks. He had given me a hug and a kiss on the cheek before he took his place in the front seat.

"Ellen, thank you so much for everything. I'm so pleased with the way my house looks, I just can't wait to get back here and enjoy it every day," he told me before we slammed the door.

Abbey and I stood in the driveway and waved goodbye as Nick headed out toward the road. He was dropping Sylvia and Sophia at their home, taking Chris to his condo, then dropping off Hal at New Hope before returning here.

I heard Nick come home after we were all in bed and the house was quiet. I was lying on my side, mulling over the events of the day, when I heard the front door open and close, then footsteps on the stairs. My eyes were adjusted to the darkness, and I could clearly see him standing in the open doorway to my room. I didn't move or make a sound.

He slowly walked toward me and reached out his hand to smooth my hair back from my forehead.

"Good night, Ellie," he said, almost so softly that I couldn't hear him. Then he bent down, and I felt his lips graze my forehead.

I reached my hand up to touch his cheek.

"Good night, Nick," I whispered.

He turned and left as quietly as he had come, and I smiled and rolled over as I heard the door to his room softly close.

"Pass the sausage, please, Mom," Adam requested as we all sat at the table on the porch eating breakfast.

Abbey and I had already gone for a morning swim and had breakfast well underway before Adam and Mya had wandered down to the kitchen, and Nick had been up early fishing while the mist had still been on the lake.

I handed Adam the plate of maple sausage links, and he stabbed two with his fork and put them on his plate.

"I can't believe we're going home today," he said, "This has been one quick weekend!"

"I know!" said Mya, "I've had a really great time! I can't wait to come back!"

"Do you really think you'll have your wedding here?" Abbey asked as she refilled her glass of orange juice.

"We're seriously considering it," Adam said. "We have to sit down and figure everything out when we get home."

"Mom, when do you think *you'll* be home?" he asked.

I really didn't know the answer to that, and I really didn't want to think about it yet either.

"I guess it depends on Hal," I responded, looking across the table at Nick.

He drizzled syrup on his blueberry pancakes and glanced up at me.

"After this weekend, Dad is thinking he'll be home in three weeks. What the doctors think is another story," he said thoughtfully. "I actually think that after all the companionship he's had at New Hope, he's going to find it lonely living here by himself."

"I'm sure Sylvia will make sure he's included in all the activities at Lakeside," I said.

"I haven't discussed it with Dad, but I was wondering if he would like you to stay on a bit once he gets home…for a couple of weeks maybe, just until he gets used to living on his own again," Nick said as he popped a bite into his mouth. "Providing you wouldn't mind that kind of arrangement, Ellie."

Well, that request took me completely by surprise.

"Oh, I wouldn't mind at all, and it sounds like a good idea to have someone here for Hal at first." I was excited at the prospect of prolonging my stay, and looked over at Abbey. "But I'm not sure how long my employer is going to keep my job open back home."

Abbey was swishing a piece of pancake around in a puddle of syrup on her plate, listening to our conversation.

"Well, we'll be coming up on Easter, and that usually starts our busy time, but I'm sure I can find someone to fill in."

I wasn't quite sure how to take her answer. I thought she'd tease me right back and be as excited for me as I was about being able to stay longer, but instead her answer was serious and thoughtful. It occurred to me that it was just a job to me, a wonderful job that I loved, but it was a business that she owned,

497

and she had to do what was best for that as well.

"I was just thinking out loud. I haven't even asked Dad yet, so that gives you both some time to think about it when the time comes," Nick said.

"You're still planning on staying with me when you come home, right?" Adam had pushed his chair away from the table and his empty plate.

I noticed Mya looking at me with interest as she was finishing off her strawberries.

Oh, things had changed while I was gone! I bet Mya had more than her own toothbrush at Adam's house now.

I chose my answer carefully.

"That was the original plan, I guess. But maybe I need to start thinking about getting my own place soon after I return...so probably just a short time, if that would be okay."

Adam grinned. "Mom, you can stay as long as you like. Cooper misses you. You're the only one I allow to feed him treats from the table."

I knew that Adam's invitation was genuine, but I certainly didn't want to be a third wheel. They had probably settled into their own little routine, and now they would be planning for their wedding, too.

Seems that I am now being forced to come to terms with the decisions that I had been avoiding for months. I had been given a nice reprieve from having to deal with the unpleasant things in my life, and I could sense that the time for facing my demons was closing in quickly. And you know what...I was ready. I almost shook my head to make sure that *I* was really the one thinking that thought! But it was true. I felt like all that fog had finally lifted, and I was seeing my life with a clarity that was almost foreign to me...when did that happen?

As I walked with Nick out to the garage, I could see Abbey sitting on the bench at the end of the pier talking to Rick on her cell. She noticed us too and lifted a hand in farewell to Nick. He waved back to her and reached down to grab the garage door handle. It rumbled its way open and we stepped into the shade of the building. I sniffed at the stuffy, stagnant air that had the distinct odor of a garage. Many years of oil changes, dried grass on the lawnmower, and plant fertilizer, all mingling together…not entirely unpleasant. In fact, rather soothing.

"I like your friend," he was saying. "Abbey's a real hoot!"

I smiled as I answered him. "Yeah, she's the best! She brings out good things in me."

"Do I do that?" he asked me seriously.

"Do what?" I replied.

"Bring out the good things in you."

I put my index finger to my chin and looked up at the rafters for a moment.

"I think you bring out the *best* in me."

He had a satisfied grin on his face when I lowered my eyes to his.

"Do I do that for *you*?" I returned the question.

He spoke without hesitation. "Darlin', you bring out things in me that I never even knew were there!"

He bent his head down and captured my lips in a quick kiss.

"I like Adam and Mya, too," he continued as he tugged on

his riding jacket, and I savored the feeling of his lips on mine.

Adam had jubilantly shook Nick's hand and clapped him on the back, and Mya had given him a goodbye kiss on the cheek. They were fans.

"You have great kids, Ellie."

"I do , I know...they're a joy to me beyond belief, and quite frankly, they are my life."

He looked at me curiously, like he wanted to ask me something else, then focused again on preparing himself to leave.

Nick was reaching for his helmet, and I was reaching for his hand, suddenly not wanting him to go. This had been such a whirlwind weekend...full of great joy and great heartache, laughter, and tears.

Other than the moment that Casey had been witness to, we hadn't really had much private time together, and my need for him was pressing.

He looked down at my touch and seemed as affected by it as I was. His arms immediately circled around me and pulled me close. I felt the air whoosh out of his chest in a loud sigh as my head rested against him and my hands gripped the shirt on his back.

"Ah, Ellie," he said, sensing the thoughts I had not put into words, "I don't want to be away from you either."

He bent his head and kissed me, a lingering, passionate kiss of two people who wanted and needed to be together. Then he pulled away, and his troubled blue eyes locked on mine. I didn't trust myself to speak a word...tears were imminent.

"I *have* to go, or I wouldn't. You have to know that."

I shook my head up and down, then rested it back against his chest.

He stroked my hair and gently rubbed my neck as I slowly ran my hands back and forth across his lower back.

"Don't worry, Ellie, this will all work out. I wish I didn't have such a damn mess to clean up back in Memphis," he said resignedly. "While I was here this weekend, I didn't have to think about my business or my finances, or the nastiness of divorce. I was just starting to feel good about myself again, and now I have to go back to it all."

I knew exactly what he meant, and I felt bad that he had to go back to that, too. I still had a mess to clean up back in Jeannette as well. Time for both of us to do some housecleaning so we could start fresh.

I resurrected my fake smile for his benefit as I pushed away. I didn't want to be another burden on his heartstrings; I wanted to be a place where he could find strength and inspiration, not be a whining, sniveling emotional weakling he needed to worry about.

I reached over and picked up his helmet, and as he accepted it from me I could almost see gratitude in his eyes.

"Thank you, Ellie," he said, and then added more softly, "I admire you for what you've done. If you got through all this, then I can too."

My smile became genuine as I looked at the wet spots on the front of his tee shirt left from my tears of just a moment ago, and as I reached my hand up to run over them, I could feel his heart beating underneath my palm, steady and sure.

"You drive safely, and call me when you get home, okay?" I requested as I moved back outside into the bright sunlight.

He pushed the Harley out into the driveway and winked at me as he pulled the helmet over his head. I watched as he straddled the bike, and just before he cranked the engine, he

501

looked over at me.

"I love you," he blurted out quickly, then the Harley immediately rumbled to life, and he was off.

Wow. I stood there staring after him for a full minute after he disappeared beyond the orange grove.

I heard flip flops approaching from behind, then a warm arm wrapped around my shoulder.

"I came to see if you were okay, but judging by the huge smile on your face, I guess you are," Abbey said.

"Abbey! He said the "L" word!"

I felt her hand squeeze my shoulder.

I wanted to jump up and down, but didn't want to appear childish. Oh, what the hell.

I grabbed her hands in mine, and we both began jumping up and down right there in the driveway.

"Yes!" I shouted.

Abbey indulged my behavior, and as we walked back to the house arm in arm, she shared my excitement in a little more subdued manner.

"I'm happy for you, Ellen. He really is a great guy," she said. "So where does it go from here?"

I shrugged my reply. I was too happy living in the moment to want to think about how the future was going to be. He loved me, and that was enough for today.

Adam was carrying two suitcases down the stairs when we entered the house, and Mya was out on the porch collecting her shells that had been spread out over the picnic table and putting them in a plastic container.

"Is the car open?" Adam asked, walking toward the door.

"Nope, I'll meet you out there with the keys," I replied and went in search of my purse.

A moment later, I beeped the doors open with the remote, and Adam flung the two cases in the trunk and turned to face me.

"Mom, thank you for everything this weekend. It was really great to see you and to see that you're so happy."

"Adam, even though I'm having a great time, I still missed you *so* much!" I told him, already starting to feel sad that he was leaving. I wish it could always be that we'd all be together, but I knew now that we could be apart and still love each other and things would be fine. It was inevitable in this day and age…jobs, school, and romances were tugging us in different directions. It was unrealistic to think things would always remain the same in our lives, and perhaps some change is good. I've definitely revised the way I look at life since Jack left. Which reminded me of something I wanted to ask Adam.

"I'm so happy for you and Mya. She's adorable, Adam, and you both seem very happy. Please let me know if I can help in any way with your wedding plans, or with anything, for that matter."

Adam grinned. "Oh, you'll probably be retracting that offer because we'll be bothering you *so* much!" and then he added in a more serious voice, "I really love her, Mom."

I reached out to touch his arm and smiled.

"I can tell, sweetie, and I'm just so thrilled that you've found someone to be so happy with. I was just wondering… did you tell your dad yet?"

The smile vanished from his face and he looked down, studying the toe of his sandal as he dug a little hole in the sandy soil.

"Not yet," he replied. "He hasn't even met Mya, Mom. We really don't keep in touch much."

"Oh, I see. Well, maybe someday you could just give him a call and let him know that you're engaged. I think it would be the right thing to do. Who knows, maybe that will bring the two of you closer."

He was still looking down at his toe and blew a burst of air out between his lips. "Fat chance of that, Mom. He pretty much has never approved of anything I've ever done, why would he start now?"

"Maybe he's changed," I offered weakly.

His head snapped up and he looked me in the eye. "Do you really believe that?" he asked sarcastically.

"Not on your life," I replied laughing, "but it felt like the right thing to say!"

My comment had broken the serious tone of the conversation, and Adam laughed with me.

Abbey and Mya came out the front door, Mya waving Adam's cell phone in the air.

"Honey, it's your sister for you!" she said as she handed it to him.

Adam put the phone to his ear, then looked over at me.

"Do we have time to meet Casey for a quick lunch near the airport?"

I looked down at my watch.

"Sure, as long as we leave right now," I replied nervously, wondering why she was making the call. I thought she was working today.

"Great, Sis, we'll see you there in about an hour?" he asked, looking at me for confirmation.

I shook my head up and down, happy that Casey wanted to see her brother before he went back, but apprehensive about how she was going to be with me.

In just under an hour, we were pulling into the little Mexican restaurant that Casey had suggested. She was waiting outside near the front door, looking so pretty and professional standing there in her navy pinstripe suit and gray pumps. Her hair was swept up in a casual up do and she clasped her designer handbag with both hands in front of her.

"Hey everyone!" she greeted us with an easy smile.

Adam whistled a cat call. "Wow, Sis, you clean up real nice!" he teased.

She punched him in the arm. "You should try it sometime! Come on, I made reservations."

We followed the hostess to our table and somehow Casey managed to sit next to me. After we were seated, I felt her cool, slender hand grasp mine below the tablecloth. I looked over at her, and she gave me an apologetic smile, giving my hand a little squeeze before releasing it.

So what did *that* mean? Darn it, the menu began swimming before my eyes.

It turned out to be quite an enjoyable lunch after all; Casey insisted on picking up the check.

Just as we were all stepping from the subdued lighting of the restaurant into the bright sunlight, Casey put her hand on my arm.

"Hold up, Mom," she said holding me back, "You guys go ahead, we'll be right out."

Oh, boy.

"Mom, I owe you an apology for the things I said to you the other night. I was really out of line."

"Oh, sweetie," I said as we hugged. "I should have told you about the feelings I had for Nick."

"Well, it took me by surprise, that's for sure, but I jumped to conclusions about how Chris would feel about it without regard for *your* feelings, and I'm sorry about that."

"Thank you so much, Casey…I couldn't bear it that you were upset and disappointed in me."

"After Nick and Chris talked to me, I understood. It's okay with me, if it's okay with them…or should I say if it's okay with you, Mom."

Wait a minute.

"Nick and Chris talked to you about us?" I asked. "When?"

"Last night; they dropped Hal off, then Chris had me come over to his condo so Nick could talk to us. I really like Chris's dad, Mom, and I think he would be perfect for you. He really likes you…it's just sort of weird, ya know? Like, do we compare notes on father and son?"

I started to laugh. "Well, I wonder if they will compare notes on mother and daughter!"

Casey laughed with me. "We'll talk more about it later. I have to get back to work now. I never should have left the other night. I missed spending time with my little bro and Mya, and I wanted to see them again before they left…and I wanted to see you too."

"I love you, Casey."

"Love you too, Mom," she said as she held the door open and we walked out into the blinding sun.

CHAPTER THIRTY FIVE

It had been almost a week since I dropped Abbey off at the airport.

"I wish you could stay longer," I had told her the morning of her departure as we sat together on the bench at the end of the dock. True to form, the sun was shining and the gentle breeze from the lake was refreshing.

"I wish I could too, but you know how it is with cheese and houseguests...after a week, they both get old and start to stink," she joked. "Actually, as much as I'd like to stay, I'm missing Rick and Natalie ... and Amazing Glaze," she said as she stood and stretched.

"What do you think I should do?" I had asked her.

"About what?"

"Oh, just everything," I replied laughing.

She had stood above me considering her answer.

"I think you have some big decisions to make, girl. I know you think you want to come back to work with me, but realistically, you're probably going to need more income than I can afford to pay you."

I had sighed and slowly nodded in agreement.

"And I think you could have a good thing going with your Harley guy, but that relationship comes complete with complications. Is he going to live in Memphis or Florida? Where are *you* going to live? Can you handle a long distance romance?"

I had nodded again.

These questions, and the answers that are still escaping me, are swirling around in my mind as I made the drive to Casey's office. Annee had called yesterday and told me that she was going to overnight the documents for the closing on my Jeannette house. I was to sign and have them notarized at Casey's office, then overnight them back to her so she would have them for the closing tomorrow.

I stopped as the attendant in the parking garage entrance approached me, and after I told him that Casey was expecting me, he waved me on through.

It had been a good week, although I had to admit the house really seemed empty after everyone left, and I thought about Hal and what a good idea it would be for him to have some company for awhile when he came home. It's hard to switch to complete silence when you're used to so much commotion.

Abbey had called two days after she left and told me that she was already needing another vacation! I knew it was the birthday party that she had just hosted talking, and I smiled in understanding. As much as she enjoyed herself with me, she was in her element now and the miles between us couldn't disguise the happiness in her voice. She had enjoyed her time off, but she was happy to be back home.

I had talked to Nick every night, sometimes briefly and sometimes for hours, and I still tingled when I heard his voice. Things were slowly progressing for him, although all the meetings with his attorney and accountant and trying to run his business were exhausting him.

The workers had come back yesterday to start on the laundry room, and by the end of the week, the whole project should be completed. I was very proud of the job we had all done together.

I pulled carefully into a parking space, and as I walked away from the car, I beeped it locked and slid the keys into my purse. I was excited to see Casey today. Things were back to normal between us now…maybe even better! Even though I hadn't seen her since the day at the restaurant, we had several in-depth phone conversations and now found humor in the situation, and perhaps sharing our feelings about our relationships has made us closer.

Casey was waiting for me in the lobby, and as we rode alone in the glass enclosed elevator, I watched with trepidation as each floor passed by. Casey must have sensed my nervousness, and grasped my hand.

"So, it's your big day today! Are you excited, Mom?"

I glanced over her way.

"Well, I'm feeling *something*…I don't quite think it's excitement though," I answered as the door silently opened. My stomach felt like it was still on the floor below us.

Casey explained each document to me in detail, impressing the heck out of me with her expertise. I signed my name about fifty times, with her secretary notarizing the appropriate places. The blank signature line above mine with Jack's name boldly typed in black mocked me with every pen stroke. Finally, Casey stacked the papers and handed them to Lauren.

"Please make us a copy and send them off!" she said to Lauren, and then to me, "Well, that's it! Congratulations!"

I had to admit, I did feel better now that the papers were signed. It was just an impending obstacle that I'd been thinking about for so long, and there was nothing I could do to change the ultimate outcome, so I may as well get it over with. I felt relieved that it was finally over and I wondered if I would feel that way when my divorce was final too.

"Thanks, I guess," I told her.

"I feel a little sad too, Mom, but it had to be done. At least now you can look forward to getting some money to buy your own place. Adam will help you find something that you like even better!"

"When do you think we'll be able to get the money?" I asked. I hadn't really had a penny to my name when I came to Florida, but I've been saving my pay from Hal in my new bank account, and it was surprising how it was adding up. I knew once I had to start paying for my lodging and utilities though, it would be gone in a flash.

"Let's call Annee while you're here. I'll put her on speaker."

Casey made the call, and after only a short minute of pleasantries, we got down to business.

"Ellen, since your divorce settlement isn't final, we can't disburse the profit on the home sale yet. You and Jack have to come to an agreement on that. Have you talked to him about it?" Annee asked.

Casey looked at me with the question in her eyes.

"No, Annee, I haven't talked to him much since I've been here, really. Have you found out anything about his finances yet?"

"They're still being difficult, but I think tomorrow will be a breakthrough. He's probably expecting his share of the profits and that may be our leverage to get them to give us the information we need to get this wrapped up for you. In fact, I think I'll call his attorney right now and see if I can schedule a private meeting with them right after the closing. Since we'll be in the same place, it makes good sense."

"I'd appreciate that, Annee," I told her. I was ticked that after all this time he still hadn't furnished his financials. "What gives? Why can't we make them cooperate and just be done with it?"

"Well, it seems like it should be an easy thing, but there's probably a reason he's holding them back, and we're just playing the waiting game," Anne told me.

"Well, I'm tired of playing by his rules. Can you please try really hard to get things moving, Annee? I'll probably be coming home in a month, and I'm going to need a place to live. I really need to know how much money I'm going to have so I can make some plans." I practically felt like I was begging her, but I didn't care; I just wanted it to be over. It felt like an eternity since my first trip to Annee's office.

"Anything you can do will be appreciated," Casey added. "Call us tomorrow?"

"Absolutely. And, Ellen, stay near your cell phone tomorrow from four o'clock on, just in case we run into a snag and I need to speak with you."

A snag?

"Okay, how long do you think the closing will last?" I asked.

"No way to tell, probably a little longer than the time it took you to sign the papers today."

As soon as we disconnected, I asked Casey, "A snag? What is she talking about?"

"Don't worry, Mom, everything will be fine," she assured me.

The next day I was a nervous wreck, and as the clock ticked closer to four, the worse it got. A picture in my mind of Jack sitting at the closing and throwing a fit about something fixated itself in my brain. I had a gut feeling that he wasn't going to make this easy for me.

Although no matter how difficult it was to sit here and wait, I would prefer it any day to sitting in the same room with Jack at the closing. That thought ran a shudder through my body.

I paced back and forth across the kitchen floor, made a cup of tea, let it get cold, reheated it…and at six o'clock it sat, stone cold, in the mug in front of me. They should be done with the closing by now. Maybe they were having the private meeting afterward that Annee had requested.

I stood up and dumped my tea out in the sink, then walked to the back porch to look at the lake. The days were noticeably getting longer, and I could still see the pier in the gathering dusk. Dora hadn't made an appearance since the day she brought her brown feathered friend to visit. Hal had been so disappointed that he didn't get to see her when he was home, and I feared the worse for her.

I jumped as the sound of my cell phone ringing interrupted my thoughts, and with shaking hands I flipped it open and accepted Annee's call.

"Hi, Ellen, I have good news. The closing went well!"

I put my hand to my forehead and rubbed back and forth.

"Thank you, Annee."

"You're welcome. However, I met with Jack and his attorney afterward, and that meeting didn't go quite as well."

I started pacing across the floor in the den. I knew it!

"Let me guess, Jack wasn't cooperative and wanted the money on the spot."

Annee's laugh jingled over the distance.

"I guess you do know him well after being married to him for so long," she said.

I sighed and closed my eyes.

"So what's going on?"

"Well, he wanted to split the profits equally, and I declined that offer on your behalf. I hope you don't mind, Ellen, but the only fair split would be at least seventy percent of the profit coming to you, especially when we don't have the rest of the assets documented for distribution."

I nodded, even though I knew she couldn't see me.

"He seems anxious to get his share of the money for the house sale, but he's still dragging his feet on the rest of the issues. I proposed that the profits from today be kept in an interest-bearing account held by the attorneys until the rest of his financials are provided and we can come to an agreement that will finalize your divorce."

"If that's what you think we should do, then I'm with you. So, if we were to split the house money now, I'd still be in the same boat as I am now with the divorce proceedings, except that I'd have some money in my bank account," I asked her.

"That's pretty much it, Ellen. It's a shame that you and Jack can't come to terms with this yourselves. Have you tried to talk to him about it lately?" she asked. "Maybe a short conversation between the two of you would save hours and dollars of attorney time and get you a better end result."

"Annee, I haven't talked to him since we got the offer on the house."

"Well, maybe give it a thought. Meanwhile, what do you want me to tell them? They're actually waiting in the other room for an answer."

"What? I didn't realize…I'm sorry Annee, I didn't know they were waiting. I guess for today I want you to put the money in that account and see if we can stir up some results."

I felt her smile through the phone.

"Good decision, Ellen. I'll let them know, and we'll call it a night here. I'll call you in a few days or if there are any new developments. Think about talking to Jack, though, if you can handle it. I'm sure his attorney is giving him the same advice."

"I'll think about it," I told her, but I really hoped it wouldn't come to that. "Annee, out of curiosity...did Jack ask why I wasn't there?"

"He did," she replied instantly, "and I told him that you were out of town."

"Oh."

"I'll give them your answer. Goodnight, Ellen."

"Goodnight, Annee...and thank you."

I didn't have much time to think about talking to Jack. By the time I had poured myself a glass of wine and sat down at the kitchen table to sketch, my cell phone was already ringing.

I was half tempted to not even answer it, but what could it hurt? The last time I talked to him it actually *did* do some good and we countered the offer on the house, leading to a better end result. So I flipped my cell open.

"Hello?" I said firmly.

"Hey, Ellen." His familiar voice travel over the miles, and as much resolve as I had not to let him get to me, just those two words did.

"Hey, Jack."

"So...I guess congratulations are in order. We closed on the house."

Where was he going with this? Sure, Jack,

congratulations on being a jack ass too.

"Yes, we closed on the house," I answered, acknowledging his statement.

"Well, you don't have to be so short with me. Why can't we just have a nice conversation?"

The word, "sorry," was forming in my mind, but thankfully never made it to my lips. I was *not* going to play these mind games anymore.

I let the silence drop like a bomb in the conversation.

"So, why weren't you here, anyway? Where the hell are you?"

"Is this your *nice* conversation?" I rebutted.

"I was worried about you. Are you sick or something?" he asked in a kinder voice.

Sheesh. Now what do I tell him?

"No, I've *never* been better, actually. I'm just out of town. Why should *you* care?"

"*Now* who's not playing nice?" he asked smartly.

So, he did draw me in and I had become a player. I sighed and started over.

"Jack, we have some things to discuss. Why don't we just try to get through this?"

"Yeah, what's the deal with holding the check for the house? I thought you'd be chomping at the bit for money by now. What'd you do, score a good job or something? Win the lottery? Find a rich boyfriend?"

My blood was boiling, and I couldn't help myself.

"Jack, I *know* about your bank account. I *know* about your post office box. I *know* you built a new house. Where did all *that* money come from?"

There was a moment's silence on Jack's end, and I smiled. It felt good to finally challenge him on these issues. I should have done it from the beginning...the first day I found out about the post office box...the day I opened the bank statement. Maybe back then I was afraid that if I asked him I would start an argument that I couldn't finish, or that I would really lose him. Now I didn't have those same fears.

"Well, aren't *you* something?" he spat back at me.

I found that I really *did* want to know where the money came from.

"Jack," I began, using every ounce of restraint I had to keep my voice calm, "where *did* you get all that money and why did you keep it a secret from me?"

"I *am* in investments, Ellen! Let's just say I made some good ones. Why didn't I tell you? Why do you think? Do I have to spell it out for you?"

So he'd been creating a plan to leave me for a lot longer than I thought. As much as I didn't want to be in a relationship with Jack now, it still hurt me to the core to know that. The phone line was silent for a moment while his words sunk in.

"Listen, Ellen," he said in a softer voice, "it's complicated. The money wasn't all mine to share. That's all I can say right now. I made sure you never wanted for anything though, isn't that true?"

Sure, the only thing I had wanted was a husband who wasn't a lying bastard.

"That doesn't excuse what you did, Jack."

This time the silence was on his end.

My phone signaled that I had another call coming in, and when I looked at the screen I saw that it was Nick.

"Hey, Jack, I have to go, but could you please just get your information to my attorney so we can finalize our divorce?"

"So, what's the big hurry to get the divorce? You got a boyfriend now?" he asked.

This coming from a man whose winky was making house calls before the sheets on my bed were even cool.

The little devil on my shoulder wanted to tell him, "*Yes! Someone who is much better than you ever were!*" But my good senses won out and I held myself in check.

"Jack, I have to go. Just do it, okay?"

"So, you don't want to talk about splitting the house sale money then?"

"*Jack.*"

"Damn, Ellen, you've changed. You used to be so reasonable."

I almost laughed.

"Good night, Jack," I said as I flipped my phone shut, and tipped my glass up to finish the last drop of wine.

I poured another glass and called Nick back.

"Hi, Ellie," his deep voice resonated over the line, and I smiled as I replied.

"Hi there, Nick."

"Your voice sounds happy tonight. Have a good day?"

"Yes, actually, I did."

I carried my wine up to my room and curled up on my bed as I shared the details of the closing and my conversation with Jack.

"Ellie, I'd like to show him a little southern hospitality, and I don't mean that in a nice way," I could sense the frustration in his voice.

"Ah, it's okay, Nick. I can see how he operates now, and it's hard to believe that for so many years I didn't. Every time I stand up to him it gets a little easier."

"Well, I'll be glad, for your sake, when this is over and you don't have to deal with him anymore."

"That's just it, though. There probably never *will* be a time when I don't have to deal with him on some level. We have kids together, there's always going to have to be some interaction."

"Boy, Ellie, you sure have a good attitude about this whole thing."

"Well, today I do. Maybe it's the wine helping me out right now. Next time I might not fare as well. Adam didn't even tell him yet that he's getting married. I'm sure I'll have to run interference for him on that one."

"I can't imagine not being close to my son. Chris and I have such a good relationship...always have. I feel kind of bad for Adam."

"I do too, really. Jack just never seems to appreciate Adam, and he's always been such a good kid. I'm so proud of him," I told him as I touched the cross Abbey gave me.

Nick was silent for a moment.

"I guess that's kind of how it is with Chris and J-Rae. Chris adores her, but I've always felt that she didn't return affection at the same level. She just wasn't the coddling type of mother. But in her defense, she was a good mother."

I guess now was as good a time as any to broach the subject since he had mentioned her.

"Nick, does J-Rae have any investments in Florida?" I asked.

"She could, I have no idea. That's what I'm trying to uncover here. She's acting just the opposite of your Jack. He's dragging his feet on your divorce, and J-Rae is plowing full steam ahead on mine. I want one as soon as possible too, but I want to make sure all of our financial eggs are in the same carton. Once you get that divorce certificate, it's too late to recoup something you missed. It's a done deal. I just don't trust her now, and I think she's trying to do the hurry up so I overlook something. Why?"

"Oh...well..." I didn't want to incriminate Casey just in case she was wrong. "Just wondering. Did you say she started her own company?"

"Yeah, a while back, but now I'm finding out that she has real estate all over the place."

"Wouldn't you be entitled to some of her profits too then? Just like I think I should be entitled to Jack's?"

"I'm just amazed, Ellie, that she was able to keep so much from me. Maybe if I'd been a more attentive husband..."

"Oh, don't go down that road, Nick," I jumped in, "Dr. Burke said never to play the 'what if' game. There is no way you can win it."

Nick laughed. "Okay, doctor, good advice."

A few days later, Nick called as I was taking a load of towels out of the new dryer.

"Nick, I've never been so excited about doing laundry!" I told him as I held the bundle of warm towels against my chest and pushed the dryer door shut with my elbow, enjoying the fresh scent of fabric softener that drifted up to my nose.

I flopped them down on the kitchen table and admired the new washer and dryer as I began to fold.

"The laundry area is finished and it looks super! And it's so easy to get to now. Hal is going to love it!"

"I'm glad they did a good job. So that's it then. Are you going to miss having all the workers around?" I heard him ask through my Bluetooth.

"It's been nice company, and I'll miss that, but all the dirt that comes with remodeling? Absolutely not! By the way, I've decided that if you and Hal would like me to stay on a bit longer after he comes home, then I'm game. I agree with you that it may just be too much of an adjustment for him to be alone right away."

"Boy, am I glad to hear you say that! Dad called about an hour ago, and he was so excited! His doctor told him that he can be released next week as long as someone is in the house with him and he comes to physical therapy twice a week, and if he promises to use his walker and cane."

My hands stilled momentarily, holding a towel in midair.

"Nick, that's just wonderful. Did you mention to him that you asked me to stay on?"

"Sure, I told him that a while ago. I think he used that for leverage with the doctor! I know he's so anxious to get home, especially after the tease of being home for the weekend. It's been a long haul."

I smoothed my hand over the folded stack of towels, picked them up and carried them to Hal's new bathroom, placing them on the open shelving. I stood back to admire the effect. The stack of blue and cream stripes added the homey touch the room had been lacking.

"So, what did you and Abbey decide about your job?" Nick asked.

I went back to the kitchen and poured a glass of iced tea.

As I took a sip, I thought about the conversation I had with Abbey last night that lasted until the wee hours of this morning. "We both agreed that it would be a good idea for me to stay here a little longer. The mom of one of Natalie's friends was inquiring about a job, so Abbey is going to hire her to take over my position. Then when I go back I can work with them part time until I find a new full time job."

"Are you sure you're okay with that?" he asked.

"Nick, I *have* to find another job when I go back anyway, so it actually makes me feel better to know that I'm not screwing Abbey. She was good enough to let me have all this time off, so I don't want to keep her in limbo any longer. I'm really going to miss working with her though. I loved that job," I said as I squeezed a slice of fresh lemon into my tea.

"Any thoughts on what you're going to do?"

"I know what I'd *like* to do…" I began, and I could hardly believe I was saying this out loud. The thought had been forming in my mind for several weeks now. "I would like to start my own business. I've loved working on this house and I think I could make a go of decorating or staging, something like that. I just haven't thought it through entirely yet."

"You definitely have the talent, Ellie. I think you can do whatever you set your mind to."

"Do you know where you would like to have your business?" he added.

As I thought about how to answer that question, I heard a knock on the front door.

"Nick, someone's at the door," I said as I peeked around the corner of the hallway. "Oh, it's Sylvia!"

"Go ahead and get it then, I'll talk to you tonight."

I removed the Bluetooth from my ear and laid it on the counter as I went to unlock the door. This was different, usually Sylvia came right up to the back porch door.

"Hey, Syl!" I said as I held the door open for her.

"Hi, Ellen! Come on out here, I want to show you something."

I followed her out to the driveway, where a black and silver golf cart was parked.

"What do you think?" she asked as she waved her hand toward the cart. She folded her arms across her chest and was evidently very pleased with herself.

"What happened to your pink cart?" Knowing her style, I couldn't believe she would prefer this model to her snazzy pink one.

"It's at home, silly, I can only drive one at a time!"

I was surely missing something here. "So, now you have two carts?"

She unfolded her arms, placed her hands on her hips instead, and looked at me tilting her head. She was adorable today in her denim capri pants, and pink lace tank top.

"This one is for *Hal*! I bought it for him as a comin' home present. He'll be home next week, ya know. I figured it would be easier for him to come and visit at Lakeside if he had his own cart. Do you think he'll like it?"

What a thoughtful idea!

"Sylvia, he's going to absolutely *love* it!" I was sure of it. "Actually, Nick just told me the good news on the phone a few minutes ago."

"You got time to take a spin?" she asked, already getting in the driver's seat.

I climbed aboard and she maneuvered it with ease through the orange grove.

"So, I hear you're going to stay awhile and help Hal. I'm very glad to hear that," she said and reached over to pat my hand.

"This is a really expensive coming home present, Sylvia. Are you sure you can manage it?" I asked.

"No problem there," she assured me as she laughed. "I didn't sell my body or anything."

I shook my head as we pulled onto the pavement at Lakeside.

"So, how is it going with you and Hal?" I asked.

Sylvia glanced quickly at me, and I saw her blush.

"Well, things are progressing nicely," she finally answered.

"Sylvia, it's *me!* You can tell me!" I joked.

"Oh, I'm really sweet on him, Ellen. I just can't wait for him to come home! It's getting tiresome driving over there all the time. And we get *no* privacy!"

I laughed out loud as we swung around the lake and then headed back toward the orange grove.

"So, what are we going to do about this Brooklyn character?" she asked me as she straightened up a bit in the seat.

"Syl, we don't really know if Shoresale is his company or not. We're just speculating. Has Casey got back to you yet?"

"She did, but it's going to cost more than we thought to buy it outright. Some of the folks just don't have that kind of money, living on fixed income and all. They're just not in a position to make that commitment. They were all excited before, but now they're kind of just accepting the inevitable."

"So, you're giving up on the idea?" I felt bad that they couldn't make it work.

"Give up is not in my vocabulary, but I guess the idea is shelved for now."

Sylvia pulled quietly up onto the driveway in front of Hal's house.

"Well, maybe even if Shoresale buys it, they won't make anyone move," I said hopefully.

She shrugged as I stepped out of the cart.

"Thanks for the ride. Hal will love it!"

I waved goodbye to Sylvia and strolled down toward the lake, stopping to admire the yellow hibiscus, which was now in full bloom. As I neared the water, I heard splashing under the dock. I leaned over the side, gingerly grasping the wooden handrail, and saw the rear end of the brown and white duck. He righted himself in a flurry of webbed feet and splashes, then tipped himself over again, submerging his head and leaving his backside and tail feathers above the water.

Deciding to help him out in his quest for food, I reached below the bench and pulled out my can of cracked corn, giving it a good shake to get his attention. Something rustled in the tall grasses.

Oh my gosh, it was Dora! She squawked loudly as I scattered a handful of corn across the wooden planks, and seven little balls of yellow fluff followed her out of the brush.

"Dora, you're a *mom!*" I squealed.

I watched as the brown duck paddled out from under the dock and joined Dora and the ducklings. This was too cute! My fingers were itching to sketch them and I pulled my cell phone out of my pocket to snap a picture.

I stood leaning against the rail, watching and enjoying, until my phone, which was still clutched in my hand, began to ring. I looked down at the screen, and my mood shifted immediately.

"Hello?" I answered, reluctantly.

"Hello, Ellen," Brooklyn's voice boomed into the phone. "How are you?"

And before I had a chance to answer, he continued.

"I haven't seen you around lately. I'm going to be over in your neck of the woods later in the week to look at some property and was wondering if I could take you out to dinner."

What a loaded question. I certainly didn't want to go out with him, or give him the *impression* that I wanted to go out with him…but it would be a good opportunity to do some detective work for Sylvia.

"Okay, we could meet for dinner," I answered, and I could almost hear the thought in his head that his persistence had finally paid off.

THIRTY SIX

Two days later I was still trying to remind myself that I was having dinner with Brooklyn for the good of all…taking one for the team. It wasn't even noon yet, and my stomach was churning. I tried to calm myself by working on my sketch of the ducklings, but so far I hadn't succeeded.

I debated about whether to tell Nick about the dinner, and I ended up spilling the beans to him on the phone last night. He wasn't pleased. He actually seemed jealous, which was kind of cute, but I assured him that it was strictly for investigative purposes.

"Here I am hundreds of miles away from you, feeling a bit randy, and you're going out with that leech," he told me.

I was smiling to myself now, thinking of where our conversation went after that, when I heard my cell ringing in the den. Putting down my charcoal pencil, I pushed my chair away from the table and jogged into the other room, unplugging the phone from the charger and putting it to my ear.

I barely got out, "Hi, Syl," before she plunged into the conversation.

"He's here! You have to come over!" she blurted out breathlessly.

"*Who's* there?" I asked, sitting on the arm of the leather couch.

"*Brooklyn!*" she yelled into the phone. "He's here with some lady and they were walkin' around Lakeside lookin' at everything. Now they're in the office. It *has* to be him. They pulled up in a big, fancy car and acted like they owned the place, or nearly own it!"

I let my rear end slide over the edge down into the soft

cushions, and let out a sigh. That must be the reason he was coming over to *my neck of the woods* today…to do business at Lakeside and then take me to dinner to celebrate. Brooklyn was big on celebrating, I already knew that.

"I don't know what I can do, Syl," I began, and then I remembered what Casey had told me about seeing Chris's mom in the car with Brooklyn that time, and curiosity got the best of me. "I'll be right over."

"They're down by the pool now," Sylvia said as I parked the bicycle in her driveway.

"Are you stalking them?" I asked, jabbing at the kickstand with my sneaker, remembering the day that Abbey and I supermarket stalked Jack and his girlfriend.

"No! I sent Sophia to do that!" she said as she started walking toward the street. "Come on!" She waved her hand at me.

We walked side-by-side toward the clubhouse, passing the shiny black Lexus parked in the office lot. Sophia was hunkered down next to the window of the clubhouse, resting her chin on the ledge and pressing her nose against the glass. She turned to look at us as we approached.

"Shhhhhhh!" she said, holding her finger to her lips.

Sylvia and I stood to the side of the building, out of view.

"What's goin' on in there?" Sylvia asked, pushing her shiny, purple visor higher and wiping the sweat from her forehead with the back of her hand.

Sophia stood up and joined us at the side of the building, hiking up her pale pink elastic-band pants.

"They were all sitting at the conference table looking at papers and then they all wrote something with a pen. Just now they were shaking hands."

Sylvia blew a gust of air out between her lips.

"Well, that's it then. Ellen, maybe you can convince him that this is a good investment just the way it is, and that we don't need any of those fancy houses built over here."

"Okay, I'll talk to him at dinner tonight and see what I can do," I answered. "Let's get out of here before he sees us. I don't want to confront him now."

"Yeah, he'll probably listen to you better after he has a few drinks. Wear something sexy, Ellen," Sophia said in a hushed voice.

I shot her a look.

"Sophia! I'm not seducing him, this is strictly a business dinner!" I replied, but had to smile at her anyway.

She pursed her lips and shrugged her shoulders. "Looking sexy couldn't hurt."

We were just about to round the corner of the building when we heard the clunk of the front door opening and snatches of conversation, as the group of people exited the building. I reached out and pulled Sophia, who was starting to walk toward the street, back behind the building. Then we all peeked carefully around the corner.

"There they are...Brooklyn, the woman, and the park owners," Sylvia whispered.

They had their backs to us, standing on the sidewalk talking.

My hand flew to my mouth as I instantly recognized him,

and the familiarity hit me like a punch in the stomach, knocking the wind right out of me. I squeezed my eyes shut and hoped that when I opened them I would be able to breathe again.

A gasping sound escaped from my throat and Sylvia tore her gaze away from the group and motioned for me to keep quiet. When her eyes met mine a look of concern immediately replaced the one of annoyance on her face.

"Ellen! What's wrong?" she asked taking my hand.

I had to move. I had to get away. I pulled my hand out of Sylvia's grasp and started walking back toward the pool.

Sophia and Sylvia scurried after me. "Ellen! Are you okay?" Sylvia called after me.

I kept walking and put my index finger up, indicating for them to give me a minute. Heat was washing through my body and my head felt like it was full of all the air that I couldn't breathe. My brain was floating and my thoughts were disjointed.

I walked quickly, wringing my hands, staring straight ahead and trying to pull my thoughts inward and gain control, trying to regulate my breathing. Finally, after three laps, I could feel the hammering of my heart slow down to a normal thumping and the light-headed sensation was replaced by a more grounded feeling.

I sank onto the bench between Sylvia and Sophia, feeling exhausted.

Sylvia put her arm around me, and I rested my head against her shoulder.

"Was that a panic attack, dear?" she said as she lightly rubbed my arm.

I shook my head and involuntarily quivered.

"Oh, my," she said gently. "I'm sorry I asked you to come

over. I didn't realize that seein' Brooklyn would upset you so much."

I stood up again and started to pace back and forth, not feeling panicked this time, just trying to figure it all out.

"Sylvia, that was *not* Brooklyn," I said, stopping to face her. "It was *Jack*."

They looked at me wide-eyed.

"Who's Jack?" Sophia asked.

"Ellen's almost ex-husband," Sylvia explained.

We were all quiet for a moment while the words sunk in.

"Are you sure it was Jack? You only saw him from the back," Sylvia asked me.

"Syl, I was married to the man for almost thirty years. It was him."

"So is he in cahoots with Brooklyn?" Sophia asked.

"I have no idea, but I intend to find out. Let's go!" I announced as I grabbed each of their hands and pulled them up.

A million thoughts bumped against each other in my head as we made our way back to Sylvia's house. The space where the Lexus had been parked at the office was empty, and I was relieved. I wasn't ready for a confrontation with Jack until I did a little homework and got my nerves settled down.

"Maybe you shouldn't ride the bike home," Sylvia said as I straddled the seat.

"I'm fine now, really," I insisted. I felt invigorated and wanted to get home to think this through.

"Well, call me when you get home!" I heard Sylvia call

after me as I pedaled down the street.

The speed of the bicycle and the wind in my face chased away any remnants of the panic attack, and by the time I pulled the bike in the garage, I felt renewed and recharged.

I ran into the house and punched Casey's number into my cell phone.

"You're not going to believe who I just saw at Lakeside!" I sputtered before she could even get out a hello. "Your dad."

"*What?* No way! What is *he* doing at Lakeside?" she asked.

"From what it looks like to me, he's trying to *buy* the place!" I filled her in on the details that Sylvia had given me, sketchy as they were.

"You've got to be *kidding* me! Mom, who was the woman with him?"

I drew a blank. "As soon as I realized the man was your dad, I freaked out and didn't even look at them again. Can you believe that I have no idea?"

"Could it have been his girlfriend?" she wondered aloud.

"All I can tell you is that she had blond hair, and that's all I remember. I only saw them from the back anyway, but I guess it *could* have been her," I said trying to rummage through my brain for any recognition.

"Hey, did you ever find anything on the flash drive I gave you from our home computer?" I asked her.

"I'm sorry, Mom. I got busy with tax season at work and totally forgot about it. I'll look tonight for sure. Now I'm really curious too, and mad at him! He's this close and he never called to visit me? I'm going to call him right now!"

"Well, don't tell him any of this or that you know he's here, okay?"

"Sure. Are you still going to dinner with Brooklyn?"

"Yep, in fact I have to go get ready. I'll call you tonight and let you know what I find out."

Brooklyn clunked his glass to mine, and I peered at him over the rim as I slowly sipped. He was on his second rum and coke. Not that I was taking Sophia's advice or anything, but I figured I'd let him get good and relaxed before I started asking my questions. The time was now.

"So, Brooklyn, tell me about your latest property acquisition," I began, as I swirled the blush wine around in my goblet.

He finished his drink and signaled the waitress to bring another. This was going well.

He proceeded to tell me about a building he had just purchased over in Lakeland, an older hotel that he was going to renovate into condos. I listened patiently as he took pride in explaining his plans in detail.

I actually found myself getting excited about it, too, and began offering him suggestions. Then I remembered the reason for accepting his invitation in the first place.

"Is Lakeside a property you are interested in?" I asked.

He looked a little startled. "No, I'm more into the condo thing. I don't want to be a landlord for a trailer park."

I felt insulted. "It's not really a trailer park...they're

modular homes, and very nice ones at that!"

He studied my face as the waitress put his drink on a white paper napkin.

"Why do you ask, Ellen?"

I have never been good at hiding my feelings, and today was not the exception.

"Well, my very good friends live there, and they've heard that the property was being sold. They're worried that they'll have to move," I answered as I watched his expression for any sign of deceit.

All I saw was genuine concern.

"That could always be a possibility I suppose. When someone buys a choice property like Lakeside, it might turn more of a dollar to re-sell the lots and build new homes on them than to collect rent from existing structures. It's just the reality of it, Ellen. Most developers are in the business to make money, not to be emotional or sentimental."

"I understand that, but when you're dealing with throwing senior citizens out of their homes, then it becomes a personal issue with me," I said with a toss of my head. "I heard a company did that to the residents at Lake Pete."

"I know that property. Beautiful homes over there."

"I heard that the same company was buying Lakeside," I decided to put it all on the table. "A company named Shoresale."

"You're right about that, Ellen. That's exactly what happened over there."

"So, are you a part of Shoresale?" I blurted out.

He laughed and swished the lime around in his drink just as the waitress served our salads.

"Hell, no! The guy who owns that is a real jackass!"

Or a Jack Stern. The realization hit me like a lightning bolt. Jack could be Shoresale.

Brooklyn drizzled balsamic dressing on his salad and began to eat. I had lost my appetite and still had so many questions unanswered.

"So, you know the Shoresale guy?" I asked as I feigned eating by pushing the lettuce around with my fork.

"Not really. Met him once at an investor's seminar. Real cocky guy."

I almost laughed out loud. Kind of like the pot calling the kettle black. Had to admit that Brooklyn was different than Jack though. Brooklyn wasn't condescending, he was just self-confident.

"Does he have a partner?" I asked as I actually put a bite of salad into my mouth and forced my jaws to chew.

Brooklyn pushed his empty plate to the side of the table and wiped his mouth with the cloth napkin.

"Think so, not quite sure of the whole arrangement. He's not from around here though."

Huh.

"Do you ever have partners in your investments?" I asked, taking another bite.

He took a sip of his drink and gave me a lazy smile. *Oh no.*

"Well, Ellen, I wouldn't mind having *you* as a partner…in business *or* pleasure. Are you looking for an *investment?"* he asked as he covered my hand with his.

I casually removed my hand and pushed my half empty plate next to his.

I laughed nervously. "Maybe not so much of an investment, but I'll be looking for a new job soon, and I'll be going back to Pennsylvania in a few weeks. Hal is coming home."

He looked genuinely crestfallen, and I almost felt sorry for him.

"You're going back to *Pennsylvania*? What have you got there that you don't have here? Why don't you just stay?"

"Well, my son lives there," I began.

"But your daughter lives here," he interrupted.

I was ready to rally back, but I came up with nothing. I shrugged my shoulders.

"It's where I live, Brooklyn."

His reply was quick and to the point. "I thought you sold your house. You don't *have* a place to live yet, do you?"

"Well, just pour salt on the wound, why don't you?" I blurted out. This wasn't the direction that I wanted this conversation to be going.

"I'm sorry, Ellen. Hey! I have lots of condos I can show you! Really nice ones, and I'll give you a special deal."

I'll just bet he would.

The waitress delivered our dinners, forcing a lull in our conversation and a chance for me to recover.

Brooklyn's face lit up and he snapped his fingers.

"I have it! I can offer you a job as a consultant on my new condo project…the one I just bought in Lakeland. I have to hire someone anyway. I pay well." He looked very pleased with himself.

If it were anyone else, I would have jumped at the opportunity. Isn't that just what I was telling Nick I would like to do? And here it was, dumped right in my lap. If he was sincere, that is.

My hesitation in responding showed him that he had captured my interest, and he went on to describe what the job would entail. I felt like I was practically drooling. It sounded like the perfect fit for me, and I could feel myself jumping on the bandwagon…those butterflies of anticipation were flying around in my stomach, but I had to set one thing straight before I would even consider working with him. I can't believe I'm even contemplating that option, but in any event, I needed to let him know where I was coming from.

I took a deep breath.

"Brooklyn, I really enjoy your company, but I don't see us ever being romantically involved. In fact, I'm sort of in a relationship right now."

There, I said it. I hoped he didn't think that I was using him by agreeing to come to dinner with him.

He laughed his robust laugh, and seemed unfazed as he cut his steak.

"Oh, I know. You're seeing Chris Blackwell's dad."

I thought I was going to surprise *him* and he turned it back on me. I looked at him wide-eyed. How the heck did he know that?

"Oh, I make it my business to know things about people," he said, as if reading my thoughts.

"He's a good man, I'm just better," he said with a grin.

This time I laughed out loud!

"I don't know how you knew, but yes, Nick and I are in a relationship."

"Not too hard to figure out, Ellen. The day he ran into us at my place...well, he was flexing his punching hand. I asked Chris about it later," he admitted.

I remembered that day, hoping that Nick wouldn't punch him out.

"So, you're okay with us just being friends, then?" I asked, finding it hard to believe.

"Well, I'd much rather be your lover, but they say that sometimes you have to be friends first. You're worth waiting for."

Was he serious? I searched his face for my answer.

"I meant it about the job, Ellen. It's yours if you want it."

"Well, you've given me a lot to think about, Brooklyn."

Somehow I don't think Nick would be tickled about me working for Brooklyn, but if we could keep it purely business, it was something I might consider.

"Oh, you want to hear something funny?" He broke into my thought process. "You were asking me about Shoresale, and Chris Blackwell's *mom* is involved with that guy."

Wait. *What?*

My head jerked up and the smell of food was suddenly nauseating.

"Yeah, she started her own investment company a while

back, and sometimes comes to me for real estate advice. She wanted my opinion on a property she was considering in Orlando. Not something I'd be interested in, but I can see the potential there. On the way over, the guy called her like three times."

This could not be happening.

"So, you mean involved *professionally?*" I forced myself to say.

"Maybe, but he's definitely getting some," and he made a crude hand gesture. "That's how I met him at the seminar, she introduced us."

But Jack's girlfriend's name is Jessica. I was sure of it.

"What's her name again?" I asked meekly.

"J-Rae…I think it's short for Jessica Rae. I'm surprised you didn't know that, didn't Nick ever mention her to you?"

I felt like I was going to be sick.

"Excuse me a moment, Brooklyn, I need to use the ladies room," I said as I pushed my chair away from the table.

"Did I upset you, Ellen?" I heard him say as I bolted to the restroom.

I wet a paper towel and held it to my forehead. Could Jack really be involved with Nick's almost ex-wife? What exactly had Nick told me…that she was seeing someone that she had an affair with a few years ago and then got back together with…if that's true, then Jack had been cheating for years. It took everything I had to keep the contents in my stomach.

I sat on the chair in the lounge area, moving the cool towel to the back of my neck.

This was bizarre. *What are the odds?*

Maybe I was all wrong. Maybe Jack's Jessica wasn't Nick's Jessica. Maybe Jack wasn't involved in Shoresale at all. But I saw him at Lakeside with my own eyes…he was definitely involved in something. And knowing what I know about Shoresale, that would explain all the money in the mystery account, and why he had a post office box. He wanted to keep his business a secret. Oh my gosh, I can't believe how blind I had been! And moreover, I can't believe that it was going on for so long.

Then I started to think beyond myself. If Casey had a hard time seeing me with Nick, she was going to be totally overwhelmed when she saw Jack with Chris's mom. Oh my gosh…*Casey!*

I pulled my cell from my purse and punched Casey's number, holding the phone to my ear with a shaking hand.

"Hey, Mom, if you're calling about Dad, I left him a voicemail and he didn't answer, but I can't talk now though…in the car with Chris. His mom is in town and invited us to dinner. I think she wants Chris to get to know her boyfriend."

"Casey–" I tried to interrupt.

"He's not sure that he wants to be involved, but I told him that he was okay with his dad seeing you, so he should be open to his mom's relationship. Aren't you proud of me?"

She finally came up for air, and I hated to tell her this way, but I didn't want Jessica or whatever her name is, to spring this surprise on an unsuspecting Casey.

"Are you driving?" I asked.

"Nope, Chris is, why?"

"I have something to tell you…I think Chris's mom is seeing your dad."

Silence.

"*What?*"

"I'm having dinner with Brooklyn, and he told me that Chris's mom is involved with the guy from Shoresale…and I think that guy is your dad."

"Mom, how many drinks have you had?" she asked bluntly.

"Casey, I'm serious."

Silence.

"How is that *possible?*" she asked me, my words finally sinking in.

I briefly explained what I knew.

"So, now what am I supposed to do? We're almost to the restaurant."

I didn't know if she expected an answer or if she was just thinking out loud.

"Mom, do they know that Chris and I are dating? Would Dad be expecting to see me?"

I wondered that myself. "I don't know. It may be a huge surprise when you walk through the door."

"Then that's exactly what I'm going to do! Thanks for the heads-up, Mom. I'll call you later, I need to talk to Chris."

"Wait! Casey!" I said into the already dead air space.

Just as I put my cell back in my purse, the hostess poked her head in the door.

"Are you feeling okay? Your date said he thought you

might be ill, and asked me to check on you," she said as she approached me.

"I'm fine, thank you. Would you please tell him I'll be out in a moment?"

I stood at the mirror and applied fresh lip gloss, ran a brush through my hair, then asked my reflection, *"Can you freak'n believe this?"*

Brooklyn was waiting at our table, my full dinner already packed up in a white Styrofoam box. He was actually being very thoughtful and attentive. He stood as I approached the table, and took my hand.

"How are you feeling?" he asked. "I'm really sorry to have upset you, Ellen. Maybe I spoke out of turn."

"No! No, you were fine…it's me. I'm sorry to have spoiled dinner for you."

"You didn't spoil anything, Ellen. I'm sorry you didn't get to enjoy yours. The food here is excellent," he said as we made our way through the parking lot.

Back in the quiet darkness of his car, I felt inclined to offer him more of an explanation. As he pulled onto International, I decided to tell him the whole story.

"What you told me really took me by surprise. Maybe this is the kind of situation that one laughs at later, but I'm still in the 'I'm shocked' part of it. Brooklyn, I think the guy from Shoresale, the one Chris's mom is involved with, is my ex-husband."

"Whoa! You're kidding me! Jack is your ex?"

Well, that pretty much confirmed it.

"Is his name Jack Stern?" I asked.

He made a sort of grunting noise in his throat. "Good Lord, Ellen, how were you ever married to that guy? Jessica has the kind of abrasive personality to keep him in his place, she's every ounce the player that he is. But you...you are so sweet, I'd imagine he'd step all over you and squash you like a bug."

Was that a backhanded compliment?

"Sorry, honey. That makes the scenario even funnier," he looked quickly over my way. "I mean funny, as in weird. If you don't mind me asking, do they know about you and Nick?"

"Brooklyn, I didn't even tell Jack that I was in Florida! As far as I know, neither one of them know about us, and then throw Casey and Chris into the mix..." suddenly I started laughing.

"See, honey, I told you you'd find the humor in it! I just didn't expect you to find it so quickly," he said as he put his hand on my knee.

I removed his hand, and he joined in my laughter. I couldn't stop. It was like all my nervous energy needed an outlet and had thrown me into hysterics. Tears were rolling down my face and I started to hiccup.

By the time Brooklyn pulled into my driveway, I had settled down. I was anxious to get inside to call Nick. I wondered how he'd take the news.

Turns out I wouldn't have long to wait.

"This just gets better and better," Brooklyn said with a smirk, as he stepped out of the car.

I waited until he opened my door, then got out just as Nick was coming down the front porch steps.

"Thanks for returning her home safely," Nick addressed Brooklyn.

"My *pleasure*," Brooklyn replied, giving me a quick kiss on the forehead before heading back to the driver's side of the car.

"Thank you for the dinner, Brooklyn, and ...everything," I called to him.

"You're welcome, Ellen, any time...consider my offer," he said with a wink before he slid into his seat and put the car in reverse.

As he headed down the driveway, I ran to Nick and wrapped my arms around him, holding him tight. He spun me around in a circle, lifting my feet off the ground.

"This is a surprise! I had no idea you were coming!" I said right before he captured my lips in a kiss. It was an all consuming kiss, fire right from the moment our lips touched. A possessive kiss that said, "You are mine, and I want you." A passionate kiss that said, "I've missed you, and I need you." An erotic kiss that said, "Let's forget our plan and get busy."

And get busy we did. I smiled as I lay beside him now, running my fingernails gently through his hair, remembering how he had swooped me up and carried me to my room. By unspoken consent, we had given to each other what we have been depriving ourselves of for so long. His caresses had been gentle, and his technique...magic.

I truly loved this man.

Now, as we lie wrapped in each other's arms, I knew that I had to tell him what I found out tonight. I sat up, pulling the sheet with me and tucking it under my arms.

"I have some news, sweetie, and I'm not sure how you're going to take it," I began.

My tone of voice got his attention, because he sat up as well and focused on my face, but his finger ran a line from my jaw, down my neck, and tried to find its way under the sheet. I playfully swatted it away.

"Seriously, I found out some interesting stuff from Brooklyn tonight."

He snorted. "Brooklyn. Can't we not talk about him right now? And by the way, what did he mean about thinking about his offer? The nerve of that guy!"

His hand had returned and was tracing outlines of my body parts on the sheet. I grabbed his hand and held it, as I smiled.

"Listen, you are not going to believe what I'm about to tell you."

He folded his hands on his lap, school boy style, and looked at me expectantly.

"I'm giving you five minutes. That's all the longer I'll be able to sit here without touching you."

I rolled my eyes at him, and started talking.

Turned out he was able to last at least fifteen minutes without touching me.

"Ellie, I can't believe it! Of the gazillions of people committing adultery on this planet, our spouses found each other to do it with."

He was taking it much better than I had.

I tried to picture Nick being married to the woman that I had seen with Jack at the super market. They just didn't seem to fit.

"Jessica doesn't seem your type," I told him flat out.

"Well, didn't we already agree that they were both donkey's behinds? They deserve each other, as far as I'm concerned. Ellie, we're gonna take 'em down," he spoke with conviction.

"Now let's forget them for awhile and get back to business here," he said, and pulled the sheet away from me with a flourish.

CHAPTER THIRTY SEVEN

"Mom! Call me back!" Casey's voice rang loud and clear on the voice mail she left for me several hours ago.

I had padded down to the kitchen to get a drink of water, leaving Nick sleeping soundly upstairs. Seeing my purse on the table, I remembered with a start about Casey's dinner with Jack. I grabbed it and rummaged around until I found my cell, then listened to her excited voice.

How could I have possibly forgotten something that important? Man, I was losing it. Was it too late to call her?

Now that I had returned from planet ecstasy, I really wanted to hear what had happened. I dialed her number and she answered immediately.

"Why didn't you call me back right away?" she accused. I could tell she was really wound up.

"Nick surprised me and was here when I got home, and I just got distracted…sorry," I explained.

"Too much information. Just stop there," she replied. "I can't take any more of my parents and their sex lives tonight."

"So, what happened?" I was pacing the kitchen floor.

"Well, I briefed Chris about the possibility of my dad being his mom's boyfriend, and when he said that he had met him for about half a second a while back, I took our family picture out of my wallet to show him and he confirmed what you had suspected," she began, sounding like the lawyer that she was.

It surprised and saddened me to think that she still carried our family photo around in her wallet.

"So...*we* went in knowing what to expect. Mom, it was great! You wouldn't believe the look on Dad's face when he saw me! At first I think he thought I just happened to be in the same restaurant as him, and then when we walked up to his table and Chris hugged his mom, Dad just about had a cow!"

So, he had no clue that Jessica's son was dating his daughter.

"Don't they *talk*?" I asked as I sat down at the kitchen table. "All this time they never disclosed anything about their kids to each other?" I found that very hard to believe.

"I know, right?" she answered.

"Then what happened?" I prompted her to continue.

"Well, after he figured it out, he gave me a hug and asked why I hadn't called him lately."

I shook my head.

"I told him to check his voicemail."

I smiled.

"It was *so* weird, Mom. I was so angry with him at the beginning, then as we sat there eating dinner, I started to feel sad. I've missed him, ya know? And it sort of felt like old times, except Chris's mom was there where you would have been. Just kind of surreal."

I pursed my lips and felt a little stab of jealousy, then berated myself for it. How could I be jealous of Jack being with someone, when I had Nick right upstairs in my room? Well, the difference was that at least I had waited until we were separated before being with someone, and if what Nick said was true, then Jack had cheated on me years before this.

"So, what was she like?"

This brought a laugh from Casey.

"I figured you'd be asking that! Well, if she wasn't Chris's mom, I'd probably have a different opinion, but I'm giving her the benefit of the doubt and saying that she was okay. Kind of ditsy, but I could tell that she was smart, so I don't know if it's an act or if that's just the way she is. She was pretty, but not as much as you, Mom."

Now I laughed at her. "It's okay, sweetie, it doesn't bother me if she's prettier than me."

And my nose probably grew two inches.

"Well, seriously, she's not. You are genuine and naturally attractive. She's just…fake, I guess, and very *boobular!* They were hanging out like nobody's business! But, like I said, it was weird to see Dad with her. He looked the same though."

Well, that was too bad. I had hoped he looked nasty.

"Did he ask about me?" I had to ask that as well, I'm only human.

"He only said that he hadn't seen you in a while. I just sort of changed the subject, since I didn't think you wanted him to know where you were."

"Thanks, Casey."

"So, get this. She was all kind of bragging about the property they had just bought, and it was Lakeside for sure. Too bad Sylvia wasn't successful in getting the group to buy it, because it does sound like they eventually have other plans for it."

My heart sank, and I slid down onto the kitchen chair.

"Ah, that's such a shame. Isn't there anything we can do?"

"Well, I've been thinking about that, Mom. Give me a couple days, okay? I may have a plan."

"What did Chris think of all this?" I asked as I noticed some crumbs on the table and brushed them into my hand.

"Oh, he's going with the flow and trying to be open-minded. He said Dad was okay, but it's weird for him to see his mom with someone else too. It'll just take a while for everything to gel."

I stood up and threw the crumbs in the trash can, and stifled a yawn. "Well, I'm going to go up to bed now. We can talk more tomorrow, or should I say later today?"

"Yeah, I'm heading to bed myself. Thanks for calling me back. I love you, Mom, and don't worry, everything will be fine. You've made some good choices for yourself. I see how you are around Mr. Blackwell, and I think that he's good for you. You seem happier and just more relaxed than I remember you being with Dad."

"Ah, thanks, Casey. That means a lot to me. I love you too."

I drank a sip of cool water, and padded back up to bed. I snuggled against Nick's warm body and fell asleep smiling to the sound of his gentle snoring.

Hal came home with bells on…literally. Sylvia had tied jingle bells on his walker so we could keep track of him. She was playing the part of nurse to the hilt, and I think they were both enjoying the heck out of it. It had been fun having her around this week. She pretty much came at dawn. Not that I was up that early, but she was already here at the house by the time I woke up, so I assumed that's when she arrived.

She and Hal would be sitting on the dock with mugs of steaming coffee, or at the kitchen table with their heads bent together, concentrating on the crossword puzzle in the morning newspaper, or out on the porch poring over travel brochures. It was cute.

I was beginning to feel like a third wheel, that I really wasn't needed to take care of Hal, but I guess at least I was here during the night if he needed anything. Quite honestly, I wondered if Sylvia would spend the night if I wasn't here.

Nick had stayed for several days after my eventful dinner with Brooklyn, and I really missed him now that he had returned to Memphis. We were anxious to get our divorces over and done with. The financials were an annoying roadblock for both of us…but at least we had some facts to go on now, and we had fed this information to our attorneys.

I talked to Annee and she felt confident that she could research Shoresale's profits and put the pressure on Jack's attorney now that she knew Jack was involved. Casey had been an enormous help. She finally looked at the flash drive that I gave her and was able to retrieve some bank account information, with staggering deposits and withdrawls. Once again, I felt cheated and betrayed by Jack's secrecy.

The other night I called Abbey to give her the latest.

"Holy shit!" she had blurted into the phone. "You've got to be *kidding* me! Holy shit!"

We talked for quite a while, and during that conversation I made my decision that it was time to go home. I knew the day would come when this job would come to an end, but I hadn't wanted to think about it. I love this place, and the people who live here, It had become a part of me, and I had grown so much since my arrival. In fact, some days I hardly recognized myself! Never in a million years would I have thought that I would ever be happy again.

The woman who hugged her first palm tree was one

whose world was falling apart, and so was she, emotionally and physically. Over the course of these few months, I had become a woman who felt more confident than ever. My creativity had exploded and I felt passion again for my drawing. And of course Nick had ignited my passion to love and be loved. I felt good about the way I looked too. I had lost the weight I'd gained, and then some. I felt healthy and strong from all the exercise I've been getting, and my smiles came easily once again.

Nick. I still didn't know what would become of our relationship. He had his hands full trying to salvage what he could of his company. Let's just say that the financial state of affairs had turned into something very complicated for both of us. Now that Hal's health wasn't a distraction for him, Nick could concentrate more on the matter at hand.

Although Nick wanted me to make my own decision, which was a refreshingly new concept to me, he really wanted me to stay at Lake Juliet for awhile. As much as I would have loved to do just that, I felt that I had unfinished business back home. I just needed to wrap up the loose ends of my life and see where that took me. Besides, I needed to think about another job. It wouldn't be right for me to stay here and expect Hal to pay me any longer. Nick said that I could just stay here anyway and look for another job, but I knew that I needed to go home, as hard as it would be.

It was with a heavy heart that I decided to share my decision with Hal and Sylvia over breakfast this morning. I had been sitting on the window seat in my room, looking out over the lake. The morning mist had already evaporated, and the sun was glistening on the water. Sylvia and Hal had walked hand in hand down to the dock and were sitting on the bench feeding Dora and her brood. Hal had been using only a cane this morning, and I smiled as I watched him pour some corn in his hand and coax one of the ducklings to come close enough to nibble it out of his palm.

I sighed as I made my way down the steps and out the front door. After pausing to touch my finger to a red hibiscus blossom, I continued down to the lake.

"'Mornin', Miss Ellen!" Sylvia called out to me.

"Ellen, look at this little rascal eat!" Hal exclaimed, as the duckling continued to peck away at the cracked corn in his hand.

I took a seat on the bench next to Hal and watched quietly.

"What's wrong, dear?" Sylvia asked, pushing her jade green visor higher on her forehead and scrutinizing me with her gentle blue eyes. "You look like you lost your best friend!"

I shrugged, not knowing how to begin, and then just blurted it out.

"I think it's about time for me to go home."

There. I said it out loud. But instead of feeling better, I felt worse.

"Oh, my! Why?" Sylvia prodded. "Aren't you happy here?"

"Well, I think my job of house sitting has been completed, and Hal, you are doing so much better now! Sylvia, you're here to see that all is well. I just think I need to go."

I lowered my head and studied the remaining kernels of corn scattered on the wooden planks.

Hal covered my hand with his.

"Ellen, you're welcome to stay as long as you want. You're family."

I could feel tears welling up. This was so hard!

"I thought you were considerin' takin' the job that Brooklyn offered you?" Sylvia asked. "You could do that and live here."

Brooklyn had called a couple times, trying to persuade me to accept the job of helping him plan the new condos, and I have to admit that each time, the offer got a little sweeter and harder to refuse. The salary was amazing, and the job description made me salivate. It was an awesome opportunity. Had it been anyone but Brooklyn offering it to me, I would have jumped on it immediately. I just didn't know if Brooklyn and I could work professionally or not, plus I knew that Nick wasn't exactly thrilled at the prospect of me working so closely with Brooklyn. Even though I would never betray him like Jessica did, he still had a way to go with trust issues.

"I just think that I need to go home…to see Adam, and help with the wedding plans. Don't forget, we'll all be back for that!" I felt a littler brighter at that thought, at least I would be coming back. "Regardless of my long term plans, I need to wrap things up in Jeannette. I have my car and furniture stored in Adam's garage. I can't leave things there forever."

Sylvia looked me directly in the eye, her features softened, but her gaze direct.

"Miss Ellen, you have to do what is right for *you* now. This is a big step in your new life and you can't be frettin' about what Nick's opinion of you workin' with Brooklyn is."

She briefly turned her attention to Hal, who was focused on a group of gulls on the lake, but he nodded his head in agreement.

How did she even know that Nick's opinion was weighing in on my decision?

"Is the job something that you really want to do?" she asked, once again scrutinizing me.

I answered without hesitation. "It's perfect, Syl, but things are complicated."

"No, it's really very simple. Who's the one makin' it

complicated...*you* are!" she said with a huff. "Just do it and everyone else will have to find their way to deal with it."

Hal laughed out loud at her display of emotion and covered her hand with his, giving it a little squeeze. Then he looked over at me.

"I think what she's trying to tell you, Ellen, is that you have to trust yourself to make the right decision for *you*, and you have to trust the people who love you to let you do that. If you are truly happy, then we'll all be happy too, no matter what you decide. If you're worried about Nick, well, I can tell you that he would never want to hold you back from doing something that you are passionate about, even if he has to adjust to the idea. He's still figuring things out, Ellen, but maybe if you point him in the right direction, he'll follow your lead and learn from it too. Both of you are good people, and heaven knows you both have bent over backwards to please the people in your lives. Now it's time for you both to take stock and move forward."

"That's exactly what I meant," Sylvia said softly, "only Hal said it better." She patted his knee, her slender fingers perfectly tipped in pale pink polish.

I sequestered myself to my room for the afternoon, but had talked to everyone on the phone...Abbey, Casey, Adam, Brooklyn...and now I only had one more call to make.

"Hi, Ellie, I was just thinking about you."

The sound of Nick's voice made me smile. I sat at the window seat and watched a speedboat zoom across the lake, bumping up and down and leaving a wake of ripples behind it.

"Hi there, yourself," I replied. I knew that he was probably at work when I dialed his number, and my suspicions were confirmed when I heard the beeping of a construction vehicle going in reverse.

"Sorry to bother you on the job, but I needed to talk to you about something," I apologized.

I heard the clunk of a door shutting, and the construction noises disappeared.

"It's okay, I needed a break anyway. I'm in the job trailer now, what's going on?" he asked. I heard the pop of a soda can being opened, and I could imagine him taking a long swig as he waited for my answer.

"I've decided to go home this weekend."

He didn't answer right away, and I could tell that he was wrestling with saying what was on his mind, and saying what I wanted to hear. The latter won out.

"Well, I'm sure Adam and Mya will be happy to have you home again..." his voice trailed off.

"And I've asked Brooklyn to hold the job in Lakeland open for two weeks, while I make my decision on accepting it."

This time he said what was on his mind.

"*Really?* You are seriously thinking about working for that clown?"

I heard a can hit the table hard, and I smiled.

"Nick, I love you."

His voice softened, and I could imagine his shoulders slumping, the fight gone out of him.

"I love you too, Ellie, and I want you to be happy. I'm sorry, I just don't trust the guy."

"Well, you trust *me*, don't you?"

He answered without a pause.

"Of course I do."

"Well then, there is nothing to worry about," I told him firmly.

"I want to see you before you go home. When are you leaving?" he asked urgently.

"Saturday."

"Man, Ellie, I can't get out of here by then."

I was disappointed in that too, but tried to shake it off.

"I already made my plane reservations. I need to go home and see how I feel there so I can get on with my life," I replied honestly, as I ran a hand through my hair.

"I understand," he said in a subdued voice. "This is the last project we're working on under the company that J-Rae and I own. I need to get these punch-list items completed so we can sign off on the job and get our final payment. Then we can dissolve the company and get on with the damn divorce. We're close, but it won't be done this week for sure."

I knew that was just as important to him as Brooklyn's job was to me. Nick had plans of starting a brand new construction company on his own, but he couldn't do that until his former assets were settled.

"And I understand that, too," I told him honestly.

"Nick, we'll make this work. We just have to be patient and finish all of our old business so we can start fresh with each other." I really needed a hug right now, but I felt in my heart that I had made the right decision, or at least was giving myself an option of making the right one for me.

"I guess it *would* be better for us if you lived in Florida instead of Pennsylvania. Where are you planning on living if you take the Lakeland job?"

"I hadn't got that far in my thinking yet. Brooklyn has offered one of his condos at a reasonable–"

"*No way!*" he interrupted. "I'm willing to accept the fact that you might be working for him, Ellie, but I'm only human. Don't expect me to like you living in one of his places too!"

I laughed at his outburst. "I wouldn't be living *with* him, silly!"

"I don't care, Ellie, we'll work something else out. At least pacify me with that much of a promise."

To be honest, I wasn't crazy about being indebted to Brooklyn any more than I needed to be anyway. I didn't think he'd be one to call in favors, but you just never know.

"Okay we'll work something else out, *if* I accept the job."

"Thank you," he replied and I heard him expel a deep breath, then someone else talking in the background.

"Ellie, I have to go, sweetheart, the guys need me out there, but I'll call you tonight."

The rest of week was spent gathering up the things that I had accumulated, including my sketching supplies. I took some bike rides with Sylvia, and had a crate of oranges shipped to Adam's address. Every morning was spent sitting on the dock, and every evening on the porch with Hal and Sylvia.

On my last day, Sylvia invited me to lunch. Casey was coming over after work to spend the night with me, and then take me to the airport in the morning. I sat on the front steps next to Hal, waiting for Sylvia to pick me up.

I had noticed little black bugs flying lithely around the past few days, but today they just seemed to be everywhere. Hal swatted one that had landed on his sandal.

"These horny little bugs! Hope they don't stay long this year," he said.

"What?" I laughed at his choice of words.

"Oh, you've never heard of love bugs?" he laughed back at me.

"Don't think we have those at home," I told him as I inspected one that had just landed on my purse. "Are they like mosquitoes? We don't have much love for them."

"No, they're harmless, just a pain in the rump. All they want to do is mate! See?"

I looked more carefully and noticed that it was not one, but *two* bugs stuck together.

"Ewww! Get a room!" I exclaimed as I brushed them off my purse.

Hal laughed a huge belly laugh.

"Ellen, they won't hurt you, they just fly around mating all day. They're a little early this spring. Usually they're only here a month or so, then they're gone as quickly as they arrived."

The sun glinted off of Sylvia's Cruiser as she pulled up in the driveway, she had the top down and Sophia waved from the back seat. Sylvia got out and approached us, bending down to give Hal a quick kiss.

"Wow, your car looks really shiny today!" I told her.

"Herb said that the love bugs won't stick to your car if you cover it with cooking spray. I was out, so I just put some vegetable oil on a sponge and wiped her down! Those bugs will just ruin the paint on your car if you don't get 'em off right away."

"Never heard of that remedy, honey," Hal told her with a doubtful look on his face.

He walked us over to the car and I noticed he wasn't using his cane this morning. Hal looked so different than the first time I met him. Now he was tan and had put on a few needed pounds. As he bent over the door to kiss Sylvia goodbye, I could tell that he was a very happy man.

"You gals have a good time!" he said, backing away from the Cruiser.

Sylvia handed me a purple visor, and I decided to appease her and actually wear it for the drive today.

Before I knew it, we were pulling in to the Gator Buffet in Lakeland, and I couldn't help but look around to see if I could spy the building Brooklyn was renovating.

The three of us had a great lunch, and for dessert today I chose a slice of red velvet cake. I closed my eyes as I savored the first bite.

"You are such a cake slut!" Sylvia said, her humor almost making me choke.

"We haven't heard anything more about the creep who bought Lakeside," Sophia said. "Have you heard anything, Ellen?"

"No, I haven't talked to Jack or heard any more from my attorney, but I promise I'll look into it when I get back home."

"By the way, Soph, I guess your clue on the buyer was wrong. You said his name was something from New York, that's why Ellen and I thought it was Brooklyn, like the bridge," Sylvia said with a smirk.

"No…no, I was right," Sophia said with mouthful of cheesecake.

"How do you figure?" Sylvia challenged. "His name is Jack Stern."

I cringed at the mention of his name.

"The Stern part," Sophia replied.

Sylvia looked at me and I shrugged, then she looked back at Sophia expectantly.

Sophia signed and set down her fork.

"The radio guy, Howard Stern, he's from New York!" she said with a look that implied that we were a couple of knuckle heads.

"Oh, for Pete's sake," Sylvia finally said.

We were still laughing about it as we strolled through the parking lot arm in arm.

"Sylvia, what happened to your car?" Sophia asked as we rounded the corner.

We all froze in our tracks and stared at Sylvia's Cruiser. It was pretty much entirely polka dotted in black, crunchy love bugs.

"Oh…. my….gosh!" Sylvia whispered, and her hand flew to her mouth.

"The sun heated the oil and fried those honeymooners to a crisp!" Sophia exclaimed. She flicked a few off with her fingernail and crunched them with her Croc.

"That's just disgusting!" Sylvia finally managed to say, "Thank goodness I put the roof up before we went into the restaurant!"

I shivered just imagining her whole interior covered with those pesky little bugs.

"All aboard for the car wash," Sylvia called as we got in the car.

By the time Sylvia pulled the sparkling, clean Cruiser into the driveway at Hal's house, the front grille was already re-plastered with love bugs.

"I'm takin' this baby right home," Sylvia said. "Tell Hal that I'll ride the golf cart over later, would ya?"

"Sure thing," I replied as I reached over the back seat to give Sophia a hug.

"I'm going to miss you!" I told her honestly.

"I'll miss you too, honey, but you'll be back soon," Sophia said as she patted my hand.

"I'll see y'all later," Sylvia said as she put the car in drive.

I found Hal sitting on the back porch reading a gardening magazine, and he looked up when I opened the door. After giving him Sylvia's message, I told him what happened to her car.

"Somehow, I knew that wasn't a good idea, but I just didn't want to burst her bubble. She looked so darn proud of herself!" he said once he finally stopped laughing.

"Hal, it's so good to see you home and healthy!" I told him as I plunked down beside him on the glider.

"Well, I have to tell ya, it's darn wonderful to *be* home, happy and healthy!" he replied.

"I'm going to miss you, Ellen," he added softly. "You've

become like a daughter to me."

I felt a tear trickle down my cheek, and I rested my head on his shoulder, but I didn't trust my voice to respond.

"I'm indebted to you for taking such good care of my place, and I hope you consider this your home as well."

"Oh, Hal," I finally managed to say.

"And let me just say this. That son of mine had just better not screw this up! You are the best thing that ever happened to him!"

At that I laughed and turned to look at Hal.

"I love you, mister!" I exclaimed, and threw my arms around his neck.

Casey arrived shortly after Sylvia returned, and we sat around the pool eating takeout Chinese for dinner.

I was really starting to rethink my decision to leave. I didn't want to go. I toyed with a piece of glazed chicken, pushing it around in the rice and broccoli.

"What's the matter, Mom? Don't you like it?" Casey asked as she speared a piece of my chicken and ate it.

"Just feeling sad about leaving, I guess," I told her as I laid down my fork.

"Don't worry, I have a feeling you'll be back soon. Just think of it as a vacation to Pennsylvania," she suggested. "I know that Adam is looking forward to seeing you."

"I know, and I'm looking forward to seeing him too. It's just…I don't know. That's it, I guess. I still just *don't know* what I'm doing or where I'm going."

"Sure you do. You know inside what you want to do. You just have to find the strength to do it!" Sylvia said as she helped herself to more rice.

"There's a slug in every garden," Casey read from her fortune cookie. "What the heck kind of fortune is that!"

"Vegetable oil is for cooking, not for waxing cars," Hal joked as he pretended to read his fortune.

Sylvia playfully slapped him on the arm.

"Here, read yours, Mom," Casey said as she handed me a cookie.

I crunched it open and removed the thin paper strip.

"Time will tell...be sure to listen," I read aloud.

We were all quiet for a moment, pondering my fortune.

"I think that's a good one," Sylvia said finally, popping a piece of cookie into her mouth.

I folded the paper up and slid it into my pocket. I thought it was a good one, too.

CHAPTER THIRTY EIGHT

Another airport trip. Only this time *I* was the one who was leaving. With my bags curbside, I had hugged Casey with every ounce of strength that I had. The fresh scent of her perfume still lingered on my clothes as I sat looking at the clouds drifting by the airplane window, and I breathed it in gratefully.

I hate goodbyes. My farewell to Lake Juliet was short and sweet. I was adamant that I was not going to have a drama-filled scene. It wasn't like I was leaving forever. I *would* be back, if only to visit. However, it was so much harder to put up a good front than I ever would have imagined. It was agony saying goodbye to Sylvia and Hal, and then leaving Casey behind.

The last few months had been a fairy tale existence for me. I had grown and changed so much. Would I have progressed as well if I hadn't left Jeannette? Dr. Burke had told me that it was up to me to make the choice to be happy, and I'd like to think that I would have been able to make that choice had I stayed home.

But I know that it was the people and the surroundings of Lake Juliet that had helped to mend the broken pieces of my heart so quickly. Come to think of it, Dr. Burke had told me that too...to surround myself with people who are positive and uplifting, not those who complain all the time or bring me down. She's pretty smart, that Dr. Burke. I would have to stop by and see her, or at least give her a call. I think she would appreciate a success story.

The ground below, which had been dappled with the many lakes of the Florida terrain, was now invisible as we approached a higher altitude. I stared at the white wisps of clouds outside my window, and rubbed my fingers over the cross around my neck.

Abbey...it was going to be so good to see her again! We

had talked at least weekly on the phone, but nothing can beat a good face to face conversation.

The pilot announced that seatbelts could be removed, and the clunk of snack trays being lowered could be heard from the front of the plane. I left my belt on and rested my head back against the seat, watching the miles fly by.

I thought of Nick, and how upset he was that I was leaving Florida before he could come and see me. He didn't understand why I couldn't wait a couple more weeks…but I couldn't explain it properly. It just felt like the time to go had come…and maybe a part of me knew that if I saw him I *really* wouldn't be able to leave. It wasn't that I didn't care for him enough to wait, quite the contrary! I cared *so* much that I just wanted to be with *him*, and it wouldn't have taken a whole lot of persuasion on his part to get me to stay longer.

But I knew that at some point I would have to make a decision about the rest of my life and that included finishing up the business at home. I wanted to make some decisions on my own– I'm just learning how to do that now– and not base them on my feelings for Nick. Yeah, I really surprised myself with that line of thinking.

Since Hal has come home, I've kind of felt like I've just been *existing*, even though it has been an enviable existence, and I found myself actually needing a purpose or a goal. I needed to make a choice. However, I was missing Nick plenty. I sighed as I was handed a clear plastic cup filled with ice and ginger ale, and a small, crinkly bag with about six pretzels in it.

I love Nick, I know that, and I hope *he* knows it, because I've told him a gazillion times. But I've spent my whole adult life letting Jack make my decisions for me and not thinking for myself. Maybe I'm tipping the scale too far in the other direction, but I want the chance to prove to myself that I can make a choice that's right for me, even if it's not the popular one for everyone else, and make it work.

My thoughts drifted to Jack. Would he have stayed with

me had I been the person that I've become? It didn't matter, really. *He* would still be the same person and that's not the type I want to be around. I had made an appointment with Annee for next week. I was tired of this game playing, I needed this divorce to be final.

My ears popped as the plane descended, and I heard the thud of the landing gear being lowered. The Pittsburgh skyline greeted me from the window, and I could see the parkway snaking through the hills, and the rivers meandering below. The first bubble of anticipation crept into my belly.

As soon as we touched down, I sent Adam a text. I followed my fellow passengers as we disembarked from the plane and were herded onto the tram, then to the escalator toward the baggage claim area.

I saw him from about halfway down, leaning against the wall with his hands stuffed in the pockets of his jean jacket, a black and gold baseball cap turned backwards on his head, scanning the throng of travelers, looking for me. I raised my hand and frantically waved it back and forth, my heartbeat quickening in excitement.

Finally, my feet stepped off the moving stairs and I quickly wove my way through the crowd toward Adam. He hugged me and I felt my feet lift off the ground as he twirled me around.

"Welcome home, Mom!" he said as he planted my feet firmly back on the floor and a kiss on my cheek.

For a moment, all that mattered was that I was with my son.

"Adam, it's *so* good to see you!" I told him as I linked my arm in his and we made our way to the baggage claim.

"Look at *you*, Mom! I've never seen you look better!" he exclaimed.

On the ride home he told me all about the improvements that he had done to his place, and information about another duplex in Jeannette that he currently had a bid on.

"It might be someplace you could be interested in, Mom. It's going to be a gem once I get my hands on it," he offered.

"Well, we'll have to take a look then," I told him, although I wasn't ready to envision myself staying here yet. I had to test the waters for a few days and see how I felt.

We zoomed through the Fort Pitt Tunnel and I held my breath toward the end, not in panic attack mode, but in anticipation of the view that I knew would greet me when we emerged…and it didn't disappoint! The sun glinted off the rivers and the windows of the skyscrapers that were reaching toward the white, puffy clouds, that moments ago I had been close enough to touch. I peeked over Adam to my left and saw the black and gold of Heinz Field sitting majestically near the river, and that the fountain at the point was on, and a glance to my right provided a view of the Gateway Clipper Fleet docked at Station Square, and the little, red Duquesne incline slowly climbing up its track on the side of Mt. Washington. I smiled in satisfaction.

"So, when will Mya be home?" I asked as I settled back in my seat. I knew that she was away at a trade show this weekend.

"Oh, she'll be back by Tuesday. Sorry she couldn't be here when you got home."

"No, problem, sweetie, gives us more time to catch up. So how are the wedding plans going?" I smiled over at him.

The rest of the drive home went quickly as he filled me in on all the happenings, and as he pulled into his driveway and put the truck in park, I had just one more question to ask.

I put my hand on his arm. "Adam, have you talked to your dad about the wedding?"

He put both hands on the steering wheel and gripped it tightly, and I knew the answer before he even said it.

"Nope," Then he looked over at me. "Have you?"

"Nope," I responded with a smile.

I followed Adam through the yard as he carried my luggage, taking in the fresh earthy scent. Springtime always fills me with renewal, and even though March could go either way, today was breezy and warm. Having been acclimated to Florida weather, which was thirty degrees warmer than here this morning, I still wore my winter coat, but spring was definitely in the air. The ground was soggy from the melted mountains of snow, and although the trees were still bare of leaves, the branches had the familiar reddish tint of the bulging leaf buds. Next to Adam's front steps, an early bunch of purple crocuses were in full bloom.

Cooper was so excited to see me that he did about twenty laps around the living room before bringing me his soggy Clifford and squirting a few drops of happy pee at my feet.

"Geez, buddy! I thought we had outgrown that!" Adam laughed as he went in search of cleaner and paper towels.

As I scratched Cooper's belly, I looked around in approval, and could see Mya's touch.

"Adam, the place looks super!" I called out to him.

"Thanks!" he said as he began squeezing the spray bottle and blotting with the towels.

After a tour of the other rooms, he stretched out his hand toward the guest room.

"Ta-da! Your suite awaits you," he said dramatically.

I peeked inside and was thrilled! They had put such effort

into making it a comfortable room for me. My own bed and dresser were there, along with some of my favorite belongings that he must have gathered from my stash in the garage. A fresh, new bedspread with matching curtains done in shades of yellow and blue brought new life to the old.

"Wow!" I exclaimed, as I entered the room and gently touched one of the real daffodils in my crystal vase on the dresser. "Everything is just perfect! Thank you *so* much, Adam!"

I was extremely touched that he had gone to such lengths to please me. I turned and threw my arms around his neck. "I love you!"

"I love you too, Mom. I thought you'd like it. Mya gets credit for the decorating though," he said proudly as he surveyed the room.

"I'll be sure to thank her, too, when she gets home. Are you sure that I'm not going to be a third wheel staying here? I know you guys have your routine...."

"Of *course* you are! You're going to be a *real* pain in the butt," he said.

I turned, surprised, to look at him, and he was smiling. I playfully swatted him with my purse, and Cooper joined in the game and started barking.

"I'm going to put this fella outside for a bit while you unpack. Your car keys are on the desk over there. I started it at least once a week so it should be just fine to drive."

I spent the rest of the afternoon organizing my room and sorting through boxes from the garage to find some warmer clothes to fill the drawers. Would be a while before I could wear the shorts and tank tops that were in my suitcases.

I lovingly removed the gift that Sylvia and Hal had given me and gently placed it on the nightstand. It was a Christmas village piece, a florist shop with a little greenhouse attached. I reached down and plugged it in behind the bed and the bulb inside illuminated the interior of the shop so I could see the tiny cashier behind the counter and several shoppers looking at the flowers. It was the cutest thing, and the perfect gift for me.

I could hardly believe that Hal and Sylvia were not going to be a part of my daily life. I bet they were sitting on the dock right now feeding Dora. Or who knows! Maybe they were enjoying some private time. I laughed out loud. Yes, I bet that is exactly what they were doing!

Adam ordered a pizza for dinner, then we took Cooper for a walk and settled down to watch a movie. It felt good to be with Adam, but I felt a little disoriented in my new surroundings as well. I was home, but *not* home.

Later, when I was snugly tucked in my bed, I called Nick.

"Hi ya, beautiful!" he answered in his best seductive voice.

I giggled. "Hi, handsome."

"Made it there safe and sound?" he asked.

"Yes, I had a good flight and a fun day with Adam."

"I miss you," he said.

"I miss you too," I replied as I looked at my little greenhouse. I had left it on as a nightlight. "And I miss Lake Juliet."

"I always miss it so much at first too when I get back to Memphis, then I get all caught up in my work," he admitted.

"Is that how you feel about me too? After a while you don't miss me so much?" I asked boldly.

He laughed heartily. "Darlin', there is *no way* that I *ever* stop missing you!"

My heart was pounding and I sat upright in bed.

I spoke softly into the phone, "Nick–"

"It's okay, Ellie. I know you had to go home. Hell, no one knows that better than me. I'm always the one heading back to Memphis. I'm just thinking though, that there's nothing here for me anymore. When this last job is done, I'm thinking that I need a change of scenery on a permanent basis."

"What are you saying?" I asked, pushing the cell phone closer to my ear.

"Just that I'm seriously thinking that none of the people I love live in Memphis. And now that we're dissolving the company…well, I have to start a new one anyway, no reason why I can't start it somewhere else."

I could envision him running his hand through his hair as he thought out loud.

"Are you thinking of Florida?"

"Well, that depends. Dad is there, and I feel that I want to be there for him. It's been ridiculous being so far away since his accident. It made me realize that I want to spend more time with him. And Chris is there…."

He left the thought open and I knew that he wanted me to finish it with the fact that *I* would be there too.

"Well," I began, "we both have some thinking to do then, don't we?"

I loved having Adam to myself for a couple of days, but I also enjoyed Mya's company once she got home. It wasn't awkward at all. Our conversations were filled with wedding plans, and she pulled out her stack of bridal magazines and showed me the gowns that she liked.

I was getting caught up in the excitement and it was so much fun to be here to share in the planning of their special day.

Maybe that's why I called Jack. I was just so full of happiness and goodwill that temporary insanity clouded my good reasoning. I was treating Adam and Mya to dinner at the Backyard Grille, and I figured it would be nice to invite Jack to join us and share the good news. After all, he *was* still family, wasn't he? I was a new person now and I could handle it.

I knew it was a mistake as soon as I heard Jack's voice.

"*What?*" he answered.

"*Excuse* me?" I replied, my eyes narrowing.

"I'm kinda busy, what do you want?"

"Well, call me back when you're *not*," and I hung up with a huff.

"I don't know why you bother," Adam said when I told him what happened. "I'll call and tell him sometime, Mom. You don't have to put yourself through this."

"I just thought it would be nice," I replied deflated.

An hour later, Jack called me back.

"Sorry, Ellen, you caught me at a bad time. I'm having some issues with a property I just bought. What's up?" he asked.

I took a deep breath.

"We have some family news that I thought you might like to know about. Did you have plans for dinner tonight?" I blurted out, wondering why just the sound of his voice still unnerves me so much.

"No plans. Jessica's away on business."

Yeah, monkey business, I thought to myself.

"How about joining Adam, Mya and me for dinner at the Backyard Grille?" I asked.

"Who's Mya?"

Oh brother.

"Adam's girlfriend?" I reminded him.

"Why? What's the family business, he knock her up?"

"Ya know what, just forget it." I was furious with him. Adam had been right, why bother!

"Okay, I'll come," he said before I could hang up on him.

There was silence on my end while I tried to compose myself.

"Ellen…I said I'd come," he spoke softly now.

"Six o'clock then," I said right before I hung up.

The three of us were seated at the bar waiting for our table when Jack arrived. I was able to study him before he caught sight of us.

He still looked like Jack, but different in so many ways. Of course his clothes were different; I'd never seen that black sweater before, but something about his demeanor was a bit alien to me as well. His eye caught mine, and I felt my face get hot. He held up his hand in greeting and made his way toward us just as the hostess announced that our table was ready. I was determined not to have a panic attack tonight. I had been prepping myself all day for this moment.

Jack pumped Adam's hand enthusiastically and gave Mya a peck on the cheek. If he felt as awkward as I did when he wrapped me in a loose hug and planted a kiss on *my* cheek, he didn't show it.

The table was a bit quiet as we looked over the menu, and after the waitress had left with our orders on her notepad, Jack looked at me expectantly.

It felt so very weird to be at a table with Jack. I really hoped the outcome of this evening turned out to be worth my efforts. I met his gaze head on and started to speak.

"Well, Adam has–"

And that was when Adam cut me off.

"Dad, Mya and I are getting married."

Jack must have guessed that's what the announcement would be, and I bet he rehearsed his reaction in the mirror all afternoon.

"Well, congratulations kids!" he said just a little too loudly.

He pushed his chair back and went around to Adam's side of the table to embrace him and then reached down and gave Mya a hug too. Then he called the waitress back to our table, drawing the attention of the other diners.

"We'd like to order a bottle of champagne. My son is getting married!" he told her.

Of all the reactions I expected, this was not even in the top ten.

"Thanks, Dad," Adam told him sincerely, and I could tell he was pleased that Jack seemed to approve and wasn't giving him a hard time about it.

The rest of the dinner went off without a hitch. Most of the conversation centered around Adam and Mya telling Jack about their jobs and wedding plans, so I hardly had to say a word, which was more than fine with me. We had agreed before we left the house though, that they wouldn't disclose the destination wedding plan yet. As far as I knew, Jack wasn't aware of my involvement at Lake Juliet and I wanted to keep it that way for a while.

I wondered if he'd bring up the fact that Casey was dating Jessica's son, but he didn't. I figured I'd just let sleeping dogs lie and keep quiet about that too.

When the waitress slipped the check on the table, I reached out for it since I was the one who invited everyone, but Jack covered my hand with his. My head jerked up with a snap, and I felt my eyes widen as I looked at him.

"It's my treat," Jack said as he smoothly removed the check from under my hand, and motioned for the waitress to return. He handed her the check and his bank card, and flashed her a smile.

We all murmured our obligatory "Thank you's" and I sat back in my chair and heaved a mental sigh.

Maybe it was the champagne taking my guard down, but this evening couldn't have gone any better. It was just as I'd hoped it would be for Adam. As much as I didn't want to be around Jack, it was important to me that he and Adam had something even remotely resembling a normal father and son relationship.

And I didn't even feel a panic attack lurking in the shadows. Hurray for me!

As we were walking out the door to leave, Jack grabbed my arm and held me back a moment, whispering in my ear, "I hope you're not expecting *me* to pay for this whole wedding."

Of course.

"No, Jack, all he wants is your blessing," I told him firmly, disappointment pushing out the happiness I'd been feeling. What a showboat he'd been at dinner, and then he was going to be a tightwad about the wedding. This comment I would not share with Adam.

My meeting with Annee went far better than I had expected. Casey had been in touch with her and they had concocted an ingenious plan to get the divorce finalized, and I couldn't believe that it was going to work…but I put my trust in both of them and signed the papers that Annee put in front of me.

I stopped by Amazing Glaze on the way home. The familiar bells jingled when I entered and Abbey hurried out from the back room, wearing a paint streaked smock over her tee shirt.

"*Ellen!*" she exclaimed as she all but tackled me.

I hugged her back just as tightly. "I'm home!"

"Well, yes, you are! Come on in!" she said taking my hand and leading me back toward the break room.

She grabbed two bottles of green tea from the refrigerator and tossed one to me as she motioned toward the table.

"Have a seat, sweetheart, let's catch up," she said, pushing aside some greenware catalogs.

We fell into easy conversation, not missing a beat even though I'd been away. That's how it is with best friends. Time and distance doesn't make a difference.

At least until she asked me the tough question, just like she always does.

"So, what now?"

I used the tips of my fingers to twirl my bottle around and around on the table.

"Abbey, I *love* being home, I really do! There are so many things here that I like and that will always be a part of me. I love the changing seasons, I love being with Adam and Mya, and I love being with you," I replied as I avoided her gaze.

"But?" she asked as she tossed her empty bottle in the recycle bin.

"But, I just feel like I left a huge part of me at Lake Juliet. Although Jeannette will always be my home, I feel like Florida is the right fit for me now, for my new life. And...well...Brooklyn has called twice since I've been home, and to be honest, Abbey, I *really* want to take that job!"

"So, then, what's stopping you?" she asked, although I know that she knew the answer. I think she just wanted to hear me say it.

"Nick doesn't really want me to work for Brooklyn." I *did* say it, and then got up to throw my bottle away so I wouldn't have to look Abbey in the eye.

She slapped her hand against her knee.

"Ellen! For Pete's sake, if you want that job, then take it! I understand why Nick isn't crazy about the idea, given what he's been through, but if he loves you, he has to let you follow your heart and learn to trust you. Please don't let another guy push you around!"

I sat back down and this time looked her in the eye.

"Nick sort of hinted that he might be ready to move to Florida himself and start his new business there," I told her.

She smiled. "See? Then that would be great, you two

could be together!"

I smiled too. "Yeah, that would be wonderful. So, you think I should do it?"

"Does a bear crap in the woods? Of course you should do it!" she laughed.

"Abbey, I love you!"

I jumped up from my chair and threw my arms around her.

"I love you too, and let me say that we have to make a pact to visit often, okay?"

"Absolutely! Adam told me he'd keep the guest room fixed up just for me anytime I wanted to visit. We talked last night, and he sort of felt the same way that you do. Now all I have to do is convince Nick."

"Sweetheart, the only person you had to convince was yourself. If you are happy, then the rest of us that love you will be happy too."

Abbey's comment was foremost in my mind as I called Nick. I was sitting on Adam's back porch steps scratching Cooper behind the ears with one hand, and holding my phone in the other. The sun was just setting, and the air had a chill to it, so I stopped petting Cooper long enough to pull the zipper up on my hoodie. He impatiently put his paw on my lap to reprimand my lack of attention.

"Okay, boy, give me a second," I told him as I resumed the scratching while I waited for Nick to pick up.

"Hi, Ellie! Sorry it took so long for me to answer. I was talking to Dad," Nick said excitedly.

"That's okay, what's going on?" I asked.

"Oh, ya know, just catching up. What's new at your end?"

"Well, I've made my decision and I hope you'll be okay with it. I'm going to move to Florida and I'm going to take the job with Brooklyn. At least until I find something else." There, I said it and that was that.

He replied without a moment's hesitation.

"Honey, I think that's terrific!"

"I thought…well, I didn't expect…." I stammered.

"I *know!* I've been a real horse's ass about the whole job thing, and I owe you an apology. The trust thing is *my* hang-up and that's just the thing, Ellie. I realized that I *do* trust you."

"Wow! What brought you to that realization?" I asked as Cooper pawed me again.

"J-Rae. I saw her this weekend so we could sign off on the company paperwork, and dealing with her again made me realize how different she is from you. I know that you not only speak the truth, but you act the truth. I don't believe that you would ever treat me the way that she has. It's not fair for you to bear the burden of her mistakes."

I stood up, wrapping my arm around my stomach for warmth, and Cooper took off after a rabbit in the yard.

"Nick, you just made me the happiest woman alive!" I was shivering not only from the cold but with excitement as well.

"I *love* you, Ellie."

CHAPTER THIRTY NINE

That thought kept me going for the next several weeks.

Brooklyn was ecstatic that I was taking the job! He already sent me the drawings of the building, and we had been exchanging ideas via email. I was impressed by his professionalism, and even though I had to admit to myself that a tiny part of me was worried about how he'd be, everything was completely above board and strictly business. I couldn't wait to get there to see everything in person and start my new job!

Mya and I had taken several afternoons to go looking for wedding gowns, and she finally found the perfect one at a small boutique in Pittsburgh. It was a soft ivory color, an off the shoulder style, simple, yet elegant, and looked amazing on her. At Mya's insistence, I had also indulged in trying on some mother of the groom gowns, and found one in a champagne shade that I fell in love with. We placed the orders, paid our deposits, and I promised to fly back for her final fitting. Now I could take care of the Lake Juliet details in person.

I decided to sell my car. Jack had chosen it for me and it just reminded me too much of my *other* life, so Adam took care of listing it online and it was sold within a week. The sale also afforded me some much needed back up cash in my account.

Hopefully, between the savings I'd accumulated from house sitting for Hal, the profit from the car, and the ample salary Brooklyn had offered, I would be just fine financially until the divorce settlement was finalized. Casey promised that I had nothing to worry about, so I was keeping my fingers crossed on that one.

Abbey and I had also spent lots of quality time together. I actually took one of her new mosaic classes and I loved it! She was not to be outdone by me already having my dress for the wedding, so another afternoon was spent choosing one for her.

"If I've already bought my dress, then I *have* to go, right?" She had reasoned.

I hadn't seen or talked to Jack since our dinner at The Backyard Grille, but I was okay with that. Even though he turned out to be such a shit at the end, I was glad for Adam's sake that we'd had the dinner. I was also proud of myself for being able to tolerate his antics and not have a panic attack. That was monumental!

The only really sad part was saying goodbye to Adam.

"Don't worry, Mom, we'll be seeing you real soon," he had promised. And I knew that was true. We both had lots of exciting things to look forward to.

Nick and J-Rae had sold their house in Memphis quickly, so he told me that he had been bunking with one of the guys on his crew until that last job was finished. His attorney had told him that things were going well on the financials of his divorce, so he was optimistic that would be finished soon. He promised to take a drive down to Lake Juliet after I got there and I just couldn't wait to see him! It felt so official now, like we were finally a real couple and were going to make this work.

Hal had been very generous in offering me my old room at his place until I could find an apartment of my own, and Sylvia was to pick me up at the airport when I arrived.

As I stood next to my suitcase, the heat radiating from the sidewalk had me sweating. I was amazed at how much warmer it had gotten since I'd left a month ago. Clearly, I was overdressed in khaki's and a long sleeved blouse.

Sylvia tooted the horn and waved from the convertible, pulling neatly up to the curb. Her silver studded visor glinted in the sun, and I could see hot pink tints peeking out beneath it.

582

I ran around the car and met her as she slammed the driver's door shut. We rocked back and forth in a hug that lasted a full minute.

"Miss Ellen! It's mighty fine to see you here again!" she exclaimed as she held me at arm's length.

"Syl, I've missed you *so* much!"

"Well, get yourself in gear and let's get you home!" she exclaimed as she opened the trunk and I tossed in my bag.

Home. I liked the sound of that, and that's exactly what it felt like as she pulled into the drive at Lake Juliet. My heart felt light as a feather, and I jumped from the Cruiser as soon as Sylvia cut the engine, running to meet Hal as he came down the front steps.

"Hal!" I cried as I nabbed him in a bear hug.

"Ellen! It's so good to have you back. It just wasn't the same without you!"

"No, it *wasn't*." I heard a deeper voice say, and I looked behind Hal to see Nick coming down the steps. He was wearing his well worn jeans, a white tee shirt, and the biggest smile I have ever seen!

My heart lurched in my chest as I flew into his arms. He lifted me up and spun me around and around. I was laughing and crying at the same time, tears streaming down my cheeks. Finally Nick set me back down and wiped the tears away with his thumb before lowering his face to mine and capturing my lips in a kiss.

"As if we didn't see enough of that with all the love bugs!" Sylvia joked.

"We'll let you kids have a moment," Hal said, and I heard the screen door shut as he and Sylvia went back inside.

"Let's go for a walk," Nick said, grabbing my hand and pulling me across the driveway. He sat down on a bench under the Cypress tree and tugged me down to sit on his lap.

"I have something for you," he said taking a little white jewelry box from his pocket.

I looked at it, stunned. Certainly this couldn't be....

"It's okay, I promise. Open it," he encouraged.

I took a deep breath and removed the lid, and there nestled in white cotton was... a key?

I looked up at him and my expression made him laugh.

"Come on, let's see what it opens," he said enjoying his game.

I was completely baffled and held his hand as he guided me down a flagstone sidewalk that I knew was not here before. It was landscaped beautifully on either side, pink impatiens and purple snapdragons in full bloom tucked along lush greens and small palms. The sidewalk led right up to the carriage house where we had stored the building supplies, only the front looked entirely different!

"Try your key in the door," Nick prompted.

What the heck was going on?

I inserted my key into the new brushed nickel lock and pushed the door open.

A blast of cool air greeted me as I walked inside and caught my breath. I looked to Nick then gazed around the room. It was beautiful! The carriage house had been completely redone. New hardwood floors gleamed under my feet, the walls were freshly painted, and oh my gosh...the kitchen was right out of a magazine!

I rushed over and ran my hand over the coolness of the granite countertops and spun around to look at the stainless steel appliances.

"Nick, what–" I started, but he interrupted.

"Come on, here's the best part," and he led me up the spiral staircase to the loft, and a completely remodeled bedroom with French doors leading out to the balcony. He opened the doors and we stepped outside, and as he put his arm around me we took in a perfect bird's eye view of Lake Juliet.

"This is all for you…from me," Nick said gently tipping my chin up so that he could look into my eyes.

All I could do was shake my head from side to side.

"I don't understand," I finally managed to say.

"I've been *here*, not in Memphis, the last couple weeks, and working like a dog I might add!" he laughed. "I wanted you to have your *own* place when you came back, and I wanted to surprise you so I had to fib a little bit. *This* is your home now, Ellie, as long as *you* want it to be."

I couldn't help it, I started to sob. It was just too much to comprehend. Nick held me close and stroked my hair. I couldn't believe how lucky I was to have the love of this man. What a wonderful thing he had done for me!

"Does that mean you like it?" he asked.

I choked out a laugh and finally found my voice.

"Nick, I *love* it!" I whispered into his chest.

"So, you think you'll want to live here?" he asked almost timidly.

"How could I *not?* It's wonderful, Nick! How can I ever thank you?"

"Well, I didn't buy furniture. I figured you'd want to decorate it how you'd like."

I finally turned away from him and surveyed the bedroom.

"Oh, it'll be so much fun! I can't wait to start!" I exclaimed as I looked around again and clasped my hands in front of my chest. "I'm just overwhelmed...."

"Oh, one more thing," he said as he reached back into his pocket. "Here's a keychain for your key."

He handed me a small silver keychain, and when I looked at it my eyes widened, then filled with tears again.

"Ellie, I know we haven't really talked about this, and I also know we both have a little ways to go before we're free to make it official, but...I don't want you to go away again. I love you and I want to be with you."

He gently released the ring from the keychain and slid it easily on my finger. I stared at the scrolled platinum band, sparkling with several tiny diamonds clustered on each side of a beautiful blue sapphire. It was breathtaking!

"I heard you were partial to sapphires," he whispered.

I laughed giddily through my tears, knowing that Sylvia had a hand in this.

"What do you say, Ellie? You think we can make a go of this?"

Looking deep into his eyes that were as blue as the ring on my finger, there was no doubt in my mind.

I answered by pulling him tight and pressing my lips firmly against his. I felt bound to him with an intensity that I had never felt for anyone before. This was real, this was right, and this was my choice.

As we kissed, I listened to the waves lapping against the shore of Lake Juliet, and the breeze swishing through the Spanish moss of the cypress tree told me, "Welcome home."

EPILOGUE

I sat with my hands folded on the table, pushing the sapphire ring on my left hand back and forth and tapping the air a mile a minute with my foot. Nick reached over and covered both of my hands with his, and I looked over at him and smiled.

"Relax," he said quietly.

He looked so handsome today, dressed in a navy blue pinstriped suit and a red silk tie. His crisp, white shirt accentuated his tan, and the smile on his face was totally engaging. I couldn't wait to get him home and *out* of those clothes!

Blushing at my thoughts, I looked down at my black sling back pumps, and concentrated on trying to keep them still. I smoothed the wrinkles in my white linen dress and cinched the belt a little tighter. I was never good at waiting.

I fidgeted in my chair and thought back over the last few weeks.

Annee had more than gently persuaded Jack to finally disclose the profits from all of those secret deals he'd been hiding from me over the years of our marriage, and the dollar amount was staggering. When Annee had investigated Shoresale, she discovered that most of the deals were, well, let's just say, not above board.

Instead of exposing Jack and Jessica and their Shoresale greediness, she and Casey had concocted a better solution. After all, I didn't want him going to jail, I just wanted to give him a dose of reality…and a punch in the wallet.

Since neither Jack nor Jessica had enough cash in their accounts to balance the asset scale and pay Nick and me our portion, they were forced to make a quick cash sale of one of their properties to a buyer who had offered only a fraction of what they paid for it. I heard that Jack had been livid about it, but I've always said that what goes around comes around, and he definitely had it coming to him.

So everything was finally settled, and our divorce papers could be filed.

Finally calming my foot, I reached over for Nick's hand and took a deep, cleansing breath.

I could hear voices in the hallway, and I jumped when the handle on the door turned.

Casey entered the room wearing a summer gray skirt and blazer with a pale pink blouse, her gray pumps clicking on the floor.

"Come on in, your buyers are already here," she told the couple behind her.

Nick and I stood just as they entered the room, and Casey gave me a wink.

There has never been anything quite as satisfying to me as the look on Jack's face when he walked through that door. I have replayed it in my mind a million times since and have enjoyed it every bit as much each time.

Nick walked toward them and reached out his hand, totally relishing the moment.

"J-Rae, good to see you. Jack, nice to meet you," he said as he shook their hands.

Jessica's face had gone pale, and they were both still standing in the doorway.

"Come on in, let's get these papers signed folks," Casey said, taking a seat at the head of the table and placing a manila folder in front of each chair.

I didn't feel comfortable enough to actually touch either one of them, so I didn't offer a handshake, but I nodded my head toward them.

"What the *hell* is going on here?" Jack mumbled as he yanked a chair away from the table and sat down next to Casey. Jessica pursed her lips and sat down next to him, giving Nick a death stare.

"You'll have to watch your language, this is a formal proceeding," Casey warned him in a serious tone.

"Well, you could have at least warned me," Jack told her.

Casey looked directly at him.

"I am here as a court appointed mediator. I have to follow the stipulated guidelines, and that does *not* include disclosing the names of the purchasers...*Dad.*"

Jack let out a "Hrumph."

"Well, maybe we should ask the court to appoint another mediator then," Jack shot back at her.

"That's fine, if you want to pay someone else to do this," she volleyed back at him.

Casey wore a serious expression, but I could tell that she was trying hard not to laugh. She loved her father, but she was distressed by his antics and wanted to see him make things right by me.

"Oh, let's just get on with it," Jessica whined. I saw her glance at my left hand and her eyebrows lifted as she caught sight of my ring.

Casey addressed all of us.

"I'm going to walk you through this agreement, then have

you all sign all four copies."

Twenty minutes later, Nick and I were the proud owners of Lakeside!

"Well, I hope this makes you happy, Ellen. Now you own a dumpy little trailer park and a scrappy orange grove," Jack told me as we all stood up. "Glad you could take it off our hands."

I knew he was bluffing. It was an awesome piece of property and valuable as well.

Most importantly, now our friends wouldn't have to move, and we would have income from the lot fees as well. It was a great investment for Nick and me.

"What I don't understand is, how the hell did you end up here, Ellen?" Jack asked me.

He had been duped, and he knew it.

I took a moment and surveyed all the people standing near me in that room, and I knew that we were all bound in some way…through past memories…through our children…and I also knew that we'd all be bound in the future as well…through our children's marriages…perhaps grandchildren. We may not get along or even like each other much, but the common thread would always be there.

I was so proud of myself that I had come this far…that I could realize all that and not be overcome by panic, and I reveled in the feeling of control that I had over my own life now…I had made it all the way through. I took Nick's hand in mine, and winked. Let him wonder.

Thank you for taking the time to read my debut novel. I hope that you enjoyed meeting the characters as much as I enjoyed creating them.

Sometimes I'm disappointed when I reach the end of a story I've read because I've become so attached to the characters that I don't want to let them go. I want to know more about them and find out what happens next.

That's how I felt when I wrote the last line of "All the Way Through". I want to know what happens next, and I hope you feel the same way.

I'm anxious to share more of Ellen's story with you, so my laptop keys have been tapping again….

Follow your dreams,
Deb

18359556R00317

Made in the USA
Charleston, SC
29 March 2013